THE GREATEST DETECTIVE IN ANY CENTURY is without a doubt Sherlock Holmes. And in the twenty-six original cases crafted especially for this volume by some of the finest minds in science fiction, he more than proves up to the demands of changing times, cultures, and technologies, solving each new mystery in a manner that would make his creator, Sir Arthur Conan Doyle, proud. So join the master sleuth as he takes on such fascinating challenges as:

"The Adventure of the Field Theorems"—When Sir Arthur Conan Doyle requires the services of Sherlock Holmes to solve a case it will take more than extraterrestrial visitors to throw Holmes off the scent. . . .

"The Adventure of the Missing Coffin"—A late-night visitor to Baker Street with a sad tale of a purloined coffin may be all that Holmes needs to track down a truly bloodthirsty foe. . . .

"Two Roads, No Choices"—When two time travelers inadvertently alter history, can even Holmes untangle the twisted strands of alternate futures?

"Second Fiddle"—Brought to the twentieth century to tackle a case of celebrity slaughter, the identity of a serial killer may prove easier for Holmes to find than his way through all the modern-day bureacracy. . . .

Sherlock Holmes and Dr. Watson were created
by the late Sir Arthur Conan Doyle,
and appear in stories and novels by him.

SHERLOCK HOLMES

IN ORBIT

Authorized by
Dame Jean Conan Doyle

Edited by Mike Resnick
and Martin H. Greenberg

DAW BOOKS, INC.
DONALD A. WOLLHEIM, FOUNDER
375 Hudson Street, New York, NY 10014

ELIZABETH R. WOLLHEIM
SHEILA E. GILBERT
PUBLISHERS

First Printing, February 1995
1 2 3 4 5 6 7 8 9

DAW TRADEMARK REGISTERED
U.S. PAT. OFF. AND FOREIGN COUNTRIES
—MARCA REGISTRADA
HECHO EN U.S.A.

PRINTED IN THE U.S.A.

Acknowledgments

Introduction © 1995 by Mike Resnick.

The Musgrave Version © 1995 by George Alec Effinger.

The Case of the Detective's Smile © 1995 by Mark Bourne.

The Adventure of the Russian Grave © 1995 by William Barton and Michael Capobianco.

The Adventure of the Field Theorems © 1995 by Vonda N. McIntyre.

The Adventure of the Missing Coffin © 1995 by Laura Resnick.

The Adventure of the Second Scarf © 1995 by Mark Aronson.

The Phantom of the Barbary Coast © 1995 by Frank M. Robinson.

Mouse and the Master © 1995 by Brian M. Thomsen.

Two Roads, No Choices © 1995 by Dean Wesley Smith.

The Richmond Enigma © 1995 by John DeChancie.

A Study in Sussex © 1995 by Leah A. Zeldes.

The Holmes Team Advantage © 1995 by Gary Alan Ruse.

Alimentary, My Dear Watson © 1995 by Lawrence Schimel.

The Future Engine © 1995 by Byron Tetrick.

Holmes ex Machina © 1995 by Susan Casper.

The Sherlock Solution © 1995 by Craig Shaw Gardner.

The Fan Who Molded Himself © 1995 by David Gerrold.

Second Fiddle © 1995 by Kristine Kathryn Rusch.

Moriarty by Modem © 1995 by Jack Nimersheim.

The Greatest Detective of All Time © 1995 by Ralph Roberts.

The Case of the Purloined L'Isitek © 1995 by Josepha Sherman.

The Adventure of the Illegal Alien © 1995 by Anthony R. Lewis.

Dogs, Masques, Love, Death: Flowers © 1995 by Barry N. Malzberg.

You See But You Do Not Observe © 1995 by Robert J. Sawyer.

Illusions © 1995 by Janni Lee Simner.

The Adventures of the Pearly Gate © 1995 by Mike Resnick.

To Carol, as always,

And to Isaac Asimov and Alfred Bester, pioneers of the science-fictional mystery story.

Contents

Contents

PART IV: HOLMES AFTER DEATH

Introduction

THE DETECTIVE WHO REFUSED TO DIE

The downstate returns aren't all in yet, but it looks as though the popular fiction character who will outlive all the others is Sherlock Holmes, the world's most famous consulting detective. In fact, the only other character who's still in the running is Edgar Rice Burroughs' Tarzan, who is about a quarter of a century younger and still going strong.

But consider:

While the original Tarzan stories are still popular with the masses, there has been only one Tarzan story not written by Burroughs—Fritz Leiber's *Tarzan and the Valley of Gold*. Now go to your local bookstore and count the number of authors who have tried their hands at Sherlock Holmes stories.

Trademark and copyright considerations? Of course. But there is also the fact that Tarzan exists in only one milieu— the African jungle—and there is precious little African jungle left. His particular feats of derring-do would have everyone from the World Wildlife Federation to Greenpeace on his case were he to perform them today.

But when your prey is a master criminal rather than a lion or a bull elephant, the game is always afoot. True, to many readers Sherlock Holmes will always reside at 221B Baker Street, in "a romantic chamber of the heart, a nostalgic country of the mind, where it is always 1895." But to others, he is too big to confine to a single era or a single country.

Arthur Conan Doyle tried to kill him off in the Falls at

Reichenbach, and failed. The public simply would not allow Holmes to die.

Doyle's death itself should have spelled an end to Holmes, but again, the public had such a hunger for Holmes stories that, after a two-decade hiatus, they began to reappear. The first major book was *The Misadventures of Sherlock Holmes,* edited by Ellery Queen in 1944 and featuring Holmes pastiches and parodies by Mark Twain, Bret Harte, John Kendrick Bangs, and more than two dozen other admirers of the great detective.

Doyle's son, Adrian Conan Doyle, alone and in collaboration with John Dickson Carr, then wrote a dozen new Holmes stories which were collected as *The Exploits of Sherlock Holmes.*

It wasn't just Holmes himself who continued to appear in works of fiction, but even the fans of Sherlock Holmes. Anthony Boucher's *The Case of the Baker Street Irregulars,* published in 1940, is about a group of Holmes fanatics who get involved in a series of murders on the set of a Sherlock Holmes film.

After the appearance of Nicholas Meyer's *The Seven Percent Solution,* a Holmes novel that made the bestseller lists and became a successful big-budget movie, it became almost open season for authors wishing to write their Holmes stories. Among the better ones were *Naked Is the Best Disguise,* by Samuel Rosenberg; *I, Sherlock Holmes,* by Michael Harrison; *The Giant Rat of Sumatra,* by Richard L. Boyer; *The Last Sherlock Holmes Story,* by Michael Dibdin; *Ten Years Beyond Baker Street,* by Cay Van Ash; *The Return of Moriarty,* by John Gardner; *The Private Life of Doctor Watson* and *Sherlock Holmes: My Life and Crimes,* by Michael Hardwick; and *Good Night, Mr. Holmes,* by Carole Nelson Douglas.

August Dereleth, who wrote a few Holmes stories himself, also created Solar Pons, a Holmes pastiche who survived through half a dozen books; and Robert L. Fish, himself a fine mystery writer, wrote some two dozen hilarious parodies featuring Sherlock Holmes, which were later collected in two books.

But at the same time all this was going on, an interesting phenomenon was taking place: Some Holmes authors decided to allow the great detective to interact with other characters, both real and fictional, many of which had a fantasy element to them. There must be more than a dozen stories in which Holmes hunts down Jack the Ripper, the best of which is Ellery Queen's *A Study in Terror*. But he also teams up with a young Teddy Roosevelt in *The Adventure of the Stalwart Companions,* by H. Paul Jeffers. As for his more fantastic conpanions and foes, there was 1974's *The Adventure of the Peerless Peer,* by Philip Jose Farmer, in which Holmes meets Tarzan; there was *Sherlock Holmes vs. Dracula,* written by Loren D. Estleman in 1978; and *Pulptime,* the 1984 novel by P. H. Cannon in which Holmes and H. P. Lovecraft discover some horrors beneath the sewers of New York.

The interesting thing is that Holmes worked just as well in these settings as he did in Baker Street. Even the movies, which have long been in love with Holmes, found a way to produce a gentle fantasy about him in James Goldman's brilliant *They Might Be Giants,* starring George C. Scott and Joanne Woodward.

Science fiction had been slow to get into the act, but by 1960 there were enough fantastic Holmes stories to produce a limited-edition book that is now a collector's item: *The Science-Fictional Sherlock Holmes,* edited by Robert C. Peterson and produced in Denver by a publishing company known as The Council of Four. The stories were all reprints.

There was a gap of 24 years before the next fantastic Holmes anthology, *Sherlock Holmes Through Time and Space,* edited by Martin Greenberg and published by Bluejay Books. It, too, contained nothing but reprints.

Another decade has passed and Holmes is more popular than ever. The Doyle books are constantly being brought out in new editions, Jeremy Brett is introducing an entire generation of television viewers to Sherlock Holmes, new novels featuring the great detective are appearing all the time—and it seemed that the time was ripe for another science-fictional Holmes anthology, but this time featuring all-original stories written exclusively for this book. For just as Holmes has never been more popular, the same can be said for science fiction: rarely does a month go by without a science fiction or fantasy novel appearing on the bestseller lists, the field is publishing ten times as many books as it did as recently as two decades ago, and a list of the all-time top-grossing movies reads like a science fiction fan's Christmas list.

When these stories were assigned, the authors were told

that they could place Holmes in any era or any setting they chose, as long as each story had a science fiction or fantasy element and Holmes remained recognizably Holmes. They took me at my word, and hence the stories are divided into four main groups: Holmes in the Past (his own era), Holmes in the Present, Holmes in the Future, and even a couple of stories about Holmes After Death.

In *Sherlock Holmes in Orbit,* you'll see the world's greatest consulting detective lock horns with the insidious Dr. Fu Manchu; you'll learn the secret embedded in Professor Moriarty's "The Dynamics of an Asteroid"; you'll find out what happened after Holmes fell to his death over the Falls at Reichenbach; you'll see him accept a commission from a vampire; you'll even encounter him as a computer program.

Sherlock Holmes will never die. But thanks to the men and women who write imaginative literature, who go to work each day asking "What if . . . ?" he has just been given 26 new worlds to conquer.

—Mike Resnick

PART I

HOLMES IN THE PAST

THE MUSGRAVE VERSION

by George Alec Effinger

EDITOR'S NOTE

Most of those who have read and thrilled to the accounts of the adventures of Sherlock Holmes will be familiar with Reginald Musgrave. He attended Cambridge University at the same time that Holmes was an undergraduate there, and the two men developed a friendship based on mutual respect and a common interest in the natural sciences. It was because of this friendship—and Holmes's practice of using another person as a sounding board for his thoughts concerning whatever problem he was working on (a function later filled so admirably by Dr. John H. Watson)—that Holmes brought Musgrave along on that fateful visit to the rooms of Ch'ing Chuan-Fu. It was four years later that Musgrave and Holmes came together again to solve the puzzle recorded by Watson as "The Musgrave Ritual."

This incident is only the first part of a much longer work. It is presented here so that perhaps it may explain some of Holmes's qualities that have troubled and intrigued historians. The twenty-one-year-old Sherlock Holmes whom Musgrave knew was not the same man who shared the flat on Baker Street with Dr. Watson. Musgrave's memories of the young man may conflict with the more familiar picture of Holmes, but there is no doubt that Holmes's meeting with Ch'ing Chuan-Fu—who in due time would rock the entire globe under his *nom de guerre* of Dr. Fu Manchu—was a major milestone along the road from the brash, somewhat naive Sherlock Holmes to the masterful and self-possessed consulting detective the entire world has admired and loved for decades.

Here now is Reginald Musgrave's remarkable story.

* * *

After reading the opening pages of this memoir, my son Miles said, "The Sherlock Holmes in your book is quite different from the one I've always imagined." There is good reason for that, and his name is John H. Watson. I suppose this is as good a time as any to stress an important though unpleasant truth. Dr. Watson—courageous, generous, sympathetic, by his *own* accounts—did have one or two human failings or, rather, weaknesses. One of these, sad to say, was a kind of jealousy or possessiveness when it came to sharing the friendship of Sherlock Holmes. Since the publication of Dr. Watson's accounts of Holmes's exploits, many students have pointed out errors, discrepancies, evasions, and some rather baldly obvious attempts to hoodwink the reader.

Why would the honorable doctor resort to such things? It is my informed contention that he did not like to think that anyone but he had had such a close working relationship with Holmes, and he guarded his own connection by removing from his stories all mention of others who might be considered "competition." I am the first to admit that this seems petty and a bit adolescent, all out of character for the Dr. Watson we have come to know. Still, I submit that "Dr. Watson," the actor in the dramas rather than the recorder of them, is a piece of fiction.

John H. Watson, Holmes's Boswell, created his own image and left it to posterity. The genuine Watson was less noble and more human. He is no less likable, to be sure; but it is simpler to understand the dissonances of fact that occur in the published adventures if we see how Watson disguised and altered his portrait of myself.

This is Watson's "Holmes" describing me in "The Musgrave Ritual":

> "Reginald Musgrave had been in the same college as myself, and I had some slight acquaintance with him.

He was not generally popular among the undergraduates, though it always seemed to me that what was set down as pride was really an attempt to cover extreme natural diffidence. In appearance he was a man of an exceedingly aristocratic type, thin, high-nosed, and large-eyed, with languid yet courtly manners. He was indeed a scion of one of the very oldest families in the kingdom, though his branch was a cadet one which had separated from the Northern Musgraves some time in the sixteenth century, and had established itself in Western Sussex, where the manor house of Hurlstone is perhaps the oldest inhabited building in the county. Something of his birthplace seemed to cling to the man, and I never looked at his pale, keen face, or the poise of his head, without associating him with gray archways and mullioned windows and all the venerable wreckage of a feudal keep."

"Some slight acquaintance," indeed! "Languid, yet courtly manners." In this tone, are not those words more than mildly disparaging? "All the venerable wreckage of a feudal keep." Beware! This is not Sherlock Holmes speaking, even though in Watson's story those words issue from my old friend's mouth. No, it is the good doctor himself, giving voice to his own hopelessly middle-class prejudice and invidiousness.

I charge that these are the words of a man who *wished* that he had attended Oxford or Cambridge, who *wished* that his practice were in Harley Street, who *wished* that his talents and abilities fitted him for more than the role of observer and confidant. He was Patroclus to Holmes's Achilles, and though he dare not don his friend's armor in battle, he could make certain that no one would mistake his part in Holmes adventures.

"Some slight acquaintance!" From that day in July, 1875, when Holmes and I were first swept up into the world of the Chinese devil, until the glad day more than *a year and a half* later when we returned at last to English shores, Holmes and I grew ever stronger in our friendship. We endured such trials together as bind men for a lifetime in mutual respect and comradeship. Except for the story of the Ritual, however, my name is never mentioned again in Watson's accounts. I should like to set the record straight; I intend to write the true account of the so-called "Musgrave Ritual," though I am sure that the legion of Holmes's admirers will put little credence in my new version. Yet I am not envious or resentful. It is too late for that.

If I were to follow the example of Dr. Watson, I should call this history "The Adventure of the Five Snows," or something of that sort. Dr. Watson was a practical man with a strong romantic streak in him, I suppose. I know from some of the wry remarks Holmes made in his letters that Watson had a certain talent for putting words in everyone's mouth after the fact, and for editing and rearranging the smaller details of a case to suit his more literary requirements.

I do not have Watson's experience in making literature from the dry bones of fact. However, I do have my journals, which I began to keep on first going up to Cambridge. Every aspect of this affair was examined and interpreted for me by Holmes himself during the days of our imprisonment beneath the Palace of the Opal Moon, within the inner Forbidden City of Peiping. I entered those events in my journal upon my return to Sussex almost exactly fifty-two years ago; yet each word, each image resounds again in my mind as clearly today as when I was a young man, not yet of a legal age but already tempered by the trials and terrors I had undergone.

It all began simply enough. Holmes, who, like myself, belonged to Caius college but lodged in the town, was told by his landlord that he had received a message during the day. Holmes took the notepaper and studied it. The words were written in a careful, precise, yet distinctly odd handwriting. "It was a Chinaman brought it," said Holmes's landlord. "I didn't mind taking the message, sir, but I'll thank you for not inviting them into your room. I'll not have the likes of them in my house."

"Indeed," said Holmes absently. He handed me the note, and I read it as we climbed the stairs to his quarters. The note said:

My Dear Mr. Holmes—
There has been a certain amount of talk among the underclassmen concerning your abilities of observation and deduction. Your success with some small problems brought to you for solution has led me to believe that

you may be able to provide me with similar assistance. I assure you that my difficulty is of great importance to me, but will not likely cause you a great deal of inconvenience. I am quite willing to compensate you according to whatever you consider fair and equitable for your time. I will look forward to meeting you at my lodgings tonight, or at whatever time you find more suitable.

Ch'ing Chuan-Fu

The note gave Ch'ing's address in Jesus Lane. Holmes frowned and folded the paper, putting it inside the front cover of a book he was carrying. As we paused while he unlocked his door, he said, "I've seen this Ch'ing once or twice about the town and heard various stories about the man. He had tried to be admitted to Cambridge on two occasions but had been denied admittance because each prospective student must belong to a college, and none of the Cambridge colleges would accept an Oriental student. Ch'ing matriculated instead at Heidelberg, where he studied medicine."

The door opened, and I preceded Holmes inside. "Yet he continued to apply to Cambridge for admission?" I asked.

Holmes nodded. "Just a few years ago, Cambridge changed its policy and began to admit young men without college affiliations. Ch'ing made another application, and this time he was accepted. I have heard that in his native land he had a certain amount of influence, but none of that was enough to break down some of the centuries-old English university barriers."

If I did not know it already, I was soon to learn that Holmes himself was as free from preconceived notions and prejudice as any man alive. "Prejudice is but the soot from an untrimmed wick," he once told me. "The lantern may be brilliant inside, but if the glass is blackened, the flame illuminates nothing."

Later, after dinner, Holmes and I left his flat in Lensfield Road and walked up Regent Street in the direction of the River Cam. In those days Holmes was not as comfortably well-off as he was to be at the time of his association with Dr. Watson. Although Holmes never spoke of his family and background, I often had the impression that they were less agreeably situated than, for instance, my own family. I know that Holmes was able to enjoy his college years without anything like the style of the wealthier lads. Some of these would think nothing of hiring a cab for any occasion, but Holmes often said that he preferred to walk. From Lensfield Road to Jesus Lane is a pleasant half hour's exercise, and the weather was fine.

The house in which Ch'ing resided was large, but divided up into many small flats. It was quite some distance from the university proper. It was owned by a Mrs. Richmond, who proved to be an elderly, gaunt woman with a permanently suspicious expression and an equally disapproving tone of voice. These were the campaign ribbons she had won over the years, battling with the underclassmen. "Yes?" she said, answering Holmes's knock.

"I received an invitation to call on Mr. Ch'ing this evening," Holmes said. He regarded the woman with quiet interest.

"Mr. Ch'ing," she said absently. She studied Holmes silently for a moment. "Come in, then, Mr.—"

"Holmes, madam. Sherlock Holmes. And this is my friend, Reginald Musgrave."

"Yes. Mr. Holmes. Make yourself comfortable in the parlor, gentlemen, and I'll— No. Why don't you just go up to his rooms? Second floor, first on the left."

"Thank you, Mrs. Richmond," said Holmes. We followed her directions and Holmes rapped on Ch'ing's door.

It was opened almost immediately. "Yes?"

"My name is Sherlock Holmes, Mr. Ch'ing. And this is my companion, Reginald Musgrave."

"Ah, yes. Please come in. I am so glad that you accepted my invitation. Please, sit there. Would you care for some tea?" Ch'ing permitted himself a quiet smile. "I have English and Chinese."

"Whatever you have prepared," I said, and Holmes nodded in agreement. We each sat in a comfortable armchair and looked about the room. I saw that it was furnished in precisely the same fashion as most other undergraduate rooms I'd visited. There was the same clutter and jumble of books, papers, notebooks. The room was lit by an oil lamp, which shed a soft light on the dark paneling of the walls and the bare wooden floor. There were few objects in the room that were not absolutely essential to the daily life of a university student.

"Perhaps, Mr. Holmes, you expected to see Chinese scrolls on the wall and possibly a Ming vase and a T'ang horse," Ch'ing said, as he served us Chinese tea in chipped teacups.

"I had no expectations at all," Holmes said.

"You wished to keep an open mind about me?" Ch'ing sat in a chair much less comfortable than the ones he had offered to us. He sipped from his cup of tea.

"Mrs. Richmond hesitated to have you meet me in her parlor, where anyone might see that you roomed in her house. You must certainly be weary of such bigotry."

Ch'ing shrugged. "Do you like the tea?" He seemed to have quite forgotten that I was present.

Holmes tasted the tea. "Very good." He waited, perhaps expecting that the other man would launch immediately into his problem, but Ch'ing seemed content to sit and drink his tea, gazing reflectively over the simple white china cup, saying nothing at all. A few minutes passed in uneasy silence—uneasy, at least, for this young Westerner unused to the Chinese way of doing things.

"Tell me," Ch'ing said at last, "now that you've observed me for a short time, tell me what you can about myself."

"I am not a mystic, Mr. Ch'ing," Holmes said, "nor am I some kind of theatrical mind reader. I am developing a system of observation and deduction, which already has been of some practical use to myself and others. If there is nothing to observe, there is nothing to deduce."

"I hope you do not wish me to believe that you observe nothing."

Holmes shook his head. "Quite the contrary. I thought only that I should make myself plain to you at the beginning, Mr. Ch'ing. If you expect some kind of magical solution to your problem, you may be disappointed."

"Not at all. And, please, you need not call me Mr. Ch'ing. It is a false construction based upon the European system of naming individuals. I wold much prefer it if you would address me by the name I use in my homeland—Dr. Fu Manchu."

Holmes gave a slight nod.

Fu Manchu continued. "I had been afraid that you might have claimed some kind of supernatural power beyond the understanding of science. You must realize that I am a friend of science."

"As am I," Holmes said.

The two men regarded each other once again. Fu Manchu shrugged. "Still you hesitate to speak," he said in his low, sibilant voice.

Holmes took a deep breath and let it out. "Very well, then. From what I know of you, I can say that you are from China, but I have never heard from which province or city. I have heard also that you are the hereditary possessor of some influence or position in your country, but I judge that, as in England, that does not mean that you also inherited wealth. This rooming house is quite some distance from the university, and consequently the rents Mrs. Richmond can charge for her flats must be lower than at a more conveniently situated house. Further, I perceive that beneath your academic robe you wear a suit of good material but inferior cut, as though you had little experience in dealing with tailors, either here or in China. You are still wearing your robe but not your cap, which indicates that you hurried back to your lodgings in the hope that we would make our visit this evening. You made a pot of tea but have not yet removed your robe. All tutorials today would have been concluded before the dinner hour, and I don't believe you would have made later appointments if you expected to meet me tonight. I suspect that you have some kind of extracurricular employment to help defray the cost of your education. Because of the common attitudes toward members of your race, I expect such employment would have to be menial, despite your previous education. No doubt you accepted this employment in some part of town remote from the university, so that you would not be discovered by your fellows while you were engaged in such an occupation. I observe also that the inside of your right forefinger is noticeably callused in an unusual way, as from some tool or implement. Beyond these things I can say no more. The contents of your room say little, other than that you are at great pains to adopt the ways and manners of your hosts."

Fu Manchu sipped the last of the tea in his cup and closed his eyes for a moment. "I am most interested, Mr. Holmes. Most interested. Your system is admirable. It is rare, even in a place of learning as venerable as this, to meet one such as you who seeks to know truth. Because truth is so important to you, Mr. Holmes, I must say I feel compelled to tell you that you are mistaken in almost every particular."

I saw that Holmes felt some discomfort on hearing this, but he said nothing to Fu Manchu. He waited to hear the man's story. Weeks later, while Holmes and I were both chained to an ancient subterranean wall in Peiping, Holmes would recall this moment with bitter humor.

Fu Manchu favored us with a joyless smile, an expression Holmes and I would get to know well. It is something the Chinese call "making teeth," and is used to disguise a wide range of emotions, from embarrassment to contempt to murderous rage. When this particular Oriental smiled in that way, it never failed to make me cold with fear. "You are correct, Mr. Holmes, in that I have only just arrived. I thought first of the luxury of tea, but I retained the robe so that this meeting might begin as a conversation between fellow students at a great academic institution, rather than as yet another tedious meeting between East and West. As to your estimations of my financial position, you have been betrayed by your own system. Permit me to say where I feel you fall into error. Your observations themselves are quite amazing. You are by far the most perceptive man I have come to know in the European countries I have visited. It is your deductions that are faulty."

Holmes was not visibly upset by his apparent failure. He was fascinated by this encounter, and he wanted to learn as much as possible. If Fu Manchu could correct a flaw in Holmes's as-yet-incomplete science of detection, Holmes would listen with all the attention and interest he gave his collegiate lecturers.

Fu Manchu went on. "These rooms," and the Chinese gestured about himself disdainfully, "are by no means the best I could afford. Had I the desire, I could purchase outright any house in the town. Such a thing would, of course, cause resentment and attract unpleasant attention. I have much to accomplish, much to learn here at Cambridge. I cannot afford the time to fend off the petty annoyances of your English *entetement*."

Holmes started to speak, but Fu Manchu held up a hand and continued. "I suppose you were given a nice speech by your own landlord about entertaining 'Chinamen' in your rooms. He tried it out on me first. So you must appreciate then how difficult it must have been for me to rent rooms at any more convenient location. Mrs. Richmond has no such scruples against a gentleman of my race—I doubt if Mrs.

Richmond has very many scruples at all if it comes to that. She does exact from me a good deal more than from anyone else in this palace of Occidental pleasures. As to my clothing, Mr. Holmes, you are further correct in stating that it is of the best material. I appreciate fine quality, sir, and when given the liberty I surround myself with the finest of everything. As to the cut of my clothes, I must say that this particular suit was made for me by an English tailor in my employ in Peiping, a man who has not seen England for some ten years. I understand that a suit tailored for me in London would look more pleasing to you and your companion, but this one satisfied my desire to seem unassuming and somewhat poverty-stricken. The poor man who tailored it had no idea of the recent changes in style, and my own motives were more important to me than appearing a dandy among—" He used a Chinese expression here. Fu Manchu noticed Holmes's frown. "I'm sorry for lapsing into Mandarin. That was a phrase my people use when referring to your people."

"I would hazard a guess," Holmes said, "that much about the relations of our countries could be learned if you were to translate it."

Once more Fu Manchu gave a short smile. "It means 'blue-eyed devils,' Mr. Holmes."

I was taken aback, but Holmes laughed. "And the callus?" he asked.

Fu Manchu shrugged. "No menial labor, sir, no endless toil with some strange Oriental implement. In Peiping I entertain myself with the illusion that I am something of a calligrapher and an artist. The manner and techniques of Chinese painting are quite different from the European."

Holmes finished his tea. "Ah," he said, "I seem to have made quite a complete ass of myself."

Fu Manchu made an airy gesture with one hand. "Not at all, Mr. Holmes, not at all. As I have said, your observations were keen, but the deductions to which they led were inaccurate. You must remember that two plus two always equals four here in your comfortable British Empire, but in the ancient lands of the East two plus two may equal whatever seems appropriate at the time."

"I must thank you, then," Holmes said, "for a lesson I shall never forget."

At that point, Fu Manchu elaborated upon the reason he

had summoned Holmes and myself to his room. Evidently someone had stolen a brass and enamel box, worthless but for its sentimental value to our host.

"You are no doubt aware that the term is coming to an end soon," Holmes said. "I cannot take leave of my studies at this time."

Fu Manchu nodded slowly. "Yes, of course. I rather expected you to say just that. Perhaps you will do me the very great pleasure of calling on me in my most humble apartments in London, during the long vacation."

Holmes glanced at me, and I merely pursed my lips a little. "That would be convenient to us," he said.

Just that simply began our globe-spanning series of adventures: the dreadful partnership of the League of Dragons, between this very same Dr. Fu Manchu and Professor James Moriarty; the long, harsh trek across Europe to Fu Manchu's fortress stronghold within the Forbidden City itself; our escape, our rescue, and our mad voyage aboard the submarine *Nautilus;* our meeting with the maniacal Dr. Moreau and his giant rat of Sumatra, which John H. Watson transformed into the "hound" of the Baskervilles; the murders that Holmes solved in San Francisco, and the frenzied, failed journey to rescue General George Armstrong Custer from his own murderous officers—the recording of all these things and more will have to wait until another day. I pray that my wits remain nimble and my body sound, so that I can faithfully set down all that I saw and heard. I am quite sure that it will astound the nation.

It was a time of great horror, of cruelty and savagery; and for some of us, a time of love and tenderness. I came to know Sherlock Holmes as a good and true friend. That he never made notes on this case or, if he did, never permitted Watson to write them up, indicates that Holmes regarded these happenings with particular loathing. I hope I do his memory no injustice by telling of the adventure now. I leave this history as a legacy and a warning to my sons and their children, and to my yet-unborn great-grandchildren. I pray that they may grow to live in peace beyond the shadow of Dr. Fu Manchu.

Reginald Musgrave
Hurlstone, Western Sussex
October 14, 1927

THE CASE OF THE DETECTIVE'S SMILE

by Mark Bourne

"The mundane bores me, Watson."

These were the first words Sherlock Holmes had spoken all morning—a gray, frigid January morning of 1898. His statement so startled me that my coffee was jostled from its cup, speckling the morning *Times* spread out before me.

He lounged listlessly in his armchair before the fire, a hodgepodge of books and monographs littering the floor about his feet. My friend languidly waved his pipe before his face, watching the fragrant smoke rise in ever-changing patterns that veiled his features.

"And good morning to *you*, Holmes," I retorted, dabbing up the coffee spill. I offered him a scone from Mrs. Hudson's breakfast tray, but he refused with a directed wave of his hand. Smoke swirled in graceful curls about his solemn face. By this stage in our long association, I had learned his moods well, and I had seen this one before.

"Surely, Holmes," I began, "you cannot have already forgotten that frightful episode of the princess and the bloody marionettes."

Holmes shrugged. "Trifles, Watson, trifles."

"Or the case of the spotted diplomat?"

"Hardly worthy of my unique talents, you must agree."

I was undaunted. "Well, then, that Cornish horror of the Devil's Foot—"

"Watson, Watson, Watson." Holmes turned his great

hawklike face toward me. "My blood cries out for *challenge,* for the unexpected, for anything beyond the realm of the everyday world—" He indicated the view beyond the sitting room windows "—which does *bore* me so. But I thank you for trying to relieve my black mood."

In earlier days, before the so-called Return of Sherlock Holmes, I would have worried that my friend would soon pull a tiny key from his pocket, open a certain drawer in his work desk, and withdraw a polished morocco case. A case in which he kept a hypodermic syringe with its long hollow needle. For it was while in such dark ruminations that he had sought solace in the black embrace of a seven-percent solution of cocaine.

But the Sherlock Holmes who had returned from his mysterious three-year journey abroad was a changed man.

Of course, he was still the friend I had publicly declared the best and wisest man whom I have ever known. Nonetheless, the foreign lands he encountered in his travels—during which all the world, including myself, thought Sherlock Holmes dead—had altered him in subtle ways that only I could have noticed. Chief among these was the absolute absence of the cocaine case. He had not touched it since his resurrection. What I had tried in vain to do for many years, his secret and solitary adventures had done for me.

When pressed about the details of his journeying, he would merely tell me to reread the "colorful romance" in which I recorded the events surrounding his Return. Over the years, however, troubling discrepancies had come to my attention. His account of travels in Tibet and Khartoum was rife with fallacies, anachronisms, and paradoxes. I was forced to the conclusion that Holmes's statements regarding his Great Hiatus were the purest invention on his part.

Often I wondered: what adventures could be of such profound secrecy and mystery that he would not share them with another living soul, including—*especially*—his most trusted friend?

I returned to my breakfast and newspaper, concerned but resigned. Holmes was starved for stimulation of his renowned powers, and nothing less than a case of great import could blow the dark cloud of ennui from his brain.

It was with providential fortune that a knock rapped our door.

"Mr. Holmes? Doctor?" called Mrs. Hudson.

Holmes seemed not to hear her. He remained still, eyes fixed on the smoke twisting in the air before him. With a grunt of dismay I opened the door.

"A woman is at the door, sir," said our landlady. "She insists on seeing Mr. Holmes."

"Did she offer her name?"

"No, sir. But she told me to say that she and Mr. Holmes share mutual acquaintances, and to give him this." She handed me a playing card, of the kind used in a gaming deck. I examined it for anything peculiar, such as a message written along its white border. But it was merely an unremarkable Queen of Hearts.

This portended something extraordinary. Anonymous strangers on our doorstep had become routine over the years, but they usually saved their cryptic messages until after they had entered our rooms. I turned toward Holmes. By all appearances, he was completely unaware of our presence in this hemisphere.

Mrs. Hudson peered over my shoulder at Holmes. A frown of concern tugged at her elderly features. She stood on her toes and leaned close to my ear.

"Oh, dear," she whispered so softly I could barely hear her words. "Mr. Holmes *is* a gray cloud today, isn't he?"

I whispered in reply, "You may have just provided a ray of sun, Mrs. Hudson. Please show the lady up."

She looked gravely at my companion, then exited, silently closing the door behind her.

"Mrs. Hudson has taken to predicting the weather, I see," Holmes remarked from his chair. I felt my face flush with embarrassment, and he smiled wanly. "But within every gray cloud lurks the makings of a thunderstorm. Pray, Watson, let me see our visitor's calling card."

I handed it to him. He learned forward and studied it intently. He flexed it gently between his hands and rubbed its surface with his long fingers. At last he brought it to his nose and sniffed, as if inhaling the vapors of a fine wine.

"Our mysterious visitor is between forty and fifty years of age," Holmes said. "She hails from a family with close associations to University education. Specifically Oxford, where I suggest her father was at least a professor of mathematics. She has particularly fond memories of her childhood that she treasures dearly."

Even after so many years and hundreds of cases in my

files, I was still capable of surprise. "Holmes," I said. "If I believed in supernatural forces, I would say you were of their realm. How, for heaven's sake, can smelling a playing card tell you so much about a woman you haven't even seen yet?"

"As always, Watson, you choose not to see that which is in plain sight. Notice the manufacturer's imprint." He indicated a singular symbol hidden amid the ornate decorative patterns on the back of the card. Tiny letters were printed beneath it.

"Highley and Wilkes, 1862," I read.

"Exactly. Makers of the finest playing cards ever to grace a gentleman's table. Their work was particularly popular among those in the cloisters of academia, who often commissioned limited-edition packs for themselves. The set to which this orphan belongs was such a commission, printed in 1862 for the Department of Mathematics, Christ Church, Oxford, which is represented here in the card's illustrative decor. The fact that our guest is in possession of this particular card indicates that she has a close male acquaintance associated with that department at that time. Most probably her father. This card, after more than three decades, is in remarkably fine condition. It is no forgery, for it carries the unique scent of the treating chemicals used in Highley and Wilkes paper. It has likely been kept pressed in a scrapbook, carefully isolated from both dirt and handling fingers. I infer that it was given to our visitor at a memorable time in her childhood during—or shortly after—1862. It has remained a memento of her youthful days amongst the ivy of academe."

Before I could utter an exclamation of amazement, a woman's voice spoke up behind me. "Impressive indeed, Mr. Holmes. Nine out of ten."

I turned toward the voice as Holmes rose to his feet. A handsome woman stood in the doorway. She was about Holmes's age, with streaks of gray adding mature dignity to hair that had once been deep brown. She was clad in mourning black and held what appeared to be a glass case the size of a jewelry box, tinted a smoky red.

She smiled disarmingly and looked squarely at Holmes. "What my acquaintances tell me about your gifts," she nodded toward me, "and what I read through the good doctor's reminiscences in the *Strand,* have apparently not been exaggerations. But in truth my father was a Dean. I had a beloved friend who was Mathematics Lecturer of Christ Church. *He* was the gentleman who gave me the card when I was ten years old, and yes, my memories of that time are precious indeed."

With renewed vigor, Holmes stepped over the clutter and approached the woman. "Please forgive my error, Madam. Do come in."

He offered her a chair and she sat, resting the glass box carefully on her lap. Its exquisitely crafted facets reflected the light in complex patterns. On the lid was engraved a stylized heart, similar to those on the playing card.

Holmes took the chair opposite her. "You have me at a disadvantage, Madam. To whom do I have the pleasure of speaking?"

"My name is not important just now. In fact, it would initiate a flurry of questions on your part, queries of a personal nature that would merely delay my mission here today. Let us say that your assistance in a significant case was valuable to some—" she paused, and her expression took on a pleased, far-seeing look "—*acquaintances* of mine. Five years ago."

Holmes sat up with a start. I had never before seen such an expression of shock and bewilderment on his stoic face.

"You left them," she continued, "before they had a chance to thank you adequately. That is why I am here." She paused and gazed into the red crystalline patterns of the box. A tear drifted down her cheek. Holmes offered her a handkerchief, which she accepted with a small, embarrassed laugh.

"Most kind," she said, dabbing her eyes.

Holmes waited for the woman to collect herself. Then he leaned forward, steepling his fingers in his gesture of undivided attention. "Madam, I ask you to provide specifics. At the time you indicate, I was . . . traveling extensively, so this 'significant case' could have occurred in any one of a number of, let us say, exotic locales." He indicated her mourning clothes. "And if you please, Madam, may I ask who has passed on? Is it someone known to me, a client from the case you mentioned?"

She shook her head. "No. Not the client. But the departed *was* known to you. He once found you to be a most promising student, though a tad too serious at times. He was aware of this particular mystery; however, he was not involved in its resolution, which you devised to the gratitude of all concerned."

Holmes frowned. "Madam, you speak in riddles, and I have met few individuals who do that in a manner I find engaging. Please come to your point so that I may be at your service."

The woman in black nodded. "Mr. Holmes, as Dr. Watson is your chronicler and Boswell, so too did I once have mine. He was a kind and gentle man, the only adult who found it not only *easy* but *logical* to believe the fanciful accounts told to him by a child friend. He wrote down all I told him about special places I had visited and the unusual persons I had met there."

She turned to me. "Like you, Doctor, he ... added color to my reports and altered many of the unimportant details so that they could be presented to a reading public. He knew few would believe the accounts. He even published them under a *nom de plume*. But he felt, as I think you do, that even grown-ups want to believe in something beyond the world we walk through everyday. They want to be told that maybe their own lives could be touched by the magic that surrounds us, if only their eyes saw what was before them." This last was directed toward Holmes, who nodded behind peaked fingertips.

"I understand," he said solemnly. Then a keen light of recognition shone in his eyes. He sat up straight and looked at the woman as if for the first time, as if he were seeing behind her eyes into a special realm that only they shared. Something intangible, like a wind or a whisper, passed between them. "Have you returned," he asked, "to *that place* again?"

She gave him a sad smile. "Several times. Each time, I was the only one who had changed. It was as if only a day had passed since my previous visit. Time, I think, moves differently there than in our world. Perhaps Mr. H. G. Wells knows."

"Perhaps," Holmes replied. "You have paid another visit most recently, am I correct? Your attire is connected with that journey?"

"Yes. I returned there last night. My husband believes I am visiting a sister. I spent a week there, maybe more, and still returned this morning. That's when I found out *you* had been there since my last visit. They speak most highly of you, you know. You solved a crisis of royal urgency, one that almost cost me my head. The only participant you upset was the local self-proclaimed consulting detective, who didn't take kindly to an outsider barging in on his jurisdiction."

"A successful consulting detective," said Holmes, "should never be late, *particularly* if he wears a watch in his waistcoat pocket."

The dark woman laughed, and years seemed to fall away from her. I could see the child she once was, *still* was, behind the thin veil of age. She delicately lifted the box and gave it to Holmes.

"This is for you," she said. "A small token of their gratitude, something you may use when you need it."

Holmes took the box, but his eyes never left the woman as she rose and strode gracefully toward the door. He followed her and opened the door for her.

"It has been an honor finally to meet you," she said as Holmes took her hand.

"I was going to say the same, Madam. I hope to have the pleasure again."

"Perhaps. If we're both in the same place at the same time." She looked at me. "Doctor. Thank you for your reminiscences." Holmes gently closed the door after her.

He brushed his fingers over the beautiful cut glass container, held it up to the light and studied the fine filigree in its wine-red surfaces. Woven into the reflective facets were the words OPEN ME.

A silence hung between us for a long moment. What had just transpired between Holmes and that woman? He was keeping something from me, and I was not going to stand by and let him carry it further.

"Blast it, Holmes! Who was she? What on earth are you waiting for? Open the box!"

He looked me in the eye with an intensity I had not seen since his Return. "First, my dear Watson, I must ask you to hand me the *Times*. I suspect it holds the one item our visitor did not reveal. Though, sadly, I believe I know what it will tell us."

I passed the newspaper to him. He put the box on the table and shuffled the pages with restrained urgency, letting them fall like leaves to the floor until, at last, he found what he was searching for. A weight seemed to settle about his neck, and he sank into his chair.

"What is it, Holmes?" I asked.

He handed the page to me. Amidst reports concerning the Sudan campaign, Indian finance, and the situation in Cuba, the most prominent item was a narrow column that covered the right-hand side of the page. It read

OBITUARY.
—◆—
"Lewis Carroll"

We regret to announce the death of Rev. Charles Lutwidge Dodgson, better known as "Lewis Carroll," the delightful author of "Alice in Wonderland," and other books of an exquisitely whimsical humor. He died yesterday at The Chestnuts, Guildford, the residence of his sisters, in his 64th year. . . .

When I finished reading, I turned to find Holmes inserting a tiny glass key into the box's lock. With a delicate twist of his fingers, he unlocked the lid and gently raised it. Within was a sheet of stationery, which he withdrew and read in unmoving silence. The faintest whisper of amused recollection crossed Holmes's features. Then he opened his fingers and let the sheet flutter toward the floor. I snatched it out of the air.

My dear Mr. Sherlock Holmes, it began.
Our mutual acquaintances wish you to have this as a reflection of their appreciation re the Case of the Stolen Tarts. No one else, they say, could have come to the surprising truth of the mystery so thoroughly. Our friend the Caterpillar says it was certainly a three-pipe problem. The enclosed trifle is for you. You need not be concerned about the benefactor. He has plenty of them and never uses the same one more than once.
        With fond admiration,
        Alice Pleasance Hargreaves, née *Liddell*

Holmes reached into the box and pulled back a red velvet cloth. Underneath was the most astounding sight I have ever seen, and to this day I wonder if my eyes served me honestly. What I beheld was this: a floating crescent of catlike teeth, drawn into a grin like a toothy quarter moon, perpetually amused.

Before I could look closer, Holmes replaced the cloth and closed the lid.

Holmes stood from his chair. He strode to his bookcase and sorted through myriad volumes, raising a cloud of ancient dust. At last, he pulled out a tattered edition that looked as though it had been well read long ago. He returned to his armchair and for the remainder of the day said not a word nor moved so much as a muscle save for the turning of the pages and the occasional chuckle or exclamation.

Since that day, whenever black clouds settle over him, Sherlock Holmes pulls a tiny key from his pocket, opens a certain drawer in his work desk, and withdraws a wonderfully crafted, wine-red glass case. I am always relieved when I hear the sound of the key turning in its lock.

THE ADVENTURE OF THE RUSSIAN GRAVE

by William Barton and Michael Capobianco

After Sherlock Holmes retired to Sussex Downs, his interest was fixed primarily on the sublime science of bee-keeping, and, although there were nearly continuous offers from those desirous of obtaining his detective skills, he had determined that his retirement would be a permanent one. During this period, I was fully engaged in my not inconsiderable medical practice and only went down for an infrequent weekend visit, usually with my third wife.

The ever-steady flow of inquiries that still came to 221B were, of course, forwarded on to his Fulworth address, but occasionally, one would come to me. I generally would read through these letters, taking a sort of perverse interest in the usually sordid matters enclosed, and would send a reluctant refusal making recommendations as I saw fit. A few I sent on to Holmes, thinking that he would find them sufficiently interesting to contemplate; but in general I knew that his interests had focused on sciences other than detection. In fact, it had been more than four years since the affair of Count Von und Zu Grafenstein that I chronicled in "His Last Bow."

It was in early May in the year '08 that a thickish letter arrived as I was breakfasting with my wife. I opened it absentmindedly, my thoughts already engaged in the morning's schedule, but from the first compelling sentence I grew more and more intrigued. Before I had finished reading, I was resolved to deliver this strange missive to Holmes's hand in person. After asking my wife to cancel my appointments, I started immediately for Victoria Station.

I arrived at a little past eleven. The day was somewhat blustery, and the Channel was rough. Holmes was surprised to see me, but indicated he would not diverge from his morning's ritual, and started out for his constitutional walk along the beach with me in tow. It was only after we had made the difficult descent down the chalk cliff that I resumed my attempt to report the reason for my presence. Somewhat jangled, I had fallen behind, and navigating among the pebbles and shingle of that splendid beach made it difficult to catch up.

"I say, Holmes," I said. "Wait up. I'm not used to this sort of exercise nowadays."

He apologized, and for a while we walked side by side, until finally I brought out the letter. He read through it quickly, refolded it efficiently, and placed it back in its envelope.

"Well?" I asked. "What do you make of it?"

Holmes did not answer but instead thrust the letter into his greatcoat and quickened his pace. I had noted an increasing tendency toward taciturnity in my friend as he aged, so I made no further attempt at engaging him.

Suddenly he turned toward me, a look I remember well etched upon his features. "Watson, I thank you for your speed in bringing this to me. Time is of the essence. Indeed, I knew that there were bits of web left by that vile spider Moriarty that remained in place after his death; this is an opportunity to sweep away a most pernicious bit. And a piquant mystery as well. Bees can only maintain one's interest for so long, my friend. Would you care to accompany me on this one?"

I indicated I wouldn't miss it for anything.

Holmes and I returned to London immediately and took one of the new motorized cabs to the address of the Belgravia townhouse mentioned in the letter. We were ushered into a sitting room where a handsome woman of imperious appearance sat behind a desk of the old style. Her complexion was ruddy and her blonde hair was tied back into a severe bun. She motioned us to sit.

"I am very glad you decided to come, Mr. Holmes," she said, Russian accent barely noticeable. "Although I must say I did not expect that you would be so . . . swift."

Holmes leaned forward, elbows on knees, hands steepled together. "My dear lady," he said, "your letter was most remarkable. Although you do not know it, your case touches an especial response in me. I wold like to go over the elements of this remarkable circumstance with you piece by piece."

"As you have already ascertained, I am Nadya Filipovna Dolgoruky," she said. "I am the daughter of Count Filip Alekseyevich and Countess Natalya Petrovna Dolgoruky, who were brutally murdered in Baden-Baden in February of 1891. At the time I was only six. My mother, who was of English descent, had relatives in London, and I was sent to live with them. I was raised as an Englishwoman. I had almost forgotten the tragic circumstances of my youth, when, ten days ago, I received a package bearing a gold ring and a letter."

"Could I see the ring?" asked Holmes.

"Yes, of course." The countess opened a drawer of her desk and drew it out, then handed it to my friend, who examined it closely. "Go on," he said. "My attention may appear to be diverted, but it is not."

She nodded. "I have read many of Dr. Watson's accounts of your eccentric habits. In fact, the first book I ever read in English was *A Study in Scarlet*, given to me by a friend of my mother's. Well, to continue, the letter, purporting to be a last testament written by my father, explained the long and bizarre history of our family. I have had the letter translated into English and you can examine it for yourself, Mr. Holmes, so I will be brief.

"Apparently, my great-great-grandfather, Nikolai Dolgoruky, was a participant in the failed insurrection against the Tsar of December 1825. The uprising was a dismal failure, and he and his comrades were arrested and most of them exiled to Siberia. Eventually he sent for his family, who joined him in 1833. According to my father's testament, Nikolai managed to flourish in that remote wilderness and amassed great wealth. Suddenly in 1844, for no apparent reason, he sent his wife and teenage son back to St. Petersburg. Less than a year later, this ring was delivered to them with a scrawled note saying that they would not see him again. Heartbroken, my great-great-grandmother died soon afterward."

Holmes had put the plain gold band on his little finger,

lodged just above the first joint. "A woman's ring," he said. "Tell us more."

She sighed. "Yes. From here, the story skips several generations. My father, a most intrepid man, vowed that he would find out what had happened. This is what the testament says, mind you, and I have no other evidence. He went to Siberia and found a man loyal to my great-great-grandfather, who explained that Nikolai had long feared that the jealousies he was arousing amongst the native tribesmen would prove fatal, and he had sent his family away because he feared for their lives. Nikolai knew that he had been marked for death, and he took his accumulated wealth to a secure spot, where he buried it. He intended that he would be buried there as well. The night before he was murdered, he sent the message and ring.

"In 1891, my father became involved with a man named Moran. Apparently, this Moran promised that he would provide the resources for a return trip to Siberia to recover the family wealth that had been hidden."

Holmes turned to me, index finger in the air. "Note, Watson. Enter the spider."

As she told the story, the countess's face had grown progressively whiter. She put on her spectacles and referred to a sheaf of papers on the desk. "I will translate the last paragraph for you. 'They are coming for me now, Moran and that awful man named Moriarty. I have made the ultimate mistake of telling them about the ring. As my ancestor before me, I must endeavor to hide this ring and make sure that it passes to my descendants. Moriarty will not rest until he has it in his possession.' "

Holmes sat back, rubbing the base of his neck, a mannerism that I had never noticed in him before. "And suddenly, seventeen years later, you receive the testament and ring out of the blue. I note that the paper is of authentic vintage. Could I see it more closely?"

As Holmes drew a pince-nez out of his pocket and clipped it to his nose, a look of embarrassment passed across his features. I wondered how long he had needed them. "Yes, everything looks quite authentic. Postmarked Baden-Baden, February 6, 1891. You may recall, Watson, that that was only a few months before our misadventure at Reichenbach Falls. Unfortunately, we rid the world of that monster a little too late to help in this instance. The least we can do is try to rectify matters."

I mumbled agreement, wondering what I was letting myself in for.

"And the ring, my dear countess," continued Holmes, holding the object in question up to the light, "is engraved with a secret message. Ah, I can just make it out—60 55 12 101 57 55 6 16 7 ТЕНЬ КЧуbi COCHbl.' "

"The last three words are Russian, Mr. Holmes, for 'shadow of the mound of the pine.' "

Holmes chuckled to himself. "Remind you of anything, Watson?"

I hesitated. "The Musgrave Ritual?"

"Of course. Hardly a mystery to decipher. The first six numbers designate the longitude and latitude of a location in the far east of the Russian Empire. The next two are apparently a date, mostly likely in the Julian reckoning. The final one is a time, probably seven a.m."

"Amazing," I exclaimed. "Holmes, your powers have not grown dusty with disuse. Are you certain?"

"It is unmistakable, my dear friend. I have no doubt that the shadow of the mound of the pine will be as easy to unravel."

"I hesitate to ask . . ." started the woman.

"No need to worry, Countess. We will follow this thing to the end. Right, Watson?"

I frankly could not understand Holmes's enthusiasm for this project, though a desire to clean up the messes left by his former nemesis was certainly part of it. It took two weeks to prepare for the journey. Through Mycroft we quickly obtained the necessary visas and letters of passage, and it was only a matter of booking tickets on the recently completed Trans-Siberian Railway. I had been cultivating a young doctor to eventually take over my practice when I retired, and I felt confident that he could look after my patients until I returned. Though my wife was not especially happy about my leavetaking, she knew the depth of affection I had for Holmes, and let me go with the proviso that I not be gone longer than two months.

We left from Charing Cross Station on May 20, with forty days to reach the designated location. Since Jules Verne's fa-

mous adventurers had made it halfway around the globe in
that amount of time, I felt that we would not be late.

The journey across the Russian Empire was fascinating. I
have long been an aficionado of rail travel, and, at first, I
could not have been more delighted with our accommodations. A noble family, Prince Vorontsov and his retinue, were
traveling to Vladivostok at the nether end of this enormous
railway, and we were permitted to ride with them in their
special cars.

We spent ten days in transit across a magnificent, ever-
changing landscape. We traveled through the picturesque
though often rundown Russian countryside, across prairie
and steppe, finally into pristine Boreal forest, miles upon
miles of endless wilderness dotted with beautiful bright
lakes.

As we penetrated deeper into Siberia, the towns took on
a makeshift, tumbledown appearance, and the railway stations were nothing more than piles of lumber. Holmes and I
spent this time to good effect, preparing for the rough journey to come. I made friends with the Vorontsovs, and they
kindly volunteered two of their retainers to accompany us to
our destination. One, Vassily by name, spoke English very
fluently, and would act as translator. The other, of strong
peasant stock, was called Borya. Vassily indeed had some
knowledge of the Siberian hinterlands, and told me much
about what we were likely to encounter once we left civilization.

We arrived in Krasnoyarsk on the first day of June,
greeted by auspicious, clear weather. I was struck by the pi-
oneer atmosphere of this bustling town on the banks of the
Yenisey River, and was intrigued by the resemblance to pictures I had seen of the American West. The streets were
nothing but dirt tracks, made impassable by deep gullies,
and I ventured the opinion that heading cross-country would
be quicker. The hotel in which we stayed was awful, filled
with cockroaches of enormous proportions as well as every
other form of vermin known to man. For four days we
stayed in Krasnoyarsk, as Holmes and Vassily attempted to
purchase passage up the Yenisey.

No doubt the reader thinks that we must have lost our
minds to undertake such a perilous journey into the remotest
corner of this wild country. I daresay that I was a little mad,
driven so by the tedious humdrum of my practice. I can only

say that I looked forward to the adventure with an excitement that I had not felt since the earliest days of my association with Sherlock Holmes.

Finally, we managed to convince a bourgeois young river man named Gortov, normally employed in the fur trade, to take us where we wished to go. Holmes had already purchased horses and other necessary provisions, and we loaded this unpainted, ramshackle boat to the gunnels, starting out on the fifth of June, cheered on by fine weather, though the midges and mosquitoes on the river were appalling.

Because it was downriver, Gortov's boat at first made more than fifteen knots. It took several days to reach the Yenisey's confluence with the Angara, and from then on our course took us up this smaller river, still wider than the Thames at Greenwich. The evergreens pressed down to the river's edge, and this dark green barrier grew quite monotonous. Our speed dropped to between five and ten knots. As the days passed, we came to know Gortov well, and my worry that he would not wait for us at Aksenovo evaporated. Holmes appeared to be enjoying himself, taking great delight in the nature that was all around us. Each night he would take out his surveying tools and carefully measure our position, comparing it with the coordinates on the ring.

It took us more than two weeks to reach the spot that Gortov identified as the town of Aksenovo, three rough-hewn dwellings along the river, one of which purported to be an inn. As we packed our horses, I had my first sight of the Evenki tribesmen, dark, wrinkled men with gaptooth smiles. One, named Tengiz, agreed to be our guide.

According to Holmes's computations, it was a little over two hundred and fifty miles to our destination. Our mounts were small, dun-colored, steppe horses, shaggy beasts that would almost be considered ponies back in England. They were the best that could be had in Krasnoyarsk, healthy and well-shod. We started out the next morning, and the transit through those dense woods, while never easy, was manageable. We camped each night under the whispering, creaking boughs, with hardly ever a glimpse of the stars.

On the evening of the twenty-ninth, we made camp less than a mile from the spot of Dolgoruky's grave. It had been raining, and the evergreens were still damp, occasional drips falling with an eerie crackle. I congratulated Holmes on our success, barely able to confine my excitement. When we retired that night, I was for a long time unable to sleep, wondering what we would find come daylight.

We were up before dawn, which was magnificent. Holmes had already made detailed calculations of the location of the grave, with an accuracy of about two-tenths of a mile. As we made our way northeast, the ground grew a little swampy, and the trees were not so thick. Tengiz pointed out a clearing, and we made our way there with bated breath. As expected, in the center of the clearing stood a mound of rounded stones as tall as a man.

It was now 5:15. Orange sunlight slanted through the tall trees, shadows scoring the little clearing. The mound itself cast a long shadow, but there were many pine trees within its range. Holmes examined the monument carefully, then carried on a heated conversation with Tengiz through Vassily, asking ever more detailed questions, growing visibly agitated. When I asked him what was wrong, he brushed me aside, saying, "No time. No time!"

Suddenly Holmes threw himself on the mound like a wild man, pulling out the cobbles as fast as he could, throwing them aside. Without understanding, I followed his example, until we had torn the pile apart and reached the soil underneath. Holmes continued to dig with his bare hands, after a minute pulling a small rusted box out of the ground."

"But, Holmes," I stammered. "That's not right. It's supposed to be—"

"My friend," he exclaimed, "there is no grave, except perhaps our own."

From the box he drew a single sheet of heavy paper, upon which a series of mathematical equations were laid out. Beneath them, a diagram showed two intersecting ovals. Holmes held it out to me with a strange, sickly grin on his face. "Moriarty," he said. "Master mathematician. Specializing in *orbits*, Watson. His magnum opus was *The Dynamics of an Asteroid*. It all begins to make sense now."

Holmes consulted his watch. "I doubt we can escape his diabolical design, but we can try. Watson, ride for all you're worth." And with that he jumped up and vaulted onto his horse, riding headlong into the forest. My head spinning with bewilderment, I followed, with Vassily, Borya, and Tengiz not far behind.

We spurred the horses along the narrow track that led from the clearing, galloping until the horses faltered. "Fast trot now," Holmes shouted over his shoulder. "If we push them any harder, they'll go down." The ground was growing marshier, but the track widened. We kept the horses at a trot for five miles, then urged them into a canter for fifteen minutes or so. When the horses could not go on, we dismounted and led them at a fast run. We made perhaps two miles that way. By this time the horses were sufficiently rested to trot for another five miles.

Rocky outcroppings were showing through the mossy soil here, and the ground was beginning to slope downward. We suddenly found ourselves in a precipitous valley leading to a small stream. Following Holmes's example, we dismounted and led our horses down into this declivity, eventually coming to the stream itself, which was surrounded by large boulders of all sizes. It was by now almost seven, and Holmes kept looking up at the sky as if expecting some angelic visitation. He motioned us to sit with our backs against the largest of the boulders, and we did so, holding the horses as close as possible.

A minute passed, then several more. The stream made its amiable noise and birds sang in the trees, which were stirred by the gentle morning breeze. Tengiz, in particular, wore an expression of utter bemusement, as though these strange Europeans were even crazier than he had surmised.

I had almost begun to rebel when the scene brightened slightly, as though the sun were coming out of light cloud. I was about to comment on this phenomenon, when the world exploded in white light, as bright as a limelight, etching the world in my eyes, sharp black shadows everywhere. As the light faded, I noticed that the world had grown completely silent. There was a sudden sharp jolt in the ground, almost like an earth tremor but more violent. "Holmes!" I shouted, but somehow my voice disappeared. In less time than it takes to tell, an improbably fast wall of dust shot over our heads and past us into the trees on the far side of the stream. The horses were knocked down and the trees, hammered by this burning wind, whipped over, all at once, bending almost to the point of breaking before snapping back. Only then did I notice the terrible sound, a noise louder than any I have ever heard, a deafening thunderlike noise that went on and on. When the wind had stopped, I could not restrain myself any longer. I got up and looked back.

The sky above the trees had turned brassy gold. Pink

overtones shadowed the sides of my vision, striated clouds visible overhead, picked out by brilliant shafts of illumination. As it faded, the sky turned blood red, with streaks of vermilion showing here and there. Towering into the sky was a black, mushroom-shaped cloud, streaked with red, as of fire boiling in its depths. "Good God!" I said. "Holmes, you must see this!" If his ears were ringing as badly as mine, I doubt that he heard me.

The dark cloud grew larger, blotting out the sky, causing a sort of artificial evening. By this time the others, seeing that I had not come to harm, had joined me. The horses, mercifully unhurt, were also on their feet. My eyes seemed to have recovered, although there were still dark afterimages floating before me.

I turned to Holmes, who bore the same uncharacteristic grim smile I had noticed at the mound.

"Oh, Watson," he said, "We're fools . . . fools! It's so plain to me now. Perhaps I have grown old and feeble-minded while tending my bees. That devil Moriarty! Damn his soul. Seventeen years beyond the grave, and he still almost gets his revenge."

I stammered some foolish question.

"It's all here, man," he said, brandishing the document. "During the period Moriarty was a working astronomer, he observed the breakup of a comet, and calculated the exact orbits of the individual pieces. He determined that one of them was in fact going to collide with the Earth, and figured out precisely where and when. No doubt a mind like his savored this knowledge for many years. He realized that, when he and I finally came to grips, he might not be the victor; and he formulated an ingeniously simple way to assure that his vengeance would be enacted. His henchman came here, to Tunguska, and built the mound."

"But why was the box buried under the mound?" I asked.

"It shows something of the pathology of that man, that he would do such a thing. Pure egotism. I, of course, did not know what I would find under that pile of stones, but when I realized that it had been erected no more than twenty years earlier, I began to grasp what was going on.

"The Dolgorukys were murdered as part of this elaborate deception. When the time came, one of his minions contrived to deliver the fraudulent testament and ring to Countess Dolgoruky. They even made certain that she had read about my exploits, and perhaps convinced her mother to return to England. Oh, Watson, I must say this was a delicious trick!"

And he burst into the loudest, longest laugh I had ever heard.

THE ADVENTURE OF THE FIELD THEOREMS

by Vonda N. McIntyre

Holmes laughed like a Bedlam escapee.

Considerably startled by his outburst, I lowered my *Times*, where I had been engrossed in an article about a new geometrical pattern discovered in the fields of Surrey. I had not yet decided whether to bring it to Holmes's attention.

"What amuses you so, Holmes?"

No interesting case had challenged Holmes of late, and I wondered, fearfully, if boredom had led him to take up, once again, the habit of cocaine.

Holmes's laughter died, and an expression of thoughtful distress replaced the levity. His eyes revealed none of the languorous excitement of the drug.

"I am amused by the delusions of our species, Watson," Holmes said. "Amusing on the surface, but, on reflection, distressing."

I waited for his explanation.

"Can you not discern the reason for my amusement, Watson—and my distress? I should think it perfectly obvious."

I considered. Should he encounter an article written particularly for its humorous content, he would pass straight over it, finding it as useless to him as the orbits of the planets. The description of some brutal crime surely would not amuse him. A trace of Moriarty would raise him to anger or plunge him into despair.

"Ah," I said, certain I had divined the truth. "You have read an account of a crime, I beg your pardon, the *resolution* of a crime, and you have seen the failings in the analysis. But," I pointed out, somewhat disturbed by my friend's indifference to the deeper ramifications, "that would indicate the arrest of an innocent victim, Holmes. Surely you should have some other reaction than laughter."

"Surely I should," Holmes said, "if that were the explanation. It is not." He shook the paper. "Here is a comment by Conan Doyle on Houdini's recent performance."

"Quite impressive it was, too," I said. "Thrilling, I would say. Did Sir Arthur find the performance compelling?"

"Conan Doyle," Holmes said with saturnine animosity, "attributes Houdini's achievements to," Holmes sneered, " 'mediumistic powers.' "

"His achievements do strain credulity," I said mildly.

"Pah!" Holmes said. "That is the *point*, Watson, the entire and complete *point!* Would you pay good money to see him *fail* to escape from a sealed coffin?"

"I suppose that I would not," I admitted.

"Were Houdini to tell you his methods, you would reply, 'But that is so simple! Anyone could achieve the same effect—using your methods!' "

As Holmes often heard the same remark after explaining his methods, I began to understand his outburst.

"I would say nothing of the sort," I said. "I should say, instead, that he had brought the technique of stage magicianship to as near an exact science as it ever will be brought in this world."

Holmes recognized my comment with a brief smile, for I had often said as much to him about his practice of detection.

"But it is true, Watson," Holmes said, serious once more. "Anyone *could* achieve the same effect—were they willing to dedicate their lives to developing the methods, to studying the methods, to perfecting the methods! *Then* it is 'so simple.' "

When Holmes deigned to lead an amazed observer through his deductive reasoning, the observer's reaction was invariably the same: His methods were "perfectly obvious"; anyone, including the observer, could duplicate them with ease.

"Conan Doyle claims friendship with Houdini," Holmes

said in disgust, "and yet he insults his friend. He dismisses Houdini's hard work and ingenuity. Despite Houdini's denials, Conan Doyle attributes Houdini's success to the supernatural. As if Houdini himself had very little to do with it! What a great fool, this Conan Doyle."

"Easy on," I said. "Sir Arthur is an intelligent man, a brave man. An inspired man! His imagination is every bit as exalted as that of Wells! His Professor Challenger stories compare favorably to *War of the Worlds!*"

"I never read fiction," Holmes said. "A failing for which you berate me continually. If I did read fiction, I would not doubly waste my time with the scientific romances you find so compelling. Nor am I interested in the mad fantasies of a spiritualist." Holmes scowled through a dense cloud of pipe smoke. "The man photographs fairies in his garden."

"You are too much the materialist, Holmes," I said. "With my own eyes I saw amazing things, unbelievable things, in Afghanistan—"

"Ancient sleight of hand. Snake charming. The rope trick!" He laughed again, though without the hysterical overtones of his previous outburst. "Ah, Watson, I envy you your innocence."

I was about to object to his implications when he stayed my comment by holding up one hand.

"Mrs. Hudson—"

"—with our tea," I said. "Hardly deserves the word 'deduction,' as her footsteps are plainly audible, and it is, after all, tea-time—"

"—to announce a client."

Mrs. Hudson, our landlady, knocked and opened the door. "Gentleman to see you, Mr. Holmes," she said. "Shall I set an extra cup?"

The figure of a man loomed behind her in the shadows.

"Thank you, Mrs. Hudson," Holmes said. "That would be most kind."

Mrs. Hudson placed a calling card on the tray by the doorway. Holmes rose to his feet, but did not trouble to read the card. As our visitor entered, I rose as well and made to greet him, but Holmes spoke first.

"I observe, Dr. Conan Doyle," Holmes said coolly, "that you were called abruptly into the fields, and have spent the morning investigating the mystery of the damaged crops. Investigating without success, I might add. Has a new field theorem appeared?"

Conan Doyle laughed heartily, his voice booming from his powerful chest.

"So you've introduced me already, John!" he said to me. "You were looking out the window when my carriage arrived, I've no doubt." He smiled at Holmes. "Not such a clever deduction, Mr. Holmes." He wrinkled his noble brow and said to me, "But how did you know I've just come to town, and how did you know of my involvement with the field theorems?"

"I'm afraid I had no idea you were our visitor, Sir Arthur," I said. "I did not even know we had a visitor until Holmes surmised your approach."

Sir Arthur chuckled. "I understand," he said. "Bad manners, revealing the tricks of the trade. Even those as simple as prior knowledge."

Holmes concealed his annoyance; I doubt anyone who knew him less well than I would have noticed it. He gazed steadily at Sir Arthur. We seldom had visitors taller than Holmes, but Sir Arthur Conan Doyle exceeds six feet by four inches. Unlike my friend Holmes, who remained slender, indeed gaunt, even during his occasional periods of slothful depression, Sir Arthur dominated the room with his hearty presence.

"How *did* you know about our visitor, Holmes?" I asked, trying to salvage the introductions.

"I heard Sir Arthur's carriage arrive," he said dismissively, "as you would have done had you been paying attention."

Though somewhat put off by his attitude, I continued. "And Sir Arthur's outing? His identity?"

"My face is hardly unknown," Sir Arthur said. "Why, my likeness was in the *Times* only last week, accompanying a review—"

"I never read the literary section of the *Times*," Holmes said. "As Watson will attest." He pointed the stem of his pipe at Sir Arthur's pants cuffs. "You are a fastidious man, Sir Arthur. You dress well, and carefully. Your shave this morning was leisurely and complete. Your mustache is freshly trimmed. Had you planned your excursion, you would surely have worn suitable clothing. Therefore, your presence was required on short notice. You have wiped the mud of the fields from your boots, but you have left a smear on the polish. You have confronted a puzzle that has distracted you from your customary appearance, which I can easily see—anyone could easily see—is impeccable. As to the nature of the puzzle, unripe seed-heads of *Triticum aestivum* have attached themselves to your trouser cuffs. I am in no doubt that you investigated the vandalism plaguing fields in Surrey."

"Amazing," Conan Doyle whispered, his ruddy face paling. "Absolutely amazing."

I could see that Holmes was both pleased by Conan Doyle's reaction, and surprised that Sir Arthur did not laugh again and announce that his methods were simplicity itself.

Holmes finished his recitation. "That you have failed to solve the mystery is self-evident—else why come to me?"

Sir Arthur staggered. Leaping forward to support him, I helped him to a chair. I was astonished to perceive any weakness in a man of his constitution. He was quite in shock. Fortunately, Mrs. Hudson chose that moment to arrive with the tea. A good hot cup, fortified with brandy from the sideboard, revived Sir Arthur considerably.

"I do apologize," he said. "I've spent the morning in the presence of strangeness beyond any I've ever before witnessed. As you divined, Mr. Holmes, the experience has distracted me. To perceive your supernatural talents so soon thereafter—!"

He took a deep draught of his tea. I refilled his cup, including rather more brandy. Sir Arthur sipped his tea, and let warm, pungent steam rise around his face. His color improved.

" 'Supernatural?' " Holmes mused. "Well-honed, certainly. Extraordinary, even. But not in the least supernatural."

Sir Arthur replied. "If John did not tell you who I am, and you did not recognize my face, then you could only have discovered my name by—reading my mind!"

"I read your name," Holmes said dryly, "from the head of your walking stick, where it is quite clearly engraved."

Since the end of spring, the newspapers had been full of articles about mysterious damage to growing crops. Wheat stalks were crushed in great circles intersected by lines and angles, as if a cyclone had touched down to give mere humans a lesson in celestial geometry. Though the phenomena were often accompanied by strange lights in the sky, the weather was invariably fair. If the lights were lightning, it was lightning unaccompanied by thunder! No wind or rain occurred to cause any damage, much less damage in perfect geometrical form.

Many suggestions had been put forth as to the cause of the unexplained diagrams, from hailstorms to electromagnetic disturbances, but blame had not yet been fixed. The patterns were the mystery of the year; the press, in a misinterpretation of modern physics in general and the theory of Maxwell in particular, had taken to calling the devices "field theorems."

Holmes had clipped and filed the articles, and painstakingly redrawn the figures. He suspected that if the patterns were the consequence of a natural force, some common element could be derived from a comparison of the designs.

One morning, I had come into the sitting room to find him surrounded by crumpled paper. The acrid bite of smoke thickened the air, and the Persian slipper in which Holmes kept his shag lay overturned on the mantel among the last few scattered shreds of tobacco.

"I have it, Watson!" Holmes had waved a drawing, annotated in his hand. "I believe this to be the basic pattern, from which all other field theorems are derived!"

His brother, Mycroft, speedily dismantled his proof, and took him to task for failing to complete several lemmas associated with the problem. Holmes, chagrined to have made such an elementary (to Holmes), and uncharacteristic, mistake, appeared to lose interest in the field theorems. But it was clear from his comments to Sir Arthur that they had never completely vanished from his attention.

After packing quickly, Holmes and I accompanied Sir Arthur to the station, where we boarded the train to Undershaw, his estate in Hindhead, Surrey.

"Tell me, Sir Arthur," Holmes said, as our train moved swiftly across the green and gold late-summer countryside, "how came you to be involved in this investigation?"

I wondered if Holmes were put out. The mystery had begun in early summer. Here it was nearly harvesttime before anyone called for the world's only consulting detective.

"It is my tenants who have been most troubled by the phe-

nomenon," said Sir Arthur, recovered from his earlier shock.
"Fascinating as the field theorems may be, they do damage
the crops. And I feel responsible for what has happened. I
cannot have my tenants lose their livelihoods because of my
actions."

"So you feel the vandalism is directed at you," said I. Sir
Arthur had involved himself in several criminal cases, generally on the side of a suspect he felt to be innocent. His efforts differed from those of Holmes in that Holmes never
ended his cases with ill-advised legal wrangles. No doubt
one of Sir Arthur's less grateful supplicants was venting his
rage against some imagined slight.

"Vandalism?" Sir Arthur said. "No, this is far more important, more complex, than vandalism. It's obvious that
someone is trying to contact me from the other side."

"The other side?" I asked. "Of Surrey? Surely it would be
easier to use the post."

Sir Arthur leaned toward me, serious and intense. "Not
the other side of the country. The other side of . . . life and
death."

Holmes barked with laughter. I sighed quietly. Intelligent
and accomplished as my friend is, he occasionally overlooks
proprieties. Holmes will always choose truth over politeness.

"You believe," Holmes said to Sir Arthur, "that a seance
brought about these field theorems? The crushed crops are
the country equivalent of ectoplasm and levitating silver
trumpets?"

The scorn in Holmes's voice was plain, but Sir Arthur replied calmly. He has, of course, faced disbelief innumerable
times since his conversion to spiritualism.

"Exactly so," he said, his eyes shining with hope. "Our
loved ones on the other side desire to communicate with us.
What better way to attract our attention than to offer us
knowledge beyond our reach? Knowledge that cannot be
confined within an ordinary seance cabinet? We might com-
mune with the genius of Newton!"

"I did not realize," Holmes said, "that your family has a
connection to that of Sir Isaac Newton."

"I did not intend to claim such a connection," Sir Arthur
said, drawing himself stiffly upright. Holmes could make
light of his spiritual beliefs, of his perceptions, but an insult
to the familial dignity fell beyond the pale.

"Of course not!" I said hurriedly. "No one could imagine that you did."

I hoped that, for once, Holmes would not comment on the contradiction inherent in my statement.

Holmes gazed with hooded eyes at Sir Arthur, and held his silence.

"It's well know that entities from diverse places and times—not only relatives—communicate from the other side," I said. "How extraordinary it would be, were Isaac Newton to return, after nearly two centuries of pure thought!"

" 'Extraordinary,' " Holmes muttered, "would hardly be the word for it." He fastened his gaze upon Sir Arthur. "Dr. Conan Doyle," he said, "if you believe spirits are the cause of this odd phenomenon—why did you engage me to investigate?"

"Because, Mr. Holmes, if *you* cannot lay the cause to any worldly agent, then the only possible explanation is a spiritual one. 'When you have eliminated the impossible, whatever remains, *however improbable,* must be the truth!' You will help me prove my case."

"I see," Holmes said. "You have engaged me to eliminate causes more impossible than the visitations of spirits. You have engaged me ... to fail."

"I would not have put it so," Sir Arthur said.

The trip continued in rather strained silence. Sir Arthur fell into a restless doze. Holmes stared at the passing landscape, his long limbs taut with unspent energy. After an eternity, we reached the Hindhead station. I roused Sir Arthur, who awoke with a great gasp of breath.

"Ma'am!" he cried, then came to himself and apologized most sincerely. "I was dreaming," he said. "My dear, late mother came to me. She encourages us to proceed!"

Holmes made no reply.

Sir Arthur's carriage, drawn by a pair of fine bays, awaited us.

"The automobile can't be started, sir," the driver said. "We've sent to London for the mechanic."

"Very well, James," Sir Arthur said. He shook his head as we climbed into the carriage. "The motor was quite astonishingly reliable when first I bought it. But recently it has broken down more often than it has run."

The comment drew Holmes's attention. "When, exactly, did it begin to fail?"

"Eight weeks past," Sir Arthur said.

"At the same time the field theorems began to appear," Holmes said thoughtfully.

Sir Arthur chuckled. "Why, Mr. Holmes, surely you don't believe the spirits would try to communicate by breaking my autocar!"

"No, Sir Arthur, you are quite correct. I do not believe the spirits would try to communicate by breaking your autocar."

"Merely a coincidence."

"I do not believe in coincidences."

Holmes was anxious to inspect the field theorems as soon as we arrived at Undershaw, but by then it was full dark. Sir Arthur showed the strain of a long and taxing day. He promised that we should leap out of bed before dawn and be at his tenant's field as the first rays of the morning sun touched the dewdrops of night.

And so we did; and so we were.

The descriptions and newspaper engravings of the field theorems did not do justice to the magnitude of the patterns. We stood on a hillside above the field to gain an overview of the damage. Three wide paths, perfectly circular and perfectly concentric, cut through the waving stalks of grain. A tangent, two radii, and a chord decorated the circles. I had to admit that the pattern resembled nothing so much as the proof of some otherworldly geometric proposition.

"The theorems appear only in wheatfields," Sir Arthur said. "Only in our most important crop. Never in fields of oats, nor in Indian corn."

Holmes made an inarticulate sound of acknowledgment.

We descended the hill, and Holmes entered the field.

Sir Arthur looked after him. "John," he said to me, "will your friend admit it, if he can find no natural explanation?"

"His allegiance is to the truth, Sir Arthur," I said. "He does not enjoy failure—but he would fail before he would propose a solution for which there were no proof."

"Then I have nothing to worry about." He smiled a bluff English smile.

Holmes strode into the swath of flattened green wheat, quartering the scene, inspecting both upright and crushed stalks, searching the hedgerows. He muttered to himself, laughed and snarled; the sound crossed the field like a voice passing over the sea. He measured the path, the width of the stalks left standing, and the angles between the lines and curves.

The sun crept into the clear sky; the day promised heat.

"Can you feel it?" Sir Arthur said softly. "The residual power of the forces that worked here?" He stretched out his hands, as if to touch an invisible wall before him.

And indeed, I felt something, though whether it was energy spilled by unimaginable beings, or the Earth's quiet potential on a summer's day, I could not tell.

While Sir Arthur and I waited for Holmes to finish his search, a rough-shod man of middle years approached.

"Good morning, Robert," Conan Doyle said.

"Morning, Sir Arthur," Robert replied.

"Watson, this is one of my tenants, Robert Holder."

Robert's work clothes were shabby and sweatstained. I thought he might have taken more care with his appearance, when he came to speak to his landlord.

To Robert, Sir Arthur said, "Mr. Holmes and Dr. Watson have come to help us with our mystery."

"Mr. Holmes?" Robert exclaimed.

He glanced out into the field, where Holmes continued to pace and stoop and murmur.

"And you're Dr. Watson?" Robert's voice rose with the shock of finding himself in the presence of celebrity. "Why, it's a pleasure to meet you, sir," he said to me. "My whole family, we read your recountings in the evenings. The children learned their letters, sitting in my lap to listen to your tales."

"Er . . . thank you," I said, somewhat nonplussed. Though he was well-spoken for a farmer, I would not have marked him as a great reader; and, more, I consider the perils encountered by Holmes to be far too vivid for impressionable young children. However, it was not my place to correct Robert's treatment of his offspring, particularly in front of his landlord.

"Have you found the villains?" Robert asked. "The villains who have crushed my best field!"

Holmes strode across the field and rejoined us, a frown furrowing his brow. He appeared not even to notice the presence of Sir Arthur's tenant.

"Useless," Holmes said. "Perfectly useless! Here, the artist stood to sketch the scene." He flung his hand toward a spot where gray dust covered the scuffed ground. "And there! A photographer, with his camera and flash powder. Fully six reporters and as many policemen trampled whatever evidence might have been left." He did not pause to explain how he could tell the difference between the footprints of reporters and those of policeman. "And, no doubt, when the sightseers arrive by the next train—"

"I can easily warn them off," Sir Arthur said.

"To what purpose? The evidence is destroyed. No! I could conjecture, but conjecture is only half the task. Proof, now— that's a different story."

He glared out into the field as if it had deliberately invited careless visitors to blur the story written there.

"If only," Holmes said softly, "the scene were fresh."

He turned abruptly toward Robert. He had taken the measure of the man without appearing to observe him.

"You saw the lights," Holmes said. "Describe them to me."

"Are you Mr. Holmes?"

I blushed to admit, even to myself, that the rough farmer had a better grasp of common manners than did my friend.

"Of course I am. The *lights*."

"The night was calm. A bit of fog, but no rain, no storms. I heard a strange noise. Like a musical instrument, but playing no melody I ever heard. And eerie. . . . It put the chills up my back. Made the baby cry. I went outdoors—"

"You were not frightened?"

"I was. Who would not be frightened? The Folk have fled London, but they still live in the countryside, in our hearts."

"You are a scholar and a folklorist," Holmes said without expression.

"I know the stories my family tells. Old stories. The Folk—"

"The faerie folk!" Sir Arthur said. "I've photographed them, they *do* exist."

"The Folk," Robert said, neither agreeing nor disagreeing with Sir Arthur. "The ones who lived in this land before us."

"The lights, man!" Holmes said impatiently.

"At first I saw only a glow against the fog. Then—a ring of lights, not like candles, flickering, but steady like the gaslights of the city. All different colors. Very beautiful."

"Foxfire," Holmes said.

"No, sir. Foxfire, you see it in the marsh. Not the field.

It's a soft light, not a bright one. These lights, they were bright. The circle spun, and I thought—"

He hesitated.

"Go on, man!"

"You'll think I'm mad."

"If I do, I shall keep it to myself."

Robert hesitated. "I thought I saw ... a huge solid object, floating in the sky like a boat in the water."

"A flying steamship?" I said.

"An aeroplane," said Sir Arthur. "Though I would have thought we'd hear of a pilot in the area."

"More like a coracle," Robert said. "Round, and solid."

"Did you hear its motor?" Holmes asked. "A droning, perhaps, or a sound like the autocar?"

"Only the music," said Robert.

"I've never known an apparition to make a sound like a motorcar," Sir Arthur said.

"What happened then?" said Holmes. "Where did it go, what did it do?"

"It rose, and I saw above it the stars, and Mars bright and red in the midst of them." Robert hesitated, considered, continued. "Then the lights brightened even more, and it vanished in a burst of flame. I felt the fire, smelled the brimstone— At first I thought I was blinded!"

"And then?" Holmes said.

"My sight returned, and the fog closed around me."

"What have you left out?" Holmes asked sternly. "What happened afterward?"

Robert hesitated, reluctance and distress in every line of his expression.

"The truth, man," Holmes said.

"Not afterward. Before. *Before* the coracle disappeared. I thought I saw ... a flash of light, another flash."

"From the coracle?"

"From the sky. Like a signal! White light, white, not red, from ... from Mars!" He drew in a deep breath. "Then the coracle replied, and vanished."

I managed to repress my exclamation of surprise and wonder. Holmes arched one eyebrow thoughtfully. Sir Arthur stroked his mustache.

"Thank you for your help, Robert," Sir Arthur said, as if Robert had said nothing out of the ordinary. "And your good observation."

"Sir Arthur," Robert said, "may I have your permission to salvage what I can from the field? The grain can't be threshed, but I could at least cut the stalks for hay."

"By no means!" Sir Arthur roared in alarm.

Robert stepped back, surprised and frightened.

"No, no," Sir Arthur said, calming himself with visible effort.

"Sir—!"

I was astonished by the tone of protest in which Robert addressed the landowner.

"It's imperative that no one enter the field!" Sir Arthur said. "The pattern mustn't be disturbed till we understand its meaning."

"Very well, Sir Arthur," Robert said reluctantly.

"And set little Robbie and his brothers to keeping the sightseers out of the patterns. They may walk around the edge, but under no circumstances may they proceed inside."

"But, Sir Arthur, this field, every year, has paid your rent. This field keeps the roof over my family's head! Sir Arthur, the crop prices have been low going on two years—"

I did not blame him for his distress, and he was fortunate that Sir Arthur is a humane and decent gentleman.

"You'll not worry about the rent," Sir Arthur said. "I relieve you of the obligation for this year."

On Robert's open face, gratitude and obligation warred.

"I cannot accept that offer, Sir Arthur," he said, "generous though it is, and grateful though I am to you for making it. You and I, we have an agreement. I cannot take charity."

Sir Arthur frowned, that his tenant would not accept such a simple solution to the difficulty.

"We'll discuss this another time," Sir Arthur said. "For the moment, keep the sightseers out of the field." His tone brooked no disagreement.

Robert touched the bill of his ragged cap in acquiescence.

We returned to Sir Arthur's mansion, where his gracious wife Jean, Lady Conan Doyle, presided over a fine, if long-delayed, breakfast. After our excursion, I was famished, but Holmes merely picked at his food. This meant the mystery aroused him. As long as it kept his interest, he would hold himself free of the embrace of cocaine.

For the rest of the day, we accompanied Sir Arthur to other fields where theorems had mysteriously appeared over the past few weeks. They were all, according to Holmes, sadly trampled.

We spoke to tenants who had also seen lights in the sky, but the apparitions frightened the observers; each gave a different description, none as coherent as Robert's. I could not imagine what they had actually seen.

My mind kept returning to Robert's description. Cogent though it had been, something about it nagged at my memory. I put my unease down to the mystery of the phenomenon. And to my wonder. Holmes's skepticism notwithstanding, it would be quite marvelous if we were visited by beings from another world, whether physical or spiritual. Naturally one would prefer friendly beings like those Sir Arthur described, over the invading forces of Mr. Wells's scientific romances.

Holmes dutifully explored each damaged field, and listened to the descriptions of flashing lights in the sky. But as he was presented with nothing but old and damaged evidence, his inspections became more and more desultory as the afternoon wore on, his attention more and more distracted and impatient. He also grew more and more irritated at Sir Arthur's ruminations on spiritualism, and nothing I could do or say could divert the conversation. Like any true believer, Sir Arthur was relentless in his proselytizing.

Toward the end of the afternoon, as I began to hope for tea, we rested beneath an ancient oak near a patterned field.

"Look," Sir Arthur said, "at how the grain has been flattened without breaking. The stalks in the pattern are as green as the undisturbed growth. Don't you think it odd?"

"Quite odd," I agreed.

"Not odd at all," Holmes said.

He leaped from the carriage, snatched a handful of the crop from the edge of the field, and returned with a clump of unbroken stems still sprouting from their original earth. He held the roots in one hand and smashed the other against the stems, bending them at a right angle to their original position. Clods of dirt flew from his hand in reaction to the force of his blow.

But the stems did not break.

"*Triticum aestivum* at this stage of growth is exceedingly tough," Holmes said. "Exceedingly difficult to break."

Holmes pulled out one stem by its roots and handed it to me, then another for Sir Arthur. I tried to break my stem, and indeed it took considerable force even to put a kink in the fibrous growth. Sir Arthur bent his stem, folding it repeatedly back and forth.

"The field theorems would be more impressive," Holmes said, "if the crops *were* broken."

"But, Mr. Holmes," said Sir Arthur, "the forces we are dealing with are mighty. A stem I cannot break would be like a fragile dry twig, to them. Do you not think it amazing that they can temper themselves to gentleness?"

Holmes stared at him in disbelief. "Sir Arthur! First you are impressed with a feat that appears to be difficult, then, when the action proves simple, you claim yourself impressed because it is simple! Your logic eludes me."

In Holmes's powerful hands, several stalks ripped apart.

We returned to Undershaw. We drank Earl Grey from delicate porcelain cups, surrounded by heavy, disagreeable silence. Lady Conan Doyle and I tried in vain to lighten the conversation. When Sir Arthur announced a seance to be held that very evening, Holmes's mood did not improve.

A loud knock on the door, followed by shouting, broke the tension. Sir Arthur rose to attend to the commotion.

"One of your tenants to see you, Sir Arthur," the butler said.

Robert had followed the butler from the front door; to my astonishment he crossed the threshold of the sitting room. Then he remembered his place and snatched his battered cap from his head.

"There's been another field done!" he exclaimed. "Little Robbie just discovered it, coming home to get his brothers some bread and cheese!"

Holmes leaped to his feet, his gray mood vanishing in an instant. Sir Arthur called for his autocar and we hurried off to see the new phenomenon.

The automobile, newly repaired, motored smoothly until we turned down the final road to the new field theorem. Suddenly it died. Robert stepped down from the running board to crank it, but none of his efforts revived it.

Sir Arthur revealed a knowledge of colorful oaths in several languages.

"Bushman," Holmes muttered after a particularly exotic phrase.

I reflected that Sir Arthur must have acquired this unusual facility during his service in the Boer War.

We walked the last half-mile to the field. The afternoon's heat lingered even in the shade of the hedgerows. Birds chirped and rustled the branches.

"Well, Robert," I said, "you'll have the chance to observe Mr. Holmes in action, and you can tell the story in your own words instead of mine. Holmes, Robert is a great enthusiast of your stories."

"I am flattered," Holmes said, "though of course the credit goes entirely to you, Watson, and to your craft."

We had no more opportunity to chat, for we reached the newly patterned field. Robert's children—including Little Robbie, who was considerably taller and larger than his father—had arrived before us, despite our use of the motorcar. They stood in order of descending height on the bottom rail of the fence, exclaiming over the pattern crushed into the grain.

Sir Arthur made as if to plunge into the very center of the new theorem, but Holmes clasped him by the shoulder.

"Stay back!" Holmes cried. "Robert! To the lane! Keep away the spectators!"

"Very well, Mr. Holmes." Robert and his children tramped away down the path.

I marveled at the efficiency of the country grapevine, to give everyone such quick notice of the new field theorem.

Holmes plunged past Sir Arthur. But instead of forging into the field, he climbed the fence and balanced atop the highest rail to gaze across the waving grain. He traced with his eyes the valleys and gulches etched into the surface. Only after some minutes, and a complete circumnavigation of the field, did he venture into the field theorem itself.

Sir Arthur observed Holmes's method.

"You see, John?" Sir Arthur said. "Even your Mr. Holmes acknowledges the power—the danger—present here."

"Sir Arthur," I said in the mildest tone possible, "why should danger result, if the communication is from those who loved you, in another life?"

"Why . . ." he said, momentarily awkward, "John you'll understand after the seance tonight. The other side is . . . different."

Robert ran down the path, panting.

"I'm sorry, Mr. Holmes, Sir Arthur," he said. "We kept them away as long as we could. Constable Brown ordered us to stand aside."

"More devotion to duty than to sense," Sir Arthur muttered. He sighed. "I'm sure you did your best," said he to Robert.

A group of curious people, led by Constable Brown and minimally constrained by Robert's children, approached between the hedgerows. Holmes was right: Someone, somehow, had alerted the public. Sightseers who had come to see the other field theorems now found themselves doubly fortunate.

The constable entered the field just as Holmes left it. The sightseers crowded up to the fence to view the new theorem.

Holmes rejoined Sir Arthur and myself.

"I have seen what I needed," Holmes said. "It's of no matter to me if the tourists trample the fields."

"But we must survey the theorem!" Sir Arthur said. "We still do not know its meaning!" He ordered Robert to do his best to prevent the sightseers from marring the designs.

"If we depart now," Holmes said, "before the constable realizes he is baffled by the phenomenon, we will be spared interrogation."

Dinner being far preferable to interrogation, we took Holmes's advice. I noticed, to my amusement, that Robert's children had lined the spectators up. Some visitors even offered the boys tips, or perhaps entry fees. At least the family would not count its day an utter loss.

A photographer lowered his heavy camera from his shoulder. He set it up on its tripod and disappeared beneath the black shadow-cloth to focus the lenses. He exposed a plate, setting off a great explosion of flash powder. Smoke billowed up, bitter and sulfurous.

The journalists began to question Constable Brown, who puffed himself up with importance and replied to their questions. We hurried away, before the journalists should recognize Sir Arthur—or Holmes—and further delay us.

"If the motor starts," Sir Arthur said, "we will be in time for the seance."

For a moment I wondered if Holmes would turn *volte face,* return to the field, and submit to questioning by Constable Brown *and* the journalists, in preference to submitting to the seance.

To our surprise, the motorcar started without hesitation. As Sir Arthur drove down the lane, Holmes puzzled over something in his hands.

"What is that, Holmes?"

"Just a bit of wood, a stake," Holmes said, putting it in his pocket. "I found it in the field."

As he was not inclined to discuss it further, we both fell silent. I wondered if we had to contend with—besides the field theorems, the ghostly lights, and the seance—wooden stakes and vampires.

"Tell me, Sir Arthur," Holmes said over the rhythmic cough of the motor, "are any of your spirits known to live on Mars?"

"Mars?" Sir Arthur exclaimed. "Mars! I don't believe I've ever heard one mention it. But I don't believe I've ever heard one asked." He turned to Holmes, his eyes bright with anticipation. "We shall ask, this very evening! Why, that would explain Professor Schiaparelli's 'canali,' would it not?"

"Perhaps," Holmes said. "Though I fail to understand what use channels would be—to dead people."

Darkness gathered as we motored down the rough lane. Sir Arthur turned on the headlamps of the autocar, and the beams pierced the dimness, casting eerie shadows and picking out the twisted branches of trees. The wind in our face was cool and pleasant, if tinged somewhat with the scent of petrol.

The engine of the autocar died, and with it the light from the headlamps.

Sir Arthur uttered another of his exotic curses.

"I suppose it will be of no use," he said, "but would one of you gentlemen kindly try the crank?"

Holmes—knowing of my shoulder, shattered by a Jezail bullet in Afghanistan and never quite right since—leaped from the passenger seat and strode to the front of the automobile. He cranked it several times, to no avail. Without a word, he unstrapped the engine cover and opened it.

"It's too dark, Mr. Holmes," Sir Arthur said. "We'll have to walk home from here."

"Perhaps not, Sir Arthur," said I. "Holmes's vision is acute." I climbed down, as well, to see if I could be of any assistance. I wished the automobile carried a kerosene lamp, though I suppose I would have had to hold it too far away from the engine, and the petrol tank, for it to be of much use.

"Can you see the difficulty, Holmes?" I asked.

His long fingers probed among the machined parts of the engine.

"Difficulty, Watson?" he said. "There is no difficulty here. Only enterprising cleverness."

The automobile rocked, and I assumed Sir Arthur was getting down to join us and try to help with the repairs.

"Cleverness?" said I. "Surely you can't mean— Ah!" Light flickered across his hawkish face, and for a moment I thought he had repaired the engine and the headlamps. Then I thought that Sir Arthur must have an innovative automobile, in which the headlamps gained their power from an independent battery rather than from the workings of the motor.

But then, I thought, they would surely not have failed at the same moment as the motor.

And finally I realized that the headlamps were dark, the engine still, and the lights on Holmes's face emanated from a separate source entirely.

I raised my eyes in the direction of the flickering lights. An eerie radiance lit the forest beyond the road. As I watched, it descended slowly beneath the tops of the trees.

"Sir Arthur!" I cried.

His silhouette moved quickly toward the mysterious lights.

Holmes and I ran after him. I felt a shiver, whether of fear or of unearthly chill, I could not have said.

Suddenly a great flash of light engulfed us, and a great shock of sound. Dazzled, I stumbled and fell, crying, "Sir Arthur!" I thought I heard one of Sir Arthur's exotic oaths, this time in the voice of Sherlock Holmes.

I came to myself, my sight flickering with brilliant black and white afterimages. When my vision cleared, I found myself staring straight up into the night. Among the constellations, Mars burned red in the darkness. I shivered in sudden dread. I sat up, groaning.

Holmes was instantly at my side.

"Stay quiet, Watson," he said. "You'll soon be right. No injuries, I fancy."

"And you, Holmes? And Sir Arthur?"

"My sight has recovered, but Sir Arthur does not answer my hallo."

"What happened, Holmes? What was that explosion?"

"It was . . . what Robert called a flying coracle," Holmes said. "But it has vanished, and with it Dr. Conan Doyle."

"We must return to Undershaw! Call out a search party!"

"No!" Holmes exclaimed. "He has been spirited away, and we have no hope of finding the location unless I can inspect the site of his disappearance. *Before* searchers trample it."

"But Lady Conan Doyle!" I said. "She'll be frantic!"

"If we return now," Holmes said, "we can only tell her Sir Arthur is lost."

"Kidnapped!" I only wished I knew who—or what—had done the kidnapping.

"Perhaps, though I doubt he believes so."

"He could be killed!"

"He is safe, I warrant," Holmes said.

"How can you be sure?"

"Because," Holmes said, "no one would benefit from his death." He settled into the seat of the autocar. "If we wait till dawn, we may retrieve him and return him safely to the bosom of his family. Before they have any more concern than a few hours of wondering where we have got to."

"Very well, Holmes," I said doubtfully, "but the responsibility for Sir Arthur's safety lies on your shoulders."

"I accept it," Holmes said solemnly. Suddenly, he brightened somewhat. "I fear we shall miss the seance."

I confess that I dozed, in the darkest hours of the night, cold and uncomfortable and cramped in the seat of the disabled motorcar. My last sight, before I slept, was the scarlet glow of Mars sinking beneath the tops of the trees. I dreamed of a race of beings so powerful that the canals they built could be seen from another planet.

When I woke, shivering, tiny dewdrops covered my tweeds. The silence of night gave way to the bright songs of dawn. The scent of wet grass and sulfur wafted into my nostrils. I tried to remember a particular point of my dream.

Holmes shook me.

"I'm awake, Holmes!" I said. The snatch of memory vanished without a trace. "Have you found Sir Arthur?"

"Not yet," he said. "Hold this, while I crank the motor."

He handed me a bit of metal—two strips sintered together to form one curved piece.

"What about Sir Arthur?" I asked. "What about your search?"

"My search is finished," Holmes said. "I found, overhead, a few singed tree-leaves. At my feet, a dusty spot on the ground. Marks pressed into the soil, forming the corners of a parallelogram—" He snorted. "Not even a square! Far less elegant than the field theorems. Savory food for speculation."

"But no trace of Sir Arthur?"

"Many traces, but ... I think we will not find his hiding place."

I glanced up into the sky, but the stars had faded and no trace of light remained.

Holmes fell silent. He would say no more until he was ready. I feared he had failed—Holmes, failed—and Sir Arthur lay dead in some kidnapper's lair, on or off our world.

The autocar started without hesitation. I had never driven a motorcar—it is folly to own one in the city, where a hansom is to be had for a handwave, a shout, and a few shillings. But I had observed Sir Arthur carefully. Soon we were moving down the road, and I fancy the ruts, rather than my driving, caused what jolts we felt.

"And what is this, Holmes?" I asked, giving him his bit of metal. He snatched it and pointed straight ahead. I quickly corrected the autocar's direction, for in my brief moment of inattention it had wandered toward the hedgerow.

"The bit of metal, Holmes?"

"It is," he said, "a bit of metal."

"What does it mean?" I said irritably. "Where did you find it?"

"I found it in the motor," he said, and placed it in his pocket. "And may I compliment you on your expert driving. I had no idea you numbered automobile racing among your talents."

I took his rather unsubtle hint and slowed the vehicle. Hedgerows grew close on either side; it would not be pleasant to round a turn and come upon a horse and carriage.

"I dreamed of Mars, Holmes," I said.

"Pah!" he said. "Mars!"

"Quite a wonderful dream!" I continued undaunted. "We had learned to communicate with the Martians. We could converse, with signals of light, as quickly and as easily as if we were using a telegraph. But of course that would be impossible."

"How, impossible?" Holmes asked. "Always assuming there *were* Martians with whom to converse."

"Light cannot travel so quickly between the worlds," I said.

"Light transmission is instantaneous," Holmes said in a dismissive tone.

"On the contrary," I said. "As you would know if you paid the least attention to astronomy or physics. The Michelson-Morley experiment proved light has a finite speed, and furthermore that its speed remains constant—but that is beside the point!"

"What *is* the point, pray tell?" Holmes asked. "You were, I believe, telegraphing back and forth with Martians."

"The point is that I could *not* converse instantaneously with Martians—"

"I do see a certain difficulty in stringing the wires," Holmes said dryly.

"—because it would take several minutes—I would have to do the arithmetic, but at least ten—for my 'hallo!' to reach Mars, and another length of time for their 'Good day to you' to return."

"Perhaps you should use the post," Holmes said.

"And that is what troubled me about Robert's description!" I exclaimed.

"Something troubled you?" Holmes said. "You have not mentioned it before."

"I could not think what it was. But of course! He thought he saw a signal from Mars, to the coracle, at the instant after its disappearance. This is impossible, you see, Holmes, because a message would take so long to reach us. He must have been mistaken in what he saw."

Holmes rode beside me in silence for some moments, then let out his breath in a long sigh.

"As usual, Watson, you shame me," he said. "You have provided the clue to the whole mystery, and now all is clear."

"I do?" I said. "I have? It is?" I turned to him. "But what about Sir Arthur? How can the mystery be solved if we have lost Sir Arthur? Surely we cannot return to Undershaw without him!"

"Stop!" Holmes cried.

Fearing Holmes had spied a sheep in the road while my attention was otherwise occupied, I engaged the brake abruptly. The autocar lurched to a halt, and Holmes used the momentum to leap from the seat to the roadway.

Sir Arthur sat upon a stone on the verge of the track.

"Good morning, Dr. Conan Doyle," Holmes said. "I trust your adventure has left you none the worse for wear?"

Sir Arthur gazed up with a beatific expression, his eyes wide and glassy.

"I have seen things, Mr. Holmes," he said. "Amazing things . . ."

Holmes helped him to the automobile and into the passenger seat. As Sir Arthur settled himself, Holmes plucked a bit of material from Sir Arthur's shoe.

"What have you found, Holmes?" I asked.

"Nothing remarkable," replied Holmes. "A shred of dusty silk, I believe." He folded the fabric carefully, placed it into his pocket, and vaulted into the autocar.

Sir Arthur made no objection to my driving us back to Undershaw. It was as if he had visited a different world, and still lived in it in his mind. He refused to speak of it until we returned to his home, and his worried wife.

A paragon of womanhood, Lady Conan Doyle accepted Sir Arthur's assurances that he was unharmed. She led us to the morning room and settled us all in deep chairs of maroon velvet.

Sir Arthur commenced his story.

"It was amazing," Sir Arthur said. "Absolutely amazing. I saw the lights, and it was as if I were mesmerized. I felt drawn to them. I hurried through the woods. I saw the ring of illumination, just as Robert described it. Brighter than anything we can manufacture, I'd warrant—never mind that it floated in the sky! I saw the coracle. A flying vehicle, turning slowly above me, and windows—and faces! Faces peering down at me."

Holmes shifted and frowned, but said nothing.

"Then I saw a flash of light—"

"We saw it, too," said I. "We feared you'd been injured."

"Far from it!" Conan Doyle said. "Uplifted, rather! Enlightened! I swooned with the shock, and when I awoke—I was inside the coracle!"

"How did you know where you were?" Holmes demanded. "Could you see out the windows? Were you high above the ground?"

"I was in a round room, the size of the coracle, and I could feel the wafting of the winds—"

It occurred to me that the previous night had been nearly windless. But perhaps the flying coracle had risen higher and the wind aloft had freshened.

"What of the portholes?" Holmes asked.

"There were no portholes," Sir Arthur said, still speaking in a dreamy voice. "The walls were smooth black, like satin. The portholes had closed over, without leaving a trace!"

"Sir Arthur—" Holmes protested.

"Hush, Mr. Holmes, please," Lady Conan Doyle said, leaning forward, her face alight with concentration. "Let my husband finish his story."

"I was not at all frightened. I was strangely content, and immobile," Sir Arthur said. "Then ... the *people* came in and spoke to me. They looked like—like nothing on this Earth! They were very pale, and their eyes were huge and bright, shining with otherworldly intelligence. They told me—they told me, without speaking, they spoke in my mind, without moving their lips!"

"Ah," Holmes murmured, "so at least they had lips."

"Shh!" Lady Conan Doyle said, dispensing with courtesy.

"What did they tell you, Sir Arthur?" I asked.

"They wished to examine me, to determine if their people and ours are compatible, to determine if we can live together in peace."

"Live together!" I ejaculated.

"Yes. They did examine me—I cannot describe the process in polite company, except to say that it was ... quite thorough. Strangely enough, I felt no fear, and very little discomfort, even when they used the needles."

"Ah, yes," Holmes murmured. "The needles."

"Who were these people?" I asked, amazed. "Where are they from?"

"They are," Sir Arthur said softly, "from Mars."

I felt dazed, not only because of my exhaustion. Lady Conan Doyle made a sound of wonder, and Holmes—Holmes growled low in his throat.

"From Mars?" he said dryly. "Not from the spirit realm?"

Sir Arthur drew himself up, bristling at the implied insult.

"I'll not have it said I cannot admit I was wrong! The new evidence is overwhelming!"

Before Holmes could reply, Sir Arthur's butler appeared in the doorway.

"Sir Arthur," he said.

"Tell Robert," Holmes said without explanation, "that we have no need to examine any new field theorems. Tell him he may notify the constabulary, the journalists, and the king if he wishes."

The butler hesitated.

"And tell him," Holmes added, "that he may charge what he likes to guide them."

The butler bowed and disappeared.

"They'll trample the theorem!" Sir Arthur objected, rising from his chair. "We won't know—"

"But you already know, Sir Arthur," Holmes said. "The creators of the field theorem have spoken to you."

Sir Arthur relaxed. "That is true," he said. He smiled. "To think that I've been singled out this way—to introduce them to the world!" He leaned forward, spreading his hands in entreaty. "They're nothing like the Martians of Mr. Wells," he said. "Not evil, not invaders. They wish only to be our friends. There's no need for panic."

"We're hardly in danger of panic," Holmes said. "I have done as you asked. I have solved your mystery." He nodded to me. "Thanks to my friend, Dr. Watson."

"There is no mystery, Mr. Holmes," Sir Arthur said.

Holmes drew from his pocket the wooden stake, the metal spring, and the scrap of black silk. He placed them on the table before us. Dust drifted from the silk, emitting a burned, metallic scent and marring the polished table with a film of gray.

"You are correct. There is, indeed, no mystery." He picked up the stake, and I noticed that a few green stalks remained wrapped tightly around it. "I found this in the center of the new field theorem, the one that so conveniently appeared after I expressed a desire to see a fresh one. Unfortunately, its creators were unduly hurried, and could not work with their usual care. They left the center marker, to which they tied a rope, to use as a compass to form their circles."

Holmes moved his long forefinger around the stake, showing how a loop of rope had scuffed the corners of the wood, how the circular motion had pulled crop stalks into a tight coil.

"But that isn't what happened," Sir Arthur said. "The Martians explained all. They were trying to communicate with me, but the theorems are beyond our mental reach. So they risked everything to speak to me directly."

Holmes picked up the spring.

"Metal expands when it heats," he said. "This was cunningly placed so its expansion disarranged a connection in your motor. Whenever the temperature rose, the motor would stop. Naturally, you drove rapidly when you went to investigate each new field theorem. Of course your motorcar would overheat—and, consequently, misbehave—under those circumstances."

"The Martians disrupted the electrical flux of my motorcar—it's an inevitable result of the energy field that supports their coracle. It can fly through space, Mr. Holmes, from Mars to Earth and back again!"

Holmes sighed, and picked up the bit of black silk.

"This is all that is left of the flying coracle," he said. "The hot-air balloon, rather. Candles at its base heated the air, kept the balloon aloft, and produced the lights."

"The lights were too bright for candles, Mr. Holmes," Sir Arthur said.

Holmes continued undaunted. "Add to the balloon a handful of photographer's flash powder." He shook the bit of black silk. Gray dust floated from it, and a faint scent of sulfur wafted into the air. "It ignites, you are dazzled. The silk ignites! The candles, the balloon, the straw framework—all destroyed! Leaving nothing but dust . . . a dust of magnesium oxide." He stroked his fingertip through the gray powder.

"It did not burn me," Sir Arthur pointed out.

"It was not meant to burn you. It was meant to amaze you. Your abductors are neither malicious nor stupid." Holmes brushed the dust from his hands. "We were meant to imagine a craft that could fall from the sky, balance on its legs, and depart again, powered on flame, like a Chinese rocket! But it left the tracks of four legs, awkwardly spaced. I found this suspicious. Three legs, spaced regularly, would lead to more stability."

"Very inventive, Mr. Holmes, but you fail to explain how the Martians transported me to their coracle, how the portholes sealed without a trace, how they spoke to me in my mind."

"Sir Arthur," Holmes said, "are you familiar with the effects of cocaine?"

"In theory, of course," said Sir Arthur. "I'm a medical doctor, after all."

"Personally familiar," Holmes said.

"I've never had occasion to use it myself, nor to prescribe it," Sir Arthur said. "So, no, I am not *personally* familiar with the effects of cocaine."

"I am," Holmes said quietly. "And you show every sign of having recently succumbed to its influence. Your eyes are glassy. Your imagination is heightened—"

"Are you saying," Sir Arthur said with disbelief, "that the Martians drugged me with cocaine?"

"There are no Martians!" Holmes said, raising his voice for the first time. "There are hoaxers, who created a clever illusion, dazzled you, drugged you, and took you to a hiding placc—a raft, no doubt, that would mimic the motions of a boat floating in the air. They disguised themselves, spoke from behind masks—or behind a curtain!—taking advantage of your distracted consciousness. You saw the needle yourself, the second needle that drugged you again, so they could place you where you would be safe, and soon found!"

Sir Arthur gazed at Holmes for a long moment, then chuckled softly.

"I understand," he said softly. "I do understand."

"You understand that you have been tricked?" Holmes asked.

"I understand all. You need say no more. Some day, in the future, when you're persuaded of my complete goodwill, we'll have occasion to speak again."

Sir Arthur rose, crossed the room, and opened his desk. He drew out a sheet of paper, returned, and presented the paper to Holmes.

"This is a letter of credit," he said, "in payment for your services. It's sufficient, I hope?"

Holmes barely glanced at the paper. "More than sufficient," he said. "Most generous, I would say, from a client who believes I have been made a fool of by Martians."

"Not at all, Mr. Holmes. I understand your reasoning. You are very subtle, sir, I admire you."

"Then you accept—"

"I accept your explanation as proof of my hypothesis," Sir Arthur said. "And I admire you beyond words." He smiled.

"And now, we are all very tired. I must rest, and then—to work! To introduce the world to the wonders approaching us. I've taken the liberty of hiring a private railroad car to return you to London. A token of my esteem."

Speechless, Holmes rose.

"Your luggage is in the autocar. James will drive you to the station. The autocar will not misbehave, because our visitors have gone home for the moment. But—they will return!"

Sir Arthur and Lady Conan Doyle accompanied us to the drive, so graciously that I hardly felt we were being shown the door. I climbed into the motorcar, but Sir Arthur held Holmes back for a moment, speaking to him in a low voice, shaking his hand.

Holmes joined me, nonplussed, and James drove us away. The motorcar ran flawlessly. As we passed a field that yesterday had been a smooth swath of grain, but today was marked by a field theorem more complex than any before, we saw Robert and Little Robbie directing spectators around the patterns. They both had taken more care with their appearance than the previous day, and wore clothes without holes or patches.

His expression hidden in the shade of his new cap, Robert turned to watch us pass.

"Holmes—" I said.

Holmes gently silenced me with a gesture. He raised one hand in farewell to the farmer. Robert saluted him. A small smile played around Holmes's lips.

As soon as we were alone in the private train car, Holmes flung himself into a luxurious leather armchair and began to laugh. He laughed so hard, and so long, that I feared he was a candidate for Bedlam.

"Holmes!" I cried. "Get hold of yourself, man!" I poured him a glass of brandy—Napoleon, I noticed in passing.

His laughter faded slowly to an occasional chuckle, and he wiped tears from his eyes.

"That's better," I said. "What is so infernally funny?"

"Human beings," Holmes said. "Human beings, Watson, are an endless source of amusement."

"I do not like leaving Sir Arthur with a misapprehension of events. Perhaps we should return—seek out the raft on which he was held captive."

"It has, no doubt, been sunk in the deepest part of the

lake. We would never find it . . . unless we could engage the services of Mr. Verne's Captain Nemo."

"I'm astonished that you've read *Twenty Thousand Leagues Under the Sea*," I said.

"I have not. But you did, and you described it to me quite fully." He sipped the brandy, and glanced at the glowing amber liquid in appreciation. "Hmm. The last good year."

I poured cognac for myself, warmed the balloon glass between my hands, and savored the sweet, intoxicating bite of its vapors. It was far too early in the day for spirits, but this one time I excused myself.

"When we return to Baker Street," said Holmes, "I might perhaps borrow your copy of *War of the Worlds,* if you would be so kind as to lend it to me."

"I will," I said, "if you promise not to rip out its pages for your files. Bertie inscribed it to me personally."

"I will guard its integrity with my life."

I snorted. The train jerked, wheels squealing against the tracks, and gathered speed.

"What about Sir Arthur?" I asked, refusing to be put off again. "He believes he's been visited by Martians!"

"Watson, old friend, Sir Arthur is a willing participant in the hoax."

"You mean—he engineered it himself? Then why engage your services?"

"An innocent, unconscious participant. He *wants* to believe. He has exchanged Occam's razor for Occam's kaleidoscope, complicating simple facts into explanations of impossible complexity. But he believes they are true, just as he believes spirits visit him, and Houdini possesses mediumistic powers, and I . . ." He started to chuckle again.

"I don't understand the *purpose* of this hoax!" I said, hoping to distract him before he erupted into another bout of hysteria. "Nor who perpetrated it!"

"It is a difficult question. I despaired of solving it. I wondered if Sir Arthur wished to pit his intellect against mine. If the journalists and photographers conspired to create a story. If Constable Brown wished to draw more resources to his district—and found he enjoyed the limelight!"

"Which of them was it, Holmes? Wait! It was the photographer—only he has access to flash powder!"

"And an intimate knowledge of Surrey fields? No. The

flash powder is easily purchased—or purloined. It was no one you mention."

"Then who?"

"Who benefits?"

I considered. If Sir Arthur wrote of the events, he might make a tidy sum from a book and lecture tour. But Holmes had already stated that Sir Arthur was innocent. Still, what benefited Sir Arthur would benefit his whole family . . .

"Not Lady Conan Doyle!" I exclaimed, aghast.

"Certainly not," Holmes said.

"The butler? The driver? He would know how to sabotage the car—"

"Robert Holder, Watson!" Holmes cried. "Robert Holder! Perhaps—indeed, certainly—with help from James and the butler and other tenants in the neighborhood. But Robert was the mastermind, for all his rough appearance. A veritable Houdini of the countryside!" Holmes considered. "Indeed, he used some of my own techniques. And he almost defeated me!"

"He risked all by challenging you!"

"I was unforeseen—surely he intended Sir Arthur to conduct the investigation. When you and I arrived, Robert must have realized he would stand or fall by his boldness. He offered Sir Arthur a compelling reason to dismiss my solution—and me. Sir Arthur accepted the offering. How could he resist?"

Holmes gazed out the window of the train for a moment. Unmarred fields rippled past, like miniature green seas.

"If not for Robert's misapprehension about the velocity of light," Holmes said, "a misapprehension that I shared, I would have known *what* happened, and I would have known *how*—but I never would have been certain *who*."

"You sound curiously sympathetic, Holmes," I said with disapproval.

"Indeed I am, Watson. Robert is clearly an honorable man."

"Honorable!"

"He refused Sir Arthur's offer to relieve him of the year's rent. He has no wish to steal."

"Only to lie."

"Like Houdini. Like any entertainer, any storyteller. Shakespeare lied. You have lied yourself, my friend, in your descriptions of our adventures."

"I have disguised individuals," I said, taking offense. "I have, yes, perhaps, dissembled occasionally . . ." I hesitated, and then I nodded. "Very well. I have lied."

"Life is hard for people who work the land. You and I are prosperous, now. But remember what it was like when we were younger, scraping along from season to season, with never a new shirt or a pair of boots that did not let in the rain. Imagine seeing no better prospects. For the rest of your life."

I suddenly remembered father and sons, and their new clothes.

"Who can blame them for creating a diversion, a mystery to attract sightseers, people of leisure with money to spare. People," Holmes added, "with a blind eye to turn to the evidence lying plain before them."

"What of your commitment to the truth, Holmes?" I asked with some asperity.

"I know the truth," he said. "You know it. Sir Arthur knows it, but rejects it. I have kept the solution to other mysteries confidential; it is part of my duty. How is this different?"

I suddenly understood. Holmes's sympathy was not so much directed toward the hoaxers as away from the curiosity seekers who were willing, indeed eager, to be fooled.

"Very well, Holmes," I said. "I am content, if you are."

We rode in silence for some miles, lulled by the rocking of the train, enjoying Sir Arthur's excellent cognac and the peaceful English countryside. I wondered what the world would be like if beings from another planet *did* visit us.

"Holmes," I said.

"Yes, Watson?"

"Why was Sir Arthur so willing to pay you, when he did not believe your solution? What did he say to you, just as we left?"

"He said, 'I understand why you are such an extraordinary person. Like Houdini, you have good reason to hide your abilities, your true nature. I understand why Sherlock Holmes cannot be the one to reveal the truth about our visitors. I will do it, and you may trust me to keep *your* secret.' "

"*Your* secret?"

"Yes, Watson." Holmes smiled. "Sir Arthur Conan Doyle believes I am a Martian."

THE ADVENTURE OF THE MISSING COFFIN

by Laura Resnick

"A noteworthy moment in the annals of crime, Watson," Holmes said to his faithful companion one cold night in the autumn of 1895.

"Hmmm? What?" the good doctor mumbled sleepily.

"Wake up, Watson!" Holmes snapped at his trusty biographer. "This is another pinnacle of logic in my brilliant career. D'you suppose Boswell slept while Johnson worked?"

"According to Mr. Boswell's account, they did sleep occasionally," Watson muttered, glancing at his watch. "For pity's sake, it's past midnight, Holmes. You've been at it since dawn." He straightened his collar as he shifted his position in the old chair by the fire, then peered through the feeble gaslight. Holmes had once again littered their rooms in Baker Street with an alarming array of scientific paraphernalia and was currently engaged in heating a test tube over a Bunsen burner. The substance inside the tube was particularly odorous. "Good God, what *are* you doing?"

"Hah!" Holmes cried with an expression of pleasure that suggested he had awoken the good doctor precisely to be asked that very question. "I am engaged, my dear Watson, in determining the guilt or innocence of Mr. Ricardo Fitzgerald-Schwartz."

"Ricardo . . ." Watson frowned. "Are you referring to the infamous Adventure of the Rabbi's Rosary?"

"I am indeed. If, upon reaching boiling temperature, the

liquid in this vial turns yellow, Fitzgerald-Schwartz is innocent. If, however, it turns red, then he is guilty as sin."

"But, Holmes—"

"Ah-hah! It's boiling now, old chap."

"But, Holmes—"

"There! There we have it! Do you see? Watson, do you *see!*"

"Yes. It's turning red."

"Guilty! Fitzgerald-Schwartz is guilty! I have proved it scientifically, beyond the shadow of a doubt!" Holmes cried in triumph.

"Well, then I suppose it's a good thing that he was condemned and hanged three months ago, isn't it?" Watson said mildly.

Holmes looked pained. "Oh, Watson, Watson." Holmes rested his head upon the table, heedless of the murky red substance now freely bubbling over the sides of the test tube and staining everything with which it came into contact. "It was all so sordid, so mundane. So *degrading*. I wish they had never called me into that case."

"Yes, it is a pity that four eyewitnesses stepped forward and testified before you had the opportunity to make more than one or two brilliant deductions," Watson said sympathetically.

"People have no business going around witnessing crimes," Holmes snarled. He lifted his head. His neck and the side of his face were now stained red. "Crime is *my* territory! Do I interfere in *their* petty little lives?"

"Really, Holmes, you've been sulking about this for too long. It's time to put it behind you."

"Behind me?" Holmes cried. "Watson, how can I? Since that appalling affair, not one single new client has walked through that door!" He pointed accusingly at the entrance to their rooms. "How can I recover my wits if I am to be driven to madness with boredom and inactivity?"

"Indeed." Watson surveyed the mess. The red froth was now dribbling over the edge of the table to stain the Turkish carpet. "Nevertheless, I doubt that proving the guilt of a man who's already been hanged for the crime is quite the way to keep yourself occupied until our next client appears."

"Then what would you recommend, Doctor?" Holmes responded peevishly.

Watson gave a long-suffering sigh. "You could always—"

He was interrupted by a sound at the window. As their rooms were a good twenty feet above street level, this was surprising enough to cause them both to forget the argument at hand and rush over to the somewhat dirty window.

Peering out into the darkness, Watson murmured, "I could have sworn I heard something."

"You did, Watson, you did," Holmes assured him, also peering out into the London night. "We may have a visitor."

"A visitor? Is that possible? How could—"

"When you have eliminated the *im*possible, my dear Watson, whatever remains, no matter how—"

"Please, don't repeat *that* again. What do you suppose it could have been? A bird flying off course and hitting the window?"

"Nonsense. I am something of an authority, you know, on the sounds various objects make when hitting glass. I've even written a—"

"—a small monograph on the subject. Yes, I know. What do you think it was, then?"

"Hmmm. Given the probable velocity of the object, combined with the distinct thud it made when coming into contact with the window, which is made of a particularly—"

"Why don't we just open the window and find out?" Watson suggested impatiently.

"Good God, no! If you did that, Doctor, you would lay us both open to danger of a magnitude which, I dare say, can hardly be exaggerated. No, do not think for even one second—"

He was interrupted by yet another thud against the window. "Holmes! It's a bat." Watson chuckled, turned away from the window, and resumed his seat by the fire. "Good heavens, old chap! You really had me worried for a minute there. Danger? Hah!"

"Oh, Watson, Watson. Do not be deceived. 'Tis a very clever scheme. A deception of the most infamous nature."

Watson yawned hugely and stretched. "If you say so, my dear fellow. However, I'm afraid not even great danger and infamous deception can keep me awake any longer. I'm off to bed."

Holmes scarcely nodded as his old friend passed him by and headed for the door. His eyes were fixed on some distant place. Liverpool, perhaps.

"And Holmes," Watson added, "do have a good wash before bed. You're covered with that red stuff."

"Hmmm? Oh. Good night, Watson. Pleasant dreams."

Watson frowned, recognizing Holmes's most annoyingly enigmatic smirk, and closed the door behind him.

It was only a few minutes before Holmes heard a scratching at the door which confirmed his theory. "Just a moment!" he cried. He flew about his rooms in haste, assembling the necessary items to shield himself from his visitor, then positioned himself in a comfortable chair and called, "Come in!"

The door creaked open. In the darkness of the narrow hallway, the visitor appeared only as a sinister shadow.

Holmes narrowed his eyes. "Good evening," he said.

"I believe that's *my* line, Mr. Holmes," responded the visitor in a heavily accented voice.

"Do come in, sir, and tell me how I may be of assistance to you."

"Very well." The visitor stepped into the room. He was a tall, chubby man, wearing clothes which, though nicely tailored, had not been in fashion for more than thirty years. The door closed behind him of its own accord. When Holmes was clearly unsurprised by this parlor trick, the visitor said, "I perceive that you are a man of quick wits and cold blood, Mr. Holmes."

"It was not difficult to guess the nature of my visitor," Holmes said, lighting his pipe. "Gauging size and velocity, I was naturally able to deduce that the creature flinging itself against my window could be nothing other than a vampire bat. When I further observe that the ashes in my fireplace have fallen in a such a position as to suggest that something has recently attempted to fly down the chimney, I know that the odds are astronomically against its being a coincidence that *two* winged creatures have attempted to surreptitiously enter my rooms within the last few minutes."

"Uh-huh." The gentleman leaned forward and peered at Holmes in the dim light. "*Porca miseria!* I see that another of my kind has already been here!"

Holmes blinked. "I beg your pardon?"

"That blood, all over your neck and cheek! What a mess! It must have been that dreadful count from Transylvania. He has the table manners of a pig!"

"What? Oh. Um. No, no, there has been no other visitor, sir, I assure you."

"You have not been bitten by another vampire?"

"No, of course not. As you can see," Holmes added, displaying the crucifix around his neck, "I am well protected."

"Just a little advice, Mr. Holmes. That really won't help you. I'm a good Catholic and take Communion every Christmas at Midnight Mass."

"Really? Oh. Well, then!" Holmes held up a string of garlic bulbs he had been concealing.

"That won't help you, either. I'm Italian."

"Oh?"

"Guido Pascalini. Pleased to make your acquaintance."

"I seem to have miscalculated." Holmes was despondent.

"Do not condemn yourself. It happens all the time. But could you clean up that blood on your neck? I'm on a diet, and looking at it is making me very hungry."

"It's not blood, actually. It's an indelible stain, part of a chemical experiment." He gestured to the table littered with test tubes, beakers, powders, and potions.

"*Gesù!* Where do you mortals find the time?"

"Speaking of which," Holmes said, glad to be getting things back on track, "shall *we* stop wasting time and get to the point?"

"Yes, of course, *signore.*"

"What is the reason for your visit to me? I know nothing about you, save for the obvious facts."

Pascalini frowned. "I do not understand. Which facts are obvious?"

Holmes sighed and tried (unsuccessfully) to pretend he didn't absolutely *love* doing this. "You are at least five hundred years old, but no older than six hundred fifty. You are a connoisseur of music, art, architecture, and literature, but you loathe cricket and haggis. You've been married several times, most recently to a German woman. You are only recently arrived in London, you read the *Strand,* and you frequent the salon of the actress Miss Eponine Chaste. You have already—shall we say, *dined*—this evening, and you have very recently lost something of great importance to you."

"Excellent, Mr. Holmes! This is excellent! *Bravo!*"

Holmes smirked.

"But how have you guessed all this?"

"Guess!" Holmes cried. "I never *guess*."

"No, of course not. I should have realized that from your reputation. Anyhow, it is of no importance," Pascalini said dismissively. "The reason I have come—"

"Of no importance?" Holmes was even more annoyed now. He decided to ignore Pascalini's uncouth behavior and simply proceed as if he had, as usual, been asked with breathless admiration how he had so brilliantly deduced these facts through mere observation.

"Your age is easily detected by the calluses on your forefinger. They could only be the result of using a two-edged falchion sword with triangular pommel and finger-guard, a weapon which you surely would not have used had your formative years occurred any time after the fourteenth century. Yet you are clearly no older than six hundred-fifty years, as it is a well-known fact that no Italian vampire predates Marco Polo.

"Your love of music I observe from the program book tucked in your right-hand pocket; you have been to the opera this evening. Any Italian who failed to emigrate during the Renaissance must be a lover of art and architecture. And all foreigners loathe cricket and haggis." Holmes shrugged nonchalantly at his own genius.

Toeing the line now, Pascalini prompted, "And my marriages?"

"My dear sir, any Italian man who's lived for five centuries is bound to have been married several times, and only a German wife would have let you out of the house in such unfashionable clothes."

"How dare—"

"Clearly you are new to London; no man could wander the streets of this city dressed like that for more than a few days before some self-respecting tailor would insist upon intervening. Moreover, you smell of a particularly singular brand of perfume which only one woman in all of London wears—Miss Eponine Chaste. And the color in your cheeks suggests you have already taken your sustenance for the evening."

"A pitiful ration, I assure you, Mr. Holmes. I'm watching my weight, you know."

"So you have mentioned." Holmes sucked thoughtfully on his pipe for a moment before continuing, "You are obviously a lover of great literature, for it's plain that you learned of my reputation as a consulting detective by reading one of Doctor Watson's accounts in the *Strand Magazine;* the particular variety of ink staining your left thumb is unmistakable."

Pascalini wiped his hand on his trousers. "The truth is, Mr. Holmes, I *have* lost something of great importance."

"Yes, that is clear from the obvious state of agitation in which you attempted to enter my rooms. First by flinging yourself at my window, next by flying down the chimney toward a live fire."

"Yes, yes, if we could proceed, *signore,*" Pascalini urged through his sharp teeth.

"By all means."

"I have not merely *lost* something. I have every reason to believe it has been stolen!"

"Indeed?"

"And I do not exaggerate, sir, when I say that without this object, my life is not worth the paper that the *Strand* is printed on."

"This *is* serious," Holmes observed. "I assume the object in question is your coffin?"

"Yes!" cried Pascalini. "Filled with the soil of my native village, Vermicelli!"

"I see."

"Oh, Mr. Holmes, I beg you to help me. If I am not in my coffin at dawn, I'll—I'll—"

"Die?" Holmes suggested.

"I'm already dead."

"I thought you were *un*dead."

"Well, yes, if you want to be technical. But the only real difference between being dead and undead is your net income after taxes."

"So what *will* happen if you're not in your coffin at dawn?"

"I will endure a living hell, *signore!* My body will disintegrate in the most hideously painful manner you can possibly imagine, and my spirit will be condemned to spend all eternity in Newark!"

"Where's that?"

"America."

"Good God, man! We must act at once! There's not a moment to lose!"

"My thoughts exactly."

"Show me where you last saw your coffin."

Holmes grabbed his hat and coat, and off they went, striding through the murky London night. Holmes hailed a hansom cab on the corner, and Pascalini directed the driver to a modest Italian restaurant near Holborn Circus. When they arrived, a small, grizzled old man took one look at Holmes, clapped his hands to his cheeks, and cried, "*Madonna!* You've bitten the detective, Guido!"

"No, no, Uncle Luigi, that's just a stain from—"

"This gentleman is your uncle?" Holmes asked skeptically.

"No. A very distant cousin, actually." As the old man turned and walked away, Pascalini lowered his voice and confided, "He doesn't know I'm a six-hundred-year-old vampire. He thinks I just have strange sexual practices."

"Ah. Very well. Where was the coffin?"

"In the cellar, *signore*."

"And your uncle doesn't find it strange that you sleep in a coffin all day?"

"I told him that my chiropractor advised it."

Guido lit a lantern and they descended the steep, slippery stairs into the dank cellar. "Tell me *exactly* what happened," Holmes ordered.

"I arose at sundown, dressed for the evening, went out for a bite, attended the opera, and paid a call on Miss Chaste. Then, finding myself weak with hunger on account of this diet, and feeling myself more and more tempted to sink my fangs into a few of the lady's guests—"

"Yes, I've been to one of Miss Chaste's soirées and felt much the same way," Holmes murmured absently.

"I decided to spend the rest of the night at home working on my memoirs. I've been corresponding with an English novelist who has expressed some interest in—"

"Hmmm. And that's when you noticed the coffin was missing? Is anything else missing? Have you touched anything since returning from Miss Chaste's? Has your uncle been down here? And does this silk handkerchief belong to you?"

"Uh ... No." Pascalini took the silk handkerchief from Holmes and studied the embroidered initials. He gasped with shock, then immediately began cursing vehemently in Italian.

"Calm yourself, Mr. Pascalini, calm yourself. I perceive that those initials mean something to you."

"This is the work of that odious count!"

"From Transylvania?"

"Yes!"

"Have you any idea why he would steal your coffin?"

"Oh, the infamous, monstrous, unbridled egotism of that vampire!"

"Please, sir, do try to make yourself clear."

"He, too, hopes to be immortalized by the gentleman with whom I have been corresponding, an English author who wishes to write a novel about a vampire. The count is afraid that I, Guido Pascalini, am the vampire who will be the hero of this story and who will be remembered across the centuries. He could not bear honest competition between us, and so he sought to eliminate me from the race!"

"Never fear, sir! You shall have your coffin back ere the sun rises again."

"But how is this possible?"

"Because I, Sherlock Holmes, have deduced where your notorious nemesis has hidden it."

"Where?"

"Think, Pascalini! What is the one place in all of London where an ancient coffin filled with Italian soil could go unnoticed?"

"Kew Gardens? Trafalgar Square? The House of Commons?"

"No, no, no! It's so absurdly simple!"

"Where?"

"The British Museum, of course! Come on, man! The game's afoot!"

They proceeded with haste to Bloomsbury, where Holmes tried to talk his way past the night watchman who guarded the heavy wrought iron gates outside the ponderous pillars of the British Museum.

"Sherlock Holmes? Detective stories, you say? Sorry, I don't read that trash," the man said, returning his attention to the copy of *Frankenstein* he was reading by lantern light.

"This man's life depends upon you letting us into the museum," Holmes snapped.

"*This* man? You're the one bleeding from the jugular vein," the guard remarked.

"That's just a stain from . . . The point is—"

"Do you mind? I'm trying to read here, okay?"

"This is intolerable!"

"Uh, Mr. Holmes? Perhaps I can assist."

"How?"

Pascalini crossed his eyes and made some effeminate gestures. After a minute or two, he said calmly, "We can pass now. The guard will not see us."

"But—"

"He has already forgotten we were ever here."

"Remarkable! You must teach me that some time."

"How busy is your schedule? It took me over three hundred years to learn how to do it."

They crossed the courtyard and entered the immense neo-classical structure in which the British kept treasures stolen from all over the world. As they crept through the silent, dusty halls, Holmes whispered, "I feel certain we can safely bypass the Greek and Roman collections, and also the—"

"Arrgh!" Pascalini screamed and fell back, his eyes bulging as he gazed in terror at the colossal winged bull before him.

"And also the Assyrian and Babylonian galleries," Holmes finished. "Calm yourself, Mr. Pascalini."

"Scusi. I'm just feeling very anxious, you understand."

"If this count is as diabolically clever as I believe him to be, the medieval antiquities galleries over here should— Ah-hah! It's just as I suspected!"

"My coffin!" Pascalini cried, recognizing his beloved sarcophagus. He raced forward to inspect it, then stopped cold in his tracks when a bat swooped low over his head. "You fiend!"

Holmes fingered the crucifix around his neck. "Is the count also Catholic, by any chance?"

The bat laughed demonically, circled the room three times, then disappeared in a cloud of smoke. A moment later, Holmes found himself facing a small, dapper man dressed in fashionable clothes and wearing a tiny gold chain bearing the Star of David. "Actually, Mr. Holmes," he said with a slight, elegant accent, "I converted to please the family of my twelfth wife. I even kept kosher for a while, but I went back to biting gentiles after she died."

"I have a rare blood disease," Holmes said flatly. "Highly contagious."

The count chuckled. "Never fear, Mr. Holmes. Unlike our chubby friend here—"

"*Stronzo!*"

"—I never eat between meals." The count peered at the stain on Holmes's neck. "Did he bite you?"

"No, it's ... Never mind. We have come here, sir, to return his coffin to Luigi's Restaurant," Holmes stated.

"And if I choose to prevent you from doing so?"

"*Attenzione*, Mr. Holmes!" Pascalini warned. "The count is as violent as he is ill-mannered, dishonest, and contemptible."

"In fact, just ever so slightly more so," the count admitted.

"You won't stop me," Holmes said confidently. "You no longer have any need of this coffin."

"Ahh, I see you are rather more clever than the usual English gentleman—though this can hardly be considered a huge accomplishment."

"Well, sir?" Holmes prompted. "Will you risk causing Pascalini to suffer a fate worse than death? I warn you that I will not hesitate to prosecute you to the fullest extent of the law."

"Oh, dear, I can see you're going to be tedious about this. Very well, Mr. Holmes. Case solved, coffin found. You may take it away. As you say, I have no further use for it."

"I don't understand." Pascalini looked to Holmes for enlightenment.

"I'm afraid, sir, that the count has already secured his literary fame at the expense of your own. You will observe the celebratory cigar in his breast pocket. There is a slight bulge beneath his coat, suggesting a sheaf of papers—his signed contract, no doubt. And do you observe that flower upon his lapel? It is as rare as it is lovely. I may be mistaken—"

"Oh, surely not," the count interrupted, sounding bored.

"But I believe there is only one woman in all of London who sells such flowers, and she is usually found directly outside the Den of Iniquity in Covent Garden, a popular gathering place for writers."

"But what does it mean?" cried Pascalini.

"You *are* slow, aren't you?" the count observed.

"I am forced to the conclusion, my dear Mr. Pascalini, that after stealing your coffin, the count proceeded with

some haste to the Den of Iniquity, where he assured your
English correspondent that you were no more."

"*Dio!*"

"He then proceeded to secure an exclusive contract with
the author."

"*Non è possibile!*"

"Personally, I see no reason why the book shouldn't become a bestseller," said the count, lighting his cigar. "It has
all the necessary elements—drama, suspense, true love, murder, exotic locations, more murder . . ."

"You are infamous, sir!" cried Pascalini.

"And soon to be famous."

"Mr. Holmes, what can we do?"

"I suggest that you go in search of the author and see if
an explanation of the situation will force him to reconsider."

"Forget it," the count advised. "I made sure the contract
was ironclad."

"We'll see about *that*, sir," said Holmes. "Meanwhile, I
shall think of some way to get this sarcophagus back to
Luigi's Restaurant by dawn. Uh, I don't suppose you'd care
to explain how you managed to get it here?"

"You suppose correctly. Now if you'll excuse me, the
night is still young, and I have so many demands on my
time. It's been a pleasure, Mr. Holmes. As for you,
Pascalini . . ." He sighed and handed a business card to the
Italian. "Please. Go see my tailor. It pains me to look at
you."

"There's just one more thing," Holmes said.

"An autographed copy of the first edition? Consider it
done." The count whirled his cape around his shoulders and
disappeared in a spiral of smoke. A moment later, a bat flew
over their heads and off into the darkness.

"*Madonna,* what a colossal ego!"

"Indeed. Well, let's not dillydally. We both still have a
considerable night's work ahead of us."

"But how will you relocate my coffin? It weights over one
thousand pounds."

"I am something of a student of physics, Mr. Pascalini.
I'm sure it shouldn't be too difficult to fabricate a simple
system of pulleys and levers which I shall use to lift it onto
a hansom cab."

"It sounds somewhat complex to me."

"Well, if it doesn't work, I'll simply make the Baker

Street Irregulars carry it for me. They're not doing anything tonight."

"Very well. Before I go . . ."

"Yes?"

"I was just curious about what you intended to ask the count."

"Oh, a small matter of professional curiosity."

"Yes?"

"I was wondering if he might perhaps be the culprit in one of my earliest, unsolved cases: The Adventure of the Anemic Albino."

THE ADVENTURE OF THE SECOND SCARF

by Mark Aronson

Of the myriad cases investigated by Sherlock Holmes, one alone remains unrecorded in the vast collection of his commonplace books. Nor is it to be found among the notes I have thrust into the tin dispatch box kept far from prying eyes in the safety of a locked bank vault.

It irritates Holmes that I must resort to those notes in order to bring to mind the details of the many investigations we pursued together. He regards it as a form of mental untidiness, and I cannot fault his opinion.

Yet even without notes, this one case remains in all its particulars as clear today as it was so many years ago. And though no more than a dozen words have passed between Holmes and me regarding the singular events of the autumn of 1897, I know that his remembrance of this case, *primus inter pares,* remains equally vivid. With his penchant for understatement, Holmes refers to it as "The Case," even as Irene Adler will ever be "The Woman."

But with the recent remarkable advances made by our men of science in so many fields, the English-speaking world may at last be prepared to hear in full the astonishing tale of the greatest adventure of Sherlock Holmes's career.

Nature had determined, in the autumn of 1897, to exert her primacy over the mere works of Man. For weeks, storms of unprecedented ferocity lashed the metropolis, interrupted only by brief periods of unrelenting gloom and chill. The rain, propelled by cruel winds, became bullets of water that found their way through the most elaborate foul weather clothing. The Channel was rendered impassable to all but the stoutest vessels. And the doorbell at 221B Baker Street was heard with less and less frequency, finally ceasing altogether as even the criminal class was driven into its holes by the weather's fury.

Holmes dreads mental inactivity above all else. Lacking a client, he at one time would have been driven to the needle. With those days past, he buried himself within the thousand fields in which he has made himself expert. The stench of chemical experimentation pervaded every corner of the flat. And he undertook a critical examination of the authenticity of the extant motets of Ockeghem for the London Academy of Medieval Studies. Yet this activity was plainly a poor substitute for the passion of his chosen profession.

For my part, I had taken to visiting Holmes almost daily, for the Jezail bullet that remains within me ached incessantly from the unending damp, and I found that my old chair afforded me more comfort than any other in London. So passed the season, Holmes straining at the leash and I suffering in silence.

At last a morning dawned that was windless, warm, and fair. My pain had eased, and so, evidently, had my friend's. For scarce had I reached the pavement at Baker Street than the door flung open and Holmes appeared at the top of the stairs, his eyes brighter than I had seen them in months, and a determined smile upon his face.

"Watson," he cried, "are you up for a tramp?" Without waiting for a response, Holmes turned immediately and strode toward Oxford Street. It was all I could do to keep up.

We wandered all morning through streets scrubbed clean by the recent weather and everywhere dense with people. Holmes missed nothing, his eyes photographing every detail and remarking on every observed change as we made our circuitous way through Mayfair and Soho and along the Embankment to the City.

Finding ourselves at last at the Liverpool Street Station, I declared myself all in and pleaded for a moment's respite. Holmes, who had been, if anything, energized by our wanderings, continued a disquisition on the importance of observation.

"Facts, facts, and more facts, Watson. They are the only

means by which deductive knowledge is to be gained. Facts pour into all the senses, if you but train yourself to receive them. Knowledge cannot be hidden from an open mind. For example, Watson, what do you make of that fellow there?"

A well-appointed man of middle years had stopped at the kiosk outside the station to purchase a copy of the *Standard*.

"Open your mind and your senses, Watson, and tell me what you see."

I watched intently as the man paid for his newspaper and scanned the headlines. "Judging by his dress and choice of paper," I began, "he is a man of means, yet not of leisure, perhaps a former tradesman who now owns his business. From the position of his watch-fob and the fact that he has used his left hand to pay for his purchase, I assume he is left-handed. There is nothing more to learn."

Holmes regarded me gravely. "Excellent, Watson. You are coming along. You have, of course, missed everything of interest, but still you have made progress. The man is a jeweler, left-handed as you observed, yet curiously he plays the violin right-handed. He is to be congratulated for resuming his studies at so advanced an age, for plainly he learned the instrument in his youth, put it aside in the interest of his profession, and has only recently taken it up again. There are sundry other facts to be gleaned, but that is the meat of it."

"Really, Holmes," I protested, "this is too much!"

"I merely repeat the knowledge my senses report to me, deducing what anyone might from the evidence at hand."

"But there is no proof of your claims. This man will shortly vanish into the crowd, and your assertions will never be put to the test."

Holmes abruptly turned and strode toward the man in question. The stage lost a memorable presence when Sherlock Holmes turned his powers exclusively to the detection of crime. For in the space of a few footsteps, his demeanor became that of a desperate man. Watch in hand, he addressed his subject with considerable agitation.

"You will, I hope, pardon the intrusion of a stranger, but I have heard that the great Sarasate is to play a matinée today, and if I might check the notices in your *Standard* ... you see, I am an amateur violinist and cannot bear to miss even one of his concerts."

At hearing this, the man brightened. "A fellow player! My

word! By all means, let us search." A few moments sufficed to scan the concert notices, with no success.

Feigning disappointment, Holmes shrugged his shoulders. "Perhaps it is to be next week. Thank you for your forbearance. My card."

"And mine," replied the sometime violinist, for so he had declared himself.

"Elias Hatch," said Holmes, reading from the card he held, "Fine Jewelry, Four Pindar Street." He offered me a sidelong look of triumph.

The eyes of Elias Hatch grew round as he discovered who his importunate inquisitor had been. "Sherlock Holmes! My word, my word! What an experience to relate! My word! If I were not at this instant late for an appointment—my word!—a coincidence to be treasured! Had I not resumed my studies after so many years, this meeting could not have—my word!"

With a tip of his hat, Holmes walked back to me, leaving Mr. Hatch to hurry on to his appointment, the richer by one anecdote.

"My word!" said Holmes, grinning hugely. He stopped short and raised his hands level with my face. "Do you not see a difference between the fingers of my left and right hands, Watson?"

I looked closely. "The middle and ring fingers of your left hand nearly touch, while the fingers of your right hand are evenly separated."

"Quite correct, Watson. The pattern produces a major scale on the violin; after countless hours of practice and performance, the fingers of one's left hand remain permanently thus." He wiggled his fingers.

"Also observe, Watson, that the nails of my left hand are trimmed to the quick, and that the ends of my fingers display prominent calluses from frequent pressure against the hard strings. Our Mr. Hatch's fingers had the hallmark pattern and the trimmed fingernails, but lacked the calluses. Hence my obvious deduction that he had only recently taken up the instrument again."

"Obvious to you, perhaps."

"Obvious to anyone who troubles to look! No less so than the traces of polishing rouge on his sleeve and the imprint of the loupe around his eye that declared him to be a jeweler.

There is nothing that cannot be deduced in the presence of sufficient evidence."

I did not argue the point. My friend plainly reveled in the exercise of his intellectual powers, and I was pleased to see him lifted from the melancholy that had so recently held him in its grip.

The Metropolitan Underground being immediately at hand, we rode to Baker Street and walked the few yards to 221B. Inside, we discovered that Mrs. Hudson had prepared a joint for our midday meal. We had just set into it when we heard the clatter of a hansom coming to a halt in the street. We heard the doorbell ring, and heavy footsteps ascending the stairs.

"Music, Watson," exclaimed Holmes with anticipation, "music more sweet than that which Señor Sarasate conjures from his instrument."

The door opened and a large man, leaning heavily upon a cane, made his way to the nearest chair, sat carefully and gazed at Holmes with intensity.

"If you are able, Mr. Sherlock Holmes, tell me who I am."

He said nothing more. He had a well trimmed mustache and wore a suit of dark blue with a muted brown stripe, a high shirt collar and black boots of good quality. His cane was black with silver filigree and a patent tip. He removed neither his hat nor his gloves, but sat unmoving, staring at Holmes.

Holmes threw aside a week's accumulation of newspapers and sat on the sofa opposite our visitor, examining him minutely. Suddenly he rose, and striding to the mantel asked, "Do you mind a pipe?"

The man in the chair said nothing, which Holmes took as assent, for he collected his clay pipe and Persian slipper of shag tobacco and made his way back to the sofa. Uncharacteristically, he stumbled slightly as he passed the chair and brushed lightly against our guest's clothing.

Five minutes passed, and ten. Through the clouds of smoke swirling about the room, Holmes continued to stare at the stranger. It was quite the most remarkable tableau I had ever witnessed.

At length, Holmes broke his silence. "Watson," he said, addressing me but continuing to face our visitor, "I hold one principle above all others, as you well know. That when one has eliminated the impossible, whatever remains, no matter how improbable, must be the truth. It is the cornerstone of my existence. Yet this moment tests it to the breaking point.

"The untrained eye sees little out of the ordinary in this man. But he is really quite remarkable. His boots, Watson, are unblemished, despite the recent storms, save for a blot of our distinctive Baker Street mud. Yet they bear no signs of having ever been polished; they have never been worn before today. And their construction is quite unusual. Note the extreme width of the heel, hinting at—you will pardon me, sir—a gross deformity of both feet. Perhaps that is the reason for the cane. Yet the cane, too, is new. The tip is unworn, the head not dulled by the friction of a hand. To the hands, then, which are gloved. This is plainly a mannered gentleman, yet he fails to remove either hat or gloves. Why? Perhaps to shield us from another deformity, for it is plain as he moves his hands that while his gloves have five fingers, his hands do not, the middle finger of each being artificial. Artificial is an apt description as well of your complexion, sir. Your morning shave must have been remarkably close to yield no shadow by this hour. Impossibly close, I should judge. And you did not shave this afternoon, for the aroma of soap would still be prominent."

"Alopecia areata," I murmured.

"Thank you, Watson. But topical baldness, which is the condition you name, leaves the skin discolored as with a rash, if I am correct."

I nodded.

"Now to the suit itself. Notice the fullness of the cut of the trousers, Watson. See how they disguise, but cannot hide, the presence of a second leg joint above the knee, as well as the fact that the leg itself is not connected properly at the hip. And how the suit coat similarly disguises another joint above the elbow."

"Such a child could not grow into adulthood," I exclaimed. "Such gross distortions of the human frame are inevitably accompanied by fatal internal aberrations."

"I concur, Watson. And when I contrived to touch the fabric of his suit, I found myself unable to identify the composition of its fibers. There is more, but . . ."

Holmes now addressed the stranger directly. "Sir, your exact provenance is information which I may obtain only from your lips. But I may say, with all the certainty which is ever mine to offer, that while the earth which I daily tread contains traces of my ancestors buried within, it contains none of yours.

"Sir, you are not of the soil of this planet."

I reached on instinct for the revolver in the nearby cabinet, but Holmes stayed my hand. The stranger stared at Holmes for a moment, sighed and relaxed back into his chair.

"I am relieved that your reputation has not been exaggerated. I might have approached you directly, but those dreadful scientific romances of your H. G. Wells and others ... besides which, if you had not formed your conclusion yourself, which is of course correct, would you have believed my claim?"

"The point is moot, Mr. . . . ."

"Call me Drimba."

"Mr. Drimba, then," said Holmes, "the point is moot, for you are who you are and you are here. The question that now concerns me is why."

"Murder, Mr. Holmes, murder yesterday at the highest levels of diplomacy, murder that will compromise the negotiations of two great empires, yet has left no clue to the identity of the murderer."

"There are always clues, Mr. Drimba, if there be eyes to see them and a mind to recognize them."

"Murder many thousands of miles above the Earth. Are you willing to make the journey?"

"The newspaper informs me that a man lost his life yesterday when struck by a cab in the Edgware Road. You have made your much longer journey in safety; surely Watson and I can do as well."

The three of us departed in Drimba's hansom and in time found ourselves among the wharves and warehouses in the district east of London Bridge, not far from where we had learned the secret of Hugh Boone many years earlier. Stopping at a large, windowless building, Drimba dismissed the hansom and unlocked the door.

"As you will see, this building has been made unusually secure," said Drimba. Unlocking a steel cabinet built into the wall of the small chamber we had entered, Drimba manipulated several knobs and levers in an intricate pattern, causing a section of the nearest wall to move aside silently. The large room beyond, which plainly comprised the bulk of the building, held a large, metallic ovoid object.

"This is how we will travel, gentlemen. Think of it as a captain's gig. It is a ship whose ocean is the void of space."

As Drimba approached the spacecraft, a hatch opened, rather like those which secure the watertight compartments of steamships. Drimba entered and beckoned us to follow, I after Holmes.

"Please secure yourselves with the harnesses you will find in those chairs," said Drimba, gesturing toward two unornamented, pedestaled seats. "Time is of the essence."

No sooner had Holmes and I strapped ourselves in than we heard and felt a deep, rhythmic throbbing, as of distant, powerful engines. The instruments in the wide panel before Drimba lit up in a profusion of colors, and a large screen displayed a picture of the ceiling of the great room which surrounded our craft. Before either of us could remark on the wonders around us, the display of the ceiling grew larger, as if the craft were moving toward it, though we could feel no sensation of motion.

"We have left the ground. The harnesses are merely a precaution, for you will feel no motion on this journey," remarked Drimba, as if answering our unspoken question. "Our ships generate artificial gravity, which serves to protect us from the severe forces of acceleration."

As we watched, a section of the roof slid open, and we shot up into the brilliant night sky.

"The ship will now pilot itself," said Drimba, turning his chair to face us. "It has . . . let us call them mechanisms of disguise . . . to hide it from casual watchers, and even from your telescopes. These . . . mechanisms . . . are not perfect, but they work well enough at night.

"As you so brilliantly deduced, Mr. Holmes, this is not my normal appearance. Give me but a moment to shed this uncomfortable masquerade, and I will tell you all I know about the grave situation that has driven me to seek your aid."

Drimba rose and disappeared aft into a private cabin, closing the hatch behind him. By the view on the screen, we were hurtling upward from London at a tremendous rate of speed. In moments, the city's sprawl was left behind, and in time the whole of the Earth lay before us, half dark, for we could easily see the creeping line of night. The sight of the beclouded blue and green orb left me speechless, but not so Holmes. He had taken out his watch and was dividing his attention between it and the spectacle on the screen. Even such a sight could not stop the clockwork of his brain.

"By my calculations, Watson," he observed, "if this moving picture is accurate, we are traveling something beyond forty thousand miles per hour."

"Oh, rather more, Mr. Holmes, and accelerating," said Drimba, emerging from his cabin. "This is my natural appearance; I trust it is not so foreign as to be frightening."

Without the confinement of his human costume, Drimba was taller and less bulky than he had first appeared. His arms and legs were jointed rather like the legs of a grasshopper, with each hand possessing a thumb at either end and two fingers between them. He wore a dull golden tunic and blue trousers with a gold stripe; his ensemble and bearing struck me as military. His complexion was a curious shade of ocher, and his head was markedly wider and flatter above the ears than the human norm. No wonder he had kept his hat on.

"This is a matter of the utmost gravity," he began, seating himself and turning his chair to face us. "Altor Benn has been murdered—assassinated is the better word—in his private ship, with no possible way for the murderer to escape."

"Plainly it was possible, Mr. Drimba, for the murderer is not in your custody," said Holmes. "Who was this Altor Benn?"

"He was renowned as a mediator of great skill, one who believed absolutely in the power of reason, and had come to settle the final stages of the trade dispute between the Shalanic Commonwealth and the G'daak Hegemony."

"These are the empires you spoke of?"

"Yes. Each controls the wealth of tens of thousands of worlds, and as they are expanding in the same directions, clashes over newly discovered worlds have escalated nearly to the point of war. But both sides realize that diplomacy is far less expensive, and therefore a number of years ago jointly convened a treaty conference.

"The talks, however, have been marred by deceit and acrimony, and it is only recently that agreement became conceivable. Hence the arrival of Altor Benn, who was to smooth the few remaining disputes and preside over the actual signing of the treaty. But now each side has accused the other of assassinating Benn in order to sabotage the agreement, and relations are deteriorating. There are, in truth, radical factions on both sides who would profit from war, and I expect it is one of these, rather than one government or the other, that is responsible for this crime. In any case, only a full disclosure of the facts can save the conference and avert tragic repercussions."

Holmes nodded. "One rash act can undo the diplomacy of a generation. And you are charged with the investigation?"

"I am," he replied. "I command the station built to accommodate the negotiations. It is on the far side of your Moon, where we may come and go without observation."

"Surely," I said, "there are barren worlds within your purview where such precautions would be unnecessary."

"True," replied Drimba, "but your Earth is well situated in neutral territory between the home worlds of the two empires. And by obtaining supplies from your provisioners—London being, of course the natural choice as the center of the civilized world—we avoid the vast cost and inconvenience of shipment over stellar distances."

"You say you command the station," said Holmes. "You are, then, a military man."

Drimba twisted his mouth into what was for him a smile. "I 'command' a motley company of uncommitted Filgi mercenaries and some few others as a member of what might loosely be described as an interstellar constabulary force. Beyond these, my command is honored mostly in the breach, for the prime ministers of each government have their own large retinues over which I have little control."

Drimba glanced at the instruments surrounding the screen. "We have nearly reached Altor Benn's vessel. It is floating in what your astronomers call a LaGrange point, equally convenient to Earth and Moon, yet far enough away to escape detection."

Holmes shrugged. He has often professed a total disregard for matters astronomical, caring little whether the Earth revolves about the sun or vice versa. "How was the crime discovered?" he asked.

"We received an automatic distress signal from Benn's ship," replied Drimba. "He did not respond to our attempts to establish communications, so I assembled as many of my Filgi mercenaries as could be gathered for a rescue mission."

"There is no set procedure?" asked Holmes.

"Our function is primarily security and protocol; I confess I was ill prepared for an emergency of this nature. It is, however, understood that when the alarm is sounded, all Filgi on duty report to a designated vessel, as well as those not on duty who can get to the dock in time. I believe over half the contingent were able to respond, and we managed to race to this location within the half hour. There is Benn's ship now."

There grew upon the screen the image of a vessel similar in design to ours but, by the relative size of its entry hatch, considerably larger. There was a panel of blinking lights to the left of the hatch.

"The lights you see indicate, among other things, whether the hatch was last used for entry or exit. They are integral to the hull and cannot be tampered with, being activated electrically by the hatch itself."

"And I presume that upon your arrival, the lights indicated that someone had entered the ship," said Holmes.

"Quite correct. But they also indicated that the interior of the ship was airless. I now feared greatly for Altor Benn's life, for he breathes even as you and I do, and he had not responded to our wireless messages. My one hope was that he had managed to don his vacuum suit before the disaster struck."

"Vacuum suit?" I asked, for the phrase had no meaning.

Drimba rose. "There is so much to explain," he said, striding to his cabin. He returned immediately with three small packages. One he kept for himself, the others he gave to Holmes and me.

"Despite all precautions, the airlessness of space represents a constant danger. Should our hull be breached and our air evacuated, we would perish in moments without these." He pressed a button on one end of his package; it began to unfold itself into a silvery oversuit, open in front, with a clear visor and a set of small cylinders attached to its back. He gestured for us to do likewise, and following his lead, we climbed into our suits.

"They are far sturdier than they look," continued Drimba, "and are perfectly capable of surviving the rigors of the vacuum of space. Every member of our mission, from the two prime ministers to the lowliest private in my command, has his own suit and knows how to use it. You must learn as well."

Holmes and I found that by pressing together the edges of the opening, the suit sealed itself, and we were now quite isolated from the outside world.

"I am speaking to you by wireless," said Drimba, his voice coming from a spot near my right ear. "The hissing you hear is the oxygen that is being fed into your suit from the cylinders on your back. If you look to your left, you will see a gauge divided by eight marks ..."

I heard Holmes interrupting. "I presume that this indicates the amount of oxygen remaining."

"Correct again, Mr. Holmes," said Drimba. "A full charge is approximately three of your hours. It is normal procedure to refill the cylinders when the level drops below the halfway mark, for we have periodic drills which exhaust the cylinders. We had, in fact, just done so."

I attempted to take a step, and found my feet glued to the deck. I heard Drimba's laughter echo through my suit.

"Dr. Watson! I apologize! A problem serious enough to cause one of our vessels to lose its air is likely to disrupt our artificial gravity. Therefore we have built powerful magnets into the soles of these suits to enable one to walk instead of floating helplessly. If you will but lift your heel and slide forward ..."

I am sure that Holmes and I were quite a spectacle, gliding about the deck of a space ship thousands of miles above the Earth as if we were ice-skating on a frozen Scottish pond.

After familiarizing ourselves with the simple controls of these vacuum suits, we removed them and pressed Drimba to continue.

"As I said, finding the ship airless, all the members of my crew, myself included, donned vacuum suits."

"Do you and your crew carry them about with you?" asked Holmes.

"Only when we are off duty. Otherwise they are stored in a compartment aboard ship. Each is marked, for every man is responsible for his own suit.

"You will notice that the hatches of these two ships fit together," said Drimba, gesturing toward the screen. Indeed, the two ships were now in contact. "Altor Benn's ship now has pressure and gravity equal to ours, but that was not the case yesterday. When I entered his ship, I discovered that the main power had been shut down. There were but a few self-powered emergency lights relieving the darkness, yet they were sufficient to reveal the body of Altor Benn, floating weightless in the center of the bridge. He was not wearing a vacuum suit.

"This was plainly no accident, Mr. Holmes. The air had been deliberately evacuated from the ship—not an easy task, for in the interest of safety, it is first necessary to shut down all of the operating systems of the ship. I dispatched my company to restore heat, air, light and power, and to search for the person responsible, assuming he must still be aboard."

"But you were unsuccessful," said Holmes. "Did you consider the possibility of suicide?"

"Let us step inside Altor Benn's ship, and I will show you why that cannot be."

We entered the spacious main cabin of the larger vessel. "Excellent!" cried Holmes. "You have not removed the body!"

Indeed, the body of Altor Benn dominated the large space. Stretched out upon a table, he was five and a half feet in height, extremely rotund, with a bright red complexion and, like Drimba, four fingers on each hand. He was clad in a long green robe with an elaborate orange scarf knotted so tightly about his neck that the flesh bulged out on either side.

"Strangulation?" I asked.

Drimba shook his head. "Beneath the scarf there is a small puncture wound; he was stabbed with a long, thin object that passed through several vital organs and into his brain, causing instant death. His body has swollen from internal pressure in the presence of vacuum. We have treated it to prevent further decomposition."

"And you replaced the scarf after locating the wound?" asked Holmes.

"We used Roentgen rays to examine his body; there was no need to disturb his clothing. Yet his clothing is part of the puzzle. The scarf you see is a mark of rank. Yet among members of Altor Benn's race, it is common to wear a scarf that matches the color of the robe. In fact, at the reception honoring his arrival yesterday, this was the robe he wore— with a green scarf. Equally remarkable is the fact that he wore a scarf at all on his vessel; the Mediator was notoriously informal for his rank, and always removed his scarf as soon as possible."

"So you surmise that after the murderer struck and killed

Mediator Benn, he then capriciously placed a second scarf around his neck, initiated a call for help, exposed the vessel to the vacuum of space, and somehow made good his escape?" asked Holmes.

"I see no alternative."

"There are always alternatives. But let me examine the wound."

Holmes unwound the scarf, removed his glass from a pocket and brought it close. Peering intently, he gestured for Drimba to join him.

"This faint discoloration surrounding the wound—it is not blood?"

Drimba shrugged. "I cannot identify it. Perhaps a stain from the scarf."

Holmes grunted, then threw himself flat on the metal deck. Even to one who has seen Holmes in full cry, his methods often startle.

"Holmes! I say!" cried Drimba.

"Here," said Holmes, "and here, and here. These marks upon the deck have been made, if I am not mistaken, by you and your crew in your vacuum suits; see how they grow more distinct in the direction of travel. We are fortunate; in another day, oxidation would have rendered them invisible. There are many pairs of small markings, and one larger."

Drimba nodded. "The Filgi are considerably smaller than I; they must indeed be our tracks."

The vacuum suit tracks led to every part of the craft. In the private chamber, Holmes discovered a closet containing a number of robes and a chest containing scarves in matching colors. In another hung a vacuum suit, its oxygen gauge indicating a full charge.

"Unless I am mistaken," observed Holmes, "Mediator Benn piloted his ship alone, as there are no other vacuum suits in evidence."

"Quite true," agreed Drimba. "He took considerable pride in his skills."

Holmes spent a few more moments examining the floor between the closet and the entry hatch, then rose abruptly.

"There is no more to be learned here. But I have some few questions for the members of your crew."

"I rather thought you might. Let us depart, then, for the far side of the Moon."

The sight of the Moon swelling in the viewing screen of

Drimba's ship held my utter attention. Yet Holmes remained lost in thought. Only as we prepared to land did he shake his head and speak.

"How I wish I had thought to bring a pipe, Watson. Tobacco so concentrates the mental processes. I have facts in abundance, but no frame to surround them. It is obvious how the assassin left the ship, but to identify and capture him . . . that will be an undertaking. And the matter of the second scarf remains unresolved."

"If I may ask, Mr. Holmes," began Drimba.

"All in good time, sir. Crack the egg prematurely and the bird will die; patience will hatch us a falcon. But I need more information. If this were an earthly crime and an earthly criminal, I would have my informants, my case books, my cross-references. This is *terra incognita*—or perhaps *luna incognita*—and I have nothing to provide me with the small yet vital bits of information I require to piece these clues into a quilt that covers the crime."

A section of the lunar surface swung open as we approached it, and we found ourselves docking at an underground berth. Drimba rose to open the hatch. "Perhaps I can satisfy your needs, Mr. Holmes, even as I offer you and Dr. Watson the hospitality of my station."

Our berth connected to a wide corridor populated by strollers having an unimaginable variety of shapes and appendages. Perhaps I had been inured to wonders by our journey and continued conversation with a man not of my planet, for I found the sight more curious than frightening. Drimba directed us toward the end of the corridor.

"Few here have ever seen a human before," said Drimba, "and you may be the object of scrutiny."

"The same might be said of certain public houses I have had occasion to visit in the East End," said Holmes dryly. "Lead on."

We entered a vast room cut from the living rock of the Moon and were immediately assaulted by the sounds of alien music and by odors pleasant and unpleasant that could not be identified. The room was a riot of colored light, ranging from the dimmest red to barely visible violet. Beings of all descriptions were gathered in these vivid, coruscating pools of brightness, and nearly all with glasses in their hands (or what passed for hands).

We seemed to be in the station's social hall.

Drimba led us to a table in an area of normal illumination. "There are countless races in the galaxy," he said, "many of them so alien that commerce and communication with them are impossible. Of those races who are roughly similar in constitution, as are you and I, we find that the primary difference is the light by which they see. Your sun is highly energetic in a certain part of the spectrum; you are responsive to that light. Some see well into the infrared, still others into the ultraviolet. The Filgi, for example, fall into the latter group.

"This room is considered neutral territory. There and there," he said, gesturing to tables near to us but not to each other, "you will even find the two Imperial prime ministers and their guards."

A four-armed waiter with completely human blue eyes wheeled to our table a cart with plates of food and a variety of beverages, including what I found to be a very fine light ale. I was painfully reminded that our dinner remained uneaten back on Earth, and was suddenly ravenous.

"Please enjoy our hospitality," said Drimba. "As for the Filgi . . ."

He took a pair of dark-lensed eyeglasses from his pocket and handed them to Holmes. "Since I must often visit their quarters, I use these spectacles to see in their light, as the only color we have in common is the upper reach of violet; all lesser colors are black to them, as all of theirs are invisible to us."

Holmes held them to his eyes and scanned the room. He gestured toward an area bathed in a dim violet glow. "Filgi, I presume."

Drimba nodded. In the murkiness, one could barely discern beings that fit Drimba's earlier description. Holmes sat bolt upright. "I am several kinds of fool!" he exclaimed. "This was entirely foreseeable. Watson, if at any time in the future you hear anyone allude to my superior powers of deduction, cane him immediately! Mr. Drimba, have you a ready source of reference on the Filgi?"

Drimba frowned. "We have a central reference, a . . . you have no word for it I fear. You may think of it a highly ordered brain with a great capacity for storing facts, a central exchange, a clearinghouse, if you will. Every datum from every department and field of knowledge is pigeonholed within, and can be handed out in an instant or correlated with all other data. Your Mr. Babbage touched on its philosophy with his difference engine, but our ... call it what you will ... operates on electrical principles."

"Ha!" cried Holmes. "I have used almost the same words to describe the mind of my brother Mycroft. Let us then call your device a Mycroft; lead me to it. Watson, this is, I fear, a solitary pursuit, yet I suspect you will be of invaluable use to me here."

Holmes and Drimba departed, leaving me to discover that the preparations of this kitchen beneath the Moon's surface compared very favorably with Mrs. Hudson's.

In twenty minutes, Drimba returned alone. "A message from Mr. Holmes," he said, handing me a note and two small cards.

"Watson," read the note, "this Mycroft of Drimba's is a remarkable device. The final bit of information I required was instantly at hand, and the game is now afoot in earnest. I have gone to Altor Benn's ship on Drimba's fastest vessel to confirm what should have been obvious to me at the outset; he assures me that I shall be back well within the hour. I have made one or two other preparations as well. Take the two cards which I have enclosed and give one to each of the two prime ministers. One of them is in grave danger; there will be no mistake as to which it is. Drimba will see to his safety. You will know when I have returned, for a general alarm will be sounded. Do not panic, but meet me at the boat dock and the assassin will reveal himself to us. Holmes."

Each of the two cards was identical, bearing nothing but a simple drawing of a circle within a triangle. Drimba led me first to the table of the prime minister of the G'daak Hegemony. In a language I could not follow, save for my name and Holmes's, Drimba introduced me, and I presented one of the cards Holmes had given to me. He took it with a clawlike hand and held it to his hooded face. He said a few words to Drimba, who replied and led us away.

"It is meaningless to him," said Drimba.

The prime minister of the Shalanic Commonwealth was clad entirely in black, which provided a sharp contrast to the white fur of his face and hands. Drimba repeated his introduction, but even as I presented the card, the prime minister drew away sharply and emitted a high, keening cry that set my teeth on edge.

A gesture from Drimba brought uniformed guards of his own race to the Shalanic prime minister's table, which they immediately encircled. As Drimba spoke to his guards, all the lights in the great hall blinked and a siren was heard, together with a booming voice. The Filgi raced from the hall in a group, but the others in the hall seemed unconcerned. This was plainly the alarm Holmes had mentioned.

"Only the Filgi have duties in an emergency drill," said Drimba. "I am afraid the others regard them as no more than a nuisance. Mr. Holmes and I arranged it before his departure."

We arrived at the boat dock to find the Filgi clad in their vacuum suits and standing at attention. As he had promised, Holmes was there, as well. "Mr. Drimba," he said, "please have guards at the ready."

Within a minute, one of the Filgi began to stagger. He ripped his suit open and attempted to flee, but Drimba's guards seized and held him.

"Your assassin," said Holmes. "And your eyeglasses. They proved quite useful aboard Altor Benn's ship."

Drimba took the eyeglasses from Holmes. "I am completely at sea," he said.

"Let us start with the most obvious point," began Holmes. "The murderer could not have left before you arrived at Altor Benn's ship; therefore he was still aboard when you arrived."

"Impossible!" cried Drimba.

"No. Nor even improbable. You yourself indicated uncertainty as to the number of Filgi in your rescue party. How simple it must have been, then, for a vacuum-suited Filgi to emerge from a closet in the dark and blend into the group which had just come aboard. That much was evident from the marks on the deck. All radiated from the entry hatch throughout the vessel, save one pair, which emerged from the vacuum suit closet into the main cabin. After murdering Benn, he activated the distress signal, put on his vacuum suit, which he had brought with him, emptied the air from the vessel, and calmly waited for you to pick him up.

"If the Filgi are mercenaries, as you indicated, it is only reasonable to assume within the society the existence of an assassin cult, rather like our own dacoits. Your excellent Mycroft confirmed my assumption, although the current opinion has it that the Filgi assassin cult is myth and folklore. I, however, assumed otherwise, and used the resources of your Mycroft to compare the past assignments of individual Filgi with the travels of Altor Benn. There was but one correlation. Nine months ago, one of your Filgi company and Altor Benn were on the same world, Beta Draconis IV, I believe it is called."

"That world is now in chaos," said Drimba. "A mysterious explosion destroyed the houses of government, and a dictatorship has taken hold."

"Perhaps not so mysterious," said Holmes. "Altor Benn escaped the blast by moments; there is every probability he saw the Filgi agent responsible escaping by a similar route. Benn was undoubtedly recognized by that same agent at yesterday's reception, and fearing discovery, he stowed away aboard Benn's ship and murdered him.

"There is a symbol used by the Filgi assassins to mark their victims for death. It is both a warning and a proof—the circle within a triangle I sketched on those two cards. You may tell me later which of the two prime ministers was marked for assassination; keep him safe at all costs. I traveled back to Benn's ship to examine the discoloration around the wound, and with the aid of Mr. Drimba's converting eyeglasses the discoloration resolved itself into that same symbol rendered in ultraviolet ink.

"But before I left, I examined the oxygen gauges of all of the Filgi vacuum suits. You indicated, sir, that all were fully charged before the rescue mission. Yet if my train of logic was correct, one suit should be noticeably less full than the others, for its occupant had worn it for at least a half hour longer. That was indeed the case, and I took the liberty of completely exhausting its oxygen supply."

"So when the vacuum drill alarm was sounded . . ." I said.

"The assassin stood revealed by suffocation," said Holmes with grim satisfaction. "I hope you will pardon the dramatic liberty."

"But what of the second scarf?" asked Drimba.

"Elementary, sir. The Filgi cannot see far below the ultraviolet, and Altor Benn kept his robes and scarves in separate places. Green, orange . . . both appear as black to the Filgi. Altor Benn had already removed his scarf when the assassin struck, and his misguided attempt to restore his victim's appearance merely certified his identity."

A phalanx of guards had appeared to lead the assassin away.

"I trust more conventional methods will reveal those ultimately responsible, Mr. Drimba. And I should inquire more deeply into the background of my staff if I were you. But I assume that this arrest should allay the suspicions of the participants sufficiently to conclude a treaty."

"I cannot be more grateful," said Drimba.

"If your gratitude could take the form of a cigar," said Holmes, "it is I who will be grateful to you."

THE PHANTOM OF THE BARBARY COAST

by Frank M. Robinson

In all the years that I had known Sherlock Holmes, there were only five times when he admitted failure, when he confessed that others had gotten the better of him. The public is aware of four of them, but until recently I thought it best to keep silent about the fifth, that it was safe to relate it only when those involved were dead or could no longer be damaged by the revelations.

But though Holmes thought it necessary to admit failure to the personage who had employed him, the fact was he hadn't failed—at least, not completely.

It began one Friday afternoon in late Autumn of 1895 when I was between marriages and had once again taken up lodgings with my friend at 221B Baker Street. All week Holmes had been restless, pacing back and forth in the living room and then over to the bow window to look out at one of those execrable days that plague London in the autumn and winter, when the temperature has dropped and a million coal fireplaces contribute their fumes to the fog rolling off the Thames. The result is a choking, yellowish, poisonous substance that flows through the streets and laps against the buildings like tidewater against a levee. Streetlights are reduced to orange halos in the gloom, while those poor souls condemned to be out in the murk disappear completely once they're five paces in front of you. Even the fast clop of a horse's hooves on the cobblestones is reduced to a tentative clatter while the cab driver's "halloos" warn pedestrians and other carriages of his approach.

Understandably enough, crime falls to a low point for the year, thieves and footpads no more anxious to be out in the chilly dusk than are law-abiding citizens. As a consequence, there had been little of note in the daily papers to intrigue Holmes and no abused citizen at the door to plead for his help. Of all the ways there were to die, Holmes had once told me, to die of inactivity is perhaps the worst. Predictably, as the week wore on, he became increasingly morose, sleeping far later than usual, ignoring my questions of concern and staring into space at nothing at all when he tired of pacing to and fro on the carpet.

Imagine my surprise when on Friday I returned from my morning rounds to find Holmes in his customary chair by the window, smoking a pipe of shag and looking more cheerful than he had all week.

"Something in the papers has caught your attention," I said, half in jest. "The theft of a valuable jewel, no doubt, or some outlandish murder."

"My dear Watson, you read the papers as well as I," he reprimanded. "If there had been anything of the sort, you would have called it to my attention as soon as you entered." He handed me a square of blue paper. "It may be something better than a jewelry theft or a murder. This came by messenger this morning."

From the initials "M. H." at the top, I knew immediately who had sent it. The words were brief and to the point.

"Expect me at Friday, four p.m. Important matter but of no great urgency. Mycroft."

"What on earth!" I protested. "Apparently of great importance but 'not urgent'!"

Holmes refilled his pipe, then glanced up at me with a thoughtful expression.

"I'm always delighted to see Mycroft, Watson. As you know, our paths don't cross that often—I'm frequently busy and he seldom has the energy to leave the Diogenes Club or his Pall Mall lodgings except on government business."

"Then this is undoubtedly government business," I said. "No wonder you're anticipating his visit."

He hesitated. "I'm not so sure, though naturally I *am* curious. It is highly secret since otherwise he would have asked me to meet him at the club rather than venture out himself. As to government business, I do not think so. All government business to which he has called my attention in the past has been both important *and* urgent. Since he does not characterize this particular endeavor as urgent, I am forced to assume that there are personal aspects involved but no particular villainy." A wry look crossed his face. "Lacking that, I'm afraid I may not be the man he wants."

There was the sound of the bell downstairs, the faint murmur of Mrs. Hudson's greeting, and a moment later the pad of heavy footsteps on the stairs.

"We shall know the mystery soon enough," I murmured. Barely had I said it when Mrs. Hudson opened the door and Mycroft Holmes filled the doorway. His girth had increased considerably since last I had seen him, and the walk up the stairs had set him to wheezing. But the steel-gray, deepset eyes in his massive head were as alert as ever, sweeping the room to note any changes that had been made and alighting on me with a faint glare of disapproval.

Holmes noticed the look with some annoyance. "You know I trust Watson with my life, Mycroft. I'm sure we both can trust him with whatever you have to tell me. Pray sit down. Some brandy? Your doctor has warned you against exertion, and your climb up the stairs was faster than usual."

"Only to get out of the chill, I assure you."

Mycroft settled himself with a sigh into the chair opposite Holmes. I stood by the breakfast table, giving them a modicum of privacy but still within the conversational circle.

Holmes studied his brother a moment. "Important but not urgent?"

"I am not here on government business," Mycroft said curtly. "You must have deduced that by now, Sherlock. I come on a matter of some personal delicacy."

"Personal?" Holmes didn't bother to hide his surprise. Though there was an affection between them, they seldom traded on it.

Mycroft looked irritated by the assumption. "It concerns someone else, not me. I will try to be brief. There is a lady who has disappeared. Her family would like her found. They approached a high-placed friend, who in turn approached me and as you can see, I have approached you. It was not my suggestion, it was his."

"Your high-placed friend?"

Mycroft turned his attention to his glass of brandy, avoiding Holmes' eyes.

"I would have preferred to spare you."

Again, the hint of some sort of personal relationship. I knew of no other relatives that Holmes had, aside from Mycroft, and though he was not without friends, they were few in number and, I don't hesitate to say, I chief among them. In short, I knew of no relationship from which Holmes needed to be spared.

"The papers have reported no lady of note missing during the last few weeks," Holmes objected dryly. "I can't imagine they would have refrained from printing it if there had been."

"She didn't disappear in London, Sherlock. For that matter, she didn't disappear in England. She disappeared in America. A cessation of correspondence. No replies to either letters or wires. Inquiries to the local authorities have produced no information as to her whereabouts."

Holmes raised an eyebrow. "An abrupt cessation may suggest foul play or possible kidnapping."

Mycroft held out his glass for more brandy. "Not necessarily. Over time her letters became less and less frequent and finally, about a year ago, they just stopped."

"And where was she last heard from?"

"San Francisco. Apparently she had been living there for quite some time."

"By herself? No husband, no companion?"

"I don't believe so."

Holmes stared at his brother in surprise. "And the family wishes me to go to San Francisco to find her, is that it?"

Mycroft shrugged, as if the inconvenience to Holmes was of no importance. "You have no current cases, am I correct? And you have never seen the States."

"I've liked most Americans I've met, but that does not mean I wish to visit their country." Holmes stalked over to the window, his hands clasped behind his back, then suddenly turned. "I see no necessity for me to go; certainly the local authorities can handle it."

"I told you it was of some delicacy," Mycroft said testily. "Even more so if—although I don't think so—there was foul play of any kind and the papers got hold of it."

Holmes stared at him for a moment, then asked abruptly: "Your high-placed friend. Who is it?"

"The Prince of Wales. The family asked him as a personal favor. And he asked me to ask you."

"And why did he presume I would be interested?" Holmes' voice was sharp, not hiding his irritation.

Mycroft glanced uneasily at me, then decided he had no choice but to trust to my discretion.

"Some years back, despite his marriage to the Princess Alexandra, the Prince had a liaison with another woman. If it had become known, it would have been a scandal to rival that of his affair with the Irish actress in '61. But the lady withdrew and was unusually discreet, especially considering her age at the time. She was twenty-two, he thirty-nine. He loved her then and loves her memory still, though breaking off the affair was relatively easy for her. She was just starting her career as an opera singer and La Scala had beckoned. I believe you met her some time later—Irene Adler. The missing woman is her sister, Leona."

Holmes's face had suddenly gone gray. "I apologize for my slowness. The moment you said you wanted to spare me, I should have known. But I was not aware that Irene Adler had a sister."

"You knew very little about her," Mycroft said, a note of pity in his voice. He sounded, I thought with surprise, like any older brother might under similar circumstances.

It was Holmes's turn to fill a glass with a splash of brandy. "Your sympathy is noted but not really necessary, Mycroft. Tell me about the sister."

"Leona was two years younger than Irene but in all other respects, they were very much alike. They were both beauties, they were both highly sought after, and they both were interested in careers in music. Unfortunately, there the similarities end. Irene had a great deal of talent. Leona had a pleasant voice but nothing more, though her ambition was just as great. Irene left New Jersey for the Continent to make a name for herself. Leona journeyed to the western states, where she anticipated the audiences would be appreciative but the reviewers less critical than those in New York and its environs. She never returned. Over the years her letters became shorter and more somber and as I have told you, a year ago they ceased completely."

"Then it is obvious she wished to break off relations, that she had become estranged from her family."

"Perhaps. But the family still wants her found and to ascertain her well-being."

"She never asked them to send her money?"

"It would have done no good, they have little."

Holmes was lost in thought for a moment.

"You have her letters?"

Mycroft patted a leather case by his side. "I have taken the liberty of glancing through them. They're remarkable in their lack of particulars. There is one mention of a possible marriage and then she says no more about it."

There was a sudden gleam in Holmes's eyes.

"Had she an inheritance?"

Mycroft shook his head. "As I have said, the Adler family is not wealthy. Their only good fortune in life was their two daughters." He pushed to his feet. "I have an appointment with the Prince this evening. What should I say to him?"

"That I am not enthused."

"But you will look into it?" Holmes hesitated, then nodded. At the door, Mycroft said: "All your expenses will be covered, and you will be well rewarded despite whatever you discover. There is an American packet, the *New Hebrides,* leaving for Boston, Tuesday next. With their fast transcontinental railroads, it shouldn't take you more than another week to reach San Francisco. Nor should the trip be all that onerous. I understand the new sleeping cars are quite comfortable." He paused in the doorway. "The Prince will be very appreciative, Sherlock."

Holmes raised his glass. "For God, country and good Prince Edward," he murmured.

And the memory of Irene Adler, I thought.

After Mycroft had left, Holmes sat quietly for a long moment staring at the fog outside the window, I knew that Mycroft had opened a wound both of us thought had healed long ago. I poured myself a small tumbler of brandy and sat opposite him, respecting his silence.

He suddenly drained his glass and turned to me with a slight smile on his face. "As I recall, Watson, you spent some time in America and in that very city. 1883, wasn't it? Or was it 1884?"

"From November of '84 through the end of spring of '85 I had a small practice in Post Street." I tried to cheer him up. "It should be a welcome change for you, Holmes. San

Francisco is a pretty city, not without its attractions—and distractions." And then it was my turn to fall silent, held prisoner by a sudden flood of painful memories.

"Then I take it you would not mind seeing it again." Holmes stoked his pipe for the third time with shag. "I imagine your partner could handle your practice; we should be back in London in less than two months."

"You can't ask me to go!" I protested. "The city holds nothing but unpleasant memories for me!"

Holmes was startled by my outburst, and I felt it necessary to explain.

"I met my first wife there, Holmes. She worked as a nurse in the Marine Hospital, and we fell deeply in love and married within a fortnight. Two months later, she was dead of cholera."

"I am sorry, Watson," he murmured. "I had no idea, you never told me."

"It is not the sort of thing I talk about," I said stiffly.

We continued to sit in silence, nursing our respective wounds and watching the fog swirl past the panes. For once I wished there were a seven percent solution that might help me bury the painful past if only for an hour or so. Finally Holmes said simply, "My dear Watson, I should be lost without you."

It was the closest thing to a plea that Holmes had ever made to me and so, of course, I agreed to go. Three weeks later we were sitting in front of a fireplace in San Francisco's Palace hotel, drinking sherry and listening to the clop of the carriages outside, the ringing of the bells on the cable cars and, of course, the low moaning of the foghorns on the bay. I noticed with some amusement that outside the gaslights were mere blurs of light, as useless in a San Francisco fog as their counterparts were in one that was London made.

The furnishings of our suite were lavish while the dining room of the Palace was the equal of any restaurant in London. We had been there for the better part of a week, dining sumptuously at Prince Edward's expense but, alas, no nearer to solving the riddle of Leona Adler's disappearance.

Holmes fiddled with his pipe, unhappy that he hadn't been able to find his favorite shag in San Francisco.

"This morning, Watson, you said you were going to Leona Adler's rooming house, her last known address, but instead I see you spent your time rummaging through files of the local newspapers."

I stared at him in surprise. "The landlady was absent and the two roomers I talked to—both ruffians—were not disposed to give me any information about Leona Adler. But how did you know I had read through the papers?"

"I could not help but notice your waistcoat and your sleeves. Those little specks of paper could only have come from searching through stacks of newsprint. And your cuffs, Watson—they are black with printer's ink where you've rubbed them across a hundred different pages!"

I inspected my cuffs with shock, then brushed irritably at the tiny pieces of paper clinging to my waistcoat.

"You can repair your appearance later, Watson. What did you find out?"

I dug around in my pockets for my notes, adjusted my reading glasses and moved closer to the light of the fire.

"Leona Adler gave her first concert at the Opera House, October 2, 1884. She sang a number of arias from Puccini's *La Boheme* and *La Traviata* and reprised the role of Arsace in Rossini's *Semirande*. From the reviews it is obvious the audience was no more than polite. The critics were less so, especially her assaying of Arsace."

Holmes looked at me impatiently. "It is a role for a contralto, and she undoubtedly sang it because it was in Irene's repertoire and Irene excelled at trouser roles. Don't forget the rivalry between the two, Watson. How long was the review, incidentally?"

I wondered what on earth that had to do with anything. "As I recall, almost a full column. She was new to the city then and they went into some detail."

"And the reviews for recitals after that?"

By now, I was thoroughly confused.

"Her reviews varied, Holmes; at times she was better received than at other—"

"I meant the length of them, Watson!"

"They seemed to get shorter and shorter, when I could find any reviews at all."

Holmes looked grim. "Then I imagine the theaters got smaller and smaller as well. Whoever was her impressario would not have paid for empty seats—one who deals in birds always knows the commercial value of his canaries. I think we can assume that, all in all, her trip to San Francisco was a failure. She had neither the glamour nor the talents of her sister and contrary to our own naive beliefs of the American West, San Francisco audiences are hardly culturally illiterate. They have a reputation as the most sophisticated in the West, and the best performers in the country have made a point of playing here. I am afraid Leona Adler misjudged the city."

I glanced at my last note. "Her final recital—the review was very short—was a collection of American favorites that she delivered at an establishment called the Bella Union."

"And that was when?"

"Approximately two years after she arrived in the city." I hesitated. "If she was not a success here, I fail to see why she didn't try elsewhere, say Seattle or Vancouver."

Holmes stared intently into the fire as if he could somehow see Leona Adler among the dancing flames. The firelight outlined his narrow face, emphasizing his hawklike nose and casting heavy shadows over his dark brows, now creased in thought.

"Because she did not wish to leave. Because something was holding her here—I suspect the possibility of marriage that she briefly mentioned." He prodded at the fire with the poker. "There is always the possibility that we may run into her when we least expect to, Watson. From time to time you should refresh your memory and study the studio portrait Mycroft gave us."

I remembered the photograph quite well and resented Holmes suggesting I memorize it as if I were a schoolboy. At the time of the studio sitting Leona Adler had been a young woman with chestnut hair—at least, that is what the colourist had given her, wasp waist, and a flowing gown that formed a small train behind her. Her hair had been piled high atop her head, revealing prominent cheekbones and a faint but firm smile of great determination. She was holding a bass viol while on the wall behind her hung several other musical instruments, an obvious attempt to stress her chosen vocation and point out that she could play as well as sing. She looked, I thought, very much like Holmes's description of her older sister.

Slightly nettled by his interrogation of me I said, "I assume that you were busy as well, Holmes?"

"A short visit to what they call the Barbary Coast." He smiled with a grim pleasure. "As fine a collection of beer halls and brothels as I have ever seen. It would make London's East End look like the wellsprings of civilization."

"A tourist's trip, Holmes, they all fake it. But I fail to see the relevance to the disappearance of Miss Adler."

Holmes laughed. "You've accused me in the past of ignoring the social amenities. I took your advice and made the acquaintance of the local police. One of their number offered to show me around the city in exchange for lunch and for what I hope will be an informative dinner here tonight."

It was my turn to smile. "So you admit you sometimes benefit from my advice."

He took a moment to knock the dottle from his pipe. "My dear Watson, I gladly give credit where credit is due. For one so often wrong, the law of averages dictates that sometimes you have to be right!"

Michael Van Dyke, despite the Dutch derivation of his name, was thoroughly American. A tall, middle-aged, dapper man with a ruddy, fleshy face, he was elegantly dressed in a checkered coat, a silk waistcoat with a thick, gold watch chain running from one pocket to the other, and wearing a carefully brushed bowler. A heavy, melton cloth coat was draped casually over one arm and he carried a walking stick in the other. He was waiting just off the entrance to the dining room and hurried over when he saw us.

"I changed the reservation to my name, gentlemen—dinner's on the department, the least we can do for noted guests."

"Why, thank you very much," Holmes said easily. "Lieutenant Van Dyke, I would like you to meet my partner, Dr. John Watson."

Van Dyke nodded, gave his coat, hat and stick to a nearby waiter, then took us both by the arm and hustled us to a table by one side of the room so we had a commanding view of the entire dining area.

"Always sit with your back to the wall, never put yourself in a position to be surprised, that's my advice."

He immediately ordered whiskeys-and-sodas for all of us. After the second round, which Holmes refused, he motioned to the hovering waiter and ordered for us from the menu in creditable if accented French. I was impressed but noticed that Holmes seemed more reserved and speculative.

"You've come a long way from London," Van Dyke said

after we finished dinner and he had passed around cigars. "The captain told me you're on the trail of Leona Adler." He exhaled a perfect ring of smoke, then slouched back in his seat and waved his cigar. "Anything I can tell you, just ask."

"Why, we would be grateful for most anything at all," Holmes said cheerfully. He was preoccupied with his cigar, almost, but not quite, hiding his delight at its quality.

"The Adler woman," Van Dyke puffed. "Came out here from New Jersey in 1884, apparently trying to earn a living with operatic recitals. Nice voice but not top-drawer, if you know what I mean. And this is a town that loves either top-drawer or bottom but nothing in between. Her first manager dropped her and she picked up another, but he booked her into joints that were strictly low class."

"Low class?" I said.

He waved his hand. "Every now and then, a concert saloon will try to improve itself and book a higher grade of talent. Usually they can't afford it and wind up with second-best, but like I said, this is a town that's interested in the top and fascinated by the bottom but nothing in the middle."

"And then?" I prompted.

"After two years none of the better theaters would feature her. If you saw her act once, there was no need to see it again and word spread."

"I find that difficult to believe," Holmes said shortly. Van Dyke's face flushed and Holmes held up his hand. "I hardly meant offense. But I cannot see why she would not have tried her luck in another city with less exacting standards."

I was flattered that Holmes had picked up on the very question that I had raised earlier.

"One of the mining camp towns like Virginia City? No mystery there. She fell in love with a William McGuire shortly after coming to San Francisco. Nice enough fellow, I knew him briefly."

"They never married?" Holmes asked.

Van Dyke shook his head. "McGuire had gold fever. Left town in '86 for the big strike on Fortymile Creek up in Alaska. Promised to marry her when he struck it rich, but she never heard from him again. Probably got shot by a claim jumper, but I don't know that for a fact."

"So she waited for her lover to return and when he never did, she vanished," I said.

Van Dyke waved to the waiter to bring us a round of after-dinner drinks.

"Vanished isn't the word I would use." He suddenly became apologetic. "So far, everything I've told you about the Adler woman is fact. But a few months ago we fished a body from the bay and as far as we could determine, it was the body of Leona Adler. My guess is that she had finally given up waiting for McGuire to return, was too proud to go home and decided to end it all." He shrugged. "It happens more often than you might think. A lot of people come to San Francisco hoping to make their fortune. But this is the end of the continent, this is as far as they can go. You come out with dreams and then reality sets in. A lot of people can't face it." He drained his glass and waved to the waiter to bring the check. "I'm a gambling man and while I can't prove that Miss Adler committed suicide, I wouldn't bet against it."

"You should have told us immediately!" I cried, indignant.

Van Dyke's face hardened. "We don't work on supposition here in the States any more than you do back in London. She'd been in the water a long time; identification was strictly circumstantial. You're a doctor, you know what they look like when they've been in the drink for a few weeks and the crabs have been at them."

We sat in silence for a long moment, I still annoyed and Holmes sunk in thought. Van Dyke finally said, "Cheer up, gentlemen. Sorry about Leona Adler, but I don't think you really believed you were going to find her alive and kicking. Tell you what, stay for a few more days and I'll show you the town." He winked at Holmes. "When it comes to depravity, no city can match this one—it would give London a run for its money!"

Holmes scrubbed out his cigar in a nearby ashtray. "We might accept that offer. I have heard a lot about your Chinatown."

"There's a lot to see; the Chinamen live closer together than sardines. We estimate there are more than fifty thousand Chinks in San Francisco, only a few thousand of them women. And of those few thousand, ninety-five percent are whores. No surprise there, if you know the breed."

He pushed away from the table and we stood up. "You

want a guided tour of the seamy side, I'm your man. Maybe I can even show you the Phantom of the Barbary Coast."

We were collecting our hats in the lobby now and Holmes asked politely: "Phantom?"

Van Dyke slipped into his coat. "I haven't seen her myself, but by all reports, she's a real live ghost. All dressed in white, appears late at night at the mouth of an alley off Pacific Street. Get too close, she disappears up the alley. From all accounts, so does anybody who follows her. A San Francisco legend, Mr. Holmes, though not quite as solid as our former Emperor Norton."

"A fanciful tale," I snorted.

Van Dyke winked once again. "But a good excuse for a tour of the local melodeons and deadfalls."

Back in our rooms, I rang for some tea while Holmes took off his coat and tie and poked at the now cold fire.

"What did you think, Watson?"

"Of our host?" I asked. "The dinner? His comments about Miss Adler? Or that outrageous tale about the phantom?"

"First, the dinner—I'm sure that is uppermost in your mind."

"One of the very best I have had, Holmes. I'm afraid it has spoiled me for when I return to London."

Holmes fed little strips of paper under the grate where they promptly burst into flame, then made a small nest of twigs on top.

"And his comments about Miss Adler?"

I shrugged. "It does not surprise me. But I don't envy you when you have to tell Prince Edward."

"The case is hardly closed, Watson. We will pay a visit to the boarding house tomorrow—perhaps somebody there remembers McGuire. I have a feeling that at least part of the solution lies in the nature of the man."

The fire was roaring now and he pulled a chair closer to it, turned up a nearby gaslight and made himself comfortable with the evening paper.

"You surprise me, Holmes," I said after a moment. "You've offered no comments about our host."

He lowered his paper, frowning. "Because I am a fish out of water, Watson. My powers of deduction are almost useless in a foreign country. London fits me like a glove, I know its every wrinkle. I can tell the wealth of a man by the quality of the cigar ash he leaves behind, what section of town he lives in by the color of the mud on his boots. But to find my way around this city, I need a map." He shot me a glance. "I still have my powers of observation but no hook on which to hang my deductions, which makes us almost even. You have a slight advantage since you have lived here before. What did *you* think of our host?"

"A true American," I smiled. "Generous to a fault, as helpful as he can be though I suppose by English standards, a little crude and at times impolite. But you can hardly fault the man for that, it's a raw city with people to match."

"As usual, you see but you do not observe, Watson. Our friend is a bigoted dandy and more than a little ostentatious, both of which are major clues as to his character. And I am very much afraid that in this puzzle, character will turn out to be everything."

"You're faulting him for being typically American, Holmes. After all, this is not England!"

"No, indeed it is not," Holmes sighed. "But think of our noble Lestrade, Watson, and compare him to our American friend. Imagine them in your mind's eye standing side by side. What is the first thing that strikes you?"

"Lestrade is obviously thinner," I said after a moment. "And I believe not quite as tall—"

"My dear Watson, I fear there is no hope for you! The most obvious difference is in the way they dress! The suit our good Lestrade wears is at least three years old, his boots are worn, his cuffs are frayed. Our American host, unlike his compatriots in the department, looks as if he had just stepped out of a shop window. And the meal tonight—I watched when he paid the check and he settled it personally and with cash. One is led to believe San Francisco pays its police exceedingly well, which would be contrary to my experience in any city, or that police work is merely part time for our friend and he actually makes his living at a different endeavor entirely."

I looked at him, startled. "And what might that be, Holmes?"

He turned back to his paper.

"I have no idea but I suspect we shall soon find out."

"And his fanciful tale about the ghost?"

"Ah, Watson, we shall discover the truth of that together!"

* * *

The landlady, Hattie Daniels, was as different from Mrs. Hudson as one could possibly imagine. She was thin, hardfaced, with stringy gray hair tied back in a bun and an apron over her black woolen dress that was stained with the remnants of the previous night's cooking. The weatherbeaten sign out front promised both breakfast and dinner with the rent, though if I had been a boarder, I doubt that I would have looked forward to either.

The rooming house had seen better days. At one time the furniture had been of good quality but was now knocked about and covered with grime and dust while a few of the window panes were broken and covered with cardboard. Where parts of the floor were not covered with worn carpeting, our boots occasionally stuck to dark smears on the wood.

"I don't know nothing about your Miss Adler," Hattie repeated. And then, with a false show of sympathy because she thought we expected it of her: "I heard about her being found in the bay like that, poor woman."

"She didn't live here?" Holmes asked.

Hattie settled back in her kitchen rocker and folded her arms across her bony chest. "I told you that before," she said, her thin lips covering those gaps in her jaw where teeth had once been. She picked idly at a thread on her dirty apron and glared at us from under lowered lids.

Holmes took a letter from his pocket and handed it to her.

"She gave this establishment as her return address, Mrs. Daniels. One would assume that she had been living here." He glanced around. "As unlikely as that may seem," he murmured.

Hattie had been caught in a lie but refused to be embarrassed by it. She turned the letter over in her hands without really looking at the return address.

"Miss Adler got her mail here," she finally admitted. "I'd save it for her and she'd pick it up every month or so."

Holmes slowly strolled around the kitchen, occasionally picking up a dirty glass and setting it down, then glancing out the windows at the sloping hill in back.

"You told us she didn't live here."

"I never said she *hadn't*." Hattie watched him suspiciously. "She did at one time, but it was some years back." She sniffed. "She was always putting on airs, always better than everybody else."

"She never told you where she had moved to?"

Hattie shook her head. "She didn't tell me. I didn't ask her. She paid me two dollars a month to save her mail for her and I've done so faithfully all these years." She leered at Holmes. "She also asked me not to talk about her to strangers." She got up and limped over to a kitchen drawer and took out several envelopes. "These are her latest letters. Seeing as how she won't be picking them up, maybe you gentlemen will know what to do with them."

Holmes glanced at them and put them in his pocket. "Have the police ever come here?"

Hattie drew herself up in a mock display of dignity. "I run a decent house, there's no reason for any police to come around!"

"No offense intended," Holmes murmured. He raised his voice slightly. "Could we talk to your roomers? I think I saw them watching through the upstairs window when we came up the walk."

There was the sound of hurried footsteps on the landing and in the front hallway. I don't know how he got there so quickly, but Holmes was suddenly at the front door, blocking it. Facing him were the two ruffians I had talked to the previous day. One was heavyset and dressed in rough seaman's clothes. He looked about forty, with the thick, red nose of the heavy drinker. The other was younger, in his early twenties, thin and with a weasel face. He looked oddly familiar but for the moment, I couldn't think why.

"Gentlemen," Holmes said easily. He held out his hand. "I'm Sherlock Holmes and this is Dr. John Watson; we were friends of the late Leona Adler."

The older man shook his hand reluctantly. "Josiah Martin," he grumbled. The younger one followed suit, identifying himself as one "Willy Green."

"We were just asking Mrs. Daniels about Miss Adler, who used to live here. Perhaps you knew her?"

They looked at each other, then shook their heads. "Never heard of her," the older one growled. "And who are you to be asking?"

The younger one looked guilty and said sullenly, "I don't know her neither, I don't know what you're talking about."

Mrs. Daniels had followed us into the hallway. "They're decent roomers! She was gone before they ever moved in!"

Holmes stepped aside. "My error," he said. "Please forgive me."

They clumped down the steps, the words "law abiding" and "minding our own business" floating after them like smoke.

"We're sorry to have troubled you, Mrs. Daniels," Holmes said. He paused at the door as if the question had just occurred to him. "When Miss Adler lived here, did a William McGuire ever visit her?"

She nodded. "Almost every day. Even though he was a gambler I thought he was a gentleman, which only shows how wrong a body can be. After she moved, I understand he left her with a child and lit out for the goldfields and nobody saw hide nor hair of him again." She sniffed once more. "Broke her heart, I imagine. I always say if you want to keep a man, grab ahold of the purse strings so you can tie him to you."

Holmes took a five-dollar gold piece from his pocket and gave it to her. "If you remember anything else, we're staying at the Palace Hotel. Sherlock Holmes," he pronounced it very carefully to make sure she would remember, "and Dr. John Watson."

We left. I very glad to be away from the odors of yesterday's stew and the sticky floors. Holmes, as usual, was quiet and thoughtful. There were no carriages in sight so we walked a block over to a cable car.

"It probably was a decent rooming house at one time," Holmes said once we were seated. "It isn't now. And I would wager those are not roomers but her husband and son. You noticed the likeness of the latter?"

That would explain the familiarity of his features, I thought.

"What happened to them?" I asked.

"I suspect the marriage was common law. Back when the neighborhood was better than it is now, she probably passed them off as a roomer and his son for appearances' sake. Eventually, she and her husband took to drink and let the property deteriorate." He sniffed the fingers of his gloves. "Both the glasses and the floor were sticky with cheap rum." He handed me the letters Mrs. Daniels had given him. "What do you make of them?"

I turned them over in my hands. The postmark was New Jersey. They had been handled with dirty fingers and the flaps torn open.

"I would have bet the woman could not read."

"I doubt that any of them could," Holmes said. "I saw no books or newspapers anyplace. As for the letters, after they heard of Leona Adler's death, the husband probably opened them to see if there was money inside."

"Why did the Adler woman use them as a letter drop, Holmes? She could have had the postal department forward her mail."

"Because she didn't want to be traced, Watson! She desperately didn't want anybody to know where she was living or what she was doing. To protect herself, she chose a couple who could not read; her former landlady and family were a natural choice. Granted they could have had somebody read the letters for them, but then they would have lost their monthly stipend once Leona saw the letters had been opened."

"That's quite logical, Holmes."

"And what else might be quite logical?"

"What do you mean?"

"You saw both the husband and the son there yesterday and they were there again today. If I am not mistaken, when they ran down the stairs, they were still rubbing the sleep from their eyes. Obviously, if they work at all, it must be at night."

"But why did you ask if the police had ever been there? Do you suspect them of some crime?"

Holmes shrugged. "It would not surprise me if they were minor criminals. More importantly, if I remember Mycroft correctly, he said the Adler family had made inquiries, meaning inquiries of the police. Lieutenant Van Dyke said Leona Adler had probably killed herself. But you cannot have it both ways, Watson. If the police were not sure their drowning victim was Miss Adler, then they should certainly have investigated the rooming house, her last known address. And if they were sure, it would have been only common decency to inform the Adlers."

I shrugged. "I'm certain Lieutenant Van Dyke has an explanation."

"We may find out this evening, Watson. We are to meet him for his 'grand tour.' It may be a trip for tourists but somehow I don't think that is what he has in mind!"

That evening Lieutenant Van Dyke guaranteed that we would "see the elephant," as he put it. The evening started with a drink at the Bank Exchange bar and dinner at the Cliff House as the sun was setting in the Pacific Ocean. At the end of the meal, he withdrew three tickets from his coat pocket and handed us two.

"I'm quite a fan of the theater and I hope you are as well. These are for tonight's performance of the Gilbert & Sullivan opera, *Patience,* at the Tivoli." He grinned broadly. "I never did meet an Englishman who didn't enjoy them. Care to join me?"

I was entranced by the work of my countrymen, even if it was a pirated American production, and I believe Sherlock was as well. Lieutenant Van Dyke applauded as often as did I, but I noticed him occasionally glancing thoughtfully at Holmes and myself, as if weighing some unknown potential.

The rest of the night soon degenerated, beginning with a tour of an opium den in Chinatown, where my heart went out to the poor souls clustered together on dirty mattresses in the crowded, vermin-infested basement, their eyes closed in dreams that only they could fathom. This was genuine, I realized, appalled. The "tours" I had taken when living in San Francisco before had obviously been staged with actors playing the role of addicts.

After that, it was a round of melodeons and cheap grog-geries and deadfalls, the most interesting one of which was the Cobweb Palace whose interior was a mass of cobwebs with a row of cages against the far wall that contained monkeys and parakeets. Nobody, I was told, was allowed to interfere with any spider spinning its web.

The waiter girls in the establishments seemed quite taken with both the Lieutenant and myself, though instinctively they stayed away from a cold and unsmiling Holmes. The Lieutenant occasionally whispered to one of the women and at one time nudged me in the ribs and raised his eyebrows. I shook my head "no" and he shrugged and went back to whispering, no doubt making an assignation for later.

It was a good three in the morning when he said, "Well, gentlemen, I think it's time."

We followed him out to a waiting carriage and clattered noisily through the Barbary Coast to Pacific Street. It was late, but little clumps of revelers still wandered down the walks. The Lieutenant motioned for the carriage driver to stop and we got quietly out and followed him up the sidewalk, then at his signal lost ourselves in the shadows of a storefront.

"The alley across the way," he whispered. "Watch it."

It was a chill night and my skin broke out in small bumps, but not because of the temperature. The minutes crept by and suddenly I caught my breath. In the mouth of the alley, I saw a sudden flash of white and then a pale, young woman appeared, dressed in a flowing white gown from neck to ankle. She was carrying a guitar. She leaned against a nearby wall and accompanied herself as she began to sing a sea chantey in a soft, low voice. I could feel the hair at the back of my neck prickle.

"Interesting," Holmes murmured.

A group of seamen now reeled up the street, attracted by the sound. A moment later, the woman in white seemed to grow dim and vanished. The sailors hesitated, arguing among themselves over whether they should follow her, and then continued up the street, intent on more solid company.

After they had gone, the woman reappeared and once again began to sing a doleful tune. The next man to become fascinated by the sight was a sailor who was by himself. He stopped and watched for a long moment, then lurched over and reached out for her. She shrank back and I thought she would disappear once again but she had merely retreated a few feet into the alley. He hesitated, then followed her and they both disappeared into the fog.

Much to my surprise, Lieutenant Van Dyke shouted, "After them!" and dashed across the street. Holmes and I followed, running quickly through the alley mud. Then the alley suddenly turned to the left and we found ourselves in a small cul de sac, the walls of warehouses all around us.

The woman in white and the sailor had vanished.

Van Dyke loped around the tiny square, searching for any doors or exits into which they could have disappeared, running back and forth in his eager dedication to duty. Holmes inspected the muddy ground, then quietly circled the enclosure also checking, I presumed, for hidden doorways.

After ten minutes or so, Lieutenant Van Dyke came over and shrugged. His face seemed whiter than usual, his eyes wide. When he spoke, his words came out in little puffs of vapor. "I can find nothing; they seem to have vanished into thin air." He shivered. "Maybe she isn't a phantom, but at least for the moment she's convinced me."

"So it would seem," Holmes said. "If your carriage is still waiting, we might as well return to the hotel."

"Anything," I chattered, "to get out of this cold." Holmes glanced at me strangely, and I knew he doubted my teeth were chattering because of the cold.

In the carriage, the Lieutenant offered us cigars, bit the end off of his and said, "I imagine you'll be returning to London soon."

"In a few days," Holmes agreed.

"I'm sorry about Miss Adler," Van Dyke sighed. "We would have notified the family, but we had nothing to send back as proof of her death and it seemed cruel to tell them she had died when we couldn't be absolutely certain."

"Of course not," Holmes reassured him. "You did the right thing." But he was looking back at the alleyway when he said it.

Once in our rooms I dressed for bed, then came into the living room for a nightcap before retiring. Holmes was sitting in the easy chair in his dressing gown, sipping a glass of sherry and staring into the flames.

"I'm surprised, Watson. I never thought you believed in ghosts."

"Do you have any other explanation?" I protested. "Perhaps I didn't see a ghost, but it would take very little more to convince me."

"Then remember that you didn't see just one ghost, Watson, you saw two. Or had you forgotten the sailor?"

I decided not to discuss it. I had been through enough for one evening.

"Mycroft will be disappointed," I said.

Holmes looked surprised. "I hardly think so. The case of Leona Adler, as tragic as it is, is solved—though bringing the villains to justice may be a little more difficult. And there is the matter of motivations, though I imagine they will sort themselves out at the end." He yawned. "Which reminds me, Watson. Tomorrow pick up some clothing such as a sailor might wear. I think we shall return to that alleyway off Pacific Street tomorrow night and find out just how our ghost and her admirer disappeared, though I believe I already know."

"Only this time it is I who shall follow her, is that it, Holmes?" I said, outraged.

Holmes laughed. "There is nothing to worry about,

Watson—I shall be right behind you. But it might be advisable to bring along a revolver."

I glumly finished my sherry and then went off to my bedroom. I hesitated at the door. "It really *has* been quite an exciting evening, hasn't it, Holmes?"

"I would hardly deny that," he agreed.

I was suddenly curious. "What did you find the most interesting? The melodeon with all the cobwebs?"

"Not at all, Watson. By far the most interesting thing was the large quantity of mud on Lieutenant Van Dyke's boots when we left the alley!"

Early the following evening it started to drizzle, but by midnight it was clear. At two, we caught a carriage in the Great Court of the Palace and set out for the Barbary Coast and the foot of Pacific Street. Holmes had brought along a small chest, but I was too depressed to be curious about its contents. A block from the alleyway he stopped the carriage and we got out. I was dressed in a sailor's rough woolen pants and coat with an old knit sweater high around my throat and a woolen cap pulled low over my ears. It was cold and windy and tendrils of fog had already started to finger their way through the city.

Pacific Street seemed to have more than its share of drunks and roustabouts, but the alleyway itself was empty.

"Hide in the shadows a few doors down and wait for the usual revelers to wander by," Holmes said in a low voice. "She will disappear whenever confronted by a group but will try to entice any man who is alone into the alley. Make sure you are he—don't let anybody precede you."

"And if the phantom fails to show at all?" I asked.

"She is as solid as you or I, Watson. But if she fails to appear, we shall merely try again tomorrow tonight."

"And where will you be?" I asked bitterly.

"Don't worry, I shall be close by."

I shrugged and crossed the muddy street to stand in a doorway a few feet from the alleyway, my head protruding just enough so I could see her if and when she appeared.

A half hour had gone by before I saw a flash of white and heard the first few notes of her sea chantey. A few minutes later there were the sounds of roistering down the street and a group of carousers wandered by, clutching bottles and singing off-key. One of them noticed me and called drunkenly, "What's going on, Mac?"

I didn't answer but made as if I were relieving myself in a corner of the doorway. He laughed and they stumbled on, one of them suddenly crying: "D'ye hear a woman singing?" Another said, "It's the phantom!" and there was sudden silence. Then a querulous voice: "Where? I don't see nothing."

She had, as I suspected, retreated up the alleyway. I waited a minute or two more, then suddenly heard the quavering notes of a violin. I glanced, startled, down the street to see a lone violinist leaning against a gaslight. His cap was by his feet and it was obvious he was playing for any coins that passing revelers might drop into it. But street musicians were hardly unknown in the city, even at this time of night, and I ignored him. Then I heard the phantom's plaintive song once again and left the safety of the doorway to stagger down the street as if I had spent half the night drinking in some deadfall.

She was beautiful at a distance and even more so as I got closer. A thin, pale face with long, brown hair clustered around her neck and shoulders. Her dress looked almost like a white wedding gown gathered about her waist and covering her feet.

I fancy myself a connoisseur of musical instruments, and as much taken as I was by her, I was almost equally taken with the guitar she played. It was a beautiful instrument, the front inlaid with carefully worked mother-of-pearl. The small pick with which she played it was also covered with delicate mother-of-pearl. I watched for what must have been the better part of a minute, then she glanced up at me and smiled. It would have taken a better man than I not to reach out for her, but as she had the night before, she retreated up the alley, strumming a last chord and singing a final refrain.

Then suddenly she turned and ran, I hot on her heels. "No, you don't, my girl!" I cried. We were now in the cul de sac, and all at once it seemed to me she slowed. I almost had my hand on her shoulder when the ground gave way beneath us and we plummeted ten feet down to land on a thin pile of mattresses.

By the time I caught my breath, she had disappeared, but in her place were two cutthroats. I was in a small, dark chamber lit by several torches fastened to the walls and by their flickering light I recognized Mrs. Daniels's roomers, Josiah Martin and Willy Green, running at me with evil smiles on their faces and clubs in their hands.

"Villains!" I cried. Then Martin swarmed all over me, hitting me about the head and shoulders with his club, while I fumbled frantically in a pocket for my revolver. I finally fired through the cloth of my coat, and he screamed and fell back, clutching at his side.

Willy Green dropped his club and backed off a few paces. He dipped his hand to his belt and came up with a knife, tossing it into the air and catching it by the tip so he could throw it at me. I was still struggling to free my revolver from the ruins of my pocket and Willy, with a snarl, had drawn back his arm when I felt a sudden draft of air above me and there was the sound of another shot. Willy gave a high-pitched yelp and crumpled to the ground, a spreading splotch of red covering his chest.

"Are you all right, Watson?"

It was Holmes, of course, who had been playing the role of the itinerant violinist I had seen on the street corner a few minutes before. His small chest had held both his disguise and the violin.

"Quite all right, Holmes, though I fear it was a close thing."

Holmes walked over to the body of Willy Green and turned it over with his foot. "This is one scoundrel who will never dangle at the end of a rope." Martin was still groaning, and I scrambled over to see if he needed help, the doctor in me taking precedence over the angry victim.

"He'll live, Holmes, it's only a flesh wound, though painful. Halloo, what's this?" At Martin's feet was a large gunnysack and a coil of rope.

Holmes fingered it, frowning. "A few moments more and you would have been shangaied to a life on the bounding main, Watson. The mystery of the employment of Mrs. Daniels's roomers is now solved—they worked as crimps, one of the most profitable businesses in San Francisco. With their income, I am surprised Mrs. Daniels didn't force them to fix up her house."

He suddenly sniffed. "Do you smell that, Watson? Sea air! Gag our friend here. We shall put him in the gunnysack and deliver him to the head of the gang who is, I am sure, expecting Josiah Martin and Willy Green."

We stuffed Martin into the gunnysack, took one of the torches from the wall and started down the one passageway that led out of the cellar. We had not proceeded more than a few feet when Holmes suddenly frowned, held up his hand and went back into the room. I watched him as he carefully inspected the walls of what might have been my burial chamber.

"Just as I thought, Watson. These walls are at least forty years old and the timbers look like they had once been burned. This was probably the basement of an old deadfall. Upstairs would have been a rude shack with a few tables and a bar. Runners would have brought in sailors just off the boats for free drinks. Once inside, the bartender would have fed them a lethal concoction, then knocked them on the head and sprung the trap beneath their feet so they tumbled into this room below. Hoodlums would have been waiting to bag them and take them to ships in the harbor that needed crews."

I shivered. "You said the timbers had been burned?"

"Decades ago the establishment was probably consumed in a fire set by the Sydney Ducks—a gang of ticket-of-leave convicts from the penal settlements at Sydney, in New South Wales. The government gave them permits to leave and find work elsewhere, and a number of them came to the States. The gang periodically set fire to the city so they could loot the burning shops. Many of the cribs along the waterfront went up in flames as well, and I imagine some of the prostitutes died in their beds. Sailors, being a superstitious lot, found it easy to believe that one of them had come back as a phantom to haunt the city and it quickly became legend. But let us hasten, Watson, somebody is expecting a delivery!"

We hoisted up Martin, struggling in his sack, and hurried down the passageway, the smell of sea water becoming stronger by the minute. Holmes suddenly put a finger to his lips and we crawled forward to where the ruins of a small wharf jutted out a few feet below. A boat was tied up to it with a man in the bow staring anxiously up at the opening where we had suddenly appeared.

"Did you bring him?"

"Of course," Holmes growled in a voice approximating Martin's. But it was only an approximation, and the man in the boat narrowed his eyes in sudden alarm, then recognized us for who we were.

"God *damn* you, Holmes!"

He pulled a gun from his pocket and fired a sudden fusillade of shots. Holmes staggered, then fired his own revolver once. The man shrieked and clutched his shoulder. Holmes leaped in, hit him on the back of the head with the butt of his weapon, and the man slumped to the bottom of the boat.

"Lower Martin down, Watson—carefully there!"

I did so and clambered into the boat after him, then noticed a streak of red on Holmes' sleeve.

"Holmes, you've been hurt!"

"A scratch, I assure you—nothing more, Watson."

I turned over the man in the bottom of the boat. The fog had cleared now and by the light of the moon I could make out the features of Lieutenant Michael Van Dyke, still elegantly dressed in his checkered coat and silk waistcoat.

"My Lord, Holmes, it's the lieutenant! What is he doing here?"

"I imagine the man he regularly hired to ferry his victims out to the ships either is drunk or ill and he had to take over at the last minute. I confess, I'm surprised to find him here tonight, though I intended to have him arrested tomorrow."

I felt Van Dyke's head and the knot at the back where Holmes had struck him. An hour or so more and he would be none the worse for wear.

"I'm surprised you knocked him unconscious, Holmes. I would have thought you wanted to ask him some questions."

"I already know the answers to any question I could have asked, Watson. And what I don't know, I imagine somebody else will be more than willing to tell me."

We made the struggling Martin comfortable in his gunnysack, then Holmes turned toward the bay. Nearby a ship rode at anchor, its running lights bright in the gloom.

"Quick, Watson, changes clothes with our good lieutenant!"

"Holmes," I said weakly. "What on Earth are you thinking of?"

"That this city is corrupt and our good Lieutenant will certainly find a way to evade justice. But that ship out there is expecting delivery of a crewman and they will be delighted to receive two instead of only one!"

* * *

Two days later we had packed and were ready to return to London, though I was surprised to note that I was more cheered by the possibility of going back than Holmes seemed to be. Every night he had stayed out until the early morning hours prowling through the underbelly of the city, delighted by the crimes and villainy that were in evidence all about him.

"The most evil city in the world, Watson; it would put Port Said to shame!"

In a few more hours the baggage men would arrive to take away our suitcases and boxes, and Holmes had yet to tell me how he had solved the case of Leona Adler or exactly what the solution was.

I finally insisted on the answers early in the afternoon, when we both had our feet to the fire while rain spattered against the windows of our suite.

"I haven't told you, Watson, because it isn't over yet."

"You can at least tell me the role that Lieutenant Van Dyke played," I protested.

He tamped more tobacco into his pipe, refilled his glass, and loosened the laces of his boots so he was quite comfortable.

"When we first came to the city, Watson, I visited the local police department and told them of our quest. Lieutenant Van Dyke offered to help since he had handled the Adler case ever since they started receiving inquiries from the family in New Jersey a year ago. When Mrs. Daniels denied that the police had ever visited her, it seemed obvious to me that our lieutenant wanted no investigation of the Daniels family at all. It was quite natural to think he had a personal interest."

"You suspected Van Dyke of running a gang of crimps even then?"

Holmes sighed. "I suspect he ran more than one and probably had other criminal interests as well. He was far too rich for an ordinary officer in the department and operating as a crimp was only one of several possibilities. The night he took us to 'see the elephant' convinced me of that."

"I was still mystified. "I don't see how . . ."

"It was not really a mystery at all, Watson. By his own admission, Van Dyke was a gambler and he was also arrogant—and very fond of the theater, as he told us. There is a great temptation among Americans to 'twist the lion's tail,' to show up us English as either incompetent or impotent. And here we were, the famous English consulting detective and his faithful Boswell—you have only yourself to blame for our notoriety, Watson—and the temptation was too great. He paraded his villainy before our very eyes and dared us to see through it. He took us to see the phantom, and once the woman had disappeared up the alley with her victim, he dashed across the street crying for us to follow. It was very convincing but a risky thing to do. After all, we might have seen the outline in the mud around the trapdoor through which the lady and her victim had disappeared. But within a few seconds he had tramped around the cul de sac and deliberately obliterated any traces that might have given it away. Afterward, I believe I remarked on the excessive mud on his boots."

"The whole trapdoor device—" I began.

"—was obvious," he finished. "There was no exit from the cul de sac, no doorway through which the lady and the sailor could have disappeared. Since it was impossible for them to ascend into the heavens, they must have dropped down into the earth. Working for the police department, Van Dyke had probably discovered there had once been a deadfall there. But why go to the expense of rebuilding it and giving away free liquor when the essence of it remained—the trapdoor, the basement below, and the passageway leading to the ruined wharf in the bay. All he needed was to lure unsuspecting sailors into the cul de sac and over the trapdoor where Josiah Martin and Willy Green would be waiting down below with bludgeons and sling shots. It was a very profitable business—they robbed the poor sailors first, then rowed them out to ships in the harbor where Van Dyke collected not only his bonus but the two months' advance on his victims' pay. And this was probably only one operation of several."

"It seems like a complicated arrangement, the phantom and all," I demurred.

Holmes shrugged. "I remind you of his fondness for the theater, Watson. It must have pleased his vanity to have been responsible for the creation of still another legend in this city."

"You haven't explained the phantom herself, the woman in white—"

Holmes took out his pocket watch and glanced at it.

"The answers will be arriving shortly, Watson. If I have timed it right, the first to arrive will be a gentleman whom you will show into your bedroom and close the door. He may listen to what we say, but under no condition is he to make a sound. Some minutes after that, I believe a lady will show up. At least, I have asked the police to invite her here." He smiled bleakly. "Mrs. Daniels had a good deal more to say once I informed her she could be charged as part of the gang."

A few minutes later, as good as Holmes's word, there was a knock on the door and I opened it to see a man in his late thirties, quite well dressed but with a workingman's strength about him. I motioned for him not to talk and immediately showed him to my bedroom and told him Holmes's stipulations. Holmes hadn't turned around to greet him but remained by the fire, staring into the flames.

It could not have been more than a few minutes after that when there was another rap on the door, but this time Holmes opened it. The woman who entered swept into the room with all the dignity and self-possession of one who rated highly in both wealth and position. She was extremely attractive and of an indeterminate age, though I would have guessed her to be in her middle thirties. She was dressed all in black wool, sporting a black silk cape with a brilliant scarlet lining.

Then I caught my breath, finally recognizing her. She was as stunning in black as she had been in white a few nights before, though I was shocked by her cape, an obvious sign of her profession.

"You wished to see me?" she said coolly to Holmes. She was aware that he also knew her profession, but there was no trace of shame upon her face.

Holmes held out his hand, not to shake hers but to give her something.

"I believe this belongs to you," he said quietly. It flashed in the firelight, and even at a distance I recognized the mother-of-earl-inlaid guitar pick. Holmes had undoubtedly found it when he had descended into the basement room to save my life. In her haste to flee, the woman had dropped it in the straw on the muddy floor, and Holmes must have glimpsed reflections from it in the light from the torches.

She gave a cry then and I leaped forward before she could

crumple to the carpet. We helped her into a chair, and I poured a glass of brandy and held it to her lips.

"You were working with Lieutenant Van Dyke," Holmes said calmly. He said it as a statement, not a question.

"That vermin!" For a moment her face contorted with anger and lost much of its beauty. Then she was calm once again.

"Please tell us about it, Miss Adler," Holmes said. His tone was respectful, and there was no sign of condemnation in his voice.

"It's simple enough, Mr. Holmes. He was blackmailing me. The Daniels family had told him who I was. He knew I didn't wish to be found and threatened to tell my family, to tell the royal court, to tell my child."

"Your child," Holmes repeated softly.

"My daughter. She is eight now, being raised by Sisters in a convent across the bay. She lacks for nothing and knows me as her aunt." Her voice broke. "I tell her wonderful stories about her mother who died long ago."

"Your statements about Lieutenant Van Dyke," Holmes said. "I don't believe they are quite complete. How did you meet him?"

She was defiant now.

"Unlike so many others in my position, I had saved my money and was about to buy my own establishment. I approached him to purchase protection from the police. He recognized me from my former recitals and realized I could both sing and act. His scheme was now complete. He promised me both additional income and protection at a future date—and threatened to inform on me if I didn't cooperate."

"And so you became the phantom, the woman in white who lured sailors down an alley where they could be shanghaied."

She lifted her chin slightly. "I had my knowledge of stagecraft and disguise. With rice powder and lip rouge and in the evening shadows, I could make myself up to look young and attractive. And I still had my guitar. As for the men I lured ... There is no excuse I can offer except I had little choice. And I tried to make sure the men who followed me were all true sailors who would have returned to the sea in any event. I am prepared to be charged, to testify against the villainous Lieutenant Van Dyke. The worst is that my family will now find out."

Holmes shook his head.

"I doubt there will be any trial. Willy Green is dead and both Josiah Martin and Lieutenant Van Dyke are hundreds of miles away by now and in no position to return to this country any time soon. As for Mrs. Daniels, I believe the fear of God has been put into her and she will keep silent."

Leona Adler finally broke down then, and Holmes laid his hand lightly upon her shoulder.

"It is time to return home, Miss Adler."

She looked bitter. "I could not convincingly explain my daughter with no husband on my arm. My parents would be crushed. Nor could I flee to England, as my sister did. I could lie, of course, but in due time I would have had to tell still another lie to support the first one. Eventually my past would become a tissue of lies and finally the truth would out. I would then find myself in worse circumstances than I am now."

"Your profession—" Holmes began diplomatically.

Her eyes flashed. "My profession, Mr. Holmes? After two years here I discovered I had no profession and with a young daughter to raise and no husband to help me. My talents had failed to find an audience, I had no other skills of any kind, I had no money. Finally I sold the only thing that every woman truly owns—her virtue. It is very difficult for a woman to rise in this society, Mr. Holmes. It is very easy for one to sink. There is little that I haven't tried, little that I haven't experienced—including weeks of solitude in an opium den. But as of this morning, I own my own house and am a Madame in the only city in the United States that respects the profession. Nor am I ashamed of it, though I have no doubt you think I should be."

"You would not give it up?" Holmes asked quietly.

"It is what I am, Mr. Holmes, I am honest enough to admit it. And it will do you no good to charge me because of it, not in San Francisco."

Holmes smiled slightly.

"But you *will* give it up," he said. "And of your own volition." He motioned to me and I opened the door to the bedroom.

She looked toward the door, then would have fallen once again if it had not been for Holmes. The man in the doorway leaped to her side and held her against him. "My God, Leona, how can you ever forgive me!"

"You were too good at hiding," Holmes said to the woman. "Mr. McGuire has been searching for you for a year. You should be grateful for his persistence—and that he looked for you in all the wrong places."

She had buried her face in the man's shoulder and was quietly sobbing. "How can you ever forgive *me?*"

It was Holmes who led them gently to the door and quietly closed it after them. I was overwhelmed, not only by his generosity of spirit and understanding but that he had been willing to expose the heart that he usually kept so well hidden.

"I imagine they will spend the rest of their lives forgiving each other," I said. "As good a basis for a marriage as any, I suppose." And then: "How did you find him?"

"I told you before that this was a mystery of character, Watson. I made inquiries of the police and they told me that a year ago a gentleman had asked after Leona Adler and once again they had referred him to Lieutenant Van Dyke, who was handling everything to do with the Adler case. It turned out Van Dyke's ultimate villainy was to conceal from William McGuire that his lost love was still alive. She had disappeared, Van Dyke insisted, but McGuire continued his search. Just yesterday I located him at the Baldwin, staying in their presidential suite. Incidentally, Watson, he is now a very wealthy man. Eventually, he did indeed discover gold."

But there was still the last bit of the puzzle. "How did you know the phantom was Leona Adler? Did the guitar pick play a part?

Holmes smiled slightly. "The pick had nothing to do with it, Watson. I was suspicious when Lieutenant Van Dyke told us the tale of the phantom. And I recognized the guitar the moment I saw it. It had been hanging on the wall behind Miss Adler in the portrait Mycroft had given us. I was surprised you did not recognize it as well." He glanced at his watch again. "They will be coming for our bags soon. Is everything packed?"

I nodded, then said: "I imagine the Prince and the Adler family will be very pleased."

He shook his head.

"What would I tell them, Watson? I could not fill in the years any more successfuly than she could. She was right, she would have been forced to lie and eventually they would have seen through the falsehoods and it would have wounded their lives forever. I shall have to leave it as it is. I will tell them simply that Leona Adler has disappeared, which is partly true, at least for the woman they knew. Later, if Miss Adler wishes to contact her family, it will be easier with a marriage of four or five years behind her. Some things are more easily forgiven than others. But for the moment, to protect her I shall willingly confess to failure."

"But you did not fail!" I protested.

"Ah, but I did, Watson," he said softly. "My failure is that I did not find her ten years ago."

MOUSE AND THE MASTER

by Brian M. Thomsen

*In the numerous years of my relationship with the
consulting detective Sherlock Holmes, I have witnessed
his mastery of the arcane, modern science, mock
mysticism, and impenetrable impersonations. Always
awed by the vast mental resources he had at his
immediate beck and call, I was always in error
whenever I doubted his line of thinking, resolution, or
decision making . . . but there's still that one exception
to the rule for which even today I cannot see his
reasoning. It involved a particularly disreputable
fellow, an American if memory serves, whom the master
himself felt necessary to employ. . . .*

—John H. Watson

It was a typical spring day in London, and nature was be-
stowing her bounty on me once again.

It was raining, and the residual dampness in my quarters
was doing its best to remind me of the past errors of my
ways with the dull aches and pains that come from having
been bound and gagged and tossed in a cellar, all attributable
to my last case (a real dickens of one if I do say so myself).
My name is Malcolm Chandler, and if I didn't get hired for
a new case real soon, I would be tending my bodily aches and
pains in Newgate debtor's prison in no time at all. You
see, I'm a private investigator, a gumshoe, a shamus, a dick.

My friends call me Mouse, and unfortunately I really didn't fit the bill for the locals' expectations of what a great detective would look like, and, as a result, I was always having to scrounge for work.

I had just about resigned myself to having to join a strongarm group that the local constabulary was forming to track down some escaped convict named Magwitch or Magpie or something, subjecting my already battered body to further bodily abuse for low pay, "mean expectations" at best, when a kid of about twelve barged into my office all out of breath like the last surviving turkey on the day after Thanksgiving.

"Are you Malcolm Chandler, the second greatest consulting detective in all of London?" he asked, his body slightly stooped, his legs clutched together like some Ginny Jenny embracing a bottle.

"Who wants to know?" I asked cautiously, knowing that as of recently I had more enemies looking for me than friends, "and what do you mean the second greatest consulting detective?"

"The Master Detective asks that you accompany me back to his quarters on Baker Street," he continued, but then interrupted with the greatest urgency, "may I *please* use your pot? It's an emergency!"

Now, recognizing the cause of his awkward stance, I motioned him to the pail I kept reserved for those mornings when the spirits of the previous night's imbibing extracted their revenge, turned my back, and continued my questioning. "What does this Master Detective want with me?"

"I think it has something to do with the doctor," he replied as he finished his business. As he rethreaded the drawstring that held his pants in place, he started toward the door. "We must hurry," he said. "Mister Holmes does not like to be kept waiting."

Having no better prospects, and knowing that Sherlock always charged top dollar, and therefore might be in line for a little of his own medicine, I followed the kid out into the noonday drizzle.

Holmes's quarters at 221B Baker Street were just as I pictured them—as was Holmes himself.

Sherlock was of a build and a manner more akin to swashbuckling villains and Gothic mad scientists than the rugged persona of the manly art of mystery solving. His hands were stained yet effeminate with delicate digits whose discolored cuticle sheaths seemed naked without lacquer. He wasn't of the Wilde sort, but his hands sure were.

His hairline was receding, eyes deep set, and his nose was long and narrow as if inviting the reception of a pair of knuckles on a bone crushing course.

Not exactly much of a heroic figure, if you ask me, but then again it wasn't as if I ever had a clear view of him. The room was thick with pipe smog.

He met us at the door, opening it quickly, and addressing the lad who rushed by him.

"The pot's behind the bureau, Wilson," he told the lad who bolted into the other room as he undid his pants along the way. Turning to me, he invited me in with numerous salutations.

"Ah, Mr. Chandler, welcome. By your build, demeanor, and bearing I would say that you are the sort of fellow who probably has a nickname. Something diminutive, and verminesque. Have a seat," he nattered, ushering me to a chair.

"Uh, yes," I said with my usual amount of professional awkwardness. "The kid said you . . ."

"You mean Wilson. Bright fellow," he interrupted.

"Yes, I . . ."

"Has a bit of the trots. Runs in the family. Must be the water."

"Yes, I . . ."

"Weasel," he interrupted.

"What?" I said more confused than ever.

"Your nickname is Weasel," he continued in a matter-of-fact tone. "Your father was . . ."

"My nickname is Mouse," I corrected.

"Are you quite sure?"

"Yes," I replied. "Now, Wilson . . ."

"No, Wilson's nickname is not Weasel. Wilson's nickname is Wilson. Are you quite certain . . . oh, maybe not. You might have made a mistake," he nattered.

"About your case," I inserted, trying to get our conversation back on track. "Wilson said it was about the doctor. Moriarty, I presume."

"No, no, no. It's about Watson," he insisted.

"Your sidekick, Boswell, and broker of fame."

"Well, yes, and no," he explained, finally getting down to

the case. "Watson and I used to share these rooms a few years ago before he became a practicing polygamist, and . . ."

"Polygamist?" I queried.

"He has two wives."

"Oh."

"You see, Watson had just returned from the war where he had been wounded . . ."

"In the arm or the leg," I queried, having heard rumors of both.

"Neither," he replied. " 'Twas the eardrums. Left him quite hard of hearing. Anyway, my practice was just beginning to take off, and he began to function as my press agent. Very early on I realized that I could turn my powers of deductive reasoning into a profitable sideline. Problem solving for the rich and famous, tracking down unfaithful suitors, selling information to the Grub Street rags, etc."

"Excuse me," I interrupted. "That's not exactly the line of work, I would have expected of the Master Detective of all England."

"Well, that's part of the problem. Watson has misinterpreted a lot of my actions and intentions, and as a result I've come across a bit more noble than I had intended. I'm not complaining, mind you. It's just not what I had intended."

"In other words, you just wanted to be a common everyday peeper, just like me."

"Well, maybe not as common as you, but you get my point," he asserted.

"Sure. So: A) How did this happen? B) What's with the doctor? and C) What's it got to do with me?" I asked trying to get matters to the point.

"Well, as I said before, Watson has a hearing problem," Holmes continued, taking a moment to lean back in his highbacked chair as Wilson quietly and sheepishly ushered himself out, "and as a result he often mishears parts of our conversations. For example, one evening I was reading the label on a bottle of cough syrup that was meant to be taken orally. Unfortunately, it had a bad taste, which to someone with as delicate a set of taste buds as mine is not a minor problem. Watson, who had just woken from a nap, asked me what my problem was, and I said 'Alimentary, my dear Watson,' and the next thing I know he has me saying—in print, mind you—'elementary, my dear Watson' at the drop of a hat. Soon he had developed an entire fantasy world based on those things he thinks he hears. A case involving a polka-dotted polka sextet, somehow metamorphasized into a tale of terror with a poisonous snake."

"The Speckled Band," I inserted.

"The time I contemplated changing the color scheme of my den to a deep red."

"A Study in Scarlet."

"He even thinks I have a brother. One night I was ruminating over how I missed making paper animals. As I was an only child, and usually quite sickly, I'd do cut-outs to keep from being bored. At one point I may have mentioned that *my crafts* kept me company in my younger years, and somehow his addled little brain turned this around to me having a brother named Mycroft. Poor Wilson, I commented on his bowel condition once, and now Watson is sure he is the leader of a secret army of young aides I have called the Baker Street Irregulars."

"This is all very fascinating, but get to the point. What do you need me for?" I insisted, my patience long at an end.

"Up to now his stories about me have been quite harmless, and indeed my practice and status have profited from them, but now I've grown worried. He's claiming to hear voices from the great beyond, and to have dream conversations with an invisible friend named Artie. If we are not careful, everyone will know he's gone around the bend, and my reputation will be . . ."

"Back to my level," I added snidely.

"Or worse, if that's possible. I've made arrangements with his wives to have him packed off to a very nice retirement home at Reichenbach Falls on the morrow, but unfortunately, tonight he is attending a seance with a group of spiritualists in hopes of making nonsomnolent contact with Artie. We are so close, yet the threat remains that he can still foul things up, so therefore I would like you to attend the seance to make sure nothing goes wrong."

"Why don't you?" I questioned. "Aren't you a master of disguise?"

"I can't take the risk. Watson might uncover my charade, and make a scene. No, I wish to hire you for the evening. Come, come, my good fellow, it's not like the crowds are clamoring for your services, and if I'm not mistaken, there aren't many cases for a PI to solve in Newgate prison."

He was right, and as much as I hated it, I had to take the case.

"All right," I answered, "but I'm going to charge your rates."

"Mr. Vermin Chandler, that's out of the question. I know what your normal rates are. I've seen your ad in the back of *True Consulting Detective Magazine* and they will suit the occasion."

"What makes you think your services are worth more than mine?" I blustered.

"I have a press agent," he replied.

He was right.

I took the address of the seance and left.

Watson was fairly easy to pick out in the crowd. He was the one with the earhorn.

The seance was to take place in the basement of the Six Bells Tavern in the Whitechapel section of town, probably to keep things inconspicuous. Of course, no one would ever notice a party of eight swells dressed in evening finery entering a broken down gin mill through the delivery entrance. The swells were seated in a storeroom trying to not be noticed by each other.

I took a seat on a cider crate next to Watson.

After about twenty minutes, a dame appeared who resembled some lost Brontë sister who had spent the last twenty years locked in some attic somewhere. She was sheathed in black as if she were trying to host a joint wedding-funeral, and her voice reminded me of a nanny from Miss Haversham's School for Young Ladies and Attack Dogs.

"Will all the seekers of the other side please identify themselves and name the spirit they wish to contact," she declared to the huddled crowd.

A foreign nobleman stood up in protest.

"But we were all assured of anonymity," he argued. "I was told that this would all be kept secret, very secret."

"And it shall, Count Vlad," she answered. "For only by revealing your identities to each other can you share in a mutual act of discretion. After all, he who talks will soon be talked about. What better assurance of anonymity can you ask for?"

I had to admit it was a clever setup. She had put the

crowd at ease in no time at all. None of them even seemed to notice that though their secrets might be safe with each other, they were far from safe from everyone. It had the makings of a perfect blackmail scam with Madame Morbid (or some associate, who was probably hidden somewhere in the cellar free from prying eyes and suspicious minds) paying a call at some later date.

The count said his piece.

"I am Count Vlad Dracula, recently arrived from Transylvania, and I wish to contact my contact on the other side who goes by the name of Abraham."

The count took his seat and the roll call continued in clockwise fashion.

A gentleman doctor: "My name is Henry Jekyll and I wish to contact my other side friend Robert."

A blonde-haired maiden: "My name is Alice Liddell and I want to contact two friends from the other side, one named Lewis and one named Charles."

A blond-haired Adonis: "My name is Dorian Gray, and I have come to contact Melmoth."

A Charing Cross dandy who kept looking at his watch: "Phileas Fogg, looking for Jules."

Just then Watson interrupted.

"Sir, I'm afraid you must have made a mistake. You must be looking for the treasure hunting seance if you are looking for jewels," the half-deaf old codger interrupted.

Fogg replied in a huff. "His name is Jules. He speaks to me with a French accent."

"An ax sent?" Watson questioned.

"Please go on," Madame Morbid said. "Whom do you wish to contact, Doctor Watson?"

As I suspected, she did indeed already know what faces went with what names on the invitations.

Watson replied, "Oh, yes," with a stammer. "John Watson, and I wish to contact Arthur."

My turn had arrived, and I had to do some fast talking since obviously my name was not on the list.

"My name is Malcolm Chandler. Ebenezer Scrooge referred you to me, and I really want to contact"—I paused, and then blurted out the first name to come to my mind— "Brian."

Our hostess relaxed.

"Ah, yes," she replied. "Mr. Scrooge is one of our most

satisfied customers." Well, so much for keeping previous clients' identities secret.

Scrooge was the subject of one of my previous cases, and the grapevine had it that he had recently turned to spiritualism for some answers to some rather bizarre questions. I had taken a gamble that he had been a previous client/dupe, and it would appear that the gamble had paid off.

She had accepted me as just another mark, and would probably make some excuse later in the evening that contact would not be possible for me this evening and that, perhaps, I would be willing to reschedule at a later date when she would have the necessary time to do her homework.

A back-alley brute of a fellow who I recognized as an occasional bartender at the upstairs pub joined our group from some shadowy corner and set a table top on a base of crates roughly in the center of the room. Madame Morbid then spread a tablecloth over it (black of course) and set a lit candelabra in its center. The brute then faded back into the shadows, well out of sight.

"Please take your places around the table," she said firmly. "I am afraid that you will have to use these crates as seats. I apologize for these rather primitive accommodations, but discretion demands that everything be portable and inconspicuous."

Just like a floating crapgame or a backroom bookie joint, I thought to myself as we took our places around the table.

"Join hands," she commanded, and on cue the lights dimmed, leaving only the aura of the candelabra illuminating our circle of seekers.

The temperature in the room seemed to drop markedly, and a vague aroma of incense seemed to seep through the air.

"John Watson," she instructed. "Please call your friend from the other side."

"Arthur! Arthur! Are you there?" he questioned of the darkness.

"Oh, Arthur," Madame Morbid joined in. "Please contact your friend John. Perhaps there is something you wish to know from him."

"I am here, John," said a muffled voice that sounded suspiciously like the bartending brute who obviously lurked in the shadows, engineering the machinations of the 'other side.' "Please, share with me all of your worries, concerns, and secrets so that the bond between us might be stronger."

Watson then proceeded to unburden his soul of all of his secrets, including the major details of the cases that Holmes was working on at the present time (or at least as he perceived them, as I strongly doubted that there was really some spectral manifestation called a hound of the Baskervilles).

The air seemed to get heavier, and my mind started to drift through clouds of miasma.

Madame Morbid's voice pierced the delusional clouds. "Call to your friends," she instructed. "Share with them so that they may share with you."

A cacophony of voices ensued, all muffled variants of the brute's, I assumed.

In no time the other seekers had joined in. The count was talking about his acquisition of Carfax Abbey, and a new consort. Fogg was preoccupied with a trip he was about to make, and whether it would be safe to carry his fortune with him in a traveling bag, and Alice was talking about some antique mirror she found in her father's study. All of my companions were lending their voices to the din.

Suddenly one voice made itself clearer to me than the rest.

"Chandler, you ninny," the voice said. "Don't blow this case. Clear your mind. They are using opiated gas to befuddle you. It's all a hoax. Stick around after everyone has left and get to the bottom of it so we can get on with this series."

I didn't hesitate. The voice had to be right. Opiated gas. I should have thought of that. It was obvious that Madame Morbid and her henchman were using the obviously susceptible states of her clients to gain information that could be used for blackmail, larceny, or some other nefarious plot.

Just then the lights came back up, and Madame Morbid quickly began to usher everyone up the stairs, and out into the night.

"Please go quickly, and quietly. We will meet again next week," she said, and then turning to me specifically she added, "I'm sorry we didn't have any luck with contacting your friend Brian, but I'm sure we will next week. Sometimes it takes a while for a new spirit to feel comfortable with a new circle of friends."

The seekers headed to their homes, minds still a blur from

the opiated miasma, satisfied with their otherworldly interactions of the previous hour.

I ducked into a nearby alley and flushed my head clear with the chill of the night air. When I judged a safe amount of time had passed, I ventured back to the scene of the earlier night's festivities.

A cellar window that I had noticed when I first arrived there earlier in the evening was open just enough for me to slide in, which I did as quietly and cautiously as possible.

Just then the lights came up, and a blackjack connected with my temple.

The newly arrived light was replaced by darkness.

I awoke an indeterminate amount of time later, tied to a chair in the center of the cellar in almost the exact space the table had previously occupied. My head was filled with the familiar feeling of ache and pain.

Madame Morbid was standing in front of me, a gun trained on my chest.

"I was worried that you weren't taken in by our little setup since you had not made contact with your little 'voice from the otherside,' and therefore kept Lothar" (the brute I assume) "on watch in case you returned, which you did. After rifling your pockets we came across a rather nice little surprise, a PI license. Well, you're obviously no Sherlock Holmes, since you've been caught."

"Nobody's perfect," I offered. "Nice little setup. Opiated mist to blur the lines of perception. Offstage muffled voices murmuring instructions. Misguided marks spilling their guts. What were your plans? Mug Fogg for his traveling bag, buy up real estate around Carfax Abbey since nobility was moving in, maybe a little blackmail, on the side."

"Not to mention a little insurance in case the Master Detective Sherlock Holmes poked his nose into my business."

Just then a slightly familiar voice intruded into my consciousness.

"The chair you are tied to is rickety, and dried out. If you throw yourself forward hard enough, it should fall apart, and you will also be able throw Madame Morbid off balance, and land on top of her. It should then be a simple matter to wrestle the gun away from her, tie her up, and get help. Don't worry. Lothar is away."

The chair was, it did, I was, I did, and he was.

* * *

Lothar was rounded up by the gulls not too much later and turned stoolie in exchange for a lighter sentence. Madame Morbid received an indefinite vacation via the Botany Bay courtesy of the queen and will no doubt soon be the toast of Melbourne.

Watson accepted his therapeutic retreat at Reichenbach Falls, and Sherlock Holmes managed to maintain his misguided reputation as the Master Detective of the fogbound London mystery scene.

Sherlock paid me my meager fee and then proceeded to insinuate himself into the employ of the others in Watson's circle of seekers as a security consultant, explaining that I had been his employee on the night of the mayhem at Madame Morbid's.

One might say he was a master of manipulating such situations for his own benefit.

I returned to my working class digs, Newgate postponed for the time being.

Not too much later I had a dream.

A bespectacled, bearded fellow sat me down and congratulated me on a job well done, saying that we work very well together. He said his name was Brian, and vanished.

Go figure. That will teach me to overindulge in Old Appleyard Cider.

I've been invited to a holiday bash at 221B Baker Street next week. I guess I'll go ... after all, there is no place like Holmes for the holidays.

... For what reason Holmes employed the fellow I'll never know, nor do I care to. I have stricken him from my records of my involvements with the Master Detective. Sherlock is the master, I am his Boswell, and there is no need for anyone else.

I think I've had enough sun now. I hope the attendant takes me in for my nap soon. Artie is waiting ...

—John H. Watson

TWO ROADS, NO CHOICES

by Dean Wesley Smith

The hand on my shoulder seemed rough, brusque in its rush to wake me. As I roused myself from the warm comfort of my quilts and rolled to focus on the worried face of Holmes, he said, "Dress quickly. And for extreme cold. We have visitors here, possibly to take us for a voyage."

Before my sleep-fogged mind could muster a response, or even a simple question as to where we would be traveling, he turned and left me to the quiet of the late-night hour.

I finished with my toilet and dressed as quickly as I could, for such awakening by Holmes had portrayed in the past a need for haste on a new case. And since my friend had taken very few cases as of late, this new adventure must be extraordinary in nature. That thought had my hands shaking with such excitement that I took two attempts to fasten my vest.

As I emerged into the main room, I found Holmes in his favorite armchair, his fingers steepled as was his habit when wating patiently. He had started a robust fire to take the chill from the room, and the orange light flickered across his features.

Across from him sat two strangers, and immediately I was struck by their strange dress, the cut of their jackets, and the look of their hair. The one on Holmes's left and closest to the door had strikingly blond hair, green eyes, and a handsome face that showed no scars. He was also clearly the taller of the two, even though they were both sitting. At his feet was a large brown case that had the appearance of being very heavy.

His companion had long, almost shoulder-length brown hair and wore an outer coat that he had opened to the warmth of the fire, revealing on the edges of the coat a form of metal fastener with small teeth running along both sides of the opening. I had read of such a fastener before, but never seen one in use. The man had a dark complexion and seemed to be of Italian or Eastern decent.

I was shocked that Holmes had offered neither of them tea or coffee and was about to correct the oversight when Holmes said, "Oh good, Watson. Now we can start." He indicated that I should take a chair near the hearth and I did as he instructed.

He turned to the gentlemen as I sat and nodded. "Alright, please explain who you are, why you are here, where you are from, and what you want from me."

Both of the men had been staring at me in a seemingly nervous fashion, as if I were someone they had known for a long time, yet were embarrassed to greet. I knew from what Holmes had said that he had kept them from telling their story, even so much as their names, until I was present. He did that on occasion when he felt the need of a second pair of eyes and ears. Somehow, in a standard Holmes fashion, he must have deduced that they had wanted us to go on a trip and that it would be to a cold climate. Even though I had no idea how he came to such a conclusion, I would wait until later to ask him how he knew such details.

Holmes leaned forward in anticipation, and for some odd reason I found myself just able to contain my own excitement.

The short, dark-haired man cleared his throat, glanced at me and then looked directly back at Holmes. "My name is Carl. Dr. Carl Frederick. This is Dr. Henry Serling." He indicated the blond man, who in turn nodded at both of us.

Dr. Frederick's accent seemed to be American, yet of no region with which I was familiar. I would have to ask Holmes later if he knew the regional source.

Dr. Frederick went on. "Slightly over two months ago a new White Star Liner left port from Southampton."

Holmes nodded. "Yes, the *RMS Titanic*."

Dr. Frederick nodded. "I'm glad you are familiar with it."

"It would be hard not to be, considering the coverage it received. It seems to be one very magnificent ship. Exceptionally lucky that it did not meet a tragic fate on that first voyage. Even an unsinkable ship meeting an iceberg can sometimes lose the battle."

Dr. Frederick glanced nervously at his companion and then said, "I don't think luck had anything to do with it."

Holmes gave him a very sharp look. "I'm afraid, Dr., that I do not understand your comment."

Both of our guests seemed almost embarrassed, as if what they were about to say would seem so outrageous, so disgusting that Holmes would toss them into the street. I had seen that look a number of times when a person was about to confess something to Holmes. This time both men stared at their hands, then at the floor, then back at their hands.

The fire crackled and what seemed like a long time passed until finally the blond Dr. Serling took a deep breath. "Carl, we agreed." His voice was also clearly American, but again very odd.

Dr. Frederick nodded slowly, clearly making a decision. He looked Holmes squarely in the eyes. "The *Titanic* was supposed to have sunk. Slightly over fifteen hundred lives were lost when it did."

I thought that someone had punched me below the ribs at that moment and I suddenly knew the taste of disgust. It never occurred to me to question that the men were crazy, but their words instantly proved them so, and suddenly I felt worried for the safety of Holmes and myself.

But Holmes seemed to take the statement of the possibility of such an immense disaster as a fact. He leaned back in his chair, exhaling slowly, but never taking his gaze from Dr. Frederick. As his friend, I could see the thought had him shaken, but he remained composed as always.

The fire popped and flared for a moment as Holmes said in a very cold voice, "Go on."

Again Dr. Frederick glanced at his companion. Then he half shook himself and turned to face Holmes squarely. "We need your help in solving why the *Titanic* did not sink."

Holmes did not even blink at such an absurd idea, and when I started to object he held up his hand and stopped me. "And who might you represent?" he asked. "I assume you are not from owners of the liner or any government agency. What is your interest?"

Dr. Frederick almost laughed. Then he became very serious again. "Our lives. Our very future and that of this time, actually. You see, you will not believe me, but we are from the future. Actually, just over a hundred and two years in the future. But, I'm afraid we are from a future where the *Titanic* sank."

Holmes nodded. "I assumed you were not of our time from your clothes and your language the moment you stepped into this room. He nodded to Dr. Serling. You are also wearing some form of lens on your eye that I have never seen before."

Dr. Serling smiled and nodded. "They are called contact lenses. They take the place of glasses."

Both visitors seemed taken aback by Holmes's calm acceptance of their bold statment that they were from the future. I, on the other hand, was not as willing to take their word. Such fancy imagination was the domain of an early evening of pleasant reading of H. G. Wells, not of the middle of the night on Baker Street.

But Holmes waited for a response. "You have still not answered my question."

Both doctors glanced at each other until finally Dr. Frederick seemed to understand Holmes's question. "If you mean our employer, then I suppose that originally would have been the state of California. We were both on the faculty at the University of Southern California, Physics Department. Our specific research into time travel was funded mostly by the United States government."

Holmes nodded, as if he understood everything they had been saying, as I suppose he might have. "Why the interest in the *Titanic*?"

"In our time, the *Titanic* and the night it sank," Dr. Frederick hesitated with that statement, then went on, "are of immense interest. It wasn't until September of 1985 that the wreck of the great ship was found. Since then hundreds of expeditions have been launched to the site of the wreck. It seemed only logical that one of the first time travel expeditions would go back to the night the *Titanic* sank. Here, let me show you something."

He motioned for Dr. Serling to open the large case and Dr. Frederick extracted a large, colorful book. As he handed the book to Holmes I noticed the word TITANTIC stamped on the front cover in red. A beautiful painting of the great liner sailing the open seas filled the cover.

"That book was originally published in 1992. We brought it along as resource material. Little did we imagine that it would be put to this use."

Again the room grew quiet except for the crackling of the fire as Holmes inspected the front and back of the large and obviously heavy book and then opened it and started slowly thumbing through.

"Flip to page 196. That section is about the discovery of the wreck. There are photographs and such."

Holmes did what he was told and then spent the next few minutes moving through the book, his keen eyes missing nothing. I had a great desire to stand and move to his side to look at such a book, but I held my place, as I know Holmes would have wanted me to do. But as the minutes wore on, the task of remaining in my chair became very difficult, to say the least.

Finally Holmes closed the book and placed it on the stand beside his chair. "Since it is obvious that a tragedy such as this book portrays would have a large influence on the future, can you tell me what that might be?"

Dr. Frederick shook his head negatively. "I'm afraid not. You see, the future we came from no longer exists. At least to us. The only way possible to move forward in time for us and our machine is to a homing beacon, for lack of a better way to describe it. I could tell you about the future where the ship did sink, but—"

Dr. Serling broke in. "Let me try to explain what has occurred. With every event in history there are two or more possible futures leading from that event. Like forks in a country road." He glanced at Holmes and Holmes nodded, so he went on. "On the night the *Titanic* sank, the logical two main futures are a future where it did and one where it did not. Of course, there are many other possible futures where only a hundred were killed, or ninety-nine. And depending on who was saved and who wasn't, those lives lost or saved may or may not allow the futures to blend back into one. In our time we call these different worlds parallel dimensions or universes."

I caught myself shaking my head at the insanity of this man's words, but Holmes clearly was giving the man his full attention, so I said and did nothing, even though my instinct was to toss them both into the street.

"So what happened?" Holmes asked. "Did you change the past, causing the *Titanic* not to sink?"

"No." Both doctors spoke at the same time and both were emphatic, as if Holmes had asked them if they had committed a mortal sin.

"We arrived," Dr. Frederick said, "on the *Titanic* about two minutes before it struck the iceberg, and did nothing but watch. However, it quickly became obvious that history had changed. We were unable to return to our time and ended up having to hide in unoccupied cabins until the ship sailed into New York."

"Was it possible," Holmes asked, "that your machine simply moved you over onto a different 'road' as you put it?"

Dr. Serling seemed clearly impressed with Holmes. "We considered that, but we don't think so. If that were the case, we feel our homing device would still be functioning. But it isn't. We clearly went back to a fork in the road of history and are now traveling down a different road. Someone or something altered our world's history so that the world we came from no longer exists to us."

Holmes nodded. "And you want me to help you find out who altered history. Who stopped this—" he tapped the book, "—from happening?"

Both doctors nodded slowly.

"This is beyond the imagination," I said, no longer able to hold my tongue. "I have heard some crazy stories in my time, but—"

Holmes held up his hand for me to stop and then turned to the gentlemen. "How would you propose I do this task?"

Dr. Frederick pointed to the large case. "In here is the machine that moves us through time. Come back with us to the night of the *Titanic* hitting the iceberg."

"What?" I said.

But Holmes nodded. "Can you then bring us back to this point?"

Dr. Frederick shook his head. "Not exactly. We can leave a homing package here, but time will flow at the same pace as the time you spend on the ship. If we are there for an hour, you will return here in an hour."

Holmes again nodded, then turned to me. "Watson,

dampen the fire. And fetch our heaviest coats. We are going for a short trip."

"But you can't really imagine—" For the third time tonight Holmes stopped me with a sharp look and a hand gesture.

"My dear Watson. We have a case at hand." He was clearly seeing something I was missing and was willing to let these two have enough rope to prove their insanity.

I sighed rather loudly, but then nodded and did as I was instructed. Holmes and I donned our coats as Dr. Serling seemed to type on some sort of instrument inside the case, clicking like the sound of a dog scampering across a hardwood floor. Then he placed a small blue-green cube on the table on the top of the large book and nodded to Holmes and myself. "We are ready. Please step close."

Holmes did so immediately and I followed reluctantly. My mind was starting to worry at the possibility of actually traveling through time. Yet the thought was so utterly preposterous that I couldn't hold the reality of it.

As I stopped beside Holmes, Dr. Serling tapped a small button inside the case.

For a moment nothing registered. It was as if someone had turned off the lights and the fire and all the sounds and feelings of the world.

Then as quickly as it had left the world was back.

In my mind we were still standing like fools bundled against the cold inside the warm Baker Street address. But then Holmes said, "Interesting" and stepped toward the wooden rail to gaze out at the black night.

"What the devil—" The icy cold wind sucked the words from my mouth. I could not only feel the cold, but smell and taste it. Intense, biting cold mixed with the salty smells of the open sea. I spun around to look quickly in all directions as the wind messed my hair and pulled open my coat, sending shivers through my torso. We were clearly on a large ship, somewhere near the bow. The width of the ship was almost that of a city block, and a towering wall of metal rose both forward and aft of our position.

"We are on the forward well deck near the starboard side," Dr. Frederick said to Holmes.

Holmes only nodded as his intense gaze took in every detail. I, on the other hand, fought to keep my late dinner in my stomach. The very fact that we stood here on this cold wooden deck challenged every principle I believed in and lived by. I must be dreaming. Holmes had not awakened me and any moment this would all be a fleeting memory of a long night of troubled sleep.

Overhead a bell started ringing insistently. I glanced up at the tall pole and could barely see the light from what seemed to be a crow's nest. Words floated down to us through the night air. "Iceberg right ahead."

Dr. Franklin turned to Holmes. "That was lookout Fleet talking to Sixth Officer Moody who is on the bridge." Franklin pointed toward the stern and up. "All right on time."

Holmes only nodded. He seemed to be listening intently to the sounds of the night, the water slapping against the sides of the huge ship, the low rumble of the engines. After a moment he nodded and then leaned out over the rail to watch the iceberg approach.

I moved over beside him and did the same, the cold wind hitting my face and hands with a much harder intensity. Out of the shadow of the well deck, I suddenly realized just how fast the ship had been moving, and that realization combined with the blast of cold wind took my breath away.

I stood back for a moment, then again leaned out into the wind, peering into the black where the ship was headed. It took me a moment to understand that the dark shape, darker than the night, as if someone had punched a hole in the air, was a huge wall of ice, far wider and bigger than the ship. Fear twisted my stomach and for a moment I forgot the intense cold on my skin. I could see no way that a ship of this size could turn fast enough to avoid a collision.

Yet I continued to watch with fascination as every moment seemed to stretch. It was a sick fascination, as if watching a horrible fight where someone was being badly hurt, yet unable to turn away.

As my eyes watered and the tears seemed to freeze on my checks, I watched.

Slowly the ship turned, just enough, and just at the last second. The bow somehow slid by the leading edge of ice.

There was a faint rumbling lower in the ship and a distant scaping sound.

The huge gray wall was suddenly beside us and it seemed as if I could reach out and touch the rough ice. Yet I knew that if I did, the razor-sharp edges would have cut my hands.

Holmes and I instinctivly both took a step away from the rail and watched the mountain slide past the ship. When it was far beyond the stern of the ship and again fading into the black of the night Holmes turned to Dr. Frederick. "So what do you observe is different?"

"Nothing from our three times back here since we became stuck. However, the records we have said that this part of the deck where we are standing was originally covered with ice from the berg as it scraped past."

Holmes nodded.

"So we are only talking a matter of feet," I said, "maybe even inches between saving this ship and having it sink?"

It was Dr. Frederick's turn to nod. "In this world, as I am sure you read in your newspapers, the ship sustained damage, but the watertight compartments held the ship afloat until it could get to New York. In my universe the damage was too extensive and the watertight compartments did very little."

Behind us ten or twelve hearty men emerged from a door, the yellow light casting a long bright streak across the deck. They were clearly interested in what had happened and why the engines had stopped. They talked loudly among themselves and headed toward both rails to gaze into the night. I again leaned out and looked to the stern. The iceberg was now barely visible, a gray mountain looming in the night.

Holmes turned to Dr. Serling. "Is it possible to see these events again?"

Dr. Serling nodded. "Actually, yes. We can move up, and back in time, to the boat deck."

I looked at Holmes and then at Dr. Serling, who was again working on the case. "You mean that we can be up there on the boat deck at the same time we are, or were, here this time watching? I mean—" I stopped. I was totally confused and again my fear returned.

Dr. Frederick nodded and pulled his coat tighter around himself. "Yes, but there are limits. We have never been able to get close enough to ourselves in experiments to see our earlier, or later, self. But that has not been from lack of trying." He laughed. "Time travel is still new to us. We really can't explain some of the paradoxes. We just know they exist and somehow the universe stops certain things from happening."

"So," Holmes said, pointing up at the leading edge of the boat deck. "I will not be able to go to that position up there and look down at myself here, unless I am, or was, doing it now. Correct?"

I glanced up, but a later version of Holmes was not standing there, much to my relief.

"That would seem to be the rule," Dr. Serling said. "Ready?"

Holmes nodded.

"What about the passengers?" I asked, but to Dr. Serling that question didn't seem to matter.

The cold, the salt-filled air, the feeling of the wooden deck under my feet all went away for a moment.

And suddenly we were standing next to a lifeboat about halfway down the boat deck, again on the starboard side.

Without a moment's hesitation Holmes strode to the starboard side of the ship and looked in the direction of the coming wall of ice.

I glanced around, relieved that no passenger was within sight to witness our arrival. "I have no desire to get used to this mode of travel," I said, pulling my coat around me tightly in a vain attempt to hold out the wind. "How fast is this ship traveling?"

"Over twenty-two knots," Dr. Frederick said.

"Far too fast," I said.

Dr. Frederick only grunted as the alarm bell started its insistent noise from the direction of the bow. He and I moved to join Holmes at the starboard rail, leaving Dr. Serling with the heavy case.

Again we watched as the iceberg took its collision course. I found myself unable to take my gaze from that huge, growing mountain. That same sick desire as before kept my gaze frozen into the cold wind until finally, at what seemed to be the last moment, the ship slowly turned, shifting the iceberg to the starboard side of the liner.

With a fairly loud scraping the cold gray wall sliped past. No one said a word this time and again Holmes seemed to be listening.

I, on the other hand, was again trying to keep my nerves under control. I took a few quick steps back from the towering wall of ice as it slid past. There was something about this entire event that felt ghoulish, as if we were robbing graves. I shook that thought from my mind and instead thought of the warm fire at Baker Street.

The mountain faded into the distance behind the ship as Holmes stood at the railing, not watching it but instead deep in thought. I had no idea what he might be thinking. I just knew I wanted to be off this ship and back in my warm quilts, if that was not where I was still.

"Once more," Holmes said, turning and moving back over to Dr. Serling. "Only this time could we be somewhere near the bridge?"

Dr. Sterling seemed to think for a minute and then nodded. "Yes, I think I can get us to the boat deck on the port side. That was a deck above where we were on our first visit. That would be close enough for you to move to the port door of the bridge and watch what was happening."

Holmes nodded. "That would be satisfactory."

Serling went to work. A number of first class passengers now occupied the deck, staring toward the stern after the retreating wall of ice. But Serling and Frederick paid them no attention, as if they were nothing but harmless ghosts.

Serling typed in his case and suddenly the night again vanished.

And just as suddenly returned.

We now stood on the other side of the ship, on an empty boat deck, slightly closer to the bow.

Holmes immediately started toward the door of the bridge. I struggled in vain to remove the thought from my mind that I was not only standing here at this moment, but also at two other places on this same ship. It was enough to make a sane man crazy, and I was sure that insanity was where I was heading at a speed faster than the ship.

"You only have one look," Dr. Frederick said. "We won't be able to repeat this again."

Holmes glanced over his shoulder. "I understand perfectly, Doctor."

Just as Holmes stuck his head around the edge of the open bridge door the warning bell rang out through the night air.

Again we watched as the iceberg loomed closer and closer, only to be swept past the starboard side. Being on this side of the deck I felt less threatened by the entire event. Or possibly I was just growing used to it. Another thought I put quickly out of my mind.

Holmes never took his head away from the open door to

glance even once at the iceberg. As the ship slowed and drifted in the black waters he turned to us. The look on his face was one that I had never seen before. It was almost as if he had seen a true ghost.

"Holmes, are you all right?" I asked as he rejoined us.

"I need one more time here," he said. "Can you get me close enough to the main engines to watch them during the time of the collision?"

Again Dr. Serling thought for a moment while the cold cut through my coat as if it weren't there. I had experienced many cold London nights, but none anywhere near as cold as this.

"We'll have to go back five minutes sooner to give you the time," Dr. Serling said. He worked in the case for what seemed to be a long minute.

Then, again without warning from him, the world and the deck and the cold wind vanished. It would at least be courteous for him to give us a moment to prepare.

This time he had placed us in a fairly narrow hallway lit by electric lamps at intervals along the walls.

I leaned against the polished wood and took a deep breath of the warm, coal-smelling air. It was a relief to be out of the wind and the cold, but the thought of being inside a ship about to hit an iceberg had me on the edge of a slight panic.

"Through there and down the circular stairs," Dr. Serling said, pointing to a wooden door at the end of the hall. "The engine room will be down there. You only have a few minutes."

Holmes nodded and didn't waste a moment striding the distance to the door and disappearing through it.

I opened my coat to allow the warmer air to flow around my torso. Dr. Serling adjusted a dial inside his case and then sat on the carpeted floor. Dr. Frederick just paced.

Finally he stopped and turned to me. "Do you think he can solve this?"

I gave a slight, very halfhearted laugh. "If there is something to solve, I am sure he can. But I do not exactly understand what you are asking of him." I stared at Dr. Frederick and then said quietly, "If you ponder it, I am not sure you understand either."

"We are asking him," Dr. Frederick said, gesturing at the walls around us, "to simply put history right. This ship belongs on the bottom of the Atlantic. It needs to be there for history to return to normal."

I simply watched him as he started his pacing again. I knew it would do no good to remind him of the hundreds of people he said would die tonight if that occurred. In the background we could hear the seemingly distant rumble of the engines and occasionally a noise of a passenger from somewhere nearby. But otherwise the hallway remained silent until a fairly loud scraping and grinding filled the air.

I held onto a smooth edge of wood paneling and took deep, controlled breaths until the noise stopped. The engines dropped silent and then there was only quiet. Again my mind filled in the comparison between the silence of a graveyard, or the silence of the dead of night, before even the birds are moving.

Frederick looked at me and I returned his stare, saying nothing.

At the end of the hall the door opened and Holmes rejoined us. "We can go back to Baker Street now," he said, his voice sounding tired and emptied of all energy.

I glanced first at Holmes and then at the doctors as they looked at each other puzzled.

"Did you solve our problem?" Dr. Frederick asked.

Holmes did nothing but shake his head. "The fire would feel comforting against the chill."

After a moment Dr. Serling bent to the case at his feet, made a feew adjustments and suddenly the hall was gone, replaced quickly by the familiar surroundings of Baker Street.

Without removing my heavy coat, I bent to the fire and soon had it roaring again, its yellow flame overpowering the lamps.

I finished and turned to the room. Holmes had removed his coat and was again in his chair. Only it was very clear he was deep in thought. Both our guests understood his mood and both were respecting it. I removed my coat and hung it in its place, then moved back to the chair near the fire. The heat cut into the oppressive cold of the night and the feeling that the ship had been haunted. Haunted by not only our own ghosts, but more by the fact that many people might have died that night. In my years with Holmes and as a doctor I have witnessed many close calls and many deaths.

Yet none to my memory had shaken me as much as standing on the deck of that ship tonight.

Holmes stirred and picked up the book beside him. "Does this book have an account of the collision?"

Dr. Frederick nodded and Holmes opened the book and went to work studying and quickly reading. We remained silent and I spent the minutes holding my hands out in front of me so that the cold could be forced out by the warmth of the flames. The memory of being on that ship would, in time, fade into a seemingly bad vision and nothing more.

Finally, Holmes laid the book back down and sighed. "I'm afraid there is nothing I can do to help you gentlemen."

"What?" Dr. Serling said. "You mean you *won't* help us."

"I didn't say that," Holmes said, "I said I *can't*."

"But—" This time it was Dr. Frederick's turn to stop his companion.

"Mr. Holmes," Dr. Frederick asked, "are you saying you do not know what caused the switch in history?"

"Basically, yes. That is what I am saying." Holmes patted the book. "The details outlined here are exactly what occurred on that ship, except, of course, the ship we visited tonight didn't sink. I can think of a thousand factors that would have caused such a difference."

"Such as?" Dr. Serling said. He was not disguising the panic and the fear in his voice at all.

"Such as someone or something turning the iceberg just a fraction of a degree." He made a helpless gesture. "I would not think such a feat possible, yet I did not think travel through time possible until this evening either."

Before either doctor could say a word, Holmes went on. "The switch might have occurred much earlier in the evening. As the captain ordered the increase in speed, the implementation of the order could have been delayed just a few seconds, which would again allow the iceberg to be in a slightly different position at the time of the collision, thus making the damage lighter."

It was clear that Holmes's words were being understood by our guests. Finally Dr. Serling sighed. "It was a hope. Nothing more."

Dr. Frederick nodded slowly, his shoulders slumping. "A crazy, stupid hope, at that."

Dr. Serling stood and moved to Holmes, who also stood.

With an extended hand the doctor said, "I would like to thank you for your attempt and your time. It was generous of you."

Holmes only nodded and shook his hand. Then Dr. Serling turned to me as Dr. Frederick moved to shake Holmes's hand.

"Where will you be going?" I asked as he took my extended hand.

"We left a homing beacon in a hotel room in New York. We will return there and do our best to not influence the future too much."

"That seems like a very logical plan of action."

He smiled at me. "It would seem we have very few other options at the moment."

He turned and moved back to the large case as Dr. Frederick shook my hand and then moved over beside the case.

Holmes picked up the large book and handed it to him. "You might want this."

Dr. Frederick shook his head. "Please keep it as a gift. At this point it is nothing more than a work of fiction."

"I will treasure it," Holmes said and tucked the book under his arm.

Dr. Serling nodded, reached inside the case and suddenly they were both gone.

The crackling of the fire was the only sound as I stood staring at the empty place where they had been.

"Quite something, isn't it?" Holmes said.

I turned and watched as Holmes almost dropped into his chair, the exhaustion heavy on his strong shoulders. He laid the book on his lap and stared at it as if it were a monster to be tamed.

I poured us both a hot coffee and a snifter of brandy and then dropped into the chair across from him. He continued to stare at the cover of the book, not even offering his thanks for the drinks.

"It seems," I said, "that the night wore on you as much as it did on myself."

Holmes only nodded.

I took a sip of the brandy, letting it warm the deep cold inside. "It is lucky that you did not find the answer to their problem."

Holmes looked up at me and for the first time I saw his eyes, eyes watery and burning with an almost insane gaze.

"My dear Watson," he said, his voice low, barely in control, a state that I had never witnessed in Holmes. "I knew exactly what caused the change."

"What!" I almost came out of my chair, my coffee spilling a hot stain down my trousers.

He nodded slowly. "I lied to them. Actually the solution was simple." He tapped the book but made no motion to continue.

"Please, Holmes. I must know." I was sitting on the edge of my chair, facing him.

He grunted and then for the first time reached for his brandy. After a long sip he looked me square in the eye. "It is the knowledge of nightmares."

"But they will be my nightmares," I said.

He looked and me and then slowly nodded. "I first read the answer in here. It said that at the time of the sighting of the iceberg the First Officer William Murdock ordered the engines 'full speed astern' and put the helm 'hard to starboard.' Now, such a move would cause the ship to turn to port."

I nodded. I knew enough sailing to understand that basic principle.

"But," Holmes said, "putting the engines full speed astern made such a huge ship much more difficult to control and thus the turn was just slightly slower. The ship would then strike the iceberg in a direct manner, thus causing enough damage to cause it to flounder."

"I am at a loss," I said. "Is that what happened? Why did the ship stay afloat?"

"No," Holmes said. "The engines remained full speed ahead, thus giving the ship just a fraction more ability to maneuver, thus allowing it to only graze the iceberg."

"So First Officer Murdock somehow changed his order? But how?"

Holmes shook his head. "No, he ordered full speed astern just as the book says. When I heard him give that order was when I first knew that our guests were correct. That ship should have sunk that night." He took another drink from his brandy.

"That was why you needed to visit the engine room?"

Holmes nodded. "The man on the telegraph between the bridge and the engine room at that moment was not from our

time. He ignored the order and thus saved the ship. And
changed the future it would seem."

I stared at Holmes. "How could you know he was from a
different time?"

"Simple, really. Just as Dr. Serling wore what he called
contact lenses, so did the man on the telegraph in the engine
room."

I sat staring into my brandy, letting what Holmes had told
me sink in. Finally I gathered enough nerve to ask the question I knew Holmes was expecting. "If history really was
changed by someone from the future, why didn't you set it
right?"

Holmes almost laughed. "I had the opportunity to do so.
Remember what Dr. Serling told us about there being more
than one future from every decision?"

"Forks in a road," I said.

Again the insanity seemed to burn like a flash fire in
Holmes eyes as he fought for control. "We are simply on the
branch of the road where I did not stop the person from the
future."

He gulped down the last of his brandy, studied the crystal
snifter for a moment, and then with all the force he had he
threw the glass into the fire where it shattered and sent
sparks flying.

He leaned back into his chair and closed his eyes. His
hands gripped the large book in a death grip, his knuckles
white. Softly he said, "On that other road I stopped that
man, doomed a great ship, and killed over fifteen hundred
human beings in the process. I know that road exists. I know
I walked it."

My head was spinning from the very thought of what
Holmes had suggested. I took a sip of my brandy and stared
at the light reflecting off the shattered fragments of
Holmes's glass. "You mean," I finally said, "that on that
other world we are sitting talking about how you stopped
that man and the deaths it caused?"

Holmes nodded very slowly.

"But you could have never done that." I wanted to shake
him, wake him from his crazy thoughts.

He opened his eyes and I saw they were almost empty of
energy and life. "My dear Watson. I most certainly could
have. And in that other world, on that other road, I most certainly did."

He closed his eyes again and sank farther into his chair, as if a huge weight were pushing him down.

And I finally understood what that weight was. My friend had had the future of the world on his shoulders tonight. More weight than any man should be forced to carry. Even if that man was Sherlock Holmes.

THE RICHMOND ENIGMA

by John DeChancie

(Being a manuscript, one of many, found among the effects of the late John H. Watson, M.D., formerly of the Army Medical Department.)

As I look through my notes on the sundry cases on which, over the years, my friend Mr. Sherlock Holmes has been engaged as an investigator, I see many that are above the commonplace, some that are odd, and a very few that my be termed "singular." But I do believe that the case which I have decided to call, for want of a better name, "The Richmond Enigma" is the only one that may aptly be described as *peculiar.* I recount it here, not with any eye toward publication, or any sort of public disclosure whatsoever—indeed, I should think the public would make me a laughing stock—but purely for my own amusement, and in keeping with my resolve to record the salient events of every case on which Sherlock Holmes has brought to bear his formidable powers of scrutiny and ratiocination, this one being no different from any other in that regard.

It began on a spring morning in late March of 1896. I had just come downstairs and found Holmes by the far window in the sitting room, playing his violin. I recognized the tune: from the Beethoven violin concerto; third movement, I believe.

I said nothing as he finished the passage. Then he laid

down his bow carelessly on the acid-stained, deal-topped table which stood in the chemical corner, and on which lay an assortment of scientific accoutrements.

After staring out the window for a moment, he turned to me with a bright smile. "Good morning, Watson!" he said.

"Getting in a bit of early practicing, eh?"

His smile turned rueful. "I fear, Watson, that I shall never be as good a musician as I want to be, regardless of how much I practice."

"Nonsense, Holmes. With talents as numerous as yours, it's very likely you could do anything you set your mind to."

Laying down the violin, Holmes acknowledged the compliment with a nod. "I thank you, my dear Watson. But rote discipline, which great musicianship demands as much as artistic sensitivity, is not my forte. My mind rebels at the routine, the mundane. I cannot long perform tasks that require tedious repetition, endless grinding, on and on. As to this beautiful instrument, I will never be its master. I love to play but balk at daily finger exercises. The battle is therefore lost before it is begun."

Armed with a newspaper, I seated myself on one of the armchairs by the fireplace and began my frontal assault on the day's events. I had barely gotten started when Holmes said, "You are up quite late this morning."

I peered over the newspaper at him. "The devil you say. Why, it's not half past nine."

"Nevertheless, you missed the delivery of this note, from a Mr. Eustace Filby."

"Oh?"

"Yes. He's due to arrive any moment. Had you deigned to come down any later, you might have missed him."

"Really, Holmes." I tossed the paper aside. "And what does this Mr. Filby want?"

"I have gleaned only the vaguest notion from this, the vaguest of notes," Holmes said, holding up an envelope neatly slit open at one end. "Do you wish to read it?"

"I shall be satisfied with your précis, my dear Holmes."

Holmes smiled. "It is brief. I will read it entire." He pried out the folded note, opened it, and read: " 'Mr. Sherlock Holmes, Detective Investigator, 221B Baker St.' etcetera . . ."

"Oh, 'Detective Investigator,' is it now?" I twitted.

Holmes paid service to this gentle gibe with a brief upcurl

of his lip. " 'Sir: I shall call on you this morning, very early. If you are so kind as to receive me, my intention is to relate to you some rather curious business in Richmond, which you may find of interest—and then again, which you may not. Should the former be the case, I would seek to engage you in an investigation of said business, to make of it what you will, to our mutual benefit and satisfaction.' Signed, 'Eustace T. Filby.' "

I nodded. "Curious note, indeed. What time did he say he'd arrive?"

" 'Very early.' "

We had not long to wait. After but a few more conversational exchanges, we were interrupted by Mrs. Hudson's polite knock against the door jamb.

"A Mr. Filby to see you, sir," she said to Holmes.

"Thank you very much, Mrs. Hudson. Do send him up."

Our Mr. Filby turned out to be a tall, red-haired man with a raw, ruddy face. He was dressed in somber attire; that is to say, conservatively, in the darker shades and quieter weaves of material. His morning coat was black, his waistcoat a dark maroon. The gray of his trousers was a brooding shade indeed, barely set off by the darker stripes. His tie, black, was precisely tied, his collar primly starched. He came into the room and surveyed it, and us.

Holmes and I rose.

Holmes said, "Mr. Filby, I presume?"

"Yes, sir. And you are, I take it, Mr. Sherlock Holmes?"

"I am, sir. May I present Dr. John Watson—my Boswell, as it were."

"Indeed," said Filby bowing slightly. "I have read your accounts of Mr. Holmes's exploits with great interest, Dr. Watson. I am honored to make your acquaintance."

"Thank you, sir," I said.

Holmes said, "Mr. Filby, please be seated, and tell me how long you have been a solicitor."

The man halted a motion to seat himself. "How did you know I was a solicitor?" he asked with surprise. "There was nothing in my note—"

"Besides having noticed that your message was written on legal paper, I also see that you wear the uniform of your profession," said Holmes.

"Uniform? Why, I don't quite know what you mean."

Holmes laughed. "Come now, sir. There are three types of

professional men who are in the habit of wearing sedate attire: the clergyman, the lawyer, and the undertaker. I deemed it improbable that an undertaker would seek the services of a private investigator. You are obviously not a man of the cloth. Ergo, you are in the legal profession. The only decision then to face me was whether you were a barrister or a solicitor. Barristers, however, tend ever so slightly toward more conventionally colorful clothing, for when they appear in court the unbecoming gaudiness is hidden by robes. Therefore, sir, you are a solicitor."

"Remarkable," Mr. Filby said.

"Not really so remarkable," Holmes said. "I have made a hobby of studying revealing trivia. The sartorial habits of the various professions is one area of study that I find immensely useful. Regarding lawyers, I can hazard a guess as to what city a lawyer practices in by the shoes he wears. Also, I can tell whether he is in independent practice or is a member of a large firm. In addition . . . but enough. Please sit down, Mr. Filby."

Filby took his ease on the settee. We repaired to the armchairs. Holmes crossed his legs languidly, and, as is his wont when in an analytical mood, put his fingertips together and peered over them at our guest.

"I am grateful," said Filby, "that you saw fit to receive me at so early an hour. The matter I wish to discuss with you is of such a singular nature, taxing my poor powers of description, that the note which you received must have been somewhat . . . how shall I put it? Enigmatic?"

"Only mildly so," said Holmes dryly.

"I offer my apologies. But now I will explain my business, if I may."

"Please do."

"Very well, sir. I come to discuss with you a matter on which I have been engaged not only as a solicitor—for that is indeed my profession—but also as a friend of the client. In fact, I have been appointed the executor of his estate."

Holmes interjected with, " 'He' being . . .?"

"I refer to my client, Mr. ——, of the city of Richmond."

(I omit the name, for reasons which will become clear later.)

At the mention of the name, I detected an odd glimmer in Holmes's eye. At the time, I did not know what to make of it.

"Very well," said Holmes. "Go on."

"In sum, and in short, the problem is this. Mr. —— is missing. He has been missing for some six months. I wish you to find him. Short of that, I would charge you to ascertain whether he is alive or dead. If the latter, his estate can then be properly settled."

"This seems a straightforward matter," Holmes observed. "In fact, it seems more a matter for New Scotland Yard than for a private consulting detective. Have you gone to the police?"

"No, sir, I have not."

"May I ask why you have not?"

Filby let out a great sigh. "That, sir, would involve relating the circumstances immediately attendant upon his disappearance. And that . . . well, Mr. Holmes. Were I to go to the police, they might think me insane. Or they might believe me to be hoaxing them. In either case, they would lock me up and throw away the key."

Holmes' eyes narrowed to slits. "Indeed," he said softly. "Indeed."

"But," stated Mr. Eustace Filby with firm resolve, "I have no qualms about telling *you*, Mr. Sherlock Holmes. I shall relate the whole story, omitting nothing."

"Stout fellow," Holmes murmured. "Do go on."

"Very well. It began almost exactly one year ago, when I received from Mr. —— a draft of a will that contained some very unusual clauses. It appointed me the executor of the estate, which I knew to be a sizable amount—for, as I said, I am also on social terms with this particular client, and knew him to have a tidy income on some very considerable holdings. He does not work, occupying his time with the devising of unusual mechanical inventions."

"How very interesting," said Holmes. "What sort of inventions were these?"

Mr. Filby thought for a moment. "One of them, I remember, was a box affair that he purported to be capable of sending telegraph messages without the use of wires for transmission."

"Absurd," was my comment.

Filby turned to me. "My sentiments exactly. However, he claimed to have conducted experiments which proved his theories. He even demonstrated to me, and some few others, how the box worked. Actually, there were two boxes. One to send the alleged message, and one to receive it. 'Messages,' indeed. Sparks, is what were sent, if they were sent at all."

"Sparks?" said Holmes.

"A coil in one box emitted a dim spark, and almost simultaneously, a like coil in the second box did the same. My friend's claim was that the two events were causally related."

"Indeed," Holmes said with interest. "But nothing came of this miraculous device?"

"Nothing whatsoever. There were other contrivances. Dozens, which he exhibited and demonstrated, usually at dinner parties he would give, and to which he would invite a close circle of intimate acquaintances. I cannot begin to count how many of these mechanisms I have seen in the last ten years, all different, all quite obscure as to their intent or purpose, all completely mystifying. Mystifying to me, that is, and to the rest of his friends. However, as we were rather fond of him, and even, in our own way, admired him, we indulged him in these curious enthusiasms. But let me return to the matter of the will. The will stated that I would be made an executor of the estate in the event of my client's death, or, in the event he should disappear for an indefinite period, I would be made a trustee."

"That is very strange," Holmes said.

"Yes. Stranger still, there was a codicil which specified that the house was not to be sold. In fact, it was to be kept up, maintained, and looked after, though never to be let, leased, or occupied. The house was to remain as it was, down to every candlestick, every rack of furniture, untouched. Indefinitely, until its owner should return."

"And he has not," Holmes said.

"No, he has not returned in six months."

"He took a trip," I suggested.

"If he did," said Filby, "he left no clue as to his intended destination. I have done some detective work on my own, checking and rechecking steamship records. I could find no indication that he left the country. If he is still in the British Isles, he has completely hidden himself."

"No one can hide forever," I said.

Filby eyed me. "You have not heard the rest of my story, Dr. Watson. If you think what I have related so far is strange, you will be dumbfounded at the end of my tale."

"Pray continue, Mr. Filby," instructed Holmes.

"I will, sir. A most extraordinary request accompanied the draft of the will. I was not to discuss the will or its contents with anybody, under any circumstances, not even with the client himself! All communication about this matter was to be written. But that is not all. I could reply to the letter, but I was not to do so until a full year had passed. But before that time had elapsed, more instructions would come, again by way of the post."

"And what did you think about this strange business?" Holmes asked.

"Why, sir, I was nonplussed! Befuddled. Perplexed and befuddled. I did not know what to make of it. I could not even call on my client and ask him about it, for I was expressly forbidden by that same client to do so!"

"What did you do?"

"I put the will and the letter in my files, and dismissed it as an aberration of his sometimes peculiar personality. Until . . ."

Holmes had been listening with his eyes almost shut. He opened them. "Until . . . ?"

"Until he disappeared. But I must lead up to that. I have told you about his penchant for mechanical contrivances. About six months ago, at his house, among this same circle of friends, he told of a new invention he had been working on. This one . . . and here is where I began to doubt my client's sanity—this one, gentlemen, was supposed to be a device capable of conveying a traveler through time."

"Time?" I said with some puzzlement.

"Yes. He called the device a Time Machine."

"It was some sort of timepiece? A clock?"

"No, Dr. Watson. Not a clock. I don't know how else to put it. It was a machine that could travel through time, past and future. He explained the theory—something to do with four dimensions . . . I confess I did not understand much of it. However, he showed us a working model of the device, then, shortly afterward, the device itself, though the latter was not yet completed. In the main, the Time Machine was a metallic frame, inside which was mounted a seat facing a set of two crystalline control bars. Parts of the device were of brass, other components were perhaps of nickel or some other silvery metal. It was quite remarkable, and well-made."

"You said . . . a *working* model." Holmes's eyes were wide and attentive.

"Yes," said Mr. Filby. "I did say 'working,' did I not? And I saw the model work, if my client's explanation is to be believed. The curious little device, a miniature of the one in the laboratory, disappeared from a table top, and did not reappear. I saw it vanish with my own eyes, and still have trouble believing it."

"A parlor trick," said I.

"An illusion—perhaps," Filby said. "I thought so at the time. But now I am not so sure."

"And did your client travel through time?" Holmes asked. "Or, should I say, did he claim to have done it?"

"He did so claim," Filby said. "He invited me and a few others to a dinner party the next Thursday. Unfortunately, I could not attend. But I have had many corroborating accounts of what happened. And this is what happened: the guests arrived, but the host was nowhere to be found. Dinner began. Halfway through it, my client suddenly burst from his laboratory, dressed in rags and looking as though he'd come from a battlefield. He was covered with mud, and had numerous cuts and bruises on his arms and face. After gulping down two glasses of wine, he related to his dinner guests the fantastic story of his journey into the future."

"The future, eh?" I chuckled.

Holmes's countenance was completely serious. "How far into the future?"

Filby gave a mirthless laugh. "If you can believe it, his assertion was that he traveled into the future more than eight-hundred thousand years."

"Good heavens," I exclaimed. "Why, that's . . ."

"Scarcely to be credited?" said Filby. "Certainly. Nevertheless, if it was fiction, my client's literary talents are formidable. It was a long and detailed account, though I'm not sure I could—"

"As best as you can, and summarizing as much as possible," Holmes said, "please render an account of his journey."

"I shall certainly try," said Mr. Filby, the solicitor.

[If I thought this manuscript fit for publication, I would here give a more or less verbatim transcription of Filby's words, taken from my notes. But, as I deem it improbable that this will ever see print, I will simply outline the bizarre exploits of the Time Traveler (as I will hereafter call him), as told by Filby, omitting much that is as interesting as it is irrelevant.

[The world of Anno Domini 802,000 and some odd years was—or will be—a strange one. Humanity had divided into two groups. These were the Eloi, elfin creatures who lived an idyllic life in a garden-world of endless delights and pleasures—and the Morlocks, a primordial, degenerate, and bestial race that dwelt in machine-cluttered caverns beneath the earth. The Eloi, diminutive and handsome, if listless and strangely uninterested in anything but the most basic pastimes, led lives cut savagely short; for the awful truth was that the Morlocks preyed upon them, using them as food. The Time Traveler found this state of affairs as repugnant as any decent man would. He tried to do something to rectify the gross injustice of it, and succeeded in destroying many of the beasts in a raging brushfire; but it is doubtful whether he effected any great change in the future world-at-large. He did strike up a rather intimate relationship with one of the Eloi, a woman named Weena. But she died in that same conflagration. Despairing, he went on into the unimaginable future—and here the tale grows more fantastic still. He traveled almost to the end of time, and the end of the Earth itself, and saw many a strange and curious thing—the bloated, dying sun, the horrific creatures that huddled under it, the blackened skies of Doom itself. It was a world as dark as the Time Traveler's mood. Saddened and disillusioned, he returned to the present, and his long-forgotten dinner party.]

At the end of the story, Filby sighed. But he had more to tell. "One of the men who was there that night called on [the Time Traveler] the next day. My client avowed that he was determined to mount the Machine again and travel in time, armed now with a camera, and a knapsack for collecting specimens. He said he would return shortly. The visitor heard the Time Machine start up. When he went back to the laboratory to investigate, the curious vehicle was gone. It has not returned since."

"And since that time, six months ago," Holmes finally said, "you have seen to it that the house has been taken care of."

"Quite true."

"And the place is unoccupied?"

"Yes. The housekeeper, Mrs. Watchett, and the manservant have moved out. Mrs. Watchett, who now lives with her sister in Croydon, believes the house to be haunted. However, she comes every two weeks to dust and look after things."

"I see," said Sherlock Holmes. He then fell silent.

Filby and I regarded each other for a while, then looked away. Holmes was deep in reverie, his eyes closed, his head tilted back against the chair.

The silence continued. When it began to grow uncomfortable, I cleared my throat. Holmes finally opened his eyes, and I was relieved, for I thought he had fallen asleep. He rose.

"Would it be possible to inspect the house?" he asked of Filby.

"Certainly, sir."

"Today?"

"By all means. However, I must do one item of business while I am in London. Otherwise—"

"Then, may we meet you at the house later today—say, five o'clock?"

"I will give you the address," said Filby, and he did.

Filby got to his feet. "Mr. Holmes. Is it possible that you could find him? Or at least ascertain whether the fantastic tale he told is true?"

"I believe I can," Holmes said. "As for believing the tale, you say that he brought back no specimens, no evidence whatsoever, from his first trip?"

"Ah, I nearly forgot!" cried Filby, who immediately began to dig in the pockets of his waistcoat. "I do have something—given to me by one of the men who was there that night. He didn't know what to do with them. Here they are."

He brought forth a folded piece of waxed paper, and unwrapped it. Inside were two tiny white flowers, stems and all. They were flattened, withered, and dried out, but still quite intact.

"These are some flowers that Weena gave him," Filby said.

Holmes took the specimens and examined them. Presently, he looked at Filby, then at me. He then crossed the room and laid them on the chemical table.

After searching the bookshelves, he brought forth a fat volume on botany, sat at the table, and began his study. Filby and I seated ourselves as he worked. One book was not enough for Holmes. He went and fetched two more, then a third. He looked through all of these, then returned to the shelves for yet a fourth book.

After fifteen minutes, Holmes rose from the chemical table, bearing the flowers, still in their nest of paper, back to their caretaker.

Filby wrapped them up again and put them back into his pocket.

"Mr. Filby," said Holmes. "The tale your client told was absolutely true."

Filby's jawed unhinged. He swallowed hard, then said, "Absolutely astounding. If you say so, Mr. Holmes, then it must be true."

"It is," stated Holmes. "Those flowers are of no species known today. I would immediately dismiss the notion that they are of some obscure plant from a far-off jungle, for they have all the earmarks of being indigenous to a temperate, not a tropical, climate. Moreover, they are unutterably strange, showing some extremely unusual characteristics, especially as regards the pistils. No, these flowers never grew in the England we know."

"Remarkable," Filby said.

"We shall meet again in Richmond, at five, then?"

Filby looked up at him. "Eh? Oh! Certainly. Yes, yes, I must be going. Thank you, sir. Thank you." Filby got to his feet.

"Good day," said Holmes as Filby left.

"I knew him," Holmes said as the sound of the front door closing came to us.

"Eh? Knew whom? Filby?"

"The Time Traveler. I knew him during my two years at college. Moreover, I am distantly related to the man."

"Extraordinary. So that's what was behind the gleam in your eye."

"Gleam? Perhaps. A gleam of remembrance. Of recognition. I recollect him to have been a strange fellow. I did not know him well, but I do remember him."

"Holmes, are you going to tell me, now that Filby is gone, that you believe that utterly preposterous story about the Time Machine?"

Holmes turned full face toward me and fixed me with a sober look. "I do. The flowers prove it. However, I have some thinking to do on this matter. Much thinking. If you'll excuse me."

"Certainly, my dear fellow."

Holmes retired to his room, leaving me free at last to peruse the daily paper, which I did.

The day wore on. I went out to do some bank business, returning at a quarter of three. Holmes had yet to emerge from his room. I spent some time at my desk, going over my notes, then looked at my watch. It was time we were getting to the station. I went up and got dressed, came downstairs again. No Holmes in sight. I was about to go give his door a knock when he finally emerged. He went to his desk, took out paper and a pen, and began writing. Whatever the message, it was short. He folded the paper, put it in a large envelope, took a match to some sealing wax, and sealed it. He then rose, went to the door, unhung his cape-backed overcoat and deerstalker, and put them on.

"Come, Watson," he said, stuffing the envelope into an inside pocket. "We must deliver a letter."

"I'm your postman," I said as I got into my greatcoat. The weather had been chilly and wet for late March. "Perhaps you'd like to tell me to whom the letter is addressed?"

"To the Time Traveler, Watson," said Holmes.

"Ah."

It was all a lot of nonsense, of course, but I was determined to see what Holmes could make of it. After I turned down the student lamp, we left.

Finding a free cab at that time of day was a difficult proposition, but luck was with us, and we bade the cabman to make haste to Paddington Station. We made it in time to catch a train on the suburban line.

The trip out to Richmond was short and uneventful, and completely silent on Holmes's part. He stared out the window. I could only hazard a guess as to what was going through that subtle mind. Morlocks and Eloi? The mating habits of anomalous flora? The swollen red sun at the crack of Doom? Perhaps it was something completely trivial. We lesser mental beings, with our clumsy, clanking brains, can only dimly imagine the workings of a mind such as the one possessed by Sherlock Holmes. A more finely tuned, oiled, and efficient mechanism nowhere exists; but exactly how it works, how it arrives at its mental results and solutions, which it freely gives forth, is the darkest mystery of them all.

We easily got a hansom at the Richmond station, and proceeded toward the address that Filby had given us. It turned out to be a capacious suburban house with many gables and windows, sitting on a large lot surrounded by a high iron fence.

"Perfect," said Holmes. "Perfect."

Perfect for what? I did not ask. We alighted from the cab, paid the cabman, and went to the front gate which was locked. I looked at my watch. It lacked but three minutes to the hour of five.

Filby appeared precisely at five o'clock. He took a key to the gate and admitted us. We followed him to the front door, which he also unlocked, with a different key. We entered.

The place was dark and silent, shrouds covering most of the furniture. The place was impeccably free of dust, but the stale smell of disuse and abandonment was heavy in the air. The place was handsomely appointed, from what I could see of it. We walked through the house. The library was well-stocked, as I thought it would be, and favored the natural sciences over literature and the fine arts.

We came upon the Time Traveler's writing desk. Papers were piled high on it. I peered at them. They seemed to be diagrammatic drawings, engineering specifications, technical studies of some sort, all very obscure. Holmes stood at my side. He did not appear to give them much notice.

He took the envelope from his pocket.

I gave Holmes a look. "Do you expect him to return?"

"He may. It is a gamble. He may, after all, be dead, done in by Morlocks, or some other fantastical beast. But if he is alive, he will surely return to his house, and if so, he will find this envelope."

"Perhaps," said I.

Holmes nodded. "Perhaps."

"What now, Holmes?"

"We wait."

"Wait?"

"Yes. But not here. In the laboratory. Will you wait with us, Mr. Filby?"

"Certainly, Mr. Holmes."

"What are we waiting for," I inquired, "and for how long?"

"We have an appointment at eight o'clock," Holmes said. "Come, let us situate ourselves in the laboratory."

"Aren't you going to leave your letter?"

"Let me see the laboratory first."

The laboratory was connected to the house by a long passage. The door was not locked. We went in and beheld what was more a workshop than a place for scientific inquiry. Tools lay all about on work benches. Materials—lengths of pipe, metal rods, and other oddments—lay in piles in the corners.

One bench was covered with more mechanical drawings. Holmes placed the letter on top of them.

"There. If he returns, he might want to consult his drawings, in order to make repairs to his machine."

"Good guess," I said.

"And now we wait," said Holmes.

"There are no chairs, Holmes," I said. "I will go fetch some."

"Thank you, Watson."

Filby assisted. We brought three chairs into the workshop and set them at the far end. The three of us seated ourselves, and I began to wonder about Holmes's sanity. Whom did we await? I was determined not to ask. Come the hour of eight, I would either know the answer, or be confirmed in my suspicions that Holmes's finely wrought mental machine needed a bit of oiling, or perhaps a complete overhaul.

"I need a book. If you don't think the owner would mind, Mr. Filby."

"You have my permission to borrow any book, Dr. Watson."

"Thank you."

I left, returning with a philosophical treatise on the physical sciences; also, I brought a candlestick. The light outside was waning. I lighted the candle. Holmes nodded his approval.

The evening dragged on. Holmes was silent throughout. Filby made the occasional innocuous comment, at which Holmes merely nodded. I read. The stiff-backed chair prevented me from nodding off. The book was interesting indeed, and I could see how the Time Traveler might have gotten some notions from it. The author dealt with various ideas about the nature of time and space. It was all very interesting, and completely academic. Nevertheless, I forged on.

Presently, I looked at my watch. It was ten minutes after seven. Sighing, I rose from my uncomfortable seat and announced that I was going to fetch another book, the treatise having bogged down in mathematical arcana.

I was waylaid in the library by a shelf of medical books which caught my interest. I sat in a comfortable stuffed chair and pored over at least a dozen volumes, deciding which one I would take back to read. I must have lost track of time, for when I consulted my watch again, I saw that it was just shy of eight. I hurried back toward the laboratory.

I had just about reached the door at the end of the long corridor when I heard a curious sound, like the rushing of wind, but mixed with an unnerving mechanical whine. I grasped the door handle and pushed the door open. A draft of cold air washed over me.

And there was the Time Machine, sitting in the middle of the laboratory floor. Occupying the seat was a man of about forty with long brown hair. Hatless, he was dressed in a hunting jacket and trousers. He dismounted from the machine, looked at me standing in the doorway, then turned toward Holmes and Filby.

He approached Holmes with his hand extended. "Sherlock Holmes! How much time has passed since last we saw one another?"

"What is time to a time traveler?" Holmes said, taking the man's hand.

"Not much, I'm afraid," said the Time Traveler. "Hello, Filby, old man."

Filby flushed with gladness. "Welcome back! We thought you utterly lost."

"Oh? And how long have I been gone?"

Filby frowned. "Six months. But surely—"

"You forget, Filby, the dictum of which Holmes just reminded you. Time is nothing when one has a time machine. For me, only a few hours have passed since I embarked on my second journey."

"But . . ." Filby was at a loss for words. "I don't understand."

"Think on it a while, Filby. At any rate, Holmes, I got your message, telling me to meet you here, at this time, this date."

"Thank you for coming. When did you find the envelope?"

"I don't quite remember the exact date, but it likely was some ten years from now. I have taken to exploring the immediate future . . . and I am mystified. This house stands, but I seem no longer to occupy it. The place is shut up, empty. This lonely state of affairs continues for at least a decade and a half; then, the house suddenly has occupants again, unknown to me. I can only interpret these events as meaning that I never return from a future time trip. Perhaps even this one."

Filby said, "The house stands empty according to the provisions of the last will and testament which you sent to me."

"Last will and . . . Filby, whatever are you talking about?"

"Why, you mean to say you didn't . . . ?" Filby was bewildered.

Understanding suddenly registered on the Time Traveler's face. "Of course, a capital idea. Have the house stand empty but habitable while I travel through time, so that I always have a haven. Yes, sending you a document of that sort is something I should do, and probably will do. No, it is something I *most definitely* will do, for it seems that I have already done it."

Filby was baffled by this as well.

Holmes said, "So, you intend to flit about in time for the immediate future—if I may put it that way?"

"I suppose I must. For something has occurred to me. I realized it the moment I woke up this morning . . . excuse me. When I woke up the morning after returning from my first trip into the future."

"And what was this realization?"

"That the Time Machine is a danger to the world."

Holmes nodded. "The possibility of paradox looms large."

"Yes. Paradox, engendered by travel into the past. You can easily meet yourself coming the other way. You can appear in places where you shouldn't be . . . at the battle of Waterloo . . . at Agincourt . . . at the Crucifixion—"

"Heavens!" exclaimed Filby.

"Yes, Filby. Even that. I have not done it. Would it be a blasphemy? And what effect would my presence have on the course of historical events?"

I had walked across the workshop to the where the three men stood. "Why is the Time Machine such a danger?"

"Dr. Watson, is it? A pleasure to meet you. It is a danger because of the unknown effects of paradox. Can history be changed? Should it? And think of this: one Time Machine can change history. Imagine, then, the chaos that might result when every man has one. Think of every Tom, Dick and Harry with a Time Machine, gadding about History, causing all sorts of bother."

Holmes said to me, "He's right, Watson. The thing must be destroyed. I spent the day thinking along much these same lines."

"I can destroy the machine," the Time Traveler said. "I never dreamed that I would say this, but I am willing to destroy it, and all the plans and drawings for it. But there is still a dilemma. At least a dozen people know about it. One of them was that journalist fellow— What was his name again, Filby?"

"Wells," said Filby.

"Yes, Wells. So, the secret is out. Once the world at large finds out about it, investigations will be made."

"No one will believe it," I ventured.

"At first, yes. But slowly, incredulity will yield to facts. And if I am around, the secret can be coaxed out of me, if the coaxers are ruthless enough. Even if I am not around, the fact that the feat can be done might be enough to inspire future inventors. No, gentlemen. I have made my decision. I will destroy all these drawings, my notebooks . . . and then the machine itself—but only after I use it to effect one and only one change in history."

"You will eliminate the invention of the Time Machine," said Holmes.

"Exactly!" said the Time Traveler, "though I don't know just how I will do it. I may have to eliminate myself."

"Good Heavens, man," I said. "How can you do that?"

The Time Traveler grinned impishly. "Simple, take my revolver, go back before the Time Machine was constructed, and shoot myself."

I was dumbfounded. "But . . . then you'd . . . but how could you—?"

The Time Traveler laughed heartily. "Paradox! Or, if that's distasteful, I can murder my grandfather."

"This is insanity," I muttered.

"Or," Holmes said carefully, "see that your grandfather marries a woman other than your grandmother."

"Precisely, Holmes. And there are other, even more subtle ways to effect the same change. A minor historical change. It shouldn't affect the main stream of mankind's history—which, as I found out, leads to tragedy anyway. In any case, I might have to go farther back than one or two generations."

"After you do the thing," Holmes said, "will you return to the far future?"

"I might. There is a possibility that I might rescue Weena—a woman of my acquaintance. But . . . Holmes, will I have a future? I might be erased from the cosmic scheme of things, become a chimera, a ghost without a place to haunt."

"Somehow I doubt that," Holmes said. "As I said, I have done some thinking. The likely result is that the great river of history will split into two alternative streams."

"Never thought of that," the Time Traveler said. "Now that I consider the notion, though, it sounds plausible."

"We will never know," Holmes said. "One way or the other."

"Likely not," agreed the Time Traveler. "Now, will you help me? Destroy the papers, I mean."

"Most assuredly," said Sherlock Holmes.

We did the deed. All the notebooks, the drawings, the detailed plans and specifications went up as smoke through the house's great chimney. What spare parts there were we bent out of shape, or disassembled, or smashed. We made a thorough job of it.

"Done at last," said the Time Traveler. "Now I must leave you. Forever, I'm afraid."

Holmes shook his hand. "Good luck to you. May you find a place to rest, a home in some distant sunny clime, in the past, or in the future."

"Thank you. My gratitude is boundless."

The Time Traveler shook my hand, then turned to Filby.

"Filby, my old friend and advocate."

"I will keep the house as it is for as long as I am able," Filby assured his friend. "You will always have a place to come back to."

"Thank you. And now, gentlemen, I must be going."

The Time Traveler returned to his machine and mounted it. After consulting the dials between the control bars, he activated the machine. It began to whir and whine. Dust on the floor rose up, and a cold draft blew from the direction of the anomalous craft.

The Time Machine grew soft and indistinct, blurring like an image in an unfocused telescope, and the bench behind it was clearly visible through the miasma. Then the air cleared, and there was nothing.

We put on our coats, and were about to leave the workshop, when I remembered something. I looked at the bench, and was astonished all over again.

"Holmes! The letter!"

"Eh, Watson? What is amiss?"

"Your letter. Why, the seal is intact! That fellow never did read it. But how did he—"

Holmes was laughing, and suddenly it dawned on me. I felt rather foolish. "Oh," I said. "Stupid of me. Of course."

"Don't castigate yourself, Watson. Human beings are unaccustomed to thinking in terms of the Eternal. We are timebound creatures. Come, let us go home."

And that is all there is to the Richmond Enigma. Not a week goes by that doesn't have me thinking about the Time Traveler, and where he might have gone. And what he might have done. I wonder what course Holmes's historical river will take.

But I also think that we might have been hoodwinked, somehow. It is a preposterous story. I don't quite believe it myself. After all, we only have the Time Traveler's word, and Filby's. The two could be in collusion.

Oh, bother. This will do for a first draft, I suppose. Not that I'll ever polish it. Really, it's all so improbable.

(The MS. ends here)

AFTERWORD

It is not beyond the realm of possibility that Watson here was trying his hand at pure fiction. In any case, fact or fancy, "The Richmond Enigma" is a fascinating story. There are interesting things in it. One wonders, for instance, whether the "Wells" mentioned was Herbert George Wells, the young novelist who has lately made a name for himself painting our contemporary social world in bold strokes. Intriguing to speculate what he might have produced had he taken up the writing of scientific romance.

This, then is the last of the unpublished manuscripts of John H. Watson, now seeing print for the first time in this limited edition of the complete works, published by the Museum. We hope you have enjoyed them.

This last story has sparked a strange bit of speculation in me. Does Watson forget that Holmes and the Time Traveler are distantly related?—and does he realize that, should the latter go back far enough in time to do his meddling, there arises the possibility that Sherlock Holmes would be eliminated as well?

Sheer fancy, of course. For we avid Sherlockians know, to paraphrase a French agnostic, that if Sherlock Holmes did not in fact exist, as he does in our "stream" of history, it would be necessary to invent him.

A. Conan Doyle, Curator
The Sherlock Holmes Museum
London

A STUDY IN SUSSEX

by Leah A. Zeldes

It had been some years since I had last seen my old friend, Mr. Sherlock Holmes. He had retired down to Sussex to keep bees more than thirty years before, and our paths seldom crossed afterward.

At first he was greatly occupied with setting up his farm, and with his researches for his *Practical Handbook of Bee Culture*. During the Great War, of course, I was busy with my medical practice, my junior, Dr. Verner, having gone to serve at the front, and it was several years thereafter before he was again fit to take up a full load.

Holmes, meanwhile, became more and more reclusive in his habits, seldom leaving his lonely South Downs estate. An occasional weekend visit was the most that I ever saw of him.

In the decade since my own retirement, I had been greatly troubled by rheumatism in my shoulder and leg, where I was wounded during my service in Afghanistan, and had been content to spend my time reading quietly by my hearthside. I wrote to Holmes now and then, and received characteristically terse replies, to the effect that he too was troubled by the scourge of aged joints, but I feared that barring that one trait in common, we had greatly drifted away from each other.

It was, then, with some surprise that I received a telegram from Holmes last Wednesday:

Come at once if convenient—if inconvenient come all the same.

S.H.

At my age, I am unused to such peremptory summonses, and I was inclined to feel rather ruffled at first, but then I reflected that Holmes had never sent for me without good cause. I cursed the fact that his rural neighborhood is not yet on the telephone, but wired back that I was on my way.

Travel, however short, is not such an easy thing for an octogenarian, and by the time I reached Eastbourne I was feeling quite exhausted. I engaged a cab to take me the final five miles to Holmes's house near the village of Fulworth. His housekeeper admitted me.

"Mr. Holmes is with his bees just now," she said. "If you would care to rest a while, sir, he will return in time for tea."

She showed me to my room. I removed my coat and shoes and lay in my clothes on the bed, thinking to relax for a few moments and then go in search of Holmes at the hives, but my old body got the best of me and I was soon fast asleep.

When the housekeeper woke me, I had a few moments of confusion, wondering where I was. The sun was already setting, and the room was purple in the deepening gloom. The housekeeper lit a lamp and brought in a pitcher and basin.

"Mr. Holmes asks that you join him in the study, sir. The tea is nearly ready," she said.

I had forgotten how few of the amenities that we now take for granted in London, such as electricity and running water, were available in the country. I could almost imagine myself back in the old days in Baker Street.

This sense of being in another time and place deepened when I entered the study, for Holmes had taken with him most of the furnishings from our old rooms and still had them, arranged in much the same way as they had been there.

The chemical bench stood in one corner, near the acid-stained, deal-topped table. The same old sofa, reupholstered, but littered as always with papers, and my old armchair sat near the fireplace, where Holmes's unanswered correspondence was transfixed to the wooden mantelpiece with a jack-knife. The coal scuttle contained cigars, and the ancient Persian slipper lying by the pipe rack, I had no doubt, held strong tobacco in its toe.

The only indications of the change of location and the passing of time were the thatched roof above, the titles of the rows of reference books on the shelves, and the patriotic initials, G.R., picked out in bullet-pocks upon the plaster wall.

"Why, Watson!" said Holmes, as he came into the room. "I would scarcely have known you. You are as thin as you were when we first became acquainted, five decades ago."

It was true. I, who have been a heavyset man for most of my life, have shrunk in my old age to gauntness such that I only ever had before upon my return from the tropics, suffering the effects of my war wounds and enteric fever.

"But you, Holmes," I cried, "you have hardly changed at all!" The well-remembered features were a trifle sharper, the forehead a little higher, and his body in the purple dressing gown a little thinner, but that was all. And Holmes, who had always been a pale man, shone with a wonderful color and moved with the vigor of a man twenty years his junior. "How splendid you look!"

"The country agrees with me."

The housekeeper came in with the tea tray just then, and set it on the table. "If that is all you require, Mr. Holmes," she said, "I'll be going. Tomorrow being my day off, I'll see you Friday morning. I've laid out the things for your breakfast, and a cold luncheon is in the icebox. Are you sure you'll be all right for tea?"

"Yes, thank you, Mrs. Merton. We shall manage." Holmes looked at me. "As you see, Watson, in my later years, I have adopted the workingman's habit of high tea in place of dinner. But there is an excellent tavern nearby where we can sup tomorrow."

With that, we fell to on Mrs. Merton's fine repast of Scotch woodcock, thick bread and butter, sliced ham, and iced gateaux. As Holmes reached to pass me a plate, the sleeve of his dressing gown fell away from his arm, revealing it to be dotted with innumerable round, red and angry welts, as from punctures.

"My dear Holmes!"

"It is nothing," he said, drawing his sleeve back over his arm. I scanned the room for a familiar morocco leather case.

He laughed. "Ah, Watson, you fear I am back to my old unsavory habits. No, these are not the marks of a needle. They are merely remembrances from my friends, the bees."

"But so many, Holmes!"

"That, Watson," said he, "is why I sent for you. As you know, I have for the past thirty years—a longer period than I practiced as a detective—been engaged in apiarian research. Bees are curious creatures, totally devoted to their communities. The continuance of the hive is more important to them than any individual. The individual may die, but the hive goes on.

"At first I occupied myself with systematically studying the best methods of beekeeping, the results of which research I set out in my *Practical Handbook of Bee Culture, with Some Observations upon the Segregation of the Queen.* But thereafter I began to look into the properties of various substances produced by the bees. You will recall that I sent you copies of my monographs on the dangers of honey as a food for infants and the uses of beeswax in salves."

"Yes, I found them quite useful in my practice," I said. "It's a pity they were not more widely disseminated."

"The medical profession does not take to new ideas easily," said Holmes. "To continue, for a long while I studied royal jelly, the secretion that worker bees prepare to feed the larvae and the queen. I was convinced that this substance had properties linked to longevity, for the queen bee, who dines on nothing else, lives for three years, while the worker bees, who eat it only in the first two days of their lives, have a life span of only six weeks. I conducted various tests.

"I even ate it myself and smeared it over my body. But apart from a certain smoothness to the skin, I found it had little effect. The properties that have so wonderful a consequence in bees appear to have little influence on human beings."

"I wonder at your research into longevity, Holmes," I said. "I recall that after the Adventure of the Creeping Man you expressed your revulsion for those who would try to rise above Nature. Such a one is liable to fall below it, you said. 'The highest type of man may revert to animal if he leaves the straight road of destiny. . . . The material, the sensual, the worldly would all prolong their useless lives. The spiritual would not avoid the call to something higher. It would be the survival of the least fit.' "

"When have you known me to be spiritual?" Holmes asked dryly. "And that was twenty years ago. I have moderated my opinion somewhat since, in particular with regard to my own longevity.

"You see, Watson," he said, turning toward me earnestly, "I believe the world will have need of me, of my mental powers."

"I see," I said, thinking my friend had always had a monstrous ego. "But you have been refusing to stir from your retirement here these past twenty years. You have been content to let the world manage entirely without you ever since the Great War. Why the change of heart now?"

"I believe we are on the verge of another war," he said.

"Surely not!"

"Yes, war, Watson. And war with such an evil and diabolical mind behind it that the world has not seen since the death of Professor Moriarty at the Falls of Reichenbach. I will be needed, Watson."

"And the bee stings, Holmes?"

"Some years ago, on a day when my rheumatism was particularly troubling me, I went out to tend my hives. I am so used to the bees that I rarely bother with netting. But the stiffness in my joints that day made me clumsy, and the bees were disturbed and stung me. Later, I noticed that, while the stings themselves were sore and red, the rheumatic pain was gone.

"Since then, I have encouraged the bees to sting me daily, and I am as you see me." He held out his hand for my inspection. The long fingers were straight and even, with no sign of the redness, swelling and twisting that characterizes rheumatism.

"This is wonderful, Holmes!" I said. "But why have you summoned me? You know I have not practiced medicine for ten years."

"I want your assistance with an experiment, Watson. Having to be within daily reach of the bees keeps me homebound. It extracts a great toll of bees, since their bellies are ripped away with the stinger and they die. And it is not unpainful. I have developed a method of extracting the bee venom without harming the bees. It is a long and complicated process; allowing them to sting is much simpler. So far I have tried injecting myself with a month's worth of venom, and found it as effective as thirty days of daily stings, although there were some side effects.

"I have now prepared two years' worth of venom that I

intend to inject over the course of two days. I wanted a medical man I could trust and whose powers of observation were known to me to be here to record the effects." As he spoke, he reached into the pocket of his dressing gown and pulled out a case containing two hypodermic syringes.

"My dear Holmes," I remonstrated, "surely such experimentation is dangerous."

"I am determined, Watson, and will do this whether you are here or not. Will you help me?"

I could only acquiesce.

He began rolling up his cuff. "You may find me somewhat feverish and perhaps a little delirious. Do not be alarmed. I would be grateful if you would record all my reactions in that notebook on the table there. Give me the second injection in the morning," he said, handing me one of the syringes.

He took the other and adjusted the delicate needle, thrust the point into the flesh of his left arm, and pressed down the tiny piston. I turned and gathered up the indicated notebook. When I turned back, Holmes was looking flushed.

"The fever is starting. Perhaps I will lie down."

I accompanied him to his room. I set the second syringe down on the dresser and pulled an armchair over by the bed, thinking I was rather old to be conducting this sort of all-night vigil once again. When Holmes removed his dressing gown, I saw that his left arm was puffed and ruddy, swelling almost visibly as I watched. Bright spots appeared on either cheek and his skin glistened with sweat. He began to gasp for breath.

"The window, Watson, open the window!" Holmes cried. I hurried to comply.

"I must be at the fight," Holmes said. "No one else can stop him. You won't fail me Watson. You never did fail me. Protect the hive. It's unfortunate, but the queen must die."

"The queen died in 1901," said I.

"The new queens die, all but one. And then the swarm. Protect the hive! Protect the hive! Fly! Fly!" He began to thrash around until I feared he would fall out of the bed, and I looked about for something to use as a restraint. But finally, after more such ravings, he quieted and slept, breathing harshly.

I recorded all that had happened in this notebook, noting that it also contained notes of Holmes's previous experiments with the bee venom. I was reading through these when I fear I fell asleep in the chair.

I awoke, stiff and sore, to the sound of cocks crowing. I was again a bit disoriented. It took me some moments to recall where I was and why I had been sleeping in the chair. I looked over to my patient and recoiled in horror. My skin went cold and my hair bristled.

"My God!" I whispered as I beheld the dreadful spectacle on the bed where last I had seen Holmes's supine form. From head to foot the cot was a writhing mass of black and yellow, a buzzing, seething aggregation of thousands upon thousands of small, striped bees.

I stared, terrified, unable to move. The buzzing grew louder. The bees began to swarm, rising in a single movement, twisting and shifting until they formed a long and slender silhouette, hanging in the air over the bed. My heart grew cold as I saw that the mattress was empty.

The buzzing rose in volume until I thought I should go mad. And then I perceived in the writhing swarm of bees a familiar, sharp-featured profile. The hum of the bees took on the character of a well-known voice:

"Za game izz afoot. Come, Watzzon, come," it said.

And the bees flew out of the window.

I stood a long moment looking after them. Then, slowly, I reached for the syringe upon the dresser.

THE HOLMES TEAM ADVANTAGE

by Gary Alan Ruse

"The devil, you say!" I exclaimed. "Someone stole your prize pit terrier, and then two hours later, surreptitiously brought him back?"

My friend, Sherlock Holmes, fixed me with his reproachful gaze, but otherwise ignored my unfortunate outburst. "Now, then, Lord Farthington," said he to his prospective client, "if you would be so good as to provide us with the particulars of this case."

Lord Desmond Farthington shifted his stout form uncomfortably upon his chair in our London flat, an aristocratic pout setting his lips. "Very well, then. As I said, it was yesterday that this occurred. I had returned home unexpectedly early from Parliament, which had recessed due to an unfortunate incident of food poisoning at the Carlton Club. Dreadful mess, that was! At any rate, when I went out to the kennels behind my home to see Apollo, I discovered him missing."

"And you are quite sure the animal had not merely wandered off?" inquired Holmes.

"Yes, quite sure. The kennel gate was still secured, as was the gate to the yard itself."

"I see," said Holmes. "And you questioned the servants?"

"Yes, straight away," replied Farthington. "But they swore they knew nothing of the dog's disappearance."

I jotted these facts down carefully, and could not refrain from asking, "And you believe your servants?"

Lord Farthington nodded resolutely. "Yes, Dr. Watson, I do. At least insofar as this matter is concerned. I decided that I should notify the police, but as I was feeling a bit ill myself, I chose to lie down briefly until I could regain my strength. When I arose some two hours later, I happened quite by accident to look down from my bedroom window on the second floor. I have a good view of the kennel from there, better than on the ground floor, actually, due to the shrubbery. And what did I see but Apollo, being taken back to his kennel by two criminal types. They placed him back inside and secured the latch, then stole silently away."

"My word!" I exclaimed. "Did you not cry out to them . . . challenge them in some way?"

"Believe me, Dr. Watson, I started to. I wanted to. But something in their look and manner caused the words to freeze in my throat."

"But," Sherlock Holmes interjected, "you did eventually report what you saw to the police?"

"Oh, my, yes, Mr. Holmes," snapped Lord Farthington. "But they looked at me as if I was quite daft. After all, what proof had I of any crime? All that I had witnessed, assuming it was not merely some dispeptic hallucination, was my dog being returned, not being stolen. Yet I am as sure as I can be that some nefarious deed has been done."

Holmes nodded in agreement and steepled his fingers together before his brooding features. "If hallucination it were, then there would seem to be a plague of such illusions. I have this very morning read two newspaper accounts of similar 'thefts' where the stolen items were promptly and mysteriously returned."

"My word, Holmes," said I. "What can it mean?"

Holmes snapped to his feet and made for the door, pausing to gather up his cloak and cap. "It means, my good fellow, that we must accompany Lord Farthington to his home at once. There is villainous work afoot, and there may be answers to be found at the scene of the crime . . . !"

Lord Farthington's private carriage was more than large enough to accommodate the three of us as we crossed town to his residence in the West End. The afternoon light was jaundiced, but bright enough to see by.

Farthington himself led us on a brief tour of the house and grounds, allowing Holmes a chance to see with his own eyes the view from the upper bedroom. Holmes, however, was clearly more interested in a closer inspection of the kennel itself, and hurried us along to that end. Once there, he carefully examined the kennel gate, the locks, the walkways, the high fences surrounding the property, his eaglelike gaze scouring everything and anything for clues.

All the while, Lord Farthington's prize pit terrier, Apollo, growled and barked menacingly, watching every move. Holmes's gaze fell upon the dog now, a sharp and curious look.

"Tell me, Lord Farthington," said he, "is this the animal's usual behavior around strangers?"

"Oh, yes. Even the servants have to be careful. I usually feed him myself."

"Yet he allowed these two criminal types to take him away and bring him back with scarcely a whimper?"

Farthington stroked his chins. "Oh my, yes. I see your point! How strange! He actually seemed quite docile when they returned him."

"Are you suggesting," said I to Holmes, "that the dog was taken by someone he knew?"

"That is certainly one possibility," Sherlock Holmes replied. "But it is equally likely they merely threw a small chunk of sedative-laced meat into the kennel to calm him. Lord Farthington—who has been out here since yesterday?"

"Why, only myself. I expressly forbade the servants to muck about out here, lest they disturb anything."

"A wise man," Holmes commended him. "Now, there has been no rain since yesterday morning, and I see by the size and appearance of your own boots that you have stayed with the stone path in your comings and goings. Therefore these two other sets of footprints that have strayed across the dirt near the kennel must belong to the men you saw."

"Then I wasn't imagining things," said Lord Farthington.

"I hardly think so," said Holmes, who now was stooping closer to examine one of the sets of prints. His normally stoic features suddenly burned with curiosity and barely contained excitement. "Watson—have a look at this!"

Kneeling beside him, I did indeed look, but failed to see anything remarkable. My quizzical expression seemed to amuse him.

Dropping his voice to a whisper, he explained, "Poor Watson, I could not expect you to know this, but only two days ago, Inspector Lestrade was bragging to me about a case he had solved by matching an unusual bootprint to a man. He was quite proud of his detective work, and felt certain the man will be convicted of the crime."

"I fear I am still in the dark, Holmes," said I.

"Perhaps little more than I," he replied cryptically. "See here—this print of the right boot—the unusual cut across the sole, and this U-shaped gash here. And there, on the left boot's sole, see how the corner of the heel has been broken away and a small nail protrudes. I daresay there is not another pair of boots in England that could match this."

"You mean to say they will be easy to find . . .?"

"Quite so, for I have already seen them! They are the very boots the good Inspector Lestrade so immodestly showed me two days ago. Boots that are at this very moment secured in the evidence locker at Scotland Yard, where they have been for the past week!"

"But, Holmes—" I protested "—surely that's impossible!"

"At last, a worthy challenge," muttered Holmes. "Well, Hullo, what's this?"

Holmes pulled out a pencil and used the point to pry loose a tiny object buried within the dirt of a bootprint. He held it up and I could see that it was a matchstick, broken in two places so that it looked something like the letter "Z". "Ah, Watson, this will help. There is a petty criminal I have observed who breaks his matches in just this way. His name is Eddie Mangles, and I believe I know where we may find him."

"What is it?" Lord Farthington blustered. "Have you found something—?"

"Indeed we have, sir," Holmes assured him. "And I fear there is much more to this matter than either of us suspected. But I promise you we shall get to the bottom of it, and soon!"

Not wishing to involve Lord Farthington or his driver in what could become a dangerous, or at the very least, tedious, situation, Holmes and I took leave of the residence by means of a hired cab. Night had nearly fallen as we reached our destination, a three-story structure on Broad Street whose signboard proclaimed it to be the Preening Peacock Inn.

"I've heard stories about this place, Holmes," said I. "I fear it is not an entirely reputable establishment."

"Your fears are well-founded," Sherlock Holmes replied. "The tavern on the ground floor has become a gathering spot for quite a number of London's better-class criminals and confidence men, and the women maintaining rooms on the upper floors play hostess to frequent and diverse guests, some of whom are gentlemen who should know better."

"Tsk, tsk. And you think Eddie Mangles frequents this place?"

Holmes was stepping down from the cab behind me and reaching for coins to pay the cabbie. "Indeed he does, and I feel certain he is implicated in this mystery. Wait, Watson, look! I believe that is he there—!"

Holmes's tone was imperative even though his voice was low, and I immediately glanced in the direction he indicated. Someone was indeed emerging from a side entrance of the Preening Peacock, stepping into the alley which ran alongside the building. Though the light was poor, I could distinctly see three men, two of whom were supporting a stretcher between them. Some burdensome object upon that stretcher lay covered with a sheet.

"My word, Holmes!" I whispered. "Is that a body?"

"If not, it bears a strong resemblance to one."

Holmes held up his hand for the cabbie's patience, his intent gaze still fixed upon the three men and their burden. We watched as the stretcher was swiftly loaded into the back of some sort of trademan's wagon parked in the alley. Two of the men got inside, while the third took the wagon's seat and reins and promptly drove off.

Holmes held open the door of our own conveyance. "Quickly, Watson—we must follow them. Driver—keep that wagon in sight!"

The cabbie did his job well, and we soon found ourselves on a street near the East End docks, facing what appeared to be an abandoned warehouse. Holmes had the cabbie let us out at the end of the block, then paid the man and sent him on his way, lest the presence of the cab attract attention.

Ahead of us, we could see the tradesman's wagon, and the men carrying the stretcher into the warehouse. A flickering light from within ebbed out, then disappeared as the door closed once more. We took a vantage point behind a stack of crates in the alley across from the building and began to watch, and wait. And wait, and watch. I swear, this aspect of Holmes's profession has never appealed to me greatly.

Nearly an hour passed, and even Holmes was beginning to twitch with impatience. "Watson, I say let's chance it. If we can find a window open—"

Scarcely were the words past his lips, when suddenly the warehouse door flew open and out came the two men with the stretcher, which they swiftly loaded back in the trades-man's wagon once more. Then, unexpectedly, the third man, aided by a new confederate, emerged from the warehouse carrying a *second* stretcher, which also gave every indication of supporting a human body beneath its sheetlike covering. This stretcher was hastily put aboard an enclosed carriage, and then both vehicles drove off at a brisk pace, going in opposite directions!

"Which one do we follow, Holmes?"

"Neither, Watson. Both would be lost from sight long before we could find a cab. Besides, I think the answers we seek may be found within that building."

We crossed the street warily, approaching the warehouse door. Holmes and I tried to peer in through several windows, but they appeared to have been painted over on the inside with thick black paint. There was nothing left to do but to go inside.

Thankfully, the hinges were quiet as we opened the door and slipped inside. Again, we could see the flickering light we had observed before, though we could not see the source of it. It seemed to emanate around several partitions that were part of the structure.

The outermost portion of the warehouse was exactly what one would expect for an abandoned building. A few dust-laden crates and other odds and ends were scattered about the place. I am quite sure my friend Sherlock Holmes could perceive much more than I about the place, but to me it looked quite ordinary. Except, of course, for that eerie light that came from beyond the partitions, beckoning us on, like moths to the flame. I could only hope the results would not be as deadly.

Holmes led the way, cautious as he should be, and yet impelled by a weird eagerness and curiosity. As we rounded the corner of the first partition, we heard a growling sound that was at first familiar yet it became strange as we realized that it was not a single voice, but a chorus.

"Well, well," said Holmes, warily approaching the row of six wire cages which had been neatly aligned along the partition wall. "It would appear that Apollo is not as rare a hound as we thought."

"My word!" said I. For there before us, staring intently and growling at us, were six identical pit terriers, all as much like Lord Farthington's hound as if they had sprung from the same litter. "Do you think, Holmes, that Farthington's dog has been replaced by one of these lookalikes?"

Holmes smiled strangely, contemplatively. "No, Watson. I daresay Lord Farthington has his own true Apollo back."

"Then what of these fakes . . . ?"

"Fakes may be too harsh a word," replied Holmes, studying the animals intently. "But whatever the answer, I think it must lie beyond the next partition."

Screwing up our courage, we advanced farther into the spacious warehouse. Rounding the second partition brought us face to face with the most bizarre sight I think I may have ever seen.

It looked like a nightmare vision of the kind of laboratory equipment of which Holmes himself was so fond, enlarged to a giant's scale and made strange beyond belief. There were rows upon rows of something resembling enormous bell jars, containing geometric arrangements of metallic plates, aglow with amber light. A huge control panel with dials and levers seemed to be connected to them and other devices with a much heavier version of telegraph wire, or perhaps something akin to the power cables found in the new Swan and Edison electrical system.

Suspended from the ceiling were three large crystalline cylinders, filled with hazy gases and mirrored at both ends. They seemed to be focused upon a small three-sided stage whose walls and flooring were starkly painted with grid lines spaced one inch apart. An identical stage stood a short distance away, facing another set of crystalline cylinders, and all was connected to the control panel by a myriad of wires and cables.

"I swear, it looks like the devil's own laboratory," I ventured. "What on earth could be powering such outlandish equipment?"

"A better question, Watson, might well be, 'What *in* the earth?' " Holmes strode purposefully toward one side of the huge warehouse, where the flooring had been torn away.

Massive cables from the control panel stretched down into a pit dug deep into the ground beneath the warehouse, so deep that I could not make out the bottom. I thought I could hear the faint hissing of steam cylinders far, far below us, but I could not be certain.

"What do you make of this, Holmes?"

"Perhaps some form of geothermal energy, like tapping into a hot spring. But I must confess, I do not fully understand the method employed."

A strange voice came sharply from behind us at that moment. "Actually, sir, you are doing quite well. Far better than most of your contemporaries, I daresay."

Holmes whirled with a start, I a bit more slowly. Facing us stood half a dozen men with various weapons drawn, tough looking hooligans who presented a sharp contrast with the well-dressed man who appeared to lead them. A bit stout, he was wearing a bowler hat that looked a few sizes too small for his curly-haired head. Wire-rimmed spectacles perched on his nose, and his bushy mustache and beard nearly hid his ruddy-lipped mouth.

"I suppose," the man continued, "that even *uninvited* guests deserve an introduction, especially when they are the distinguished Mr. Sherlock Holmes and Dr. Watson. . . ."

Holmes gave a nod of acknowledgment. "And you, sir?"

"Sylvester Rosewarne, Professor of Physics and practitioner of various experimental disciplines, and, I might add, your captor."

Holmes seemed to ignore the implied threat, looking with admiration at the equipment beyond. "And, I presume, you are the inventor of this truly marvelous device."

Professor Rosewarne's chest swelled with pride. "Ah, you like it, do you? I thought you might. I wonder, though, if you fully comprehend what it is."

"I would not pretend to know its inmost workings," Holmes replied, "but I would deduce that it is for the express purpose of duplicating matter. Specifically, it makes exact copies of *things,* like a workman's boots, or a gentleman's pit terrier."

"You can't be serious, Holmes," I protested.

"Yes, quite," said Holmes.

"And quite correct, as well," Rosewarne stated. "The hounds are an obvious guess, but how did you know about the boots?"

"While at Lord Farthington's, I saw fresh tracks from a pair of boots that I know the police have had locked up for a week."

"What!" Professor Rosewarne went ramrod straight and turned on the hooligan standing nearest him on the left. "Ross—did I not tell you to dispose of all the duplicate boots once we had finished testing the device?"

The one identified as Ross cringed and shifted his beady-eyed gaze uncomfortably back and forth. "I did, sir. I did!"

"How?"

Ross cowered like a whipped dog. "Well . . . I gave a pair to me mate, Eddie Mangles, and the rest . . . the rest I sold to the secondhand clothing store 'round the corner."

"There goes Lestrade's case," Holmes said with a chuckle.

"We shall discuss your impropriety later, Ross." Professor Rosewarne now turned to face Sherlock Holmes with a look that was coy but no less menacing. "Now then, lest I forget my manners, I see that we have but one chair for our unexpected guests. I shall remedy that and at the same time provide the renowned Mr. Holmes with a demonstration. Ross—bring that chair to the target grid!"

"Yes, sir!" Ross scurried over to fetch the chair. It was wooden, plain and solid, hardly fine furniture, but serviceable. Ross carried it to the first of the two three-sided stages and placed it squarely in the center of the platform.

Still under the threat of the hooligans' drawn weapons, Holmes and I could do naught but watch in helpless fascination as Professor Rosewarne stepped over to the strange looking control panel and began throwing switches, turning dials, and adjusting levers. From somewhere deep in the pit behind us, the rhythmic hissing of steam pistons quickened and rose in volume.

With his pudgy body and slender limbs, Rosewarne looked incongruously froglike as he danced before his panel, manipulating controls. But then, as a droning hum began to grow ever louder, our attention was drawn to the gas-filled cylinders hanging above. It appeared that raw electrical power was being fed to the devices, for brilliant arcing began to crawl along the outer surfaces of the cylinders, like phosphorescent serpents in a frenzied rush from one end to the other. This seemed to cause a reaction within the gas-filled cylinders, making each one glow with a different hue.

Beams of radiant energy now flashed out through apertures in the mirrored surfaces fronting the cylinders, beams which converged in an intense spotlight bathing the chair as it stood upon the gridded platform. I had the fleeting impression that the light was so bright I could actually see through the chair, its inner structure revealed.

An instant later, the second set of gas-filled cylinders began to behave in much the same way, though I thought I detected a more resonant sound to the hum they produced. Their commingled beams fell upon the empty three-sided stage with such a fearsome glare of light that I had to blink and squint into it to keep from being dazzled.

A moment later, the droning sounds abated and the eerie light of the gas-filled cylinders was quenched. My eyes adjusted, and to my astonishment, a chair now stood upon the second stage, exactly like the chair which had been placed upon the first stage.

"Wonder of wonders . . ." I exhaled.

"Impressive," said Sherlock Holmes. "Quite impressive."

"And quite functional," said Rosewarne. "At least, it will be once I've stabilized its molecular structure."

The professor threw a switch on the control panel which caused a bright green beam to shine down upon the chair from some manner of heavily shielded box hanging directly above the second stage. The wood of the chair seemed to sparkle for a moment, and then the green beam was extinguished.

Rosewarne's henchmen now brought the original chair and its duplicate over to us, forced us down upon the seats, and proceeded to roughly tie us up, lashing us securely to the chairs. All the while, the professor paced about us with increasing agitation.

Holmes asked him, "I suppose you intend to sell the duplicates of Farthington's dog to other gentlemen dog fanciers?"

"Of course. Prize pit terriers fetch a pretty penny if you know where to sell them, with no questions asked. I need more money for my experiments. A great deal more. Lord knows, the British government is not forthcoming with grants for what it considers crackpot ideas."

Holmes arched an eyebrow in that annoyingly condescending look of his. "Would it not be simpler to merely duplicate gold coins or ingots?"

The professor stopped directly before Holmes with a haughty look. "Simpler? *Simpler?* Oh, my my, yes, I daresay it would be a great deal simpler, indeed. There is only one *tiny* little problem, my dear Mr. Holmes. The bloody thing won't work on gold, or anything *else* with an atomic weight above 186.22."

"Really?"

"Really!"

"Hmmm . . ." mused Holmes. "Why do you suppose that is?"

"Why? *Why?*" The color rose in Rosewarne's cheeks. "Well, now. I rather think that if we knew the answer to that, then perhaps it wouldn't be a *problem,* now would it!"

"I suppose not."

Rosewarne hastily consulted his pocket watch. "Now then, Mr. Holmes, much as I would enjoy continuing this theoretical tête-à-tête with you, I have urgent and pressing business. So, I hope you will forgive our taking leave of you. We should be back by morning, and then we can decide how best to deal with the two of you."

"I would offer to accompany you," Holmes coyly suggested, "but I fear the good doctor and I are a bit tied up at the moment."

Professor Rosewarne harrumphed petulantly, then turned and headed for the door, motioning for his men to follow. In a few moments they were gone, and the warehouse-turned-laboratory was disturbingly silent once more.

After a brief moment of futile struggle, I asked, "What are we to do, Holmes?"

"Never fear, Watson. This is but a momentary setback. But we must hurry if we are to thwart their evil scheme."

"You know, then, what they are up to?"

"I know part of it. To learn more, I must get free and investigate." He seemed to be listening intently. "There, I think they are far enough away by now."

I watched as Holmes began to violently wrench his entire body upward in a series of spasmodic jerks, twisting slightly to his left each time. Each time, the chair upon which he was lashed rose off the floor briefly, coming to rest again an inch or so from where it had been. Within a matter of several minutes, he had managed to propel his chair around in an arc, so that we were now seated back to back. Immediately, his long, dextrous fingers began to work on the ropes binding my own wrists, with a speed and skill that would have put a fishing boat's net-rigger to shame.

Though working blind, as it were, he succeeded in untying my wrists within a few minutes. Once my hands were free, I was able to release the rest of the ropes restraining me, and then work on freeing Holmes. Moments later, we were both standing.

"Now," said Holmes, rubbing the rope marks on his wrists, "to the task at hand. We can only hope that some shred of evidence has been left behind in their haste."

He immediately began scouring the area around the various pieces of equipment, the control panel, even the strange energy pit itself. Next he began to check the three-sided stage upon which we had seen the original chair placed for duplication. Down upon all fours, he searched every inch of the platform, and every crack and crevice surrounding it. Suddenly, he froze, staring hard. Then his fingers pried some tiny object loose from its resting place between two floor boards, and Holmes abruptly leaped to his feet.

"Well, Watson, I think we have the clue we need," he announced solemnly. "But it does not answer all our questions."

"You've found a trinket?" I queried.

Holmes held the small, shiny object aloft. "It's no mere trinket, Watson. It is a gold watch fob, engraved with the emblem of the British Railroad Owners Society. It is a highly exclusive club whose membership is limited to the principal stockholder of each of the major railroad companies operating in England."

I fear my puzzled look only exasperated Holmes further. "And . . . ?"

"Don't you see? This is not merely a stolen object. It was somehow knocked loose from the unconscious man that we ourselves saw carried in here, and then back out again."

"My word!" I gasped, as the significance of it all dawned on me. "Do you mean to say that the *second* body we saw carried out upon that other stretcher was in fact a duplicate of the first man?"

"Precisely," said Holmes. "Which can only mean that they kidnapped some unsuspecting railroad owner from his recreational den of iniquity and brought him here to create a duplicate copy. I assume that their intent is to return the real gentleman, so that no one is any the wiser, and to keep the copy to aid them in their nefarious plan."

"How dastardly! But, my God, Holmes—there must be at least thirteen or fourteen men who could fit that description."

"About a dozen that are presently in England," he replied. "And facing the lack of any other hard evidence to reveal their plan, the only thing we can do is visit the home of each of these men to see which one is missing his fob, and question him to determine what shipment or event might be the target of these men."

"But that could take all night," I protested. "Perhaps days, even."

"Precisely, Watson. And judging from the urgency in Professor Rosewarne's words, we must conclude there is precious little time to waste."

I picked up my chair, and was considering heaving it into the control panel. "This device is diabolical!"

Holmes quickly stayed my hand. "Yes, in a way it is. But it may yet be our salvation. Now this is what I want you to do. . . ."

What happened next in that strange warehouse turned laboratory must surely be the most bizarre event I have ever witnessed. I have long believed Holmes to be possessed of an eidetic memory, and he once again demonstrated his skills of observation by working the dials and switches of Professor Rosewarne's device exactly as he had seen the Professor manipulate them earlier, pausing only to make a few adjustments he believed necessary.

As the grotesque machinery began to power up, with the attendant hissing of the steam pistons ebbing up from below and the eerie droning hum growing in volume with each passing second, Holmes placed my trembling hands upon two levers sticking out from the control panel, then quickly sprang to the center of the first three-sided stage and drew himself up, ready to face the demons of Hades itself, if need be.

"I have allowed for the difference in mass between myself and the chair, Watson, but this is still a gamble." Holmes's gaze shot to the cylinders pointing down at him from above, gauging the intensity of the electrical discharges crawling over them. As the unknown gases within them began to glow, he shouted, "Now, Watson—throw the levers!"

I did as instructed, with some trepidation, then blinked as the beams of radiant energy flashed out upon Holmes with blinding intensity. His clothing, his body, even the very bones beneath his flesh seemed to turn incandescent.

Then, as before, the second set of gas cylinders fired up, bathing the empty second stage with their intense glow. After a moment that seemed to last an eternity, I heard Holmes's shout above the drone.

"Cease, Watson!"

I immediately pulled back on the levers, and as the glow faded, I was startled to see Sherlock Holmes standing not only upon the first stage, but now the second stage as well. The duplicate Holmes glanced over briefly at the first, then sprang from the stage and approached me. I must confess, I backed away a bit, more in awe than fear.

"I'll take over now, Watson," said the second Holmes, reaching for the controls I had just released. "If I must be in a dozen places at once to solve this case, then by God, I shall be!"

With the nodding approval of the original, the second Sherlock Holmes proceeded to repeat the process in which I had just participated. More droning hums, more blinding flashes. Moments later, a *third* Sherlock Holmes appeared, leaping off the platform to join the second, who continued to throw the levers of the diabolical machine back and forth, again and again. *Hiss, Hum, Flash! Hiss, Hum, Flash!* My mind began to reel under the steady assault of sounds and bright lights and the unimaginable thing that was taking place before my very eyes. How Holmes could bear it, I do not know.

When at last it was done, and the equipment was finally powered down, I blinked open my eyes, as if awakening from a bad dream. But the dream was not over. Assembled before me was a baker's dozen of Sherlock Holmeses; the original, of course, and twelve copies. I frankly could not tell one from the other.

"Come, Watson!" they chorused in unison. "We must make haste!"

I felt slightly ill and wondered what I might prescribe for myself in such a situation, but then the lot of them were off, running for the door like a small army detachment, their deerstalker caps snugged down and their Inverness capes flapping and swirling.

I chased after them for four blocks until they finally halted at a corner within sight of numerous cabs and gathered in a huddle. One of them, the original, I presume, was barking out orders to the rest. Then they immediately split up into groups of one, two, or three and hailed cabs to carry them to their respective destinations. The one remaining Holmes took me by the arm and hurried me off to the last waiting conveyance.

With a clatter of hooves, the team whisked us across town directly to Scotland Yard, where Holmes, after making a few introductory remarks to the officers and inspectors there, took up a position by the telephone. There we waited for perhaps fifteen or twenty minutes, though it seemed a good bit longer. When at last the phone rang, Holmes snatched up the earpiece and listened intently. He spoke briefly with the caller, then hung up the phone and turned to face the rest of us.

"We must rally a force and be off for Euston Station!" he announced. "The kidnapped man proved to be none other than the president of the London and North Western Railway. His keys and security passwords are now in the possession of Professor Rosewarne and his men, and in less than an hour a currency shipment from the Bank of England will arrive at Euston Station and be placed aboard a train bound for Liverpool. From there it is to be transferred to a ship bound for Dublin."

One of the Yard inspectors nodded. "Military payrolls for the troops stationed in Ireland."

"There is no time to waste, gentlemen!"

With that, Holmes and I were off once more, accompanied by a sizable contingent of the Metropolitan Police. Past Trafalgar Square, we raced up Charing Cross Road in a variety of official conveyances, crossing Oxford Street and continuing up Tottenham Court Road. A turn right and then a turn left brought us to Euston Station.

The train was already building a head of steam as we approached the platform. We could see the security men from the Bank of England approaching from the other side, carrying weighty valises and escorted by other members of the Metropolitan Police.

Watching them, too, and waiting by the train's open mail car were a half dozen railway security men. Some of them, in their ill-fitting uniforms, looked vaguely familiar. The Bank of England men had reached them and apparently exchanged passwords when the railway security men suddenly became aware of our approach. To a man, their faces blanched. They turned back to attempt concluding the exchange, reaching out to grasp the valises, but by now the bank agents were also aware of us and were resisting. A bizarre tug of war between the parties ensued, and then as we began to close in on them, the fake railway men broke and ran, leaving their prize behind in an effort to escape.

"Catch them!" someone cried, and needless to say, outnumbered as they were, all six were captured in short order.

Holmes surveyed the criminals, and all else he could see upon the platform, with an eagle eye. "Professor Rosewarne is not here. I fear, Watson, that while we have thwarted his scheme, we have let slip the master villain. . . ."

The passing of a week found us once more at Scotland Yard. Holmes felt duty bound to clear the innocent man who, arrested on the basis of Inspector Lestrade's boot print evidence, seemed otherwise likely to be convicted of a robbery Eddie Mangles had committed. Holmes determined that it was, in fact, Mangles by the depth and stride of the impressions. Lestrade made a show of gratitude for this kind assistance, but I suspect his heart was not in it.

"You have prevented a great wrong, Mr. Holmes," Lestrade said through his forced smile. "What a pity Professor Rosewarne and his miraculous equipment have eluded us."

"Through no fault of yours, I am sure," said Sherlock Holmes with equal politeness. "Rosewarne must have come back for something after Watson and I left and discovered our escape. Though he let some of his men continue with their plan, he and his other henchmen apparently dismantled the components of his device and drove them away. There were wagon tracks upon the floor of the warehouse when we returned from Euston Station. Only the steam pistons in the pit were left behind."

"At least we recovered the duplicate railway president unharmed," Lestrade said. "Have you any news of his condition, Dr. Watson?"

"He's quite fit, really," I told him. "He and his twin, as it were, have already arranged a schedule by which they alternate going to work and staying home. They seem quite pleased with it, actually."

Lestrade chuckled. "I wonder how his—their—missus feels about *that*."

"The jury is still out on that one," said I.

"But wait—" Lestrade suddenly interjected "What of your own duplicates. The twelve copies of *you,* Mr. Holmes?"

"Interestingly enough," Holmes replied, "in my great haste to apprehend Professor Rosewarne, I neglected to finish the last step in the duplication procedure, the green ray which stabilizes the duplicate's molecular structure. Without that step, each of my copies rapidly deteriorated within a few hours, leaving a dozen inexplicable and rather messy puddles scattered about London."

Lestrade rolled his eyes and sighed. "What a pity."

"Yes. Once more," I proclaimed proudly (and with more than a little relief), "there is only *one* Sherlock Holmes!"

ALIMENTARY, MY DEAR WATSON

by Lawrence Schimel

The scene was unnervingly familiar as I called upon my friend Sherlock Holmes to wish him the compliments of the season. He was lounging upon the sofa in his purple dressing gown, his pipe rack within reach upon his right, and the morning papers in a crumpled pile upon the floor where he had dropped them after a thorough study. Save for the fact that it was the day after Christmas rather than the second day past, and that the hat under examination was a sharp looking top hat rather than a seedy and worn hard-felt type, I would have thought I had stepped back into the events which I chronicled in "The Adventure of the Blue Carbuncle."

"And where, pray tell, is the goose?" I asked in a loud tone as I entered the room, hoping my attempt at humor might alleviate my uneasiness. "You have not, once again, eaten it before my arrival, I hope."

Holmes set the lens and hat upon a wooden chair beside the sofa and smiled at me warmly. "My dear fellow, it is rabbit this time, rather than the goose of the case you allude to. Mrs. Hudson is preparing it as we speak. Meanwhile, tell me what you can deduce from this."

He offered me his lens, and I took the hat from where it hung upon the back of chair. I recalled all that Holmes had been able to deduce of Henry Baker's identity and situation from that hat and tried my best to extrapolate similarly from the details I noticed upon the one I held. It was an ordinary, if rather large, top hat in all regards, save for a slip of paper tucked under the brim which declared: "IN THIS SIZE 10/6," and a small stain where a splash of tea had fallen against it. I pondered these facts, and at last declared, "He was not a very careful man, nor overly concerned with his appearance. He has bought himself a very fashionable hat, yet one which does not fit him properly and dips down over his eyes. Nor, having spilled tea upon his own hat, should he have then ventured forth unconcerned with such a prominent stain upon the velvet had he cared about the image he presented to the world. Unless, of course, there was an afternoon struggle which resulted in the stain, and in his haste to flee, the man simply donned his stained hat. Have we a crime to solve this time, or is this a whimsical inquiry?" I replaced the hat and lens upon the chair and waited for Holmes's judgment of my surmises.

"Very good, Watson. You are losing your timidity in drawing inferences. However, one can also tell that the man is short in stature, since the angle of the stain indicates that the hat was being worn at the time it was acquired, rather than lying besides him upon the table or a chair waiting to be spilled upon. Therefore, your conclusion that a struggle occurred is most probable. Only, the man did not retrieve his hat when he fled, since we have it before us. It was found in the residence of one Mr. Charles Dodgson, who is presently missing. Will you accompany me on a visit to his residence this afternoon?"

I nodded my assent.

"Good, then sit and share a bit of rabbit before we go. I hear Mrs. Hudson upon the stair."

"The police declared that insufficient time had passed to warrant an investigation," Holmes informed me as we walked to Dodgson's apartments, "but on the implorings of his landlady, Mrs. Bugle, and for the sake and safety of his young niece, Alice, who lived with him, I consented. I must confess, I was intrigued by the puzzle she presented: Though he had had no callers, she found the unusual hat, which we have already examined, in his study, a large crack in the looking glass, though she heard no sound of either a struggle or of glass breaking, and the white rabbit of which we par-

took just recently, lying on the floor of the study, its neck
wrung."

We had arrived at Dodgson's apartments, and I mulled the
information Holmes had given me as Mrs. Bugle admitted us
and led us up to the study, where she introduced us to
Dodgson's niece, Alice. As is quite common for young girls,
she had set up a tea party for some imaginary friends of
hers, with whom she had been conversing as we entered.
She stroked a large gray cat, who sat in her lap.

"That's a handsome watch you've got," Holmes remarked
to the girl. "Was it your uncle's?"

The girl pulled it out of her pocket to display. "My uncle's? No, it belonged to the March Hare."

As if a premonition, my stomach began to growl at the
mention of the rabbit, and I could not help wondering if we
had just eaten the girl's favorite pet.

"You realize that it is set fifteen minutes ahead of the
hour," Holmes continued, while looking about the table
where the tea service was set.

"Yes," the girl answered, "he was always late, and thus
had set his watch ahead in an attempt to arrive at the proper
time."

"Did the March Hare also wear this?" Holmes asked,
showing her the hat Mrs. Bugle had brought to him.

"Aha!" she said, when she saw it. "So that's where his hat
disappeared to. That belongs to the Mad Hatter. He's been
frantic over it since yesterday afternoon, when he left it
here. It's his only hat."

"He came to tea with you?"

"It's the only way to get him to come, you understand,
and he had to come, so they could help me. They had to
bring it with them."

"It?" asked Holmes, pointing to a little bottle that rested
on the table. A paper label round its neck bore the words
"DRINK ME" in large letters. The girl nodded.

"And what would this do?" Holmes inquired.

"It makes one smaller."

Holmes did not bat an eye at this outlandish remark. "Is
there an antidote?"

"There is," the girl replied, and pointed to a cake in a
glass box beneath the table. Bending closer to observe it further, I noticed it bore the words, "EAT ME" written upon it
in currants.

"I see," said Holmes, who proceeded to dip his finger into the bottle and taste thereof. He shrunk noticeably, around two or three inches, and all his clothing accordingly.

"Curiouser and curiouser," Holmes declared after the transformation had taken place. He looked thoughtful a moment, considering the finger he had just tasted, then continued, "It has a sort of mixed flavor of cherry tart, custard, pineapple, roast turkey, and toffee."

"And also hot buttered toast."

"Yes," Holmes agreed, "and also hot buttered toast. And why did the March Hare and the Mad Hatter need to bring it to you?"

The girl looked between Holmes and myself, her lower lip trembling. Trustingly, she decided to place her confidence in Holmes. Looking back to him, she began, "At night he would climb into bed with me and touch me and—" She broke down into such a fit of crying that she was soon surrounded by a puddle of tears. I cannot explain it, since she must have cried more water than her body could possibly have contained to produce such a puddle. But Holmes and I both witnessed it.

I wanted to reach out and comfort the child, but, especially in view of the circumstances for her tears, forbore. Holmes steered the discussion onto a different matter. "That's a lovely cat you have."

"Dinah?" The girl blew her nose delicately on the sleeve of her dress and patted at her eyes to dry her tears. "Why, yes, she is. Such a capital one for catching mice, and oh, I wish you could see her after the birds! Why, she'll eat a little bird as soon as look at it!"

"Or a man," Holmes asked, "shrunk down to the size of a mouse?"

Dinah gave a large smile, and slowly vanished, beginning with the end of her tail and ending with her grin, which remained some time after the rest of her had disappeared.

Holmes took these unusual occurrences in much calmer stride than myself. "You might," he even ventured to remark, when we were back at Baker Street, "write in your notes that he died of consumption, if you're willing to interpret the term loosely." He smiled, turned away from me, and began an alchemical distillation of the contents of that mysterious cake, in order to determine how much he should consume to return him to his proper height. I saw no evidence that his humor was an attempt to alleviate uneasiness, as my own earlier attempts had been. I was amazed at his lack of ponderings or attempts to explain the many inexplicable events we had witnessed that day. Justice had been done in the girl's favor, he had declared, and was content, evidently, to let the case rest, solved if unexplainable.

I shook my head and stared at his back a moment while he worked. "At this rate," I mused as I began to prepare my notes, "he'll have me believe in no less than six impossible things before breakfast!"

THE FUTURE ENGINE

by Byron Tetrick

Although my reputation as the chronicler of Sherlock Holmes's many adventures has brought me my own modest amount of fame, it has also carried a burdensome responsibility that becomes no less tedious with the passage of time. I speak not of the task of recording the minutiae of details in conversation and locale, the descriptive exposition, or of the underlying motivations of the crimes. No, if Sherlock Holmes has taught me anything, it is an appreciation of the trifles that make up the nature of our lives.

Nor do I complain of the dangers that perpetually seem to stalk Sherlock and me, sometimes one step ahead or one behind, but all too often joining us in a military lockstep waiting for us to make a miscalculation. Actually, I relish that part—God forbid my dear wife should hear me say this. My fellow veterans of the Afghan War and those who have waged the farflung battles of our expanding British Empire know of what I speak.

It is not even seeing the pale underbelly of the human race laid bare to me as, time after time, Sherlock Holmes has exposed the cruelty and greed that precipitates so many of the crimes he has investigated. As a doctor, I well know that the human condition contains good and evil, that the living body sustains the miracle and wonder of life even while cancers gnaw from within.

No, my readers, the burden—and my agony—lies in the

fact that I have not been completely forthright. Astute readers may recall that many years passed between the occurrence and the publication of the case of the Speckled Band—a delay necessitated by a promise of secrecy. Often I have made reference to other cases that, for one reason or another, were locked away. But always—call it a gentleman's agreement—there was the understanding that eventually, as the circumstances warranted, all would be told. In fact, Sherlock Holmes has for some time, while not outright asking me to do so, made it known that he desired that I faithfully record our adventures. Certainly he did not invite me along to draw upon my powers of deductive reasoning!

But here I sit, pen in hand, knowing that what I am going to write will never be seen by those who have so faithfully followed our adventures; that a case so startling and momentous in its consequences, and one in which, but for the skills of Sherlock Holmes, the future of the English people would have been disastrously affected, will be put away, and known but by the few of us who participated.

Two seemingly unconnected conversations, coincidentally occurring on the eve of the beginning of the case, set the pattern that would later bear great influence on what was to follow. I had stopped at Baker Street to pick up Sherlock Holmes for dinner at Simpson's, where Major-general Harold Thompson, who had been my commanding officer in Afghanistan, would be joining us. My wife had been feeling poorly as of late and was visiting family at the shore, leaving me to my practice by day and frequent dinners with my old friend at night. In his sitting room, Holmes had been in a rather foul mood and had not bothered to offer me a usual whiskey and soda. I shook off the chilly October drizzle from my topcoat, warming myself by the fire while I waited for him to dress himself in like manner for the relatively long ride to the Strand.

"Watson," said he, as we sat back in the cab of the landau, "I have long believed that Victorian England represents the culmination in achievement of the human race. As a people, we have tamed the continents, established good order under British laws, and begun the industrialization of the world. It would seem that all the pieces are in place, and we need only complete the proper organizing—which is what we English do best, I might add—and the British Empire should be on the cusp of a golden age."

"I quite agree," I said, and tried to add a comment myself, but it fell on deaf ears as Holmes excitedly continued.

"Then what is happening to our economy? I spent a good part of the afternoon with my banker, and all of my investments have declined, in some instances, drastically so."

And now, the cause of his ill humor immediately became evident as Holmes began a discourse on the pitiful state of the British economy: a deep depression in agricultural prices; trade associations cornering markets and manipulating prices; shortages of resources as pricing was assumed more and more by administrators and not the free market. Holmes had seemed to acquire more knowledge of economics in one afternoon than in all his previous years, for I have never known him to show much interest in money.

"It is almost as if some malefactor is trying to ruin me financially," he said, finally coming to a close.

I laughed. "Come, come, Holmes, you can't be serious. Manipulating markets of the empire just to ruin you? You give your enemies too much credit. My own small portfolio isn't doing that well either."

"Have *all* of your investments declined?"

"Of course not, not all," I answered.

"Mine have."

Simpson's-in-the Strand has long been a favorite of ours, and the evening soon changed moods as quickly and graciously as a forgiving wife. Holmes and General Thompson hit it off quite well, finding innumerable common interests, not the least of which was swordsmanship. Holmes seemed to have forgotten about his finances. Dinner was a superb mixed grill of wild game, served with rice from the Far East, and more than a couple of bottles of Tokay.

After dinner, sitting at a heavily carved table with comfortable leather chairs, the general laughed heartily at a witty comment of Holmes's and then said, "Before we go any further, Mr. Holmes, please dispense with calling me General. I think we know each other well enough by now. Call me Harry."

"General," said Holmes, "I appreciate the offer. I find it not surprising that you would make it, having long since deduced your character. However, I honor your rank and your service too greatly."

This brought even greater laughter from General Thompson. "Deduced that, did you! I had quite forgotten that you are a detective by trade. What else have you *deduced* about me?"

A small smile crept across Holmes's face. The battlefield was the general's forte . . . we had just entered Holmes's.

"Oh, a few things. You arrived here in London by horseback only a few hours ago . . . perhaps from your family's estate, which is north of Manchester, say either Leeds or Bradford. You come from quite a large family—very wealthy I might add—of which you are the second-eldest son. You have been wounded at least twice in battle, although your pronounced limp is not a battle wound, but an injury you acquired in the Afghan War, nonetheless. You are a modest man for one of such heroic deeds, and you are much loved by your men—"

"Enough!" he cried. "It is all true, though I can't speak for my men. I'd accuse Watson of priming you, but he knows naught of my personal life. Explain your magic, lest I go mad."

"Elementary, sir, and quite simple." Here, Holmes paused while he lit his pipe and took several deep draws. "That you only just arrived is evident by your boots, which are still soiled, though the staff of the Langham Hotel is surely mortified that it escaped their immediate attention. There is horsehair on both insteps." Holmes leaned closer to the general's boots. "A fine Arabian, I see. Your accent puts you from Manchester, but it is the mud on your boots that pinpoints the area as either Leeds or Bradford. That you come from wealth is evident by the cut of your uniform. Her Majesty pays her general officers well, but not enough that they can afford the finest cloth and Savile Row tailors. Firstborn sons usually assume the family business, leaving ambitious brothers to seek success and honor in the military. Watching you eat, I could see the influence of a large family. Even in a well-mannered one such as yours, one must not let his attention wander lest all the food be taken, eh?" laughed Holmes.

"Your right shoulder has limited movement indicating either a deep bullet wound or a poorly healed saber cut. The black mark on your cheek is powder from a pistol that was fired point-blank into your face, but misfired. Your limp is almost a hobble, unique to those who are missing both toes. The odds of losing both in battle seem remote, thus frostbite. And where but the mountain passes of Afghanistan has the British army seen service in that type of extreme cold? Your wounds indicate that you are an officer who leads by example, fighting alongside your men.

"You wear but two medals on your chest, while yon colonel sitting three tables over is bedecked with ribbons enough to tie back the hair of all the ladies at the Lyceum. One is the Victoria Cross—England's highest honor. The other appears to be a unit badge, probably the unit you are currently commanding. Finally, you reddened and stopped me when I started talking of your modesty and the love of your men. Of all my assertions, that is the one I am most certain of."

A moment of embarrassed silence passed. I have always enjoyed Holmes's theatrical displays of deduction, but this was tops. I greatly admired both of my companions, and to see them doing so splendidly together was an unexpected pleasure. General Thompson pulled out a silver case and offered us Havanas which, of course, required several minutes of sniffing, snipping, and long savoring puffs.

Finally, the general chuckled, "Have you thought of entering military service, Holmes? Intelligence could use a man with your intellect and powers of observation."

Holmes smiled. "You do me an honor, General, but I have my hands quite full battling rogues and scallywags here in London. Besides, my habits don't exactly lend themselves to military life; do they, Watson?" Holmes looked over at me and winked.

I nodded, and laughed politely. "No, Holmes. I can't envision you following a military routine."

The general's tone turned serious as the conversation evolved into a discussion of science and the startling advancements in explosives and other weapons of war. General Thompson was privy to the latest developments; and, without divulging any secrets, he described future battlefields wrought with petrol-engined carts carrying cannons, while overhead, men in flying machines dropped explosives on the soldiers below.

"My greatest fear," said he, "is that an enemy might develop a weapon so advanced that we would be powerless to defend against it. Warfare is such a delicate balance."

Holmes had gone back to his pipe as he thoughtfully sat back and listened to the general. "You paint a vivid but bleak picture, General. A sufficiently advanced weapon in the hands of an evil genius would enable him to rule the world, would it not?"

The general nodded. "Precisely."

On that note, the hour being late, we shook hands and said our farewells. A pleasant evening, albeit troubling at its finish, but well spent, nonetheless.

Holmes suggested that I spend the night in my old room, which I gratefully accepted, sleeping late into the morning. I arose to find Holmes dressed, smoking his morning pipe, and the remains of his breakfast congealing at the side table. He seemed chipper considering his economic plight.

"Ah, Watson. There you are. Mrs. Hudson will bring your breakfast shortly. Make haste!" He handed me an embossed vellum business card. "This arrived earlier. I have a client."

That explained it. Nothing lifts Sherlock Holmes's spirits like a new case!

Holmes paced the floor, looking out the windows often as I finished breakfast. "This must be he. A fine carriage and a well-dressed gentlemen stepping out," he said, returning to his humidor and repacking his pipe.

Moments later, Mrs. Hudson led the gentleman into the sitting room.

"I am Henry Babbage. You received my message, I presume," he said looking first at me and then Holmes.

Holmes ended the confusion by stepping forward and introducing himself and then me. Taking Mr. Babbage's coat and scarf, he offered coffee, and we took seats near the fire in deference to our visitor, who appeared quite chilled. He was a portly man with graying sidewhiskers that framed a fleshy face. As Holmes had already noted, he was impeccably dressed in a fine suit, set off with silk cravat and a large diamond stickpin.

"You read my note, then?" began Mr. Babbage.

"Most assuredly," responded Holmes. "You have suffered a theft and wish me to retrieve the article. No doubt you have already informed the police, and achieving no results, you have come to me."

"That's correct. Actually, two items were stolen. Where shall I start?"

Holmes arose and poured more coffee. "At the beginning, please."

"You might recognize my name, or at least my father's—Charles . . . Charles Babbage."

"Why, of course!" I interjected. "He founded the Royal Astronomical Society. I have a fondness, a hobby if you will, for astronomy."

"Yes, that was he. My father was somewhat of an eccentric and an inventor. He spent most of his life and a goodly amount of the family's fortune on the development of a machine that would be able to make mathematical calculations at an extremely rapid rate. His initial attempt was partially funded by the Exchequer and was called a Difference Engine. Its original intent was to make error-free navigational tables, but my father kept redesigning it in an attempt to create a mighty engine capable of freeing mankind from the drudgery of solving mathematical equations.

"He was never able to perfect the Difference Engine and began work on an even more complex mathematical machine which he called the Analytical Engine. It contained two main parts. One part was to store all the mathematical variables of the problem and the results of the operation. The other, which my father called 'the mill,' the guts of the machine, was to process the quantities as they were fed into it, where they would again be sent back to storage or printed for use."

"And it was this Analytical Engine that was stolen?" asked Holmes, reaching for his pipe and packing it with tobacco.

"Yes. Over a year ago. It was taken from the warehouse where it had been in storage since my father's death over twenty years ago. It disappeared overnight."

Holmes walked over to the fire and retrieved an ember, placing it in his pipe, and remained standing while he sucked noisily to ignite the tobacco. "I assume that this Analytical Engine was never perfected?"

"No. Although my father even designed his own tools in an attempt to achieve the precision needed for all the thousands of machined parts, he was never able to complete his machine."

"Why do you want it back?" asked Holmes. "It is still of some value?"

Our visitor stood and walked over to one of the large windows and stared off into the morning fog as if pondering a weighty decision. He turned back toward us and began speaking emotionally. "My father was thought a fool. The scientific community called his Difference Engine, 'Babbage's Folly.'

"Mr. Holmes, my father was a genius! I studied his notes, which led me to other files that he had secreted away. Once perfected, his Analytical Engine would be capable of astounding—nay magical—feats. With it, one would be able to predict the outcome in advance of any series of events. One could define any problem using mathematical equations and feed it into the milling unit in order to find possible solutions. Do you see the potential? The power it could give you? You could predict the future . . . or even more significantly, you could *change* the future!"

"A Future Engine," said Holmes quietly, abstractly, obviously deep in thought.

"Exactly!" cried Babbage.

"Impossible!" I scoffed.

Both men turned and faced me. I hadn't realized that I had spoken out loud.

"Impossible, Watson?" said Holmes, frowning at me. "Let me ask you this. If the wind is from the north, in what direction will you find the fallen leaf?"

I laughed. "To the south, of course."

"And if halfway down, a gust blows suddenly from the east?"

"Why, then, it would land to the southwest. I see where you're going Holmes," I said, smiling. "But what about all the leaves in swirling winds?"

"If this Future Engine can make thousands upon thousands of calculations as our esteemed guest claims, then it could tell you where each and every one would alight, including which side was turned up," said he, returning my smile.

At this, I confess he made me doubt my initial scorn for this incredible tale. "Mr. Babbage, if I might ask, what type of mathematics is used in these calculations?"

"Not at all, Dr. Watson. It is based on the Binomial Theorem."

If Sherlock Holmes had been shot with a pistol, he could not have reacted more violently. His pipe dropped from his hands, spilling its contents on the carpet. His face, which is pale to begin with, went bloodless, and I thought he might faint. Instead, he kicked his pipe across the room, stamped out the smoldering ashes, and began to mutter in ever-increasing volume, "What a fool I've been. What a fool. I knew that my investments had been manipulated, and instead I blamed myself."

I had risen from my chair, and I grabbed his arm. "What is it, Holmes? What's wrong?"

"I'll tell you what's wrong. It's Professor Moriarty. It is he behind this theft. It is he who is trying to ruin me financially. And unless we stop him, it is he who will rule the world with the Future Engine!"

"Who is Professor Moriarty?" questioned Babbage, looking confused, and not a little taken aback by Holmes's display of anger.

"He is the Napoleon of crime. A nefarious blackguard who controls much of what is evil in this great city. He is genius, gone awry. And ... he is a former mathematics professor who as a young man wrote a treatise on the *Binomial Theorem!*"

Holmes walked over and picked up his pipe, examined it minutely, and then, as if realizing that only a clear head and cool logic would prevail, he relit his pipe and calmly began to question Babbage.

"You mentioned that two items were taken."

"Yes. Four months ago to this very day, all my father's personal files and scientific papers also disappeared."

"From your home or the warehouse?"

"From my home."

"Had you made any progress yourself on the Future Engine?"

"Some. It could tabulate to six decimal places, and I was able to compute the first thirty-two multiples of pi, but then the gears kept sticking and I could not fix it. I had not worked on it for more than a year."

"Who knew of your progress?"

"Several people. I was quite excited at first and spoke openly about it at the Royal Astronomical Society."

"Ah-h-h ... including to a tall, thin, bald-headed man with sunken eyes and a beak-like nose."

"Why, yes. He seemed quite interested ... and very knowledgeable."

"You, sir, have met the vilest criminal on the planet," said Holmes, placing his hand on Babbage's shoulder. "Come. Take me to the scene of the thefts. Time is of the essence."

Babbage hesitated. "It has been a year, and Scotland Yard *did* inspect the warehouse and my home quite thoroughly."

Holmes shook his head. "And what did they find?"

"Well ... nothing."

Holmes and I exchanged glances ... and a smile. "Quite so," said he, reaching for his coat. "Let's be off."

The warehouse was nestled among several well-located buildings and factories in the industrial section away from the Thames. The Future Engine—the new name seemed to have stuck, for even Babbage called it that now—had been located on the upper floor centered in a large, high-ceilinged hall that surprisingly was heated to a comfortable temperature. Babbage explained that this was necessary to prevent moisture from causing the many gears to stick. The room contained very little else: a drafting board, some file cabinets, a desk placed over by one of the large, well-caulked windows, and several bins full of assorted cogs and gears. The outline of the machine was clearly delineated by the shading of the wood and the residual oils accumulated over twenty years of storage.

"It was quite large, I see," noted Holmes.

"You can see what a puzzle this was to the police. It weighed more than a ton. It took my father a week to dismantle, transport, and reassemble it twenty years ago. This floor has a separate entrance and stairway from the bottom floor, which was chained and locked, and had not been tampered with."

Holmes brought out his magnifying lens and examined the area. Then he inspected the door and lock.

"May we examine the lower floor?" he asked.

"Of course," replied Babbage and led us off, explaining as we departed that the building was owned by his family, but as their fortunes declined, they had been forced to lease the space below.

The lower level was a beehive of activity. It was leased by an importer-exporter whom Babbage trusted completely, the merchant having been a tenant for a decade.

"As you can see," commented Babbage, "this place is very busy, with no chance the theft could have occurred by day. At night, my warehouse, as well as the neighboring factories, is patrolled by a security service with bonded guards. Not an hour goes by without a check."

It did not take Holmes long before he was satisfied. Stopping at a pub, Holmes expounded. "Well, we know who, what, when, and how. The question before us now is, where—"

"Excuse me, sir," interjected Babbage. "Did you say we know, how? I'm at a loss . . ."

Holmes smiled. "Sometimes I despair of the police work done by Scotland Yard. Even when they find a clue, they never place it in the context of the situation. For instance, the assumption was made that one day the machine was there, the next day it was gone. Thus it had to have disappeared that night."

"Correct," nodded Babbage.

"No. Incorrect. There were no fresh scratches—even allowing for a year's passage—near the machine's location. Yet there were several gouges in the wood that had the appearance of being twenty years old that surely dated from its original move. The Future Engine was not moved overnight; it was moved over many nights. Each evening, one of the common laborers below would conceal himself in one of the many nooks-and-crannies, climb up through the central-heating vent—I observed the coal room and furnace were on the bottom floor, and being the summer months, not in use—and thereupon, under dim candlelight, proceed to dismantle small, interior portions of the machine. He would then return before sunrise to the floor below, hide his booty, and then mingle with his coworkers as work began that morning."

"I visited the warehouse often. I saw nothing amiss," said Babbage, obviously puzzled.

"But you had ceased experimentation, had you not?"

"Yes, for quite some time," he replied.

"What you saw was the shell of your machine . . . more so every day. Until finally, it was an easy matter to dismantle the remaining structure. Most of the mass was in the gears and entrails of the machine. The thieves had only to evade the watchman once on his rounds, place the frame on a dogcart, and be off. I inspected the lock on the lower floor, and it *had* been picked before."

"I must say, Holmes, I am impressed," said Babbage, lifting his glass in a salute.

A search of Babbage's home revealed nothing further, or at least nothing that Holmes shared with us. We left Babbage at his house with arrangements to meet in two days, Holmes confident that by then he would have more information, perhaps even the location of the Future Engine. On the ride back to Baker Street, I asked him how he could be so certain.

"What do we know about the Future Engine, Watson?"

"It's large, heavy, complicated, and ... apparently, now that Moriarty has tinkered with it, capable of predicting the future, or perhaps *determining* the future," I replied.

"Oh, we know much more," said he. "It must be kept as dry as possible—no easy task in London. Thus it is probably in a warehouse much like Babbage's. We know it is here in London because Moriarty must have quick access to the financial markets and news centers to properly and timely direct his infernal machine. We can gather that he had need of advanced machining in order to correct the original deficiencies of its gears. Lastly, because it is potentially the most valuable—and dangerous—machine in the world, it is well guarded, perhaps so much so that that in itself will draw our attention to it."

Though I had my practice to attend to, I offered to aid Holmes in his efforts. He assigned me a reconnoiter of the machining and tooling shops, cautioning me to be careful. We departed, agreeing to meet in two days. I doubted whether Sherlock Holmes would sleep.

Henry Babbage was already present in Holmes's sitting room when I arrived two days hence, at precisely seven p.m. Holmes directed me to fix myself a whisky and soda. He appeared to be quite pleased with himself; so I assumed he had made good progress, which I had not, and which I reported to him after taking a long, hard swallow of my drink.

"No matter, Watson," he said, waving with his hand as if my considerable efforts had been of no consequence. "I followed a different track to the same station. It's not like Moriarty to use legitimate tradesmen in the first place. I checked in with our friends at the Yard and found out which forgers had been released from Newgate or Dartmoor prison in the last year. One in particular, Willie Stokes, had been released, found employment at a tooling shop, and later disappeared with several hundred pounds worth of equipment. It took no great effort to find him."

"He led you to my machine, then?" asked Babbage.

"No ..." replied Holmes. "But he got me in the right area. I checked with some of the leasing agencies, but could not come up with any likely locations. Then I realized that with an undertaking of this import, and considering his considerable ill-gotten wealth, Moriarty would buy his own building, the better to control access. A quick check of records located several possibilities which, at least in a very cursory manner, I inspected from inside a hansom."

Holmes retrieved his cherrywood from the rack on the sidetable and carefully went through his routine of lighting up, while we waited in suspense.

"I have found it," he said, without further delay. "It is located north of the Broad Street and Liverpool Street Stations, near Tillrey. It is a small, secluded warehouse abutting a rail line with only one street dead-ending into it. A telegraph line runs into the upper level, and guards—rather I should say, thugs—patrol diligently outside."

"And the plan, Holmes?" I asked, anxious to start the chase.

"Tomorrow at midday, Inspector Lestrade of Scotland Yard will gather his forces at the Broad Street Station." Turning to Babbage, he added, "By this time tomorrow, sir, you should see the return of your property." Turning back to me, he added with a smile, "And Moriarty will be behind bars."

"Splendid!" exclaimed Babbage, rising from his chair and going for his coat. "You will contact me when it is over, then?"

"Most assuredly," replied Holmes. Holmes and I completed our plans over a simple meal, and soon after, I excused myself.

As I put on my hat to leave, Holmes admonished me, "Your service revolver, Watson. Don't forget to bring your revolver."

The forces were assembled. Lestrade seemed as anxious as Holmes to capture Moriarty, for he, too, knew of the web of crime that centered about this evil genius. Lestrade deployed a group of officers along the rail line to approach the warehouse from the rear, while we joined the main force in the attack from the front. I doubted anyone could get through the net, so tightly was it woven with uniformed policemen.

As we raced up the street in Lestrade's police wagon, I heard Holmes utter a curse, and following his gaze, I saw that the warehouse appeared abandoned. Holmes leaped from the wagon and dashed into the building, heedless of being at the forefront, determined to find Moriarty. I raced after him, my pistol at the ready.

I found Holmes on the upper level, standing next to a rectangular-shaped, oily outline where once the Future Engine sat. Rough, fresh scratches trailed across the room to where a hoist swung slowly in the breeze from an open loft.

"Once again, I misjudged my adversary," said he, solemnly. "You may return with Lestrade. I'm going to look for clues. But do come tonight, Watson. We must make plans."

I expected a dejected Sherlock Holmes when I arrived that evening. Instead, I found him buoyant and energetic. I questioned his lighthearted mood.

"This afternoon was only a setback, not a defeat," he remarked. "Once in a while I need that to keep me sharp. It seemed so easy to locate the warehouse that I didn't complete the logical process of defining all the possibilities."

"What did you omit, old chap, that you had not already considered?"

"Why, the most elemental thing, Watson. The Future Engine! Moriarty knew in advance that I would locate the warehouse. He knew to the day, if not the hour, when I would put the puzzle together, and he planned accordingly. That was why the hoist was in position; he knows me too well. No doubt he expends much of the Future Engine's calculating capabilities for the sole purpose of defeating me—his greatest threat."

I threw up my hands in frustration. "We're helpless. If he can predict our every move, how can we hope—"

"By doing the unexpected," interjected Holmes. "By moving fast and instinctively, instead of slow and deliberately."

From below came the sound of high voices, laughter, shouts, the clatter of dozens of footsteps on the stairs. Above it all we could hear the cries of Mrs. Hudson.

"Hark!" yelled Holmes, a smile on his face. "The sound of random variables."

Tumbling into the room came the most bedraggled, motley, filthy, boisterous, uncouth collection of street urchins either side of the Thames—the Baker Street Irregulars!

They lined themselves up in some primordial pecking order through a series of shoves, curses and grunts. They all doffed their caps and stood at what one might call "attention," other than the fact that one lad scratched his rump, another his privates, and they all craned their necks, rotating 'round the room to see what to their eyes must seem a wizard's den.

The tallest lad stepped forward. " 'Ere we be, Mr. 'Olmes; 'Ow may we be of service?"

"Gather around boys. I have a job for you," said Holmes, motioning them to the small table where a large tray of crumpets and biscuits lay invitingly.

I may have blinked twice. The food disappeared.

Holmes proceeded to describe the Future Engine, going into great detail about its size, weight, and structure.

"I'm not going to tell you where to look; that's entirely up to you," said he. "I *am* going to caution you though, it will be guarded by dangerous men. So be careful. And come immediately back to me once you find something. Immediately!"

Holmes looked at the leader. "Line your boys . . . er, men up."

"Atten-shun!" His yell was followed by another shoving match, though it appeared to align the boys in the same order as before.

Going down the row, Holmes placed a half-guinea in each hand. To the last, a ragamuffin no older than seven, he placed an extra shilling, whispering, "Buy yourself a warm coat, boy. Will you do that?" A nod and a smile.

"A fiver for the one who finds it. Now scat!"

Quickly, but oh so noisily, the Baker Street Irregulars ran out of the room and disappeared into the streets of London.

I stayed but a short while longer. Holmes outlined his new plan and assigned me a few tasks, but he seemed to have his most faith in the boys, explaining that Moriarty was at his most vulnerable now, what with his hurried escape last night.

* * *

The next few days were quite busy, not only with my practice, but also in the service of Sherlock Holmes as we continued our search for the Future Engine. Our nights had gotten progressively later, and I had taken up temporary quarters in my old room.

On the fifth evening following our unsuccessful raid on the warehouse, Tom, the young leader of the Baker Street Irregulars, came bursting through the door of the apartment.

"Bobby's dead!" he cried.

"Hold on, lad," said Holmes, leading him to a chair and giving him a cup of hot tea. "Now, tell us what happened."

" 'Is throat was cut through like a slaughtered 'og, 'e was; like a bloody 'og. Then tossed in the Thames."

Poor Tom looked more like the boy he was than the leader of a gang. His eyes were red, and he struggled to show no tears.

"I'm sorry, Tom," said Holmes, placing a hand on his shoulder. "We'll catch them and see them hanged. Young Bobby must have stumbled onto the Future Engine. Had he reported anything?"

" 'E was assigned the warehouses and buildings south of the river, and at our last meeting 'e said 'e 'ad worked 'is way from the Wapping Wharf to almost Waterloo Bridge."

"Then it's off to Dockland and Waterloo Bridge," said Holmes, rising from his chair. "It must be near."

"What of Lestrade and the police," I interjected.

"No time, Watson. Remember, we must act quickly now." Walking briskly to his desk, he scribbled a note and handed it to Tom. "Tom, you deliver this to Scotland Yard and then gather the Irregulars and meet us at Waterloo Bridge. I expect to have another errand for you."

As the lad rushed off, Holmes turned to me and said vehemently, "A deed most foul, Watson. A cowardly crime that shall not go unpunished. I now make a vow: I shall not rest until that blight on the earth, that child killer, Moriarty, has been removed from the realm of the living and dispatched to the everlasting torments of hell!"

Angrily, his hands shaking, he inspected the chambers of his pistol which he then placed in his coat.

"Let us see if I can honor my vow this very night, Watson!"

* * *

Holmes had the hansom drop us across the river several streets from the bridge, and under cover of darkness and a developing shroud of fog, we began our search. It seemed an impossible task as we entered an area of darkened warehouses, slop shops, and boarding houses. The only lights—there were no gaslights—came from the numerous taverns and pubs.

Holmes, too, must have realized how difficult our chore, for he said, "I think we shall have to flush our prey, Watson."

We reached a broad street lined with warehouses just off the south bank, which during daylight was probably packed with carts and drays, but now loomed ominous and foreboding. On the corner we stopped outside a bawdyhouse and tavern from which curses, shouts, laughter and song spilled forth like an opera house gone mad.

"Make a noisy entry, Watson, and offer a sovereign to anyone having information on the death of the young lad. I'll back you up just outside. If someone leaves, stay long enough not to arouse suspicion. If he lies in ambush, I'll crack his head, and we'll squeeze the information from him."

Holmes took off his scarf and, taking his knife from his coat, he cut it in strips. "If the rogue bolts for help or to report, I'll follow and leave you a trail."

I hesitated, but Holmes urged me on. I feared not so much entering the tavern—I put a hand in my coat and felt the reassuring metal of my pistol—as I did leaving Holmes alone to trail a possible confederate to the lair of Professor Moriarty.

Entering the tavern, my heart pounding, I wasted no time. "Barkeep! A pint for my dry throat," I yelled out to a room suddenly gone quiet. Looking slowly around the room, I added, "And a sovereign to the man brave enough to tell me of the child murdered on the dock last night."

The only response was a curse here and there and a noticeable movement away from me as I strode to the scarred, wooden bar and tossed coins down for my ale. I drank from my glass and turned to face the scowls and enmity of a roomful of the lowest sort: pickpockets, cracksmen, counterfeiters, lifters and palmers, and, no doubt, murderers. I had no success in an attempt to engage the innkeeper in conversation, nor with any of the ruffians who stood alongside me at the bar.

At least ten or fifteen minutes passed while I took small sips—wanting to keep a clear head—and watched for anyone to exit, but I noticed nothing. Finally, I barked another offer loud enough to be heard above the din, with the same results. Holmes had not told me how much time to allot, so I took it upon my own that enough time had passed and that it would be best to try another tavern. With a backward glance as I departed, I walked out to the street expecting to find Holmes.

He was gone!

I was frantic with worry, thinking the worst thoughts, when I came upon a strip of scarf, and then a short distance farther, another ribbon showing me the direction to travel.

How long had he been gone? I had no way of knowing, not having seen a soul depart. I had to assume it could have been a full fifteen minutes, and I cursed myself for staying so long. I started running down the street in the direction Holmes had indicated, desperately looking for another strip of cloth ... and a fragment of hope!

Whether it was luck or Holmes's skillful placement of the markings, I was somehow able to follow the trail. Every time I began to doubt my route and consider backtracking, I'd espy a glimmer of cloth and continue my course. The trail led downriver, drawing ever closer to the wharfs, until at last I reached a building whose very foundation descended to the banks, with a pier extending out over the water. Circling to one side of the age-darkened, stone foundation, I found a flight of stairs descending to a door set ajar ... and the last marker: To the body of a bound and gagged seaman was a dainty bow tied securely in his matted, bloody hair.

Stepping past the limp body, I entered and found a staircase leading to the floors above, coming across another similarly bound wharf-rat at the next level. Each level had one lit gaslight turned to its lowest intensity, casting long shadows but little light. On this floor, level with the dock, securely wrapped in oiled canvas and set on wooden skids was a large object. A knife had been run down one side of the canvas, dropping a flap that exposed a machine of great complexity ... the Future Engine!

Suddenly, from above, came shouts and scuffling noises, followed by a gunshot, then another. I raced for the next flight of stairs and had just reached the top of the landing when a bullet tore through the planking next to my head. Another bullet plucked at my coat, and I retreated to the shadows of the stairs and readied my own pistol. Though my breath came in loud, jagged gasps, I could hear the sound of running footsteps above me and the crash of breaking glass, followed by silence. Peering around the stairwell, I dimly saw where the dockside window had been crashed through, and I started for it.

I heard running from the stairs above and turned back in time to see a bloody apparition bound into the room and rush at me with deadly speed. I raised my gun to fire, and only a sudden flicker of the gaslight saved me from killing my dearest friend. It was Sherlock Holmes.

"Out of my way!" he screamed. Rushing to the window, he emptied his revolver into the night. As I, too, reached the window, I saw the stern of a modern steam launch disappear into the low-flying fog of the river. Professor Moriarty had escaped.

"The blood from my own body betrayed me, Watson. I had him, but my hands could not hold tight. He slipped from my grasp, and now he has slipped away."

I looked at Holmes. A flow of blood ran down his right arm which hung limply at his side. His face, though streaked and smeared, appeared not to be noticeably marked, apparently bloodied only from the copious fluid that imbrued his arm and hands.

"See here, Holmes!" I said, alarmed. "We must stop the bleeding."

While Holmes submitted to my ministrations, he told me how he had disabled the guards, discovered the machine tarped and ready for shipping to the continent, and found Moriarty alone on the third floor, deep in concentration, the papers of the Future Engine spread out before him on his desk.

"I could have shot him in the back, and it would have been over. The evil in the world will always have that advantage over us, Watson. I couldn't do it. After disarming him, I led him toward the stairs, when he caught me by surprise with a shiv he had hidden in his boot, slicing my arm open and causing me to drop my gun. We struggled and I had the best of him, until he slipped out of my blood-slicked hands and reached my pistol, which had been kicked near the stairs. I only had time to reach the safety of his desk before he fired. I shot back with a pistol I had taken from one of his disabled guards. Then he ran, and you know the rest."

"Come," I said. "Let us get you to my consulting room. I've stanched the bleeding, but you'll be needing stitches."

"No. We still have important work to do, my friend," he said, leading me up the stairs to the desk of Professor Moriarty. He gathered the papers, and we then descended two floors to the Future Engine. Holmes directed me to turn up the gaslight while he uncovered the machine and began to remove several large sections of the frame and commenced to extract gears, wires, sprockets, and various cams from the inside of the machine. Several times he would refer to the diagrams and sketches on the papers, returning to the machine and pulling out another odd assortment of gadgets.

Reattaching the framework and filling a piece of canvas with the parts from the inner workings of the Future Engine, he turned to me and said, "One final task, Watson."

The gaslights on Waterloo Bridge made shimmering lampshades of the river fog, and though muted, they brought a welcome glow to our environs compared to the alleys and streets of the wharf. The Baker Street Irregulars were as true as the Queen's most disciplined regiments, appearing suddenly around us as if formed by the fog.

Holmes greeted the boys and complimented them on their grand work. "You young lads did something I could not," he admitted.

The entire ragtag group of urchins stood taller and prouder, puffing out their little chests. Opening the canvas sack, he motioned the boys closer. "Each of you take as many of these gears and assorted pieces of metal as you can hold and toss them into the Thames." To each boy he handed a shilling as they filled their pockets. As they ran off, he yelled after them, "Mind you, scatter about and don't throw the pieces all in the same area!"

We walked slowly to the center of the bridge to await the arrival of the police. Holmes pulled out his pipe and thoughtfully smoked in silence as we both looked down at the black, oily river.

Finally I spoke. "What will you tell Babbage?"

Holmes replied, "The truth, of course. I removed only the parts that Moriarty had added. Babbage will get his machine back. As to the papers . . ." He withdrew the sheaf from his coat, and taking the first page, he ripped it in half and let it fall like a leaf—though no machine *now* would ever predict *its* path. "The papers . . . were lost in the struggle.

"Like all of us who live in this glorious age of science

and discovery, I have always thought that science should be free of religion ... politics ... of any restraints. Now I no longer think that." He began to tear sheet after sheet, and we watched them flutter to the water below. "General Thompson's fears are justified. Science is outracing our ability to manage the consequences. The Future Engine in Moriarty's hands—perhaps in anyone's—is a weapon of destruction ... a weapon that doesn't destroy buildings or maim, but surely one that would destroy what makes us human."

Echoing now from either side of the Thames, we could hear laughter and cries as the Baker Street Irregulars made a game of skipping the fragments of the Future Engine into the Thames. A smile came to Holmes's face. "Those boys are the future," said he, throwing the last paper from the bridge. "Let us do our part to rid England of crime, Watson, and let the future take care of itself."

Weeks later, we had just returned to Baker Street from a pleasant evening's dinner at the Cafe Royal and were discussing the ramifications of our last case. My wife was still visiting family in the South, and Holmes and I had settled into a routine much like the days when I was still a bachelor. Our conversation had—as had the case itself—taken on a disturbing aspect. Holmes—with good reason—feared that the Future Engine could yet be replicated and was more determined than ever to put an end to Moriarty. He lit his clay pipe. Drawing deeply, he puffed perfect circles in rapid succession and then watched as each ringlet lingered, and then faded into the smoky haze that now encircled him.

"You intend to write this one up, then, Watson?" he said, as he steepled his fingers in his usual manner.

"Not against your wishes. But yes, I do. Although I think it best that this case be locked away," I said, referring to the tin dispatch box I kept in the underground vaults of Cox & Co. in Charing Cross.

"I agree. Let us say, perhaps a hundred years."

At first I thought it a joke, though I should have known better. But looking at his thin, angled face, made even more gaunt by the events of our latest emprise, I heard the emotion behind his flat voice and saw the truth in his statement.

"And what of my readers?"

"Ah-h-h-h," sighed Sherlock Holmes. "They'll just have to wait."

PART II

HOLMES IN THE PRESENT

HOLMES EX MACHINA

by Susan Casper

This story is dedicated to the memory of Robert A. Heinlein.

My name is Watson. Dr. John Watson to be exact, though not a doctor of medicine. I don't think I was named after the great man of fiction, at least my parents always swore they never knew what I was talking about. I have to admit that I've never known them to read much of anything, let alone a century-and-a-half-old detective story. Still, accident or design, it certainly influenced *my* reading material. Indirectly, it even got me my job at Vid-Tech.

It was at a meeting of my college branch of the Baker Street Irregulars where the group of us sat around watching a holo of *The Hound of the Baskervilles,* swilling down large amounts of beer and even larger amounts of potato chips. Gene was, as usual, a little worse for this consumption than the rest of us. As Holmes walked across the moors, spyglass in hand, Gene started piling potato chips on the vid-table for Holmes to walk through. That was where I got the idea for "Rootie Toot."

Yes, that was me, but before you start to throw things, I have to admit that it never occurred to me that there would be problems. I thought it would be cute for kids to interact with the show. I pictured them laying string on the vid table so that Rootie could tie up the bad guys with it, or handing him popsicle sticks to help Rootie climb out of a ditch. I never realized that crayons would melt onto the screen, or that cups of water would spill into the sets. Then those big half-sized home theaters came out and, well, you know what happened.

So they moved me from creative to production, and I've spent the last five years turning out holo versions of old 2-d movies so that people could watch *Casablanca* and *Star Wars* and other ancient classics on the vid. Still, there was a germ of an idea that had been floating in my head. You didn't actually need actors to make a new film. For instance, suppose you wanted to see *The Man Who Would Be King* the way that John Huston originally intended to make it, with Bogart and Gable as stars. Well, all you really needed were samples of Huston's style, and several film clips of the actors at work. The computer would do the rest. Without realizing it, they were already doing something of the sort, using computers to change the age and weight and sometimes even the sex of an actor when the script called for it. In the last twenty years the entire makeup department had consolidated into one man with a keyboard. I'd been trying for quite a while to get someone to listen to this idea, but when you have a reputation of something of a flake, no one wants to hear what you have to say. Then, when the canisters disappeared, I saw my chance.

Personally, I had never thought of *Godzilla vs. the Smog Monster* as a very important film, but when word comes down from Landers to holo a film, it's no time to ask silly questions. The only existing copy we could find was being messengered over that morning, and I had a two-day deadline to complete the job. Hard enough to do if they arrived by ten, but when eleven rolled around and the film was nowhere to be found, I called the front desk. "Yes," Sophie told me, "the films arrived by nine-thirty. I left them on my desk for Mike and took my coffee break. When I got back, they were gone. I just assumed that Mike came and got them."

"Not me," Mike said when I found him in his office a little while later. "No one even called to tell me they were in. You don't suppose Landers has them, do you?"

"Landers?" I shook my head. "He's the one who's in such a hurry. You'd think he'd bring them to me right away. Besides, the new manuals are in. I saw him leave for production with a couple of them this morning and I don't think he's been back yet." I sank into the chair, defeat in every line of my being. It had been a good job. With the depression hitting the industry the way it was, I wasn't sure that I could ever find work in the same line.

"Well, you're the Sherlock Holmes fan. How would he figure out what was done with them?" Mike asked. He was being sarcastic, but I didn't even notice.

"Hey, that's actually quite a good idea you've got there," I said, jumping out of my seat. Luckily, I kept several books in my office.

"What on earth are you doing?" Mike asked, following me into the next room.

"They don't think you can make films from scratch, without actors, without sets. I'm going to show them, and maybe find the answer to my problem at the same time." I ransacked my drawers for the books, scattering papers all over the desk. "See these?" I asked, holding up the treasured disks. "These books are about to become a person," I said, enigmatically.

I had already written the program to create holos directly from prose, fleshing out characters from the author's descriptions alone, testing it out in those moments when Landers was gone. I'd even added a subroutine that would allow for interaction with those characters, in case the director decided to alter the plot. It was this I intended to use. The Anson 502 was, according to literature, self-programming, self-debugging, and voice activated. With luck, it wouldn't take more than a few tries to get the thing right. Since I was fairly certain I'd covered all the bases, I hit return and headed for the screening room with a puzzled Mike still on my heels.

I had set the machine to accept external stimulus while the program was running. Now, crossing my fingers for luck, I stood in range of the camera and pressed the button marked "run." The screen lit up. The camera whirred to life. Nothing happened.

"Damn," I shouted.

"Checking for damn," the computer said. "Then a second later, "Command not found."

"Debug," I said. No matter how hard you try, you never manage to cover everything, though this time I thought I had. I waited nervously to find out what I'd done wrong.

"Image not found. Conflicting information," it said, mechanically.

I sighed. "Create image from description. Use best guess sorting on conflicts." Lights lit up on the console, and I stood back, waiting to see what would happen.

The hologram formed slowly. I wasn't sure what to expect as the first vague outlines appeared against the blue-walled room. Even here it would not be full sized, but close enough that we could actually see what we were filming. Would the images be completely solid at this size? Then I began to wonder if perhaps theaters could come back into style. Large audiences watching filmed stage plays? The possibilities roamed through my mind as the images solidified. First the room. The Persian slipper on the mantle, the Stradivarius thrown carelessly on the table. The knife-pierced stack of correspondence riffling in the breeze from the open window was so real that I had to suppress an urge to go over and read it. Then, with even more amazement, I watched as the man himself began to form. He was seated on the overstuffed armchair, leaning forward in his seat, elbows resting on the arms of the chair, fingertips touching right in front of his rather prominent nose. He turned to look at me and his eyes grew warm with concern. Though I'd never had the chance to holo any of the films about Holmes, I'd been lucky enough to see quite a few in my time. Oddly enough, the computer image looked quite a bit like one of the actors who was famous for the role. I wondered, perhaps, if someone had shown the machine a picture of Jeremy Brett. To make things run somewhat more easily, I had scanned in a short note which read: "Dear Mr. Holmes, I would like to see you this morning on a matter of some small importance." This he had dropped on the table not quite stuffed back into its envelope.

"I can see, sir, that you have suffered a great tragedy. How can I be of service?" he asked.

"Tragedy?" I asked. Mike laughed. I could see by his raised eyebrows that he found all this as interesting as I did. I had set it up so that the character, Holmes in this case, would see only another wall where the camera and viewing chairs were. Mike was out of his range of vision, but not out of range of the mike that was his ears. I shushed him with a gesture.

Holmes's brows drew together and he looked positively

angry. "Oh, come, sir," he said. "If it pains you to speak of
it, then we shall say no more, but the trouble itself is obvious. You are a painter, and I might say a fairly good one,
who has recently fallen on hard times. This is obvious from
the fact that you were forced to paint upon cloth for the lack
of a canvas," he said, gesturing at my hand-painted T-shirt.
"That the fall was recent is easily deduced by the fact that
your trousers and shoes are both of very high quality, though
rather unusual style. Probably purchased abroad. But your
tragedy, whatever its nature, a fire perhaps, is evident. Why
else would you wear this masterpiece other than for lack of
any *proper* clothing?" I turned to Mike and shrugged. He
was laughing out loud by now, but fortunately his voice did
not reach the pickup. "You are a rather sentimental man, or
you would surely have sold that ring rather than paint your
picture on cloth. I can tell from here that it is quite valuable,
and since you refused to pawn it, even when needed, most
probably a present of betrothal."

Well, he was partly right. Gold, with a one-carat ruby, it
was quite valuable. He picked up the note from the table and
looked it over. "What is more, though you are an American,
you weren't brought up there," he said. "Education there is
mandatory through the eighth grade, but you were educated
at home, and by some servant or family member instead of
a tutor."

This was a bit far-fetched, I thought. I had been born and
raised in California and had gone k through 12 and four
years of college in the best schools the state had to offer. I
think I rather resented the implications, and my tone was a
but surly when I asked, "And what has led you to this conclusion?" which broke Mike up even more.

"Forgive me, sir. No insult was intended. You speak in an
educated manner, though your accent is somewhat strange. I
am sure that your learning is not the least deficient but for
one thing that a school or a tutor, even in our more casual
ex-colonies, would never have omitted to teach—a proper
hand and correct use of punctuation." He held up the note
with my spidery, uneven scrawl.

"Cut!" I called, stopping the machine.

"Cut that out!" I yelled. Mike was making this very difficult, doubled up with laughter the way he was.

"I'm sorry," he said, breaking up all over again. "I didn't

know about your great tragedy. Really I didn't. Why didn't you tell me before, Michelangelo?"

"Okay, okay, so I forgot that the computer wouldn't give him any information post 1900 or so. Still, it's exciting. I mean it works. I mean ... well, we made a person, didn't we, of a sort. If it can do this, it can certainly make a movie without using any actors at all."

Mike sat bolt upright, the silly smile gone from his face. "Hey, you're right," he said. "Hot Reds! Do you know what this means?" I was glad to see the dime had finally dropped. "Reprogram him with modern info and see if he can find the films."

"I'm not sure it's necessary. Time's short. Let's see what he can do as is," I answered. "Roll," I called to the machine and Holmes sprang once again to life. "My problem is this," I told him, outlining the basics without mentioning what was in the box, so, of course, he asked me.

"It's a pair of round cans about this big," I measured with my hands.

"Do you have one I can look at?" he asked.

"Sure," I said. There was a shelf of them under the computer. I picked one up and handed it to him. It fell to the floor with a bang. "Shit!" I said, hitting my head with my palm.

"Sir!" Holmes said, drawing himself up, eyes wide with indignation.

"Sorry, sir," I said. I put the can into the scanner and before I could even pick it up again, Holmes was holding an exact duplicate.

"And the manuals, please." I called "cut" again and sent Mike to get them, wondering what he was getting at. The manuals were new, a set of instructions for filming, selling, and storage of holos. For some reason they insisted on using old-fashioned, print media, books. These were large loose-leaf binders with, as yet, very little material in them, but plenty of room for adding the sheets that would certainly come. It went into the scanner as well. Then I restarted the machine.

Holmes opened the book, put the can inside and closed it again. "Aha!" Holmes cried as soon as he saw it. "You see what's become of your cans?" he said. I sagged into my seat. I had been counting a lot on this.

"In the manuals? Why?" I said.

"Money, sabotage? I haven't enough information on your Mr. Landers yet. But you say you've looked everywhere. On this I must take your word as I cannot now leave this room. However, if the cans are not there, and the only person who left did so holding a pair of these manuals, which are big enough to hide the item in question, then ipso facto. Eliminate the impossible and whatever remains, no matter how improbable, must be the truth."

"Cut." I called, then, "print." The image shimmered away. Once again the screen was just a blue corner of the room.

Wearily, I grabbed the book from the scanner and picked up the can. "They are just the right size," I said to Mike.

"Right, John," Mike said, rolling his eyes. "Landers stole them, hid them inside his manual and took them over to production to sell them to Moriarty for millions of dollars."

With a sigh and a shrug I trucked the book back to Landers's office. He was seated behind his desk when I walked in. I wasn't looking forward to it, but sooner or later I'd have to tell him. I braced myself for the inevitable.

"Mr. Landers, I have to talk to you," I said.

"About these?" he asked, pulling the canisters out from under his desk.

"Where on earth did you find them?" I asked.

"I didn't find them, I stole them. Well, not exactly. I was on my way out to production with these manuals, when I saw them sitting on Sophie's desk. I thought you'd need them right away, so I started to bring them up, but the box broke. I tucked them inside the manuals because I couldn't juggle everything at once. Anyway, to make a long story short, Sophie's phone rang. It was production with another emergency. So, I ran out and completely forgot that I had them. When I noticed, I rushed them back right away. I was just trying to find you," he said.

He couldn't have any idea why I was laughing. "I'll tell you later. In fact, I'll show you. There's something I very much want you to see," I said.

With Landers seated where Mike had been, I ran the tape. I don't know yet if anything will come of it, but he seemed quite impressed. Still, something felt unfinished. I waited for him to leave and pressed "run." Once again, I was facing Sherlock Holmes.

"Thanks," I told him. "You were right, of course."

"Of course," he said, matter-of-factly, but I thought he

looked grateful to have his suspicions confirmed. "By the by, do not despair of your situation. Things will improve very soon," Holmes said.

My eyes widened. I had forgotten all about my supposed tragedy. "I think that they might." I said. 'But tell me, how did you guess?"

"*I never guess,*" he said. "It is a shocking habit— destructive to the logical faculty." He stood and picked up his pipe, using it to emphasize the words as he spoke. "My reasoning is based on strict logic and on the observation of minute details that others fail to see. Observation with me is second nature. I never guess. I *know*."

THE SHERLOCK SOLUTION

by Craig Shaw Gardner

Samantha Wilson was already having a very bad day.

She had expected her vacation to rejuvenate her, to make her look forward again to her job, apartment living, and the dating game. She expected the streets of Boston to take on a rosy glow for her return. Instead, it felt as though the city had collapsed while she was away. The morning news was full of violence: a riot in a housing project, four drive-by shootings; city officials screaming at each other, every one of them trying to avoid the blame. The weather was a persistent cold drizzle, the traffic the worst she'd ever seen.

And it had only gotten worse once she got to the lab.

She'd arrived early, determined to make a fresh start on her end of the project. There was no one in the lobby. Even the security guard was gone, off, no doubt, on one of his early morning donut runs. She took the elevator to the third floor and punched the access code to allow her into the research sector. She noticed that Doris wasn't here, either. That seemed odder still. As Dr. Kinghoffer's secretary, Doris seemed to get in earlier and stay later than almost everybody else. Kinghoffer might be the head of research, but Doris ran the lab. The traffic must be tying everybody up. In fact, the entire place seemed deserted.

Her leather heels echoed on the linoleum as she hurried down the hall. It felt a little creepy. Everyone kept odd hours at SmartTech, but this was the first time she could remember being alone. She hurried to her office.

She opened her door, and her feeling of unease turned to something closer to despair. The place was a shambles. Newspapers were scattered everywhere, held down by opened books, unlabeled diskettes, and empty and not-so-empty containers from Tony's Pizza, Sid's Deli, and the House of Ling.

So much for an early start. Samantha set out to clean her corner of the office, putting a semblance of order to her work station and the surrounding counter space. What had gotten into her office mate? Brian was normally even more fastidious than she was. She'd have to have a word with that boy. Actually, as she began to fill up her second trash barrel, she decided it would be quite a few words.

She noticed that some of the newspapers had articles circled or highlighted. "FOOD RIOTS IN AFGHANISTAN," "GOVERNOR IMPLICATED IN BIZARRE KIDNAPPING SCHEME," "MORE GUNS ON STREET THAN EVER BEFORE." She put these pages aside—someone here had to be organized—next to the pile of diskettes on Brian's desk. There was something else different about this place, too. And this was particularly absurd, but, besides the stale food, the place smelled oddly musty, almost as if someone had been smoking.

Somehow, though, she didn't want to deal with that quite yet. She'd feel much better once she'd gotten back to work.

She punched in her password and called up the first of the files she wanted to review.

"Aha!" Carruthers cried as he burst into the lab. "I have the answer at last!"

"Huh?" Samantha looked up from her computer terminal. She wasn't even aware that there had been a question.

Well, she was still all-too-aware of the mess around the lab. She pushed an overflowing waste basket out of the way to look up at Carruthers.

"I beg your pardon!" he replied brusquely.

She looked up at her fellow scientist, chubby and balding, his glasses slipping down his nose as usual. Except, instead of his usual bemused grin, Carruthers was staring at her as if he had never seen her before.

"You have recently come from some southern clime," her lab mate announced.

"Well, yes," Samantha agreed, losing whatever was left of her smile. This seemed a particularly odd way to ask her about her vacation. "I did just go to Florida—"

"Although the coloration of your hair is not entirely due to the sun," Carruthers continued, his eyes darting from her to the surrounding work station and back again. "And I would guess by the lines of your clothing that your holiday has caused you to gain a few extra pounds. But we do not have time to exchange pleasantries just now." Somehow, when Carruthers paused, his stare grew even more intense. "Tell me, miss, have you come here to speak with me about—Moriarty?"

"Who?" It was Samantha's turn to stare.

"I'm afraid this will have to wait, then." Carruthers looked distractedly at the old round-faced clock on the wall. "I was expecting the others."

He turned and strode purposefully from the room.

"What?" Samantha demanded of the retreating figure. She received no further reply.

"What is going on around here?" she shouted after him.

There was no answer. But she did hear some voices from the other room. So the rest of her coworkers had arrived at last. But it was more than voices. She could swear someone was playing the violin.

"Moriarty?" she said aloud.

The only Moriarty she knew about was part of that stupid Sherlock Holmes program that Brian and Carruthers (his first name was George, but nobody called him that) and a couple of the others had been playing with in their spare time. Well, she thought a bit reluctantly, actually the game, the Holmes Program, was kind of clever: a memory-deduction program based ever more faithfully on the character, not just from Conan Doyle, but from movies and TV, too. She had played with it a bit, but never cared for it as much as some of the others, who could get wrapped up in it for hours.

There seemed to be so many excuses around here for avoiding work. Speaking of which—

She turned back to her computer screen.

The file wasn't there.

Instead, she saw the words:

MOST SECRET FOR REASONS OF NATIONAL
SECURITY.
ACCESS DENIED.

Samantha slammed her palms against the desk. Playing
with her cubicle was one thing; fooling with the computer
was something else.

Now the guys were in trouble.

She stormed from her office, headed toward the voices.

"Fascinating!" one of them said, his voice charged with
excitement. "So it got caught up in the air-filtration system?"

"Rather like Legionnaire's disease, I suppose," another
remarked with equal fervor, "but with decidedly different results!"

"Quite simple really," chimed in a third voice, a woman's
this time. "Surprising that we didn't see it before."

"But these were experimental pharmaceuticals, nowhere
near cleared for human testing!"

Samantha turned the corner to see Brian expounding to
Doris, Carruthers, and Stan the security guard.

"How could an accident of this magnitude occur with the
safeguards—" Brian paused again, turning to stare intently
at Samantha.

"And who is this?" he demanded.

Carruthers allowed herself the slightest of smiles. "The
young lady I was telling you about."

"*Young* lady?" Samantha replied. She was galloping well
into her thirties.

"From her accent," Carruthers continued, "I believe she
may originate in the Midwest. A suburb of Cleveland, most
likely—south of Cleveland."

"Wait a moment," Brian Browning announced, "I believe
I remember her."

"What are you guys talking about?" Samantha exploded.
This had to be some sort of joke. "You *all* remember me."

"Well," Doris said with a slight smile of her own, "perhaps we did remember you, before our recent difficulty."

"Difficulty?" Samantha shouted back, all patience fled.
"What in heaven's name do you mean?"

Stan the security guard gave her a smile much like the
others. "That, my dear woman, is exactly what we are attempting to determine."

"My dear woman?" Samantha repeated. Stan didn't talk like that. For that matter, they all sounded—well—*different.* "I want some answers here," she insisted. "What's been happening around this lab?" She frowned at her four coworkers. "And what is this about Moriarty?"

The four glanced at each other as if she had asked for some sort of state secret.

"Should we—" Stan began.

"Even now, he may be listening—" Doris agreed.

"He seems to be everywhere—" Brian added.

Carruthers nodded. "After all, he has been my nemesis for a very long time."

"Your nemesis?" Samantha blurted. Carruthers was talking as if he really believed he was Sherlock Holmes.

"The young lady is correct," Doris interjected. "Moriarty is the nemesis of us all!"

Even worse, Carruthers seemed to have the others playing along.

Samantha had to get a handle on this. "Wait a moment!" She pointed at Carruthers. "Time out!"

"I believe the young lady may be correct. We often do our best thinking upon quiet reflection." The security guard reached for a brown paper bag.

Ah, Samantha thought, food! While he often had trouble with such complexities as alarm systems and video monitors, their security guard certainly knew his way around a jelly donut. At least something around here was normal.

Stan pulled out an oval wrapped in foil. "I believe, after some research, that I have located the very best bagels in our area. Not that that should be our only concern." He began to unwrap the bagel. "You see, there are seven distinct types of deli cream cheese to be found in the greater metropolitan area!" Unwrapping complete, Stan paused to take a bite. "I intend to write a monograph on the subject."

Samantha's agitation popped as surely as if it had been poked with a pin.

"Wait a moment!" she cried in disbelief. "You can't *all* be Sherlock Holmes!"

Carruthers nodded solemnly. "As unlikely as it sounds—"

"Once you eliminate the impossible—" Stan added between mouthfuls.

"This is exactly what remains," Doris concluded for the

others. "When I said Moriarty was our nemesis, I was speaking quite literally."

"And how did it occur?" Brian continued. "Well, you know of course about our intelligence enhancement program—"

"The twin tracks—"

"Both the Smart drugs—"

"—and the accelerated computer learning software."

Each spoke quickly, with no pause in between. It was almost like one person with four voices.

"It all seems to have come together," Doris continued what was seeming more and more like a monologue. "Our minds are honed, analytical machines, based on the Holmes model.

"Only now," Stan insisted, "are we piecing together the parts of the investigation."

Samantha held up her hands, as if waving them might force all of this to make sense. "You refer to this—what's happened to you—almost as though it were a crime."

"Indeed." It was Brian's turn to nod. "It is a most unusual occurrence that demands exploration."

"We all agree on that." Carruthers smiled wryly once more. "But, then again, we agree on almost everything." He pulled a pipe from his pocket and began to stuff it with tobacco.

Samantha though this might not be the best time to remind them of the lab's no-smoking policy. Instead, she asked, "But why do you think your—enemy is involved?"

"How could he not be involved?" Brian exploded. "Have you heard the news broadcasts? Seen the papers? Moriarty's hand is everywhere!"

So that's why the papers were so marked up. "Well," she said after a moment's thought, "things are bad." That was easy enough to admit. "But they're *so* bad they're chaotic— totally beyond reason. How could Moriarty be behind something like that?"

"But you see," Doris insisted, "that is his genius. His pattern is the absence of a pattern, at least on the surface!"

"Until, of course, you dig more deeply," Stan cut in, "to see how he plans to control the world."

"And he might have succeeded, too," Carruthers added, "if we had not appeared upon the scene."

Brian raised a defiant fist. "Now, though, that we are

working together, the arch criminal does not stand a chance!"

The lights went out.

Somebody screamed.

"Moriarty is in our midst!" somebody else yelled.

But, of course, that somebody had to be Sherlock Holmes.

It was Samantha who thought to hit the light switch. "What was that?" she asked of the four around her. As far as she could tell, nothing else in the room had changed.

"A very dramatic statement, I would think," Doris replied coolly. "The scream, in particular, was a very nice touch."

"I think it is obvious who did it," Brian agreed.

"Moriarty?" Samantha asked, only half believing she'd bring up the name.

Stan nodded his assent. "But I don't think we've quite determined the reason—"

"Or the extent," Carruthers continued. "More has changed here than might first be apparent."

"The doors are sealed!" Doris shook a nearby knob to demonstrate.

Stan leaped upon a nearby table. He ran a hand along the overhead grille. "The air is no longer circulating through the vents."

Samantha looked from one Holmes to another. "Is he—uh—Moriarty trying to kill us?"

Doris stared at her thoughtfully a moment before replying. "No, I think if he had wanted that, we would be dead already."

Carruthers pulled his unlit pipe from between stern lips. "I believe, rather, that this is a challenge."

Brian tried a second door, with the same result. "He has trapped us in our own building. Very clever."

"But how is it possible?" Samantha asked.

Stan answered that. "It's fairly simple, at least in conception. SmartTech has a master computer. Everything in here is managed by that computer."

Well, the next question seemed obvious. "Well, if the computer controls it all, why don't we shut it down?"

Brain clapped his hands together at her suggestion. "The computer! Of course! Good man, Watson!"

"It's Wilson," Samantha reminded them, "and I'm a woman." And she had already thought of an objection to her own question. "But if Moriarty has taken over the computer, won't he try to stop us?"

"Oh, he can try," Stan said as he jumped from the table. "But nothing is impossible with the proper tools." He lifted a ring full of keys from his belt. "This will reset the entire system."

"Oh, dear," Samantha replied, "but that means it will wipe out whatever people are working on—"

Stan was unmoved. "There's something more important than those projects now. The entire system has been corrupted by a virus named Moriarty!"

Samantha frowned. There was still a lot of this which didn't make any sense. "How, if Moriarty's doing all these other things, does he have time to completely circumvent not only this computer system, but other systems the whole world over?"

All four Holmes paused to stare at her.

"Watson! You're brilliant!" Carruthers enthused.

"He would not have to take over those computers—" Brian added.

"If Moriarty already *was* those computers!" Stan concluded.

"At last," Doris theorized, "a true thinking machine! But what if that machine became bored, restless; what if it needed a challenge!"

"Improbable?" Carruthers asked, no doubt reading Samantha's thoughts. "Perhaps! But once we examine the evidence—"

Samantha had to make sense of this somehow. "So Moriarty has challenged us by—trapping us here?"

"In a way," Doris replied. "But think of it; we've been locked out—not in."

"And we are not alone," Brian added. "There are other Sherlocks out in the field. One hundred and six of them, I believe."

"One hundred and six?" Samantha replied in a voice barely above a whisper. SmartTech employed one hundred and seven.

While the others were theorizing, Stan had moved to a panel by the side of the elevator. One key unlocked an outer door. Stan inserted two more identical keys in two side-by-side receptacles. He turned both keys. A green light on the panel turned to red.

The lights went out again.

Then popped back on an instant later.

"We're on auxiliary power now," Stan announced.

"The doors are unlocked," Carruthers announced as he pushed open the nearest one, the door to Samantha's office.

Samantha stepped inside. Her computer screen was dark.

She hoped she hadn't lost anything of importance. Not that working around here would ever be quite the same again.

With a click and a whir, her workstation sprang back to life.

"Oh," Samantha said, a bit surprised, "you've reset the computer already."

"The keys are still in the off position!" Stan called from the hallway. "I've done nothing of the sort."

Words flashed across the screen:

MOST SECRET FOR REASONS OF NATIONAL
SECURITY.
ACCESS DENIED.

Then the word "DENIED" was wiped from the screen, to be replaced by the word "ALLOWED."

"I believe the challenge has been accepted," Carruthers said behind her as data began to fill the screen.

"Was there ever any doubt?" Doris added with a chuckle. "You know what they say. If Moriarty hadn't existed, it would be necessary for Sherlock Holmes to invent him."

"But Moriarty is real!" Brian continued. "And he has invented us!"

But Samantha was only half listening as the data flowed by—not the program she had called up, but facts, figures, statistics, telephone numbers, secret bank accounts—data from all over the world.

Stan stepped into the room, his arms filled with newspapers. "We will face each and every one of these challenges."

"No problem is too great for Sherlock Holmes!" all four cried together.

Samantha found a hand on her shoulder.

"But you'll have to come along!" Doris exclaimed.

"We can't do it without you!" Brian agreed.

"We will foil him at every turn!" Stan enthused.

"Come, Watson!" Carruthers called with a wave of his pipe. "The game is afoot!"

"Wilson," Samantha corrected.

Maybe, she thought, the day might turn out better after all.

THE FAN WHO MOLDED HIMSELF

by David Gerrold

EDITOR'S NOTE: Seventeen copies of this manuscript were delivered to my office over a period of three weeks. Some were mailed, some arrived by courier; three were faxed, two were uploaded to CompuServe and one to GEnie. Several arrived by messenger. All seventeen arrived under under different names and from different points of origin. I believe that more copies than seventeen were posted, but only seventeen arrived.

The following cover letter was enclosed with every copy:

Dear Mr. Resnick,

I apologize for taking such unusual steps to bring this manuscript to your attention, but after you read it, you will understand just why I had to go to such lengths to ensure that at least one copy of this will reach your desk.

By way of explanation, I am not the author of the piece, although in the absence of other heirs to the estate, I do claim full ownership of the rights. The enclosed essay, story, letter, confession—call it what you will—came into my hands in a very curious way.

I was never very close to my father; he was a stern and rigorous man, and I moved out of his household as soon as I was old enough to make my own way in the world. I even went so far as to change my name and move to another city. For some time, I avoided all contact with my father (who I shall not name in this manuscript); so you can imagine my surprise and annoyance to find him on my doorstep one evening. Although I felt little warmth for the man, I still felt obligated to invite him in. He cared with him a small parcel wrapped in brown paper and tied up with heavy twine.

"I have your legacy here," he said, by way of explanation. He placed the package on a side table and shrugged off his heavy wool overcoat and hung it on the rack in the hall. It was a familiar action on his part, and it jarred me to see it again in my own home. I felt very ill at ease in his presence, and did not know how to respond.

"I know that you believe that I have not been a very good father to you," he said. "I did not lavish the kind of attention on you in your formative years that another parent might have. I felt that to do so would weaken you and turn you into one of those men who are less than men. Now that you are grown, I can see that I was right to do so. You have a hardness of character about you that bodes well for your ability to take care of yourself. I always felt that independence was the greatest gift I could give a son. No, don't thank me. I hope you will do the same for your child someday. Never mind that now. I don't have much time and there is much that you need to know."

He took me by the arm and led me into the parlor. It was an old house that I had taken, one that could be dated all the way back to the mid-nineteenth century. He sat down opposite me, placed his parcel on the table between us, and began to speak quietly. "Perhaps you may have wondered why I have had so few friends and acquaintances over the years, and why during your childhood, we kept moving to a new place every few months. Perhaps you have wondered why I have kept such distance from you for the past few years, not even trying to seek you out. All of this has been for your own protection. I did not want *him* to find you."

"After I leave, you will be free to forget me as you will; I will not trouble you again. I will leave this package with you. You may do with it as you wish. But I must caution you, that if you accept delivery of this, your life may be in terrible danger, the worst kind of danger you can imagine. No, even worse than you can imagine. You may examine the contents of the package, as I did when I was your age. You may toss it on the fire, as I was tempted to. You may choose to pass it on to your own son, someday. Or you may feel that the time is right to reveal this information. The choice will be yours, as it was mine. Perhaps I made mistakes, but ... I did the best I could. If you must curse someone, curse your grandfather, because it was he who first accepted custody of this—this secret."

I had only the dimmest memories of my grandfather. He died when I was very young. He had always seemed a nervous man to me. Whatever secret my father was about to impart, he certainly had my attention now. I had never seen the man act like this before. In the space of the past few moments, he had said more words to me than he had said during the entire last year we had lived together under the same roof. Incongruously, all I could think to say was, "Would you like some tea?" I simply wanted to acknowledge his attention in some way, and indicate that regardless of all else that had passed between us, he still had my grudging respect.

My father blinked at me in confusion as well as in some annoyance. His train of thought had been derailed by the question. But his features eased at the thought of my hospitality; perhaps he took it as a sign that I held some gratitude for his actions, or even affection. Perhaps I did; my own thoughts were not clear to me at that point, I was so confused by his confession. I hurried to the kitchen to put the kettle on. My face was flushed with embarrassment. My curiosity had been terribly aroused by his long preamble, and now we would both have to delay the denouement even that much longer.

Shortly, however, the kettle was boiling and the tea was brewing in the ceramic pot between us, filling the room with friendly and reassuring vapors. As I placed a tray of biscuits on the table—that I had baked myself only this morning—my father resumed his narrative.

"Your grandfather," he said, portentously, "was the nephew of the famous Dr. Watson—yes, *that* Dr. Watson." He paused to let that sink in.

I had known that there was some secret about our family's past, simply due to my father's reluctance to discuss it with me; but I had always assumed it was something criminal in nature. Possibly a relative who had been hung for stealing horses or some other great disgrace. "I'm afraid I don't understand you. Why should that be something to keep secret? It seems to me that we should be proud of our ancestor."

My father tapped the parcel on the table. "When you read this, you will understand. This is the *truth* about his so-called adventures. I'm going to leave this with you. It's yours now. If you want my advice, you'll toss it in the fire and be done with it. Because once you open it, once you read it, you'll never know a peaceful night again."

He finished his tea in a single swallow, glanced impatiently at his watch—more for performance, I believe than because he had a schedule to keep—and rose immediately from his chair. "I must go now. But I'll give you one last piece of advice, perhaps the most important piece of advice I can ever give you, and you will have to take it as an acknowledgment of how much I truly do care about you and how proud I am of what you have made of yourself. Whatever you do, son, wherever you go, keep yourself secret. Keep yourself impossible to trace. Leave no record of where you may be found. It will save your life. Believe me."

And then he was gone. He slipped back into his dark old overcoat and vanished into the night as abruptly and mysteriously as he had come. The parcel remained unopened on my parlor table.

Now, at this point, perhaps I should explain a little bit about who I am. I am a single man in my late thirties; I live alone in an old house. I have never wed, I have no children, no pets, and I keep mostly to myself. I believe that this is in no small part due to the disruptive nature of my upbringing; deprived as I was of the opportunity to form attachments during my impressionable years, I have almost no social skills at all. Rather than inflict my clumsy fumblings at friendship on others, I prefer to live vicariously through the many volumes of books I have managed to collect over the years.

That my father had presented me with what was obviously an unpublished manuscript either about or by the famous Dr. Watson, was an act of overwhelming generosity to me; but the manner of his presentation was so disturbing that it left me troubled and upset beyond my ability to describe. Perhaps another person would have opened the manuscript immediately, but I was in such a state from my father's visit that it was all I could do to finish my tea and wash the cups. I allowed myself the luxury of a long hot bath to calm my nerves and then went immediately to bed. I would resolve what to do about the package the following morning.

To my dismay, the package was still in the parlor the next day. I had hoped that my father's dismaying visit would have turned out to have been merely an apparition of a troubled sleep. But no such luck. Nor had anyone broken into the house and made off with the mysterious parcel either. Whatever it contained, it was still my responsibility.

After a meager breakfast of tea, toast and marmalade, and a single soft-boiled egg, I sat down in the parlor and prepared to examine my "legacy." There were twenty-three handwritten pages. The writing was hurried and crabbed, as if the author were working under great stress. In some places, it was nearly indecipherable.

I worked my way slowly through the pages, reading them carefully, not going onto the next until I was fully certain I had understood everything before. When I finished, my thoughts were in greater turmoil than ever. Had I not been presented with this manuscript by the hand of my very own father, I would have been absolutely certain that this was the most elaborate literary hoax in history.

If even the smallest part of the manuscript was true, then my father was right; my life was in terrible danger. I could do nothing to validate the truth of this information without calling attention to myself and giving *him* a clue to my whereabouts as well as my *when*abouts.

After thinking about this matter for several days, I decided to make typescript copies of the pages, have them duplicated, and distribute them via as many channels as possible to prevent *him* from interfering with the eventual publication.

I know that most people who read these words will blithely assume that this is merely a clever piece of fiction and will casually dismiss it. However, if even one or two people who are in a position to act will take this revelation seriously, then we may be able to stop *him* before it is too late. I am sure that your curiosity is now sufficiently aroused. With that in mind, I will now get out of your way, and let you read the pages of my ancestor's last story.

Dr. Watson's Tale

Subsequent to the success of my literary efforts for the *Strand* magazine, a great deal of attention has been focused on the personal affairs of Sherlock Holmes and myself. Much of this attention has been quite unwelcome, especially those amateur analyses and salacious speculations into the nature of our relationship. I can only assume that those who waste their energies in such efforts have much too much time on their hands.

The truth is that our relationship was entirely professional in nature. Holmes and I had early entered into a partnership of convenience, which subsequently proved to be of greater mutual benefit than either of us had originally conceived. Consequently, we were stuck, as it were, with the situation as it evolved. We were holding a tiger by the tail. Neither of us could extricate himself from the partnership without the risk of considerable personal damage, and I think that neither of us really wanted to *try* to let go of the tail of this particular tiger. Together, we had both fame and fortune. Apart, who knew what we might have?

Although we shared a high regard for each other's abilities, in truth, there was little real affection between us. Mostly, we needed each other's particular abilities. Holmes had a native shrewdness and cunning which transcended his somewhat meager intellect; I had some skills, not as a reporter, but as a fabricator of tales.

Indeed, this is the substance of my confession—that Sherlock Holmes as he was known by the general public on both sides of the Atlantic *simply did not exist.* He was a total fabrication.

Let me state it clearly at the beginning that I make no claims of innocence in this accounting. I am as guilty of fraud as the man who posed as Holmes. (For simplicity's sake, I shall refer to him as Holmes throughout the rest of this manuscript.) Although most of the physical circumstances of Holmes's illustrious career were engineered by the man who was generally known as Holmes, the literary creation of Sherlock Holmes as a superlative intellect, skilled in the art of criminal deduction, was entirely a work of fiction, and that is the part of the fraud for which I must claim authorship. It greatly amused both of us to have created such a remarkable public figure as Sherlock Holmes, eminent detective.

This is not to say that Holmes did not solve the cases he did. In fact, he had the most astonishing degree of success in resolving criminal matters of any detective then or since, a fact which brought no small degree of distress to the late Inspector Lestrade. Even those incidents which were never fully described in my public writings, such as the curious affair of the Giant Rat of Sumatra, were well-known among the investigators of Scotland Yard as evidence of Holmes's incredible facility with the facts.

There was a remark I gave to Holmes in one of my stories, *The Sign of Four.* "When you have eliminated the impossible, whatever remains, however improbable, must be the truth." Holmes found this epigram so clever that after he read it in print, he began using it in his daily conversation; he was not without vanity, and on more than one occasion, I had to literally drag him away from gathering admirers. This frequently annoyed him. He enjoyed the swoons of impressionable young women and the hearty congratulations of naive bystanders; but I was afraid that he might inadvertently say something so at odds with what the public believed about him that he would trigger a cascade of embarrassing questions and investigations that would leave us both destroyed. I felt then, and I still feel, that an impenetrable air of mystery would serve us both.

Even with this instruction waved so blandly in the face of the authorities, not a single one of them ever followed the thought to its natural conclusion and realized that Holmes was taunting them to figure out the real reason for his remarkable string of successes.

I must pause here to acknowledge that even at this late date, I find it difficult to discuss the matter of the curious belt candidly. It seems to me a betrayal of everything that both of us worked so long and hard to create. Nevertheless, I feel compelled to impart to paper the real explanation of Holmes's skill.

The man the public later came to know as Sherlock Holmes first approached me after the death of my beloved wife, Tess. He said he had a proposition for me. He was an American; he had that dreadful flat nasal quality in his voice that identifies the speaker as a native of that nation where the King's English has been systematically abused for generations. His name was Daniel James Eakins and he said he was from the state of California. When I pointed out to him that California was still a territory, not yet a state, he flushed with embarrassment and begged my apology; sometimes he forgot *when* he was.

" 'When?' What a curious way of phrasing," I remarked. Then he told me a curious tale.

"Imagine," he said, "that all of time is laid out like an avenue. If we walk west along this way, we shall find ourselves in Thursday next. But if we walk east far enough, we may travel back to last Sunday's partridge dinner. What would you do if you had such a power?"

"A fanciful conceit," I admitted. "You should try your hand at writing. Perhaps the *Strand* might be interested in such a fantasy."

"But what if I told you it was not a conceit, Dr. Watson? What if a device existed that would allow you to walk the avenues of time?"

"It strikes me as a very dangerous invention. What if you killed your grandfather before your father was born?"

"Nothing happens," he said. "I tried it. Paradoxes are impossible. He died. I remained." He then lifted up his waistcoat to reveal that he was wearing a most curious belt and harness affair. "This is a timebelt," he said. "With it I can travel anywhen I want to."

This was such an outlandish claim that I was immediately certain that the man had escaped from one of those facilities used for detaining the dangerously insane.

"I know what you're thinking," he said. "I shall give you proof. Right now." He pulled a newspaper out of his pocket, the *Evening Standard,* and placed it before me. "Look at the date," he said. The newspaper was tomorrow's evening edition. "Keep this paper. Wait twenty-four hours. Then buy a copy of the *Standard.* If the two are identical, you will have to ask yourself, how did I come by this paper before it was printed? I went forward in time and brought it back. That's how."

I examined the paper carefully. If this were a hoax, it was an elaborate one. And if it were a hoax, why invest so much time and energy in the creation of a document that could be proven false so easily?

It was at this point that my eye fell upon a small article in the lower left corner of the page. The headline said "TREVOR MYSTERY REMAINS UNSOLVED." I pointed to that and said, "Perhaps your machine would allow you to travel backward to the day of this tragedy and prevent it?"

He took the paper from me and studied the article. "Perhaps indeed," he agreed. "I shall be back momentarily," and he stepped out the door with never a by-your-leave. He returned almost immediately, but this time he was wearing a totally different costume, something he had no doubt picked up in one of the more expensive booths at Harrods: a deerstalker cap and cane, a baroque pipe after the German fashion, and a long gray fogcoat. I had seen quick-change artists in the theater before, but off the stage, such a feat of physical prowess was startling. Mr. Eakins was also carrying another newspaper which he brandished at me proudly.

It was the same newspaper, only this time the headline read, "PRIVATE DETECTIVE SOLVES TREVOR MYSTERY." I read it aloud. "Mr. Sherlock Holmes of 221B Baker Street—" I looked up at him, dismayed. "Why that's my address."

"Yes, it is," he said. "That's very astute of you, my good Watson. I had to tell the reporters something. If you don't like it, I will tell them something else. Come, the game is afoot. This is tomorrow's newspaper. If this story is to come true, we must go to the police now and tell them about the code in the mysterious message. If you read every third word in the note, you'll see that it says something quite different altogether."

I shall not repeat the details of that case here. It is fully reported in my story, "The Gloria Scott." I wish only to establish that this was the first case in which Eakins-who-became-Holmes involved himself, much to the annoyance of the police.

As we walked, I observed a curious transformation coming over Mr. Eakins. He had somehow lost his dreadful American twang and was sounding more and more like a proper gentleman. When I remarked on this, he acknowledged that he had studied stagecraft for many years and had developed an impressive skill at adopting the speech mannerisms and dialects of others. He said he found the "English accent" charming. *Charming* indeed! Nevertheless, to give him credit, within a very short time, his speech had become as clear as a native-born gentleman's.

Eakins reported the basic facts of the case to Inspector Lestrade without explaining how he had come to learn them. The good man listened politely at first, then with growing irritation. "Who are you?" he demanded. "Why should I take you seriously?"

At this point, Mr. Eakins bowed politely and introduced

himself as, "Sherlock Holmes, at your service." He had a most self-satisfied expression as he did. "And this is my associate, Dr. John Watson. We are private investigators, and we are happy to make our services available to you, Inspector."

It was here that Lestrade asked the question that shaped all of our later destinies. "How did you find this out?" he demanded. "My top men have been working on this case for a week and a half."

For just a moment, Holmes-né-Eakins appeared flustered. He had not considered how he would explain the manner in which he had obtained his knowledge, and it was obvious that he did not want to reveal to anyone else the secret of his time traveling device. I felt sorry for him at that moment; he had demonstrated such power, and he did not know how to use it. That is why I came to his rescue. "Mr. Holmes has developed a methodology of criminal deduction. Over the years he has worked on his theories and philosophies about the nature of the criminal mind, and he finally feels confident enough to put his hypotheses to the test." Both Holmes and Lestrade were looking at me curiously now. I bulled ahead. "For instance, it is obvious even to an untrained eye like mine that you have a stain on your waistcoat, Inspector. But to Holmes's trained powers of observation, that is clearly a stain from a steak and kidney pie purchased from the stall on the other side of the mews. Indeed, as we made our way across the street, Holmes pointed the meat pies out to me and predicted that an investigation of police vests and waistcoats and ties would probably reveal the entire menu of comestibles available in a three-block radius."

Lestrade stared at me speechless. Holmes (as I was now beginning to think of him) was beaming with pride. To Lestrade, he said, "Dr. Watson is correct. Others only see, but I *observe*. That is the difference, Inspector. If you wish a full accounting of *how* I applied my deductive techniques to solve the mystery, you shall have to purchase a copy of next month's *Strand*. For Dr. Watson intends to write it for publication." And with that, we swept out.

That is how the whole affair began.

Over the years, Holmes became quite the talk of London. He used his time machine and his acting skills to whisk himself back and forth about the scene of a crime, observing everything he could. Then, taking the raw facts of his observations as grist for my literary mill, I would carefully craft about them a tale of deduction and intellect to inspire even the dullest of readers. Holmes was delighted at my invention, and I was equally pleased to be a part of such a delicious game at the expense of the authorities.

I do not ask for forgiveness. I believe that both Holmes and myself passed beyond forgiveness very early on. On more than one occasion, I asked Holmes if instead of *solving* the mystery, could he use his time machine to *prevent* the tragedy. Every time I raised the question, Holmes reacted angrily. "If we did that, there would be no mystery to solve!" He snapped in annoyance. "We would be out of business. I would have no fame and you would have no stories to write."

"Nevertheless, Holmes," I said, "you and I are taking a profit on the miseries of others, and I cannot help but feel that we are acting immorally. It is abhorrent to me."

Holmes regarded me dispassionately for a moment, as if trying to decide just what he should or shouldn't say. Abruptly, he apologized for his flash of irritation. "I am tired and I'm feeling a bit peckish. Please forgive me." Then he added, "Besides, my dear Watson, we *cannot* change the timestream. Not without serious risk to ourselves and others." He then expounded at length on matters totally incomprehensible to me; I remember only a few of the words and phrases, ". . . continuity disasters, the dangers of cross-cutting, unbegun happenings . . ." I was not totally convinced by all of this fancy explanation, for I remembered his casual remark on the first day I met him that he had killed his grandfather, and it occurred to me, seeing his anger on the subject, that he would be equally willing to kill anyone else who opposed him. His time device gave him the power to murder with impunity, and I often justified my participation in the whole affair by telling myself that at least this way, we were serving the cause of justice.

There were, however, several who suspected that Holmes was not all he appeared to be. Moriarty for one. The affair at Reichenbach Falls caused no small amount of distress to a great many people. Afterward, Holmes told me that he knew he was never in any danger because he had observed the whole incident several times before he actually allowed himself to participate in it.

While I have elsewhere detailed the blackguardly behavior of the arch-fiend, Moriarty, I must now confess a strange admiration for the man, and in fact, on several occasions, I found myself wishing that he would actually succeed in killing Holmes and free me from the velvet trap in which I had found myself. But over and over again, Moriarty's intricate schemes came collapsing down around his shoulders at the hands of Holmes, until finally I realized that Holmes was toying with the villain as a cat toys with a frantic mouse. Holmes never had any intention of capturing the man and ending his crime spree once and for all. Rather, he needed Moriarty to succeed just enough so that he, Holmes, could continue to flourish as his justice-serving opponent.

It was at this point that I realized the absolute corruption of power. Holmes had developed such an arrogance toward other mortals that he no longer regarded himself as bound by their rules. And, likewise, I recognized that my life depended on my ability to provide continued service to him—at least until he tired of the game.

I have realized that there is no way that I can make any of this information public. Not even after my own death, not even after Holmes's. For with his time-traveling device, he can easily travel far into the future to see how history has regarded both of us. Should he discover the publication of any manuscript detailing the truth of our exploits, he would know that I had been the ultimate source of the revelation. It would be a simple matter for him to return to our time and strangle me before these pages could even be written. My only protection, indeed the only protection for any of my heirs, is for us to keep this secret throughout all time. For I have no doubt in my mind that the man who is known as Holmes will track us down and kill us to prevent this truth from becoming known.

After observing his ability to escape death over and over again, I have no choice but to assume that Holmes is effectively immortal, at least as immortal as it is possible for any man to be. If there is a way to immobilize the monster, I have not yet devised it.

But, now it is time for me to complete this piece and put it in a safe place. My next paper will detail my thoughts on how it may be possible to stop Holmes once and for all.

I shall now give this manuscript to one whom I trust and ask him to pray for us all. May God have mercy on my soul!

EDITOR'S NOTE: The manuscript ends here. No second part has yet been found, and all attempts to contact the author or owner of the piece have met with failure. If anyone has any information on how to find the heirs of Dr. John Watson, please contact me c/o this publisher.

SECOND FIDDLE

by Kristine Kathryn Rusch

Holmes looked out of place as he crouched on the pavement, staring at the streak of blood. I had already put Vicks on my nose and lit a cigarette. The stench on the side of the road had nearly gagged *me*—a ten-year veteran of homicide and fifteen on the force. The area smelled as if someone had run over a herd of deer three days ago, then left them in the sun. Holmes had merely wrapped a scarf around his face before examining the blood streak as if it contained the secret of the ages.

I had already followed that blood streak. It led down an embankment to a mutilated female body lying in the drainage ditch against the chain wire fence. The killer had been daring this time, dumping the body next to one of the busiest interstates in the area, only yards away from Cabot Hill, Santa Lucia's newest—and ugliest—housing development.

But the location didn't seem to catch Holmes's attention, and neither did the rusted-out 1970 Oldsmobile abandoned on the roadside, with blood on its fender. A member of the forensics unit was scraping off the blood into a plastic bag. The photographer was straddling the drainage ditch, snapping pictures of the body. Three men from the unit were scouring the car, and two other detectives were scanning the roadside looking for other clues.

I was standing beside the squad car listening as Rae Ann,

the only woman on the team, hunched over the radio, requesting a few more hours at the crime scene. It would play hell with the morning commute, but Holmes had requested it. And since the department had paid over a quarter of the budget to get the only privately run time travel company to bring the Great Detective to Santa Lucia, it had to honor his requests.

I had been watching him since they brought him into the force twenty-four hours ago. He was thin, of average height, with a hawk nose. I had expected a taller man, and perhaps by Victorian standards he had been. His suitcoat was a bit more tailored than I had expected, but he did wear a deer-stalker cap, and he carried a curved pipe which he put away when he discovered that a person who owned something made of elephant ivory was subject to verbal abuse in California.

I had protested Holmes's arrival, but the chief insisted. Our small department had had a running rivalry with the FBI for years, and since there was no actual proof that the murderer was kidnapping his victims and running them across state borders, the chief was doing all he could to prevent FBI involvement. Holmes was merely the ace-in-the-hole, a last-ditch effort to prove to the feds that the homeboys could solve one of their own.

From the moment Holmes arrived, he listened a lot, asked few questions, and asked for information on the era, on California, and on Santa Lucia in particular. I had snorted when they told me that. He may have been the greatest detective that ever lived—although I would wager greater detectives had existed in relative anonymity—but his information was one hundred years out of date. How could a man who had made his reputation by observing the small details discover a twist none of us—good detectives all—had failed to see?

And believe me, we had looked. I had had four hours of sleep a night since the task force was formed a month ago. That's when we realized that Santa Lucia was as much a victim as the mutilated bodies we found. The killer was preying on the rich and famous—two young movie stars, a former child television star, a Princeton football player who was this year's number one draft choice, and the wife of one of the state's most famous senators—a well known sculptor in her own right. Each of his victims was famous enough to make the evening news across the country, and all of the bodies had been found here, in Santa Lucia, even though most of them had disappeared—alive—from somewhere else.

Holmes followed the bloodstain to the crusted grass on the embankment before putting a hand over his nose. Then I nodded. He seemed to have a diminished sense of smell, probably from snuff, or his pipe smoking.

"What the hell you think you're doing, Ned? You too good to scour the crime scene?"

I glanced over my shoulder. Birmar was standing there, his tiny eyes running and his round face pale and greenish. He was a different kind of detective than I was. Holmes had been his idol as a boy and Birmar had been the brains behind calling the Santa Cruz Time Wizards for help in this case.

"I'm working," I said in a tone that brooked no disagreement.

"Looks like you're watching Holmes," Birmar said, but he walked away, his overcoat clinging to his frame like wet sandpaper.

I had been watching Holmes, but I had already surveyed the crime scene. I had been the first member of the team to arrive. My house was a block away. That galled me. I was the spokesman on this case. If the killer was following the press coverage, he knew about me. And even though my address and phone number were unlisted, it wouldn't take a lot of effort for a guy this smart to figure out where I lived.

"Officer Zaleski." Holmes was looking up the embankment at me. "Would you join me for a moment, please?"

I sighed, leaned over, and stamped out the cigarette in the squad's ash tray. Then I approached the embankment, careful to avoid the blood streak. A low irritation was building in my stomach. Whenever this guy wanted a consult, he chose me, not Birmar. And I had better things to do than babysit someone who was wasting more of the department's money than the chief was.

"Do we know whom this unfortunate woman is yet?" he asked.

Even with the Vicks and the cigarette, the smell was nauseating. A body, decaying normally, shouldn't smell that strong. "No," I said.

"Well," he said. "This one may be exactly what we have been looking for. She does not have much in common with the others."

I looked down, reluctantly, holding up all my training as

a shield. The body was not a person; it was the king in a chess game, the reason for the fight and no more. But the killer had left her face intact, and the look of horror in her wide blue eyes would haunt me if I let it.

I made myself examine her for the clues Holmes was talking about. Her teeth were uneven and discolored—certainly not the product of million dollar attention. The remains of the dress she wore showed a store-bought label. Holmes reached down and held out a piece of fabric to me. The cuff of a sleeve. One button was missing. The other had been sewn on rather ineptly.

"Jesus," I said. "Copycat."

Holmes leaned on his haunches and peered up at me from beneath the brim of his cap. "Copycat?" He clearly didn't understand.

I pulled myself out of the embankment. "We got two of these nuts on the loose. One of them is killing for weird personal reasons and the other is reading the press coverage and imitating."

Holmes clambered up beside me, remarkable at ease with his body although he looked as if he never exercised. "Nonsense," he said. "Such a thing is preposterous. The odds of having two killers with the same—"

"It happens all the time," I said. I walked to the squad. Rae Ann's cheeks were flushed. She was fighting with dispatch.

"They're already rerouting because of a multicar pile-up on I-5," she said.

"Let me talk to them."

"There is no need." Holmes was standing behind me. "As long as your photographers are finished, we may return to the station. You and I must discuss the way these copycats work."

WEDNESDAY, 11:53 A.M.

The last thing I wanted to do was sit at my desk and talk basic criminal theory with a man who had died three decades before I was born. But he absolutely refused to work with Birmar ("I am afraid, my dear sir, that the man does not understand nuance"), and the chief told me my job was on the line if I ignored Holmes. Wonderful. It seemed that the Great Detective needed a foil, and he had chosen me as this century's Watson.

The chief was using his office to brief a new team that would handle a double murder reported to the Gato Apartments. No privacy anywhere. So I took Holmes to my favorite dive, a bar just off Fifth that had been passed over by ferns, gold piping, and neon lights. The place hadn't seen daylight since 1955, and the windows were painted shut. The interior smelled of cigarette smoke layered so deep that the walls were half an inch thicker. The floor was littered with popcorn and sticky with spilled beer. Someone had to be bribing the city health authorities because logically the place should have been closed in its first year.

To my surprise, Holmes said nothing as we walked in. He followed me to a booth and slid in as if we were both regulars. I ordered a light beer and he ordered an iced tea "heavy on the sugar and cream," then smiled at me. "I have grown quite fond of that in the last few days," he said.

I was in no mood for idle conversation. "So you want me to explain copycats."

He shook his head, a slight smile on his narrow lips. "I think I grasp the concept. However, I thought I should let you know that I believe you are wrong."

I felt a heated flush rise in my cheeks. The man knew how to get to me. I had been decorated three times by the State of California for my work, recognized as one of the best detectives in the nation by the *New York Times,* and had been portrayed in a TV movie based on one of my cases.

"Look," I said. "I've investigated more homicides than I care to think about, and I've been on teams that have captured six different serial killers. Someone who doesn't follow the pattern is inevitably a copycat."

"But the pattern was followed," Holmes said. "All the way up to and including the directions of the knife wounds, as well as the advanced odor of decay. Some of the flesh was not hers, and beneath her were the bits and pieces of another corpse. An animal, as in the other instances. In the past the killer has used this technique so that a hidden body will be discovered, and has done so this time. I do not believe you have put these details in the press, have you?"

The cocktail waitress set down my beer, sloshing some of the foam onto the scarred wooden table. Then she put down a glass of iced tea for Holmes, followed by a pitcher of milk and a bowl of sugar. With a sarcastic flourish, she produced a spoon and handed it to him, scooped my five dollar bill off the table, and left.

"No," I said reluctantly. "We haven't."

"In addition, there was a small print from an—athletic shoe—and it had come from the opposite direction away from the car. I think you will find that the killer splashed the blood on the bumper as a way to lead us astray. The blood streak was a similar ploy, for it is too even and straight to have been caused by a body dragged to the edge of the embankment. The killer walked through the embankment in the pre-dawn hours, walked from one of the sidestreets, carrying the body with him. Since the incline from the road is so steep, I would doubt that anyone saw him."

I took a sip of the beer. My hand was shaking. I had noticed those things, but had not put them together. Holmes was right. I guess some details didn't change over the span of centuries.

"I believe," Holmes said, "that if we discover who this woman is, we will have found our killer."

WEDNESDAY, 2:33 P.M.
We sent the victim's fingerprints and photograph to crime labs nationwide. Then we gave her picture to the press, who published it nationwide, then we hired a temp to monitor the phone calls.

Holmes was amazed by some things: the amount of data we had at our fingertips; the way that information could travel across country in a matter of seconds. Of course, he expressed that amazement with calm, letting us know that such changes were logical extensions of the era in which he had lived. He also told me privately that he believed such intellectual ease had made us lazy.

Birmar thought the remark funny. I didn't. Holmes wasn't making any points with me at all.

By this point in the investigation, we had eight different psychological profiles on the killer. The profiles assumed the killer was male and strong (which seemed obvious, given the football player), deficient in social skills and with a deep-seated hatred of famous people. Holmes disagreed with all of the experts on all of the points but two. He conceded that the killer had a hatred of the famous, and that the killer was strong.

We had returned from the bar after a lunch of burgers,

heavy on the grease. I had had the one beer and Holmes had downed four cups of tea, making him jittery. When we returned, we were summoned to the chief's office, along with Birmar, for an analysis of the case.

The office smelled of reconstituted air and old gym socks. The chief kept his workout clothes in his filing cabinet—"that way no one will snoop," he would say slyly—and never opened his windows. His desk was littered with papers, and a computer hummed continually on the edge of a nearby table. The chief sat in an overstuffed chair behind the desk. Holmes and Birmar had taken the only remaining seats. I leaned against the closed door, arms crossed in front of my chest.

The chief had gone over the newest psychological profile—which said nothing different from the others—and then asked for our opinions.

"I would disagree with your experts," Holmes said. "It would seem to me that our killer is quite socially adept. After all, he managed to get close to people who are continually surrounded by others—and in the case of the—stars—are heavily guarded. No, this is a person who has enough resources to be able to travel great distances quickly and unseen, a person with the ability to get close to the unapproachable, and a person with ties to Santa Lucia."

The chief and Birmar were watching Holmes as if he were god. I was beginning to resent the sound of that resonant accented voice. I had already figured out the Santa Lucia part—that seemed obvious—and I had told the chief about my theory that the killer had a job that attached him to the famous. I had missed Holmes's third point, and I shouldn't have. Maybe Holmes was right: maybe my access to technology was making me intellectually lazy.

"It's got to be a private plane," I said. "He brought three of the victims in from the East Coast in less than two days."

"I'll call the airport," Birmar said.

The chief shook his head. "Our killer would be too smart to land in Santa Lucia. We need to check the airports that handle small planes. Get some help on this, Birmar. Get the logs from all the airports within a day's drive from here."

Birmar blanched. "Sir, I don't believe he would drive all the way here from, say, Utah."

"One must never let one's own preconceptions interfere with an investigation," Holmes said.

I stared at him. He looked perfectly at ease, sitting in a plastic chair, his feet outstretched, the chief's computer humming from the table beside him. No wonder Holmes was not ruffled by being leaped into the future. When he was involved in an investigation, he checked his expectations of the world at the door.

Holmes looked at me. "What type of job would a man need to get close to the famous?"

I shrugged. "Journalists get passes. Police, security guards, hairdressers, drivers, caterers—there's a whole list of support personnel that could get inside any citadel as long as they know how to open the door."

"Yes," Holmes said, steepling his fingers, "but that door must be the same for each of these unfortunates."

"We already have a team investigating the links between our victims."

Holmes smiled. "We will find nothing yet. Until we know the name of our final victim, our killer has us at a disadvantage."

I deliberately uncrossed my arms, and let them drop to my side. "What makes you say that?"

"We have all assumed the killer is male," Holmes said. "It wasn't until this very moment that I realized we are looking for a woman."

WEDNESDAY, 3:15 P.M.

I was very glad that Rae Ann wasn't in the office with us—or any of the other women in the department for that matter—since Holmes spent the next half hour explaining that the "fair sex" can be quite brilliant. He relayed his experiences with one Irene Adler and, while he implied that she was an exception to most females, he assumed that each century must produce at least one similar mind. Only this mind, the one we were seeking, was diabolically fiendish.

The thing which convinced him that our killer was a woman was the shoeprint. Holmes claimed he had been turning the pattern over and over in his mind while we talked. Forensics had confirmed that the shoe was a bargain brand, bought at a discount shoe store, and that it was a male size four. Holmes said he had watched footwear for the next day and noted that many of the female officers preferred men's tennis shoes to women's. No men wore a size four, but a number of the women did.

"That's not proof!" the chief snapped. "That's supposition. Besides, serial killers are always men."

Holmes sighed. "I understand that you have a lot of data on these killers. But there is nothing to prevent a woman from using these techniques for her own gain. There are several other things that point to a female hand. The victims were clothed, not naked, as seems to be common in these cases. And, while she seems to have done a lot of lifting— which I believe possible for the women I have seen since I have come here—the method of murder, the knife attack, relies more on surprise and a victim's abhorrence of knives than any need to physically overpower someone. The knife, by the way, is an angry weapon, often chosen by people who have kept a great deal of fury buried inside for a long time. A woman's weapon, if you will, since women are trained not to express their feelings." Then Holmes smiled. "That much, at least, has not changed between our time periods."

Holmes leaned back in his chair and pressed his steepled fingers against his lips. He spoke softly, as if he were speaking to himself. "In fact, I would suppose that a number of the unsolved serial killings you have in this nation are unsolved simply because you are unwilling to admit that the fair sex is as capable of atrocity as we are."

At that comment, I turned my back on the discussion and left the office. Holmes's contempt for our methods sent an anger through me that was counterproductive. He had worked on a handful of cases in Victorian London, a city with a population half that of Santa Lucia, Santa Cruz, and San Jose combined. Murder was a parlor game then, and the only serial killer, the infamous Jack the Ripper, had never been caught. If I had remained in the room, I would have said all of those things.

Instead, I went to my desk, took deep breaths, and thought. The precinct was nearly empty, with most of the department working on various cases, and another group handling the Gato Apartment murders. In the background, a phone rang incessantly. Behind bubble glass at reception, a uniformed officer argued with a woman about wasting the department's time searching for a lost cat. One of the dispatchers, a slender woman with black hair, wandered out of the radio room, and poured herself a cup of coffee.

I wished there was more noise. I thought better when I had to screen out distractions.

I hated to acknowledge that Holmes had a clarity of vision which I lacked. That our killer was a woman made sense. It would explain the two anomalies to our statistical analysis: the football player and the senator's wife. A young man in his early twenties could be lured anywhere by an attractive woman—and not feel threatened by her. The senator's wife with feminist leanings simply needed her sense of sisterhood invoked.

That made our search easier. We weren't looking for hairdressers or caterers or even journalists, which had been my initial bet. We were looking for someone who fit more into the profile of a person who owned a private plane. Someone who would have contact with all of these people and yet remain anonymous. A driver. For short promotion tours, a lot of studios, and publicists relied on a handful of people who were screened to drive the famous about. Most preferred women because women were perceived as nonthreatening. A driver with a private plane could be on call in several communities, under several aliases.

I went over to the departmental computer, mounted and chained onto a desk in the middle of the room (someday maybe the department would spring for individual computers for all of us—a more cost-effective solution than hiring the Santa Clara Time Wizards) and pulled up the victim files. They didn't go into the kind of depth I wanted, so I went into the newspaper logs instead, looking for any recent mention (before the murders of course) of the victims' names.

The door to the chief's office opened and closed. I heard footsteps behind me and knew who they belonged to. I wasn't surprised when Holmes pulled up a chair and sat next to me. He watched as article after article scrolled by on the screen.

"Are you finding anything?" he asked.

I nodded. The football player had been to three different cities so that he could meet the owners of the team that had picked him and get wined and dined separately by each. Both movie stars had been on promotional tours for films they had just completed, and the senator's wife had been accompanying her husband on a junket around his home state. "Finding the driver who handled all of these shouldn't be hard," I said. "The companies should have resumes on file complete with photographs. But it is not illegal for someone to use an alias—as long as they're using the correct social security number."

I grinned at Holmes's look of confusion. I wished I could see that look more often.

"But," I said, "even if we show the link, we still don't have enough to hold up in court."

Holmes leaned back in his chair. "I do not understand the fear with which you all seem to view your legal process," he said. He had heard enough about it—I had heard the chief warn Holmes twice not to mess with evidence or interfere with forensic procedure—but I thought he had been ignoring the warnings until now. "But I do agree that we need more information. A case is not closed until we understand the motivation for our killer's actions."

I had had enough. Too little sleep, too much coffee, and too many lectures. My patience snapped. "First of all, this is not 'our' killer. Secondly, I have worked on cases in which the killer's only motive is a hatred of the color yellow. Thirdly, real life is not a murder mystery. Here, in the 1990s, we rarely tie up all the loose ends."

"Loose ends," Holmes said softly, "are a luxury a stable society cannot afford to have."

Rae Ann's arrival saved me from replying to that. She held out a fax, the cheap paper curling into a small roll. "We found her," Rae Ann said. "Our latest victim. Kimberly Marie Caldicott. A housewife from Bakersfield, California."

"Bakersfield?" I said. I frowned. Bakersfield. Holmes had to be wrong. A housewife didn't fit into this scenario.

"Does she have any ties to Santa Lucia?" Holmes asked.

Rae Ann nodded. "Born and raised here. Graduated from Santa Lucia High in 1970. Homecoming queen, valedictorian, and voted most likely to succeed. Teenagers aren't good at predicting that sort of thing through. Who'd've thought she'd've ended up a divorced secretary, mother of two?"

"She doesn't fit the profile, Holmes," I said. "I think we really have to entertain the idea of a copycat and look for information leaks in the department."

Holmes shook his head. "You are overlooking the obvious, my friend. Before we assume two killers with the same strategy, we must investigate this as a related death. My dear—" he looked at Rae Ann"—answer a question for me.

I assume the items you mentioned in reference to Kimberly were honors."

Rae Ann nodded. "That's the top of the heap in high school."

Holmes smiled. "Then we need to find out who got stepped on in Kimberly's rise to the top. We need to find the young lady who came in second."

FRIDAY, 4:10 P.M.

The Santa Lucia High School Annual had only one picture of the salutatorian from 1970: her official graduation photo. Lorena Haas was a pie-faced girl with coke-bottle glasses and a mid-sixties bouf-do, the kind of bookish intellectual girl who sat quietly in the back of a room and remained unnoticed even after twelve years with the same classmates. A few of them remembered her, and used words like quiet, shy, and moody. Only one classmate kept in touch, and she claimed Lorena lived back east, and drove a taxi for a living.

"Lorena may have hated Kimberly," the classmate said, "but there's no way she woulda killed her."

Holmes had smiled at that. "Jealousy," he had said to me, "is, perhaps, the most destructive of human emotions."

Whatever the motive, the evidence against Lorena Haas was mounting. Within a day of looking at the annual, we had found Haas's pilot's license, matched her voice prints to airline logs, and through that tracked her various aliases. We even had enough evidence to tie her to each victim—she had chauffeured all of them in company limousines.

The discovery put the remains of the investigation in the FBI's purview, although the Santa Lucia Police Department Special Homicide Unit would always receive credit for solving the case. The FBI found Lorena in a D.C. suburb, living under the alias Kim Meree. They brought her to San Francisco on Friday morning, for an interview, before they officially charged her with the crime.

Holmes insisted upon seeing her. The chief had had to negotiate for that. Finally, Holmes's fame had prevailed. Holmes was going to be able to speak with Haas alone.

Holmes insisted that I accompany him. I was tired of being his Watson. Ever since Holmes arrived, I had played second fiddle. I really didn't care why Lorena Haas had murdered a bunch of celebrities and her high school rival. I had already been assigned to a murder/suicide that had been called in this morning—easily solved, of course—but the kind of case that generated a pile of paperwork.

I was still protesting as we climbed the steps of the FBI building in San Francisco, where they were holding her for questioning.

"We've got enough to make a case, Holmes," I said. "There's no reason to talk to this nut."

I had been making the same argument all day. Holmes had brushed it off before, but this time he stopped at the top of the stairs and looked down at me. On this afternoon, he appeared taller, and I suddenly realized what a striking presence he really made—in any century.

"My dear sir," he said, "one must always discover if one's suppositions are correct."

"And if they aren't?" I asked.

Holmes looked at me gravely for a moment. "Then we solved the case by luck and happenstance, not by intellect."

I sighed to myself. "She's not going to confess anything, Holmes. She's too smart for that."

"I don't need a confession," Holmes said. "Merely a confirmation."

He pulled open the door and went in. I followed him. I would be so glad when he was gone. That patronizing tone, as if he and he alone saw the details of the universe, grated on me so badly that I tensed each time he opened his mouth.

The inside of the building had a dry metallic dustless scent. Our footsteps echoed on the tile floor, and the people we saw—all wearing suits—did not meet our gaze as we passed. We passed door after door after door, all closed as if hiding secrets we could never be privy to.

When we reached the designated room, Holmes took the lead, and had the agent show us directly to the interrogation area. Before we went in, we were instructed that our entire conversation would be taped.

A guard stood outside the interrogation room. The guard nodded at us as we went in, as if memorizing our faces. The room itself was white, except for the one-way glass on the back wall. Even the table and chairs were white. Lorena Haas stood in front of the glass, peering at it, as if by doing so she could see the people hidden behind. She turned as the door closed behind us.

Although I had seen recent photos, I was unprepared for her physical presence. She had come far from her coke-

bottle glasses days. Contact lenses had made her eyes a
vivid blue. She had shoulder-length blonde hair, high cheekbones, and a small upturned nose. She moved with a lithe-
ness of an athlete. She could easily have carried those
bodies. If I hadn't known, I would have matched the 1970
Kimberly Caldicott graduation photo with the 1990s version
of Lorena Haas.

"I'm not talking to anyone without a lawyer," Haas said.
She had the flat nonaccent most Californians specialized in.
She leaned against her chair instead of sitting in it, and she
kept gazing at Holmes as if he were familiar.

"I merely wanted to meet you," Holmes said, and stuck
out his hand. "I am Sherlock Holmes. I am sure you read
about my involvement in the case."

She didn't take the offered hand. "Oh, yeah," she said.
"The world's greatest detective. I suppose I should be honored. Well, I'm not. People like you, they make their way by
focusing on the inadequacies of others."

Then her gaze met mine. Those intense blue eyes sent a
shudder through me that I couldn't hide.

"You must be Ned Zaleski. The newspapers mentioned
you, too. You were the one who led the investigation until
Mr. Holmes came and took it all away from you." Her words
had an accuracy that hurt. I had never mentioned my dis-
placement to Holmes as a problem, but I had resented it.
More than I ever expressed.

She smiled, slowly, as if we shared a secret, and I remembered that morning, so long ago it seemed, when Holmes
took his first action on the case. The last body had been discovered near my home. And until that point, I had been the
focus of the investigation, the cop made famous by Lorena's
work.

She knew. She saw. And worse, she understood.

Jealousy, Holmes had said, *is, perhaps, the most destructive of human emotions.*

Lorena Haas had allowed jealousy to destroy her. Who
would know what remark one of her famous passengers
made that set her violent emotion free. But once freed, it led
her back to Santa Lucia, to her home, the place where coming in second had destroyed her life. It didn't matter that
Kimberly Marie Caldicott had not succeeded. What mattered
was that in high school, Kimberly Marie had become a symbol of everything Lorena could not have.

A symbol she killed over and over again with the weapon of anger. A knife.

Holmes had been right again. Without asking her a single question, he had managed to confirm both her guilt and her motivation.

He was right, and I despised him for it.

Lorena's smile grew and I had to look away.

Holmes half-bowed to her, ever the English gentleman. "I thank you for your time," he said, and knocked on the door. A guard let us out of the room.

I said nothing to Holmes as we walked back to the car. My skin was crawling and I was deeply thankful that he was scheduled to leave with the Santa Cruz Time Wizards the following morning.

When he returned to his home, he would not remember me. But, like Lorena with Kimberly, I would always remember him.

FRIDAY, 6:05 P.M.

It should have ended there, but it didn't. As I dropped him off at the chief's house for a celebrity dinner that I was not planning to attend, a voice pierced through the static on my police radio, announcing a body had washed on shore from the Santa Lucia River. The body was that of a young girl, missing for two days, and she had obviously been strangled.

As the dispatch fed the information, I imagined the scene: the bloated, black-faced body, tongue protruding, the neck of mass of welts and bruises washed clean of evidence by the river herself. A homicide unrelated to any other that would probably go down in the books as unsolved.

Holmes was watching me. "Loose ends happen," he said, "only when we permit them to exist."

My mouth worked, but I said nothing. Who had appointed him my teacher, anyway? I was just as good as he was.

He took his pipe out of his pocket and then pulled out a pouch of tobacco. "What Miss Haas failed to realize," he said, "is that such jealousies prevent us from seeing ourselves clearly. She already had the perfect revenge: a good income, several jobs that put her in touch with something your society values. She had an interesting life, but instead, she constantly compared herself to an imaginary figure from the past."

My jaw was clenched. After this evening, I would never see the man again. Yelling at him would do me no good.

He filled his pipe, and put it in his mouth, then shoved the tobacco in his pocket. Then he reached out a hand. I shook it, more out of a desire to get rid of him than courtesy.

"I am quite sorry," he said, "that I will not be able to take my memories of you back to Baker Street. You have one of the keenest minds I have ever encountered."

Then he let himself out of the car, and walked up the sidewalk to the chief's house. The face of Lorena Haas rose in my mind. History would never record what the young Kimberly Marie Caldicott had thought of her. Perhaps Kimberly looked at her with respect and admiration, or perhaps she had noted, once too often, a talent that went unused.

I could follow Lorena's path, and make Holmes a hated icon on which I could blame all my inadequacies. Or I could move forward.

I glanced out the car window. Holmes stood on the steps, his pipe in his mouth, his cap pulled low over his forehead. I nodded once to him. He nodded back.

Then I wheeled the car onto the road, picking up my mike and reciting my badge number. I would go to the river, with no preconceptions, and forget about technology. I would look for details, and I would open myself to nuance.

I never wanted to see Holmes again, and there was only one way I could make sure that happened.

I had to stop relying on suppositions, experts, and computers. I had to sharpen my own mind, and think for myself.

PART III

HOLMES IN THE FUTURE

MORIARTY BY MODEM

by Jack Nimersheim

"That's right, sir. You're a machine. In fact, you've always been a machine. A damn amazing one, too, I might add."

"And tell me again, my good man," a disembodied, emotionless voice asked, "exactly what kind of machine was it that you called me?"

"A computer."

"A computer. An odd name, that. An analysis of its structure, assuming that the word reflects a traditional etymology, leads one to speculate that this particular device is able to perform certain types of mathematical calculations, which it then extrapolates into numerical values. Am I correct?"

"Only partially, sir. Well, no. Forgive me. Now that I think about it, your description is unerringly accurate. Strictly speaking, that's exactly what a computer does. However, the manner in which it can manipulate and apply the results of any operations it performs elevates a computer far above the status of a mere calculator."

"I would hope so. Your revelation that I am more machine than man is disturbing enough without placing further restrictions on my capabilities. Rare would be the individual who could anticipate discovering that his entire existence has been . . . Has been what? I suppose the only way to state it would be to call the life I once thought I led an illusion.

"And yet, here I am, living proof—if this is itself not an illusory turn of a phrase—that such incredible events can, indeed, occur. Where I once believed myself to be human, the very pinnacle of evolution's handiwork, I now find that I am, and ever have been, a mere machine, some mysterious device which you call a computer."

"Actually, sir, that's not quite correct, either. To be more precise, you're what's referred to as a computer program—a series of coded instructions that, when executed by a computer, allow it to accomplish a specific task."

"Hmmm. All of this is beginning to sound quite complicated." In my mind's eye, I could almost visualize him (for I still thought of Holmes as a *him,* having no desire to relegate the famed detective to *it* status) drawing upon his familiar pipe, sifting through the information now in his possession, contemplating its significance. "And just what was the designated purpose of the particular computer program that you claim defines my being?"

"Stated simply, you were, um, created to assist in the collection, collation, and analysis of evidence associated with selected criminal investigations. That's an undertaking, I might add, for which a well designed computer program is ideally suited. And as I implied earlier, sir, you are an amazing piece of work."

Several seconds of silence followed this observation. This time, I could conjure up no image of how Holmes might be reacting to my comments. How would I feel, I pondered, were someone suddenly to reveal to me that *I* was not the man I'd always believed myself to be? Indeed, that I was not a man at all!

To his credit, once Holmes assimilated this information, he responded with his customary poise and the insatiable curiosity that the legendary detective displayed throughout his long and illustrious (and, yes, he was correct, largely illusory) career.

"Well, there you have it, then. If what you say is true— and ignoring for the moment the natural aversion any rational entity would feel toward the situation you describe, I see no reason to doubt your veracity—the only practical course open to me is to accept the facts of my existence as you've outlined them and continue performing those tasks for which, apparently, I was, ah, constructed.

"It seems logical to postulate, therefore, that you have summoned me, however such a summoning might be accomplished, so that you can consult with me on matters relating to some criminal activity. So explain to me, my good man, the exact nature of the crime that has presumably confounded you. I trust the investigation of it shall prove worthy of my unique talents."

"Oh, it will, Mr. Holmes. I assure you, it will—assuming, of course, that you're at all curious as to the recent activities of your most notorious antagonist, Professor Moriarty."

Holmes, that incredible piece of programming which I still tended to perceive from a decidedly human perspective, had a lot to catching up to do. The techniques and technology employed by both the criminal element and those charged with containing it had changed dramatically in the century since he was first created. I spent the greater part of two months upgrading him (*it*) to state-of-the-art status. My efforts produced some pretty impressive results, if I do say so myself.

"Good morning, young man," Holmes—or, rather, a three-dimensional image representing the famed detective—mumbled, as I entered the study.

"Good morning," I responded.

When I opened the door, the holographic Holmes had been leaning back in a virtual armchair, eyes only half open, fiddle thrown across his knee, carelessly scraping the bow across its strings. I must admit, I briefly considered eliminating this musical subroutine. It was pleasant enough when replicating identifiable passages. Like Watson had before me, I rather enjoyed Mendelssohn's *Lieder* and several other pieces it contained; on a whim, I even added a semiclassical interpretation of *Strawberry Fields Forever*. The effect was quite the opposite, however, on those occasions when, as was the case this morning, the simulated violin generated random tones, indicating the parallel execution of some other, unrelated algorithm.

"I hope my playing did not awaken you prematurely," he said.

"Oh, no, sir," I lied.

"It is kind of you to say so, but I suspect a lack of honesty in your reply. Having recognized that I no longer require sleep, I'm afraid I've developed an unusual tendency to lose track of the time. I find it quite easy to slip into meditation and melancholy, regardless of the hour of the day or night."

Carefully laying down his violin, Holmes pushed himself

upright from the chair. Slowly, deliberately, he assumed his full height of rather over six feet. His sharp, piercing eyes, which previously appeared to be contemplating some imaginary point far beyond the room's physical boundaries, focused on me intently.

"Take this morning, for example. I've spent almost the entire night pondering your dilemma. Certain aspects of what has transpired, I must confess, trouble me."

"Such as?"

"You claim that my most dreaded nemesis, Professor Moriarty, is once again loose upon the land. Is that not so?"

"It is."

"I must inquire of you, then, how can this be? Professor Moriarty and I were adversaries almost from the commencement of my professional career. He was the organizer of half that was evil in my beloved London. As I once explained to Watson, he was a genius, a philosopher, an abstract thinker, a man with a brain of the first order. On these points, there can be no argument. For all of his formidable talents, however, the ex-professor was not immortal! Surely, death would have claimed his damnable soul by now! How is it possible that the devil has survived into the present era?"

Thus arrived a moment I had been dreading since shortly after I reactivated the Holmes program. There was no way I could answer this question without also admitting that *I* bore direct responsibility for the resurrection of one of the greatest criminal masterminds of all time.

"Perhaps you had best sit down again, sir. For the tale surrounding Moriarty's reappearance is quite convoluted and involves technical information which I suspect will require a considerable amount of explanation for you to fully comprehend."

What followed could best be described as a crash course in Computer Science, revised syllabus. For nearly two hours I tutored Holmes, the consummate student, on a wide range of matters pertaining to the heretofore secret evolution of digital technology.

I explained to him how, while cataloging a recently uncovered cache of obsolete government records and materials retrieved from a deteriorating warehouse in south London, I stumbled across a box marked "Project 221B." I described to him the excitement I experienced when, upon opening this box, I discovered a series of monographs authored by

Charles Babbage. I attempted to convey to him my mounting sense of wonder as I realized that these previously unpublished papers indicated that, contrary to the "facts" as reflected in historical records, the prominent English mathematician had, indeed, constructed a working model of his analytical engine—one which the Queen's government, citing reasons of national security, immediately decreed to be classified item of the highest order. I then inflated Holmes's ego by informing him that *his* legacy traced its genesis to a prototype program clandestinely created to run on this 19th-century precursor to all modern computers.

Please understand that what I've recounted here is an abridged version of a rather lengthy dialog. Lack of space forces me to gloss over many aspects of Holmes's creation and subsequent evolution. For example, I've all but ignored Watson's role in Project 221B. Contrary to what you may believe, it was extremely minor. I will tell you this much: Holmes became quite despondent when, in response to his queries about Watson, I informed him that the man he believed to be his friend and trusted companion for so many years was actually a low-level government clerk assigned to transcribe and record data relating to specific crimes. His natural inquisitiveness resurfaced, however, when my narration finally touched upon the subject of Moriarty.

"Yes, yes. Professor Moriarty," Holmes muttered, the first time I mentioned this name in our conversation. "I need to know how that rogue has managed to return."

I determined it a vain effort to evade the truth with Holmes. The master sleuth would detect immediately any attempt on my part to falsify the facts in this matter. And so I plunged forward, prepared to accept the outrage I was convinced Holmes would direct toward me, once he learned of my role in Moriarty's revival.

"In truth, sir, the professor's longevity is no more a mystery than your own. For, like you—and forgive me for bringing up what I realize may still be a sensitive subject—his life does not comprise a corporeal existence. You see, Moriarty, too, is a computer program; indeed, you and he were both conceived—metaphorically speaking, of course—within the same electronic womb."

"Are you implying that, in some ungodly and perverse way I cannot begin to fathom, Professor Moriarty and I are brothers?"

"Well, I can't say that I ever considered the matter from that unusual perspective, but I imagine there are those who would characterize in such a manner the relationship that exists between the two of you. In some ways, Moriarty might even be considered your evil twin."

"Moriarty and I, twins! What an absurd notion!"

"Absurd? Perhaps, sir. Nevertheless, it does reflect a certain, admittedly convoluted, logic. Just as you were designed to record the nuances of criminal investigation, Moriarty—or, more correctly, the program personified by Moriarty—was created to identify and catalog those less noble attributes of humanity that lie at the core of the criminal intellect. He represents a darkness, in the absence of which your light would not shine nearly so brightly."

I don't know whether a computer program can exhibit pride, but the look that crossed the normally stoic countenance of Holmes's holographic image in response to this comment implied an emotion closely akin to that deadly sin. "Hmmm. I see your point. You still haven't revealed, however, the nature of Professor Moriarty's latest misdeeds. Nor have you enlightened me as to how he managed to escape this peculiar chamber in which I seem to find myself held prisoner."

For reasons that seemed to make perfect sense at the time, I'd isolated my systems following the unfortunate incident involving Moriarty. In hindsight, doing so boiled down to an excellent example of bolting the barn door *after* the horse had already bolted. Unknowingly, I now realized, it also served to penalize Homes for what was, in truth, my blunder.

"Regarding your first question, Moriarty's intentions remain a mystery at this time. Concerning the second point, however, I'm afraid that it was *I* who set Moriarty loose on the world again."

"You? But you have presented yourself to me as an ally! How could you do such a thing?"

"I didn't mean to, sir. You must believe me when I say this."

His square jaw remained set, an indication of his disapproval at my confessed impropriety. Nevertheless, Holmes waved his hand in a nonchalant manner, his thin, delicate fingers extended to their full and considerable length, signifying that I should continue.

"Do you see the wire over there, the one lying on the floor next to my desk?" I pointed behind him and to his left. The image of Holmes swiveled within the image of his chair, following my lead. He nodded. "Well, it's designed to be plugged into that small hole located in the wall just above it. Can you see it, also?"

Once again, he indicated that he did.

"Connecting the wire to that socket allows me to transfer information stored on my systems to any other computer that's similarly equipped, virtually anywhere in the world."

"Amazing. How is this possible?"

"It's all quite complicated, involving a piece of computer equipment called a modem. Without getting too technical, a modem converts the electronic signals a computer generates into audible tones which can then be transmitted through the wire I pointed out earlier. I'll be happy to provide you with a thorough explanation of the underlying principles at some future time, but not now. The specific procedures involved contribute nothing to our current conversation, and I know how you abhor superfluous details. 'Useless facts,' I believe you once called them, 'elbowing out the useful ones.' Suffice it to say that a modem functions much like an electronic gateway through which my computers—and, by extension, any data they contain—can gain access to the outside world."

"Are you telling me that, even though I'm not truly alive—a condition I have come to accept, I assure you—it is still possible for me to move beyond this room? And that I could achieve this miraculous feat by traveling through that tiny wire?"

"In a manner of speaking, yes. Which is precisely how Moriarty managed to escape, if you will."

"Again I have to inquire, how was this possible? The wire that you say is so critical to accomplishing what you describe is merely lying on the floor. It leads nowhere."

"That wasn't the case when I began researching Project 221B. Back then, I used my modem regularly to access other systems, trying to lay my hands on any and all information that I could locate relating to your career. What I failed to realize in those early days was that, as I set about rebuilding the program that ultimately resurrected you, I was also rebuilding Moriarty's electronic persona.

"Indeed, because of the order in which I started reconstructing Project 221B, I completed what turned out to be the Moriarty subroutine first. The next time I contacted a remote system to research one of your more celebrated cases, that subroutine, well, it disappeared."

"Disappeared? Where did it go?"

"That's the problem, sir. I'm afraid I don't know."

The two of us set to work immediately trying to determine where it was that Moriarty might have fled. At Holmes's request I reconnected my modem, thus allowing him access to the amazing electronic world that has come to be called cyberspace. He reveled in his new-found freedom.

"There is so much information, truly useful information, out there," he remarked, upon returning from one of his early sojourns. The virtual Holmes had taken on the practice of replicating his familiar deerstalker cap and Inverness for these digital excursions. I must admit, the latter made him look somewhat absurd. I mean, how much soot and road mud could one expect to encounter moving through a modern-day electronic switching system? "Did you know that a computer exists in Washington, D.C., the sole purpose of which is to collect and catalog the fingerprints of known criminals? An immense organization called the Federal Bureau of Investigation then makes these records available to law enforcement agencies around the globe, through telephone wires! And in a place called Columbus, Ohio, there is a system that people from all the nations of the Earth can use to communicate with one another. Why, even here in England . . ."

On more than one such occasion I had to restrain Holmes's exuberance. I accomplished this feat with relative ease by reminding him of the grim circumstances that originally motivated his excursions into cyberspace. To his credit, given the obvious allure of this brave new universe he suddenly found himself exploring, Holmes never lost sight of his principal quarry. The pursuit of knowledge may have fascinated Holmes; his pursuit of Moriarty, however, bordered on obsession.

Whenever Holmes accessed a new system, he scoured it first for any indication that the professor had visited there before him. Working from the assumption that an incursion by the Moriarty subroutine would resemble a typical computer virus, I provided Holmes with several telltale signs he could look for, to determine whether or not such an attack had occurred.

Within a period of a few weeks, Holmes became the world's leading expert on computer viruses. He could recognize and identify each and every one of them, from *Anthrax-b* to the *Zherkov* virus, an estimated 2,500 examples of malicious—or, in many instances, merely mischievous—programming. It fell on my shoulders to anonymously alert the authorities to the probability of virtually every Internet node shutting down precisely at noon on December 28, this odd date presumably having been chosen because it corresponded to John von Neumann's birthday, but it was Holmes who discovered the innocuous piece of code that would have initiated this catastrophe lurking within a backup VAX system used to archive student records at a small Midwestern university.

Three months into our search, however, we had yet to uncover a single clue as to Moriarty's potential whereabouts.

"Maybe I was wrong from the beginning. Maybe this whole idea of Moriarty being a part of your original program is nothing more than the product of my own overactive imagination. I wouldn't be the first hacker to find electronic fantasies more appealing than the real world. Spending every waking hour of your days interacting with a bunch of machines tends to be pretty boring, you know."

"Should I take that comment personally?"

"Oh, no. I wasn't talking about you, sir. Believe me, these past few months have wonderful. I can't remember when I've enjoyed myself so much. But I'm beginning to think that I may have been mistaken about Moriarty. Maybe he *was* a real person, a criminal genius who died almost a century ago, just as you first suggested."

"That would indeed be a welcome hypothesis, were it only true. Sadly, it's not. Moriarty's out there, somewhere. I know he is. I know this as surely as I know that you and I are discussing his existence here, at this time, in this room."

"How can you be so sure of that? You've been scouring cyberspace for weeks with nothing to show for your efforts. Surely, some indication of Moriarty's presence would have surfaced by now!"

"You do not know the professor, young man. Moriarty is a creature of extraordinary stealth. He thrives in the shadows, rarely if ever abandoning them. If he is indeed orchestrating misdeeds once again, I would be more surprised were I to uncover any trace of his activities."

"But if you can find no sign of him, and don't anticipate that you ever will, how can you say with such certainty that he's back?"

"You must realize that Professor Moriarty and I are rivals of the most intimate kind. Our lives and destinies are so tightly intertwined that we have developed an intuitive awareness of each other's ambitions and enterprises. Was it not I who sensed Moriarty's hand directing events those many years ago, long before others—admittedly, others less skillful than I—could detect the slightest hint of his involvement? Even in the absence of any compelling evidence, I know that Moriarty is out there. Manipulating. Maneuvering. Moving through the shadows like the creature of dark influence that he is. I have no need to verify this hypothesis with empirical proof. I can *feel* it."

Shortly after the conversation recounted above took place, Holmes also vanished. He was gone for nearly two weeks. Each day throughout this period I held lonely vigil in my study, worrying about where he might be, wondering if and when he might return. Every morning, upon awakening—for unlike Holmes, I still required rest—I would open the door to that room, expecting to see his stoic yet strangely comforting mien, hoping to be greeted in his noncommittal manner by that now familiar voice. Each time I encountered only silence and solitude.

As the second week following his disappearance drew to a close, I must confess that my faith in the famed detective was beginning to falter. I found myself considering the possibility that something untoward had happened to him and, much as it pains me to make such an admission, seriously contemplated the prospect that Holmes might never reappear. Such concerns prompted me to great distress.

"Living is easy with eyes closed, misunderstanding all you see . . . " I woke up from yet another fitful sleep with these words running through my head. For the briefest of moments, lost in that gray and murky realm between slumber and sentience, I could not discern their source. Then, sud-

denly, I recognized the song that had so gently been nudging
me awake.

"Holmes?" I muttered, flinging off the covers and leaping
from my bed. I bolted down the hallway and threw open the
study door.

It was Holmes, indeed! Standing there in the middle of the
room, violin tucked beneath his chin, bow in hand, he appeared quite preoccupied with the quiet strains of the melody he was attempting to master.

"Holmes!" I shouted.

Startled by my abrupt entrance, he stopped playing and
looked up. At first glance Holmes appeared none the worse
for wear, following whatever events may have transpired
during his absence. Upon closer examination, however, I observed the outline of his simulation to be fading slowly in
and out of focus, much like the scene in a camera's view-
finder appears as you make final adjustments to the depth-
of-field. And every few seconds, ever so briefly, an almost
imperceptible interference disrupted his image.

"Good morning, young man. The more I play this song,
the more I seem to enjoy it. The two young composers who
wrote it, Lennon and McCartney, you say they were originally from Liverpool?" I nodded mutely, still somewhat surprised by Holmes's sudden reappearance. "It's reassuring to
realize that the Queen's subjects have maintained their tradi-
tionally high standards of artistic achievement during the period that I was inactive." His voice was weak. It sounded
tinny, lacking any bass. Each time the holograph flickered,
static interrupted his speech. The overall effect was not unlike viewing a television station which has not been tuned in
quite properly.

"But I have been selfish again, haven't I? Once more I
find myself in the somewhat awkward position of wondering
whether I have awakened you prematurely."

"You did, but that's okay. There's no need to apologize.
It's good to see you again, sir. I was beginning to worry
about you."

"I did depart rather suddenly and without any advance notice, didn't I? You must be curious as to where I've been."

"A little." I understated my concern.

"I tracked down Moriarty."

I can't say that this revelation surprised me. As the days
following his initial disappearance drew out, I suspected a

tenacious pursuit of his nemesis to be the reason for Holmes's extended absence. "As always, much as I loathe the professor himself, I feel obligated to tip my cap to his genius. He selected the site of his sanctuary so masterfully that I could have searched for decades and found only frustration, had I continued my initial pursuit of him."

"Don't keep my in suspense, sir. Exactly where was it that Moriarty escaped to?"

"Therein lies the true beauty of my enemy's strategy," Holmes stated matter-of-factly, taking his violin and laying it down on the chair behind him. As he did so, his figure broke apart a bit more noticeably than before. This time, it took several seconds for the holographic image to return to sharp focus. "In truth, Moriarty never fled at all. He has been with us the whole time, concealing himself in plain sight, as it were."

I glanced about nervously, half expecting to see the gaunt and brooding visage of the so-called "Napoleon of crime" staring back at me from some shadow or shrouded corner within my study. Other than Holmes and me, however, the room held no one.

"You can relax, young man. The professor is no longer in a position to harm anyone. Whatever threat he may have posed has been contained."

"Am I to assume, then, that you've finally succeeded in eliminating your infamous adversary? That's wonderful, sir!"

As static once again disrupted his image, Holmes almost appeared to wince. "I fear your elation is premature. I did not say Moriarty was vanquished. Had you listened closely, you would have observed that I stated specifically that he has been contained. I chose this word with great care, I assure you."

"I'm afraid I don't understand."

"Allow me to clarify my comment, then. The obvious place to begin is with an explanation of the manner in which luck combined with logic to assist me in my attempts at solving the mystery of Moriarty's feigned escape.

"The professor was, you may recall, quite accomplished in matters mathematical. It embarrasses me now to admit that I did not give much consideration to Moriarty's familiarity with this subject, as I attempted to track him down. Instead, following what at the time seemed to be sound advice on your part—for there was no way you could have recognized the association I ultimately made—I initiated an organized search of those remote systems you identified as likely targets my nemesis might select for infiltration. As we both know, this approach proved fruitless. Then, sitting here alone one evening, contemplating our lack of success, I happened to spy an unusual device on the table next to your desk."

The top of the table to which Holmes referred held several pieces of computer hardware I used only rarely, among them a dot-matrix printer, a hand scanner and a CD-ROM drive. He was indicating none of these, however. Holmes pointed instead to the table's lower shelf, which contained a single item.

"You mean my Bernoulli drive?"

"That is the one."

"Wow! That's an antique. I bought it years ago, on a whim, when a local computer store was selling off some obsolete equipment at incredibly low prices. Since then I've used it primarily to keep archive copies of files that have, for the most part, outlived their usefulness. Are you telling me that that old disk drive was somehow involved with Moriarty's escape?"

"What I'm trying to explain to you, young man, is that the professor did not 'escape' at all. As I stated previously, he never left this room. Once I saw the name on that object, Bernoulli, I knew precisely where he had fled."

"I'm sorry, sir. I still don't understand."

"Nor would I expect you to. For unlike me, you probably are not familiar with the binomial theorem, a branch of algebra first demonstrated by Sir Isaac Newton. I once believed, back when I also believed both Moriarty and I to be human, that the professor possessed a keen interest in binomials. I realize now that this was merely my interpretation of a mathematical procedure incorporated within the original Moriarty program.

"This procedure, called the Bernoulli probability function, relies on a binomial formula to estimate the relative likelihood of two mutually exclusive results associated with a given condition. I can only speculate as to the reason for its inclusion within the Moriarty program. I presume it was used to evaluate the probability of success or failure—or, stated another way, the two possible outcomes—for proposed criminal activities.

"As I once told you, I have through the years developed an intuitive awareness of what drives Moriarty. I understand him almost as well as I understand myself. Because this is so, I know that he possesses, among other attributes, a profound sense of the ironic. It suddenly occurred to me, therefore, that the professor would have been unable to resist concealing his presence within a device bearing the same name as a procedure that contributed to his own creation.

"Moriarty never traversed the thin wire through which I have traveled so often, over the past few months. Indeed, he never journeyed outside of this room. That is where Moriarty fled, my good man. There, within that device you called a Bernoulli drive."

Holmes ended this revelation with a flourish, waving his arm in a expansive gesture toward the table he'd pointed out earlier. Then, without warning, his image flickered once, twice, and collapsed in upon itself, disappearing from sight.

I disassembled the Holmes program completely—reducing each command, statement, operator and variable to its lowest common denominator. A few algorithms survived relatively intact; this is what permitted Holmes enough time to recount the events leading up to his solving the mystery of the professor's whereabouts. Most, however, contained a mismash of Holmes's original code and minute fragments of the Moriarty subroutine, one intertwined around the other, like so many vines scaling a chainlink fence; they were the ultimate cause of his demise.

As I struggled to segregate that which defined Holmes from the few remaining remnants of his most reviled adversary, I also attempted to reconstruct in my mind's eye the final confrontation between these two implacable foes. It required no great genius to figure out Holmes's strategy. His plan was both obvious and elegant.

Bit by bit, byte by byte, he must have examined the sectors and tracks recorded on the Bernoulli drive. Each time Holmes encountered a trace of Moriarty, however, he scrubbed it from the disk, absorbing the rogue code into his own program.

Had I been so inclined, I could have spent hours admiring the great detective's handiwork. Here was digital surgery worthy of a world-class hacker. In the end, though, I denied myself this luxury, for I had set about to complete another, more critical task.

"It appears that I am once more in your debt. I certainly did not anticipate returning to life yet again, following my last encounter with Moriarty."

"It was touch-and-go there, for a while. You and the professor managed to tangle yourselves up pretty well, during your little tête-à-tête. I'm just grateful that I was able to separate the pieces and reintegrate you into a functional program."

"And Professor Moriarty? What has become of him?"

Anticipating this question, I had come up with what I believed to be a logical way of eliminating forever the near-paranoia Holmes exhibited toward his most fearsome foe. Now seemed as good a time as any to put my theory to the test.

Walking over to my desk, I opened the top drawer and pulled out a disk I'd prepared a few days earlier. "He's here, sir. As I extracted portions of the Moriarty code from your program, I transferred them to this disk."

Somewhat dramatically, I must confess, I inserted the disk into my floppy disk drive.

"This particular computer contains a voice-recognition card, a device that allows it to accept spoken commands. And so, if you will do the honors by reading the phrase I've written on the paper before you, what do you say we get rid of the bastard once and for all?"

He studied for a moment the contents of the paper I'd indicated. I couldn't remember ever seeing Holmes smile before. He did now, however, as he looked up and announced with a strong, clear voice: "Delete MORIARTY.DAT"

I saw no need to tell Holmes that he had just deleted an empty file. I'd already erased all vestiges of the Moriarty code, a feat easily accomplished as I reconstructed the Holmes program. Nor did I tell him that none of this would have been necessary, had Holmes only informed me of his discovery and subsequent plan before confronting Moriarty on his own. What he didn't realize, what he couldn't have realized, was that the Bernoulli drive in which Moriarty sought refuge contained a *removable* disk. Had I known the professor's whereabouts, I could have taken this disk out of the drive at anytime and destroyed it, thus ending the threat.

What would be the point of telling Holmes this? Why not allow him to believe that he had vanquished his greatest foe alone, in the only way possible? He deserved it. The way I figure things, Holmes's life already contained more than its fair share of illusions. What harm could be done by burdening him with one more—a positive one, this time?

THE GREATEST DETECTIVE OF ALL TIME

by Ralph Roberts

The silver-suited figure, for once, was late in materializing.

Sherlock Holmes laid aside his pipe and journal. In the latter, he had been writing what he knew of the latest machinations of our archenemy, the despicable and dastardly Professor Moriarty—that evil and bent man who was always trying to trap or discredit us in some manner, an annoying and inconvenient activity that called for some sort of retribution when time allowed.

As was his wont when uninterrupted, Holmes took the small bottle from the mantelpiece and his hypodermic syringe from its neat morocco case. Three times a day for many months I had witnessed this performance, but custom had not reconciled my mind to it. You have perhaps read my description of this act in previous writings—"The Sign of the Four" comes to mind—but there is now a difference, a wonderful but fearful difference in our lives.

For this moment, however, the result was the same. With his long, white, nervous fingers Holmes adjusted the delicate needle and rolled back his left shirt cuff. For a brief period of time—seconds to him, an eternity to me—his eyes rested thoughtfully upon the sinewy forearm and wrist, all dotted and scarred with innumerable puncture marks.

"Which is it today?" I asked. "Morphine or cocaine?"

Holmes glanced only briefly at me, then back to the

poised needle. "It is cocaine," he said; "a seven percent solution. Would you care to try it?"

"No indeed," I answered, a bit brusquely I'm afraid, being somewhat testy that he had ignored my advice as a medical man and continued his deleterious habit.

Finally he moved to thrust the sharp point home, thumb poised in anticipation of pressing the tiny piston that would release the narcotic into his bloodstream.

There was no discernible sound, but suddenly the silver-suited figure was there. He plucked the needle from Holmes's fingers before the sharp point had so much as indented the skin. With a practiced gesture, he pressed a 24th-century spray hypodermic against Holmes's bare arm and activated it. Holmes sighed in resignation and sank back into the velvet-lined armchair.

"There!" the figure said, his voice muffled by the silver hood, "cured, by God."

"Yes, cured again," Holmes said. "This is becoming rather a nuisance. No free time to engage in one's pastimes at all anymore, eh, Watson?"

I nodded in agreement to the obvious. We both watched as the figure removed his silver coveralls. The garment was nothing special but simply the standard protective garb for time travelers of the next three millennia. Holmes and I each had several such coveralls concealed in the back of our closets.

A distinguished appearing older gentleman of regular features was revealed. He was dressed in a white uniform with red trim and plastic boots, also red. Badges of apparently high rank adorned his shoulders and several decorations rode proudly on his chest. Obviously, our visitor, this time, was a personage of the first order. His expression bordered on the haughty and was, perhaps, somewhat tinged with contempt. He did not seem to be overly intelligent either, more the stiff and punctilious bureaucrat. Obviously he was uncomfortable—pale and nauseated as he looked around. I took an instant dislike to him.

Holmes had an unfocused look in his eyes as he groped the air before his face as if searching through a file cabinet. I hastened to fill the void and, since one seldom gets the opportunity when Holmes is about, demonstrate my own detective powers.

"Mars Constabulary," I said, somewhat smugly. "Twenty-fourth century. Rank: Chief Inspector. Service includes: the Food Riots of 2354, the Great Air Shortage of 2360, and four citations of additional meritorious service, plus the Order of Tourism, a rather important decoration from your government. And, you have taken the unusual action of walking outside the domes in the past few hours."

The inspector did not appear surprised. "Yes, yes. I know you two are great detectives, hence my journey here at some personal inconvenience. Ah ... I can understand you reading the decorations and interpolating my service record, but how did you know of my extra-dome activities?"

Holmes was now paying attention to us and spoke. "He saw a few specks of sand on your boot, old chap. Watson knows that an officer of your high rank has robotic valets and goes on duty immaculately turned out. Hence, any imperfection—even one so minor as a speck of sand—could only have occurred in the past few hours. Since the Mars domes are also kept extremely clean in the twenty-fourth century, you would only have picked up sand outside. Now, what may we do for you, Chief Primary Inspector Charles LeBeck?"

LeBeck, finally, was taken aback. "You know my name?"

I sighed. Holmes, if not cut short, would drag this out forever, and I was quite curious about what the Inspector wanted with us.

"The general period and service organization being established," I said, "it then remains but a simple matter to examine the files of all high ranking officers. I dare say Holmes knows more about you now than you do yourself."

Holmes passed the file to me. I quickly scanned it as LeBeck watched our mystifying maneuverings in what was, to him, nothing but thin air.

"Virtual reality, Chief Inspector," Holmes condescended to explain. "Gift of a grateful police force in the thirty-third century—in fact, our most consistent and delightful clients."

"We're just returned from an extended and successful stay there only minutes ago," I added.

"Quite so. Anyway, Watson and I both have computers implanted within us. To facilitate ease of use, we 'see' file cabinets, desks, paper, pen, and so forth whenever we make use of a particular function. Our databases cover all of recorded history through the fifty-fifth century."

I finished scanning the file and transmitted it back to

Holmes. "The Black Dome murders," I said. "Tourists killed at random over a number of years. Very bad for the main industry of Mars—tourism."

He nodded. "Of course. Elementary, my dear Watson. The only case of import the good Chief Inspector never solved. He nears retirement now and wishes to leave a clean slate. Also, the situation has heated up and his superiors and the Board of Tourism—an organization with extreme clout—have placed considerable pressure on him."

LeBeck raised his arms, then let them fall in disgust. "If you two already know everything, kindly consult your computers, and tell me the culprits so that I may return uptime and arrest them. Probably one of those dirty tourists themselves. Always stinking up our beautifully pure domes."

Holmes and I exchanged glances. The blatherings of amateurs in detection—which included, alas, most law enforcement officers of all millennia—never ceased to amuse us.

"My good Inspector," I said, "it is a common misconception of the layperson that Time is some black and white construct."

"You think that, for want of a nail, a horseshoe was lost," said Holmes. "For want of a horseshoe, a rider was lost."

"Yes, yes," LeBeck said impatiently. "I know the theory. The battle was lost; history was changed."

"Not so," Holmes said triumphantly. "It's actually somewhat the opposite. Time is *not* black and white, but rather many shades of gray."

"Not unlike Life," I said. "There are no absolutes."

"In other words, Chief Inspector," Holmes concluded, "mysteries are not solved until they are. No matter when they occur in Time."

LeBeck looked confused. "But . . ."

I took up the explanation. "There are a number of happenings we call the Major Mysteries: murders and other events that would remain forever unsolved unless they suffer the attentions of the greatest detective of all Time, Mr. Sherlock Holmes!"

"Ably assisted by his boon companion, Dr. Watson," Holmes staunchly and immediately inserted.

LeBeck nodded hesitantly.

"Naturally," I added, "only those Major Mysteries that Holmes and I have already addressed appear in history as solved. Yours is not yet one of those, but we have already done five this week, twenty-six so far this month, I believe. All this has created quite a demand for our services throughout the various millennia. Rather a good business wholesale-wise, and a good bit of nice uptime fringe benefits, such as our implanted computers. And, since we return here usually only a minute or two after we leave—even if the case took weeks to conclude—it doesn't interfere all that much with our regular cases and life in this era."

"Time travelers in and out of here in droves, though," Holmes said. "Our landlady, Mrs. Hudson, does look askance at us from time to time. You are all, for the most part, an unsavory appearing lot, I fear."

"I see," LeBeck commented, looking around as if seeing Holmes's lodgings for the first time. "Rather a dreary and dirty place for it," he added in obvious distaste. "Why are you so popular, Holmes? A primitive detective from a filthy, practically prehistoric era?"

Holmes took no overt offense, warning me with a glance to do likewise. "Dr. Watson's fault, of course," he said, tempering it with a smile. "It didn't take future generations very long to discern that the supposedly fanciful tales he wrote under his *nom de plume* of A. Conan Doyle were actually true stories of our exploits. It is a burden I must bear, but for many, many centuries into the future I am considered to be the premier detective of all Time. Since they come downtime to us with the cases, which we consequently solve, this reputation is maintained."

LeBeck came close to sneering, but said nothing.

"The nineteenth century," I said, "has, thus, become the very zenith of the art of detection, despite the technological advantages of future times."

"Many of which we now employ, ourselves," Holmes added.

"On the other hand," I continued, "we have also become the veritable nadir of vallainy. Just as Sherlock Holmes is the greatest detective of all time, this century is also home to Time's most diabolical evildoer, that arch villain, Professor Moriarty. He, alas, is as consulted as we are, only by the future's criminal elements instead of its law enforcement agencies."

"Enough of this," was LeBeck's reply. "If, indeed, I must put up with you on this case, let us, by all means, get it over with as soon as possible."

Holmes and I rose to our feet.

"Nothing for it except a little trip to Mars," Holmes said. "The game is afoot, Chief Inspector. Off we go, eh?" But he paused for a moment, looking down at LeBeck's mirror-polished footwear. "Watson, do be a good chap and clean the Chief Inspector's boots before we leave. Must have him looking his best, what?"

I glanced at him, but his face remained impassive. Foregoing my dignity as a medical man, as one often must in assisting the great Sherlock Holmes, I took a small brush and a blank sheet of white note paper from a side table. Bending—I must admit with a bit of effort, as Holmes and I are often regally wined and dined after solving cases in this era or that—I carefully brushed a few bits of sand onto the paper and stood again. Holmes held out his hand, and I gave him the page.

LeBeck snorted impatiently as Holmes held the paper at eye level and, with his other hand, did the groping in air that showed he was accessing the files in his virtual reality computer.

"I have been guilty," Holmes said, somewhat distracted as he leafed through the invisible-to-us files, "of several monographs, all on technical subjects related to the solving of crimes. At first, before Watson and I became in such demand on the temporal circuit, they were on such local time subjects as 'Upon the Distinction Between the Ashes of the Various Tobaccos.' In that one, I enumerate one hundred and forty forms of cigar, cigarette, and pipe tobacco, with colored plates illustrating the differences in ash."

"What is *tobacco?*" LeBeck asked, genuinely confused.

Both Holmes and I sighed; a good smoke was one of the few things missing from most future eras. It was, I might also add, precisely why we maintained our headquarters still in Baker Street during the nineteenth century instead of some more luxurious uptime address, numerous of which had been offered to us as rewards for successful detective work.

"More to the point," Holmes said, "is my treatise on Martian sand . . . ah, here it is . . . in which I detail some fourteen thousand and fifty-six varieties, including high-quality holograms of each and every type of grain, and where that sand is found. Wonderful how computers augment our abilities."

LeBeck, for once, showed at least a modicum of respect. "You're *that* Holmes as well? I thought you nothing more than some primitive playing at detective work. University of Hermes Press? 2150? I collect works relating to police and detective work, you know," he added, in a modestly arrogant manner.

"Ummm, 2155, I believe," Holmes said. He made a gesture that put away his files and dumped the few grains of sand into the fireplace, along with the piece of note paper, which flared up briefly. "The sand is from outside Black Dome," he concluded.

LeBeck was now fully back to his haughty, contemptuous self now. "Of course it is. I investigated a murder there only this morning. It was necessary to step outside the dome for a few minutes. Then, before I could properly clean my boots, my superiors demanded I go get Sherlock Holmes and solve these murders once and for all. Something I could have done easily enough on my own."

He paused and looked at each of us in turn. "You'd think I was a suspect," he said, huffing.

Holmes raised his eyebrow. "Well, of course you are, my good fellow. Everyone is until we unravel your little mystery. Except Watson, naturally. I can vouch for him, he was here with me."

LeBeck puffed out his cheeks in disgust, but beckoned us to follow him through Time. And, to close the book on this string of serial murders over a twenty-year period, Holmes and I donned silver suits from Holmes's closet and followed.

On the southern edge of Mare Australe, between that great red plain and Ogygis Regio, the first Black Dome had been built by Swiss colonists in 2054—a dark bump on the red landscape. That original construction had been long since replaced with several much larger domes. Now, in 2368, the central dome was still colored black, thus maintaining the tradition that had given this large city its name.

Holmes and I had materialized in LeBeck's wake in a customs post. Our clothes and persons were subjected to a rigorous cleaning. To our mutual disgust, Holmes's pipe and pouch of tobacco were confiscated, as were the cigars from my coat's breast pocket. Even as we rode through the city's streets, past rows and rows of tourist hotels, in a small cab to LeBeck's office, the smell of lavishly applied antiseptic

dominated the air. Everything was unbelievably clean, reflecting the habits of that culture. The streets were literally
sanitary enough to eat off of—although, naturally, the Mars
Constabulary would prevent one from soiling those pristine
surfaces in such a manner.

Seeing and experiencing this religiously purified era for
the first time brought home to me, and surely to Holmes as
well, the enormity of LeBeck's move in seeking our assistance. For LeBeck to have appeared before us, as he had,
with a few grains of sand still on his boots, was a massive
social and regulatory transgression. The pressure upon him
to solve these murders must, indeed, be tremendous for him
to forgo even a moment's time for the cleaning of his boots.
Unless, of course, he wanted us to think *he* was the murderer, then eliminate him as a suspect because, based on the
sand, it would be too obvious. I shook my head. Such a convoluted and sophisticated ploy might be employed by the
likes of Professor Moriarty—LeBeck, on the surface, appeared to lack the intelligence for it.

LeBeck's office was not exceptionally large, despite his
position as the chief investigative officer for the entire city.
It was, of course, spotless. All surfaces gleamed and were
totally dust free. One whole wall was taken by shelves displaying LeBeck's collection of items and books relating to
police work down through the centuries. His pride caused
him to first show us that collection before getting down to
business. There was, as there should be in any good collection of such a sort, an entire shelf of books about Sherlock
Holmes.

I tapped one of the leather-bound spines. "I'm pleased to
see that you have some of my works here."

LeBeck unbent with a brief smile, his pride in his collection momentarily overcoming his haughtiness. "Yes, all
under your pseudonym of 'A. Conan Doyle,' of course. Did
the people of your time really believe that Holmes was just
a fictional character?"

"A few of the editors, at least," I said.

The Inspector leaned forward and removed one book from
the shelf. I recognized its form as that of a memory block,
the type of book prevalent in the mid-twenty-first century.

"Here's an interesting oddity, Holmes," LeBeck said. "An
expanded but limited edition of 'The Final Problem'—the
story of your death."

Holmes broke off another absentminded and futile search of his pockets for his pipe, and raised one eyebrow slightly.

"Yes, Moriarty and I supposedly went over a waterfall, locked in each other's embrace. That was, however, merely a device that Watson used, writing as Conan Doyle, to gain us some breathing space. Unfortunately, the popularity of my purportedly fictional adventures were such that poor Watson was forced to bring me back to life, so to speak."

I took the book from LeBeck's hand and glanced at its cover. "The editor," I said softly, "is a certain Professor Moriarty."

Holmes once more raised his eyebrow, and took the book in his own turn. He adroitly activated the memory block—we work quite often in that era—and scanned its contents.

"Most interesting, indeed, Watson. He relates your original story in essentially an unadulterated format, but adds a long afterword."

I stepped closer to look over Holmes's shoulder, while bemoaning the fact that my work was long since public domain. Surely some sort of copyright law to protect time-traveling authors could be formulated? Why must I continually suffer seeing my work in print without a farthing's worth of payment?

"See?" Holmes said, running his finger rapidly down the book's display.

"Indeed," I said, taking it in almost as rapidly as he.

LeBeck was lost. "What?" he asked.

"It's a commentary on Holmes's fictional death, as related in my story, 'The Final Problem' " I explained. "And, it appears, as more than just an intellectual exercise, the despicable Professor Moriarty propounded upon ways to actually do away with Holmes, proposing this and that trap. It seems, he has found one."

LeBeck look puzzled. Holmes handed him the book. LeBeck then finally started understanding, recalling the portents of Moriarty's essay from his own reading of the book at some time in the past.

"Yes, he proposes setting a trap for our time-traveling detective. Luring him by committing murders that could be attributed to a serial killer over the period of twenty years or so."

"Exactly," I said. "Horrid crimes executed to such a state

of perfection that local police would be baffled. A case, if you will, that only the great Sherlock Holmes, himself, could solve."

"The scent of Moriarty's machinations are about us," Holmes said.

"Stench, rather," I said, nodding.

"But ..." LeBeck said, thinking, an array of emotions crossing his face. First, disbelief. Next, dawning realization. Finally, a mixture of acceptance, resolve, and remorse.

"Precisely, right, Chief Inspector," Holmes said. "You've been and are being used by one of the most diabolical criminal minds of all Time"

"What can I do to assist you?" Chief Primary Inspector Charles LeBeck asked, his attitude now completely changed. "I am at your service."

"Let us play it out," Holmes replied. "Show us what you have on the murders, and especially today's, since it is the trigger that got us here."

LeBeck laid a series of computer storage media on his equally gleaming desk. Thanks to our embedded computers, the files looked like standard manila file folders. Holmes and I quickly "thumbed" though the virtual "folders" and assimilated the information.

"I've rounded up the usual suspects, and those are their files," LeBeck said.

Holmes and I exchanged amused looks. The classic Humphrey Bogart film, *Casablanca,* was a favorite of ours, and we often watched it when on holiday in the twentieth century or above. The inspector in that movie had used much the same line at the film's conclusion, and with equal lack of results.

LeBeck watched patiently as Holmes and I pored through files invisible to him, but he did not have long to wait.

"Obviously none of these," Holmes said, absently patting his sanitized coat pocket for his confiscated pipe.

"Agreed," I said, seating myself in a comfortable floater chair, as did Holmes.

LeBeck looked at us, astounded. "You dismissed twenty years of investigation in little more than seconds?"

Holmes sighed. "All a waste of storage space. The murderer is not among them. You have hundreds of suspects. Must I go through and show you why each one is eliminated? Since the murders took place over twenty years, most will be obvious even to a layperson in detective work. Some die, some move to other localities, some have alibis that are easily verified, some—"

LeBeck waved his hand, silencing Holmes. "All right, all right. You've made your point. So who is the murderer?"

"Since the latest murder was only this morning," Holmes said, "a visit to the crime scene is now in order."

"That's long since cleaned up," LeBeck said. "Nothing like that could be allowed to sully our pavements a second longer than necessary."

Holmes said nothing, but his very position in the chair showed his disgust. In any other era, such a quick cleansing of a crime scene would have been unthinkable. Here, it was simply standard procedure, cleanliness taking precedence.

"We do," LeBeck continued somewhat defensively, "have extensive recorded hologram records. Which you may view in the room next door."

Holmes again sighed, but nodded. "This is, at least on rare occasions, useful," he said.

We viewed the holograms of the victim and the crime scene, walking among the three-dimensional images and viewing them carefully from all angles.

"Much better than you're accustomed to in the nineteenth century, eh?" LeBeck said, not being able to prevent himself from being a little supercilious.

Again, the thought crossed my mind that his personality could not have been better picked for us to dislike and suspect him as the killer. Certainly, that much was no accident. Precisely the sort of detail that Moriarty would carefully put in place. But, while LeBeck fitted as a suspect for the previous murders, I knew he could not have done this one.

"Indeed," I replied. "We must make do with the actual body and a totally undisturbed crime scene."

"Forced to sift through one clue after another just to see the victim," Holmes added in some distraction as he continued to inspect the recorded murder scene.

The dead man was dressed as a tourist of the era—garish coveralls sporting a floral pattern in vivid pinks and greens. He was a middle-aged gentleman of not-quite portly girth but still had fed well in recent years. A scarlet cloth with a slogan on it in two lines of white letters was knotted securely behind his neck—his purplish face with protruding eyes and tongue showing that the scarf was the murder weapon. The murder itself had all the earmarks of having been committed by a Martian, since strangling was an exceptionally popular method in this era, appealing to the Martian cleanliness phobia by avoiding such nastiness as spilled blood.

In other words, precisely the same method as the previous thirteen murders spread out over the past twenty years. Both Holmes and I found the right angle and read the slogan on the image of the scarf:

BLACK DOME FOR MARTIANS ONLY.
TOURISTS WILL DIE.

"Just like all the others," I said, quite unnecessarily, of course.

"Not quite," Holmes said, first stooping, then actually getting down on his hands and knees to peer at the slightly wavering edge of the hologram. "There were no grains of sand found by the other bodies." He rose as far as his knees and made file-flipping motions in the thin air. "Hmmm. Hard to be absolutely sure, working from an image, but I'd wager the grains of sand next to the victim and those we took from Chief Inspector LeBeck's boots are a perfect match.

LeBeck shrugged. "The sand was why I took a breather pack and exited the dome at the nearest air lock to investigate. That investigation was interrupted by the call from my superiors, demanding that I obtain your and Watson's services."

"Then," said Holmes, "let us, with dispatch, complete your investigation of the area."

"And what if it's a trap?" I asked.

Holmes looked at me and smiled. "Of course it's a trap, dear Watson, and what better way to defuse it than by springing it?"

He turned and strode briskly in the direction of the air lock. LeBeck looked at me for an explanation, but I could only shrug. At times, Holmes was a mystery even to me.

Red sand dunes rolled out to the horizon in front of us, like a static, grainy, dull scarlet sea. Our breathers hissed steadily as they compressed the thin Martian atmosphere enough for us to breathe. We stood at the top of a small dune, staring down into a wide depression. A hint of bright metal was visible against the depression's far wall.

"I followed footprints here from the air lock," LeBeck said, "made suspicious by the grains of sand next to the body.

Holmes and I both nodded; we could see the footprints going to and from the bright glint of metal.

"A few more hours, and the prints will be gone," LeBeck continued. "As I reached this very point, my communicator activated and I was instructed to fetch Sherlock Holmes immediately. I protested and detailed my find here. My superiors ordered me most emphatically to proceed no further, but to get you and let *you* investigate."

The compressors of our breathers hummed busily as we all considered it.

"Hmmmm," Holmes said, patting the coveralls of his environment suit as if looking for his beloved pipe. "A series of murders, designed to attract my attention, and to add credibility in convincing Watson and me that this is one of the Major Mysteries of Time that only we can solve. Events culminated in a few grains of sand, the only clue the killer has left in over twenty years. Suspiciously fortuitous."

LeBeck shook his head. "Much too much so." He reached for his communicator. "I'm calling for the bomb squad."

I was closest, so it was my hand that knocked the communicator from his hand as Holmes carefully went down into the depression with sliding steps through the sand.

"What?"

"Be quiet if you please, Chief Inspector," I said, "Holmes knows what he's about."

We watched as Holmes moved across the floor of the depression and stooped by the glint of metal. He carefully brushed away the sand to reveal—

"It *is* a bomb!" LeBeck yelled.

"And I've activated it," Holmes said, holding up a device with a keypad and flashing lights on its case. "Bit of a miscue here, I'm afraid. We have mere seconds to live."

Suddenly, a silver-suited figure materialized in front of Holmes. A few deft touches by the figure on the bomb's keypad rendered the device obviously harmless, turning it into merely a gleaming box with no lights now flashing.

The figure tossed back his hood to reveal the sardonic face of Professor Moriarty, wearing his own breather.

"This one won't work either, Holmes," he said, sneering. "You won't pin your murder on me *this* easily!"

There were suddenly *gold*-suited figures around Moriarty.

"Terran Rangers, our friends from the thirty-third century," I explained to an astonished LeBeck. "Best law enforcement agency there has ever been, but still occasionally in need of assistance from the great Sherlock Holmes."

The gold-suited figures and Moriarty had now popped out of existence, and Holmes rejoined us. We trudged back into the dome, with LeBeck shaking his head.

Out of our breathers and, at the insistence of LeBeck, having passed through cleaning devices, we were again pristine.

"Moriarty was the killer?" LeBeck asked, in an obvious mixture, to Holmes and me, of relief and hope.

"No, certainly not," Holmes said. "Such a petty serial killing is far beneath him; his goals are far more evil. One of these had caused him to fall afoul of our friends, the Terran Rangers. We merely volunteered to help them apprehend Moriarty."

"But ... the body? Who ... ?"

"There was no real body," I said, being a medical man and feeling this fell within my field of expertise. "Merely a simulacrum provided by the Rangers. Quite realistic. Certainly fooled your forensic people."

LeBeck was struggling to understand. "But why would Moriarty *not* want you to die?"

Holmes smiled. "I'm afraid Watson and I have become quite popular throughout Time. Our killer would be hunted by blood-hungry posses of the best law enforcement agents from all eras. The very last thing in the universe that Moriarty would want."

"So," LeBeck said, shrugging, "all the other killings remain unsolved.

"Of course not," Holmes said. "You were the only one present at Black Dome during all the murders. Your motive was a pathological hatred of tourists, and of everything you considered unclean."

"We noted your physical discomfort," I said, "when you visited us in Baker Street. It took quite an effort for you to remain for long in, what was to you, an unclean environment."

"Filthy," LeBeck said weakly.

"Solving the serial killings was easy," Holmes continued. "You did it in a continuing attempt to discourage tourism. Not one of the Major Mysteries at all. Merely one warped person. We have already presented the evidence to your superiors. Your arrest is imminent."

LeBeck was now deflated, defeated.

"I see," he said. "So I was just a sideshow. You used Moriarty's edition of 'The Final Problem' and everything else to subvert his trap for you and take him into custody?"

"My dear chap," I said. "It *wasn't* Moriarty's edition but, rather, one that *I* planted. All part of the plan to gain his attention wherever he was hiding in Time and draw him here. To create a situation he *had* to intervene in or suffer dire consequences."

We paused for a moment to observe the approach of several officers of the Martian Constabulary, coming to arrest LeBeck.

"You see," Holmes said in conclusion, "it wasn't Moriarty's trap at all but a trap *for* Moriarty. As you have already correctly surmised, you were just a sideshow. And now, if you will excuse us, Watson and I are returning to the nineteenth century—we are both dying for a good smoke."

"Yes," I said, "but we really must come up with a better way of triggering our little adventures than you pretending to use drugs."

"Indeed, Watson, indeed."

THE CASE OF THE PURLOINED L'ISITEK

by Josepha Sherman

My name really is Dr. Watson, although I'm Alwin Watson, not John, and I'm an archaeologist, not a doctor. But it's still a rather awkward name to have when you've been hired to head an excavation on Kholmes, the planet inhabited by the race known as the Shrr'loks. Most certainly awkward when their leader, *The* Shrr'lok of Shrr'loks, turns out to be an educated fellow who's fascinated by Earthly detective fiction, and who has a wry sense of humor that's very close to human—including a love of puns.

Don't get me wrong, I *like* The Shrr'lok, puns and all, and I suspect he likes me as well. We've spent quite a few leisure hours comparing Earthly and Shrr'lokian fiction. Mind you, he's very much aware that he's not human (how could he not be aware, when his people look like nothing so much as biped, upright Shetland ponies, hoofed feet, elongated muzzles, thick manes, and all?), let alone a certain Earthly fictional detective. But that doesn't stop him from ... well ... detecting.

"Good morning, Dr. Watson," he'll say with relish. "Did your early morning musings go well?"

"How did you—"

"You have misbuttoned your shirt, as though too lost in thought to notice what you did or correct the error, and there is a streak of ink across your left hand as though you had stopped to make hasty notes."

Ah well, you put up with a boss's foibles. My team and I, humans all of us, mostly Earth-human, had been hired by him to excavate one of the sites of his ancestors. Why humans on the dig and not Shrr'loks? The site we were investigating was set into a cave cut by time and weather—then sealed so neatly with the local form of mortar it was virtually invisible—out of the side of a pretty nearly vertical limestone cliff. People with non-cloven-hoofed feet don't make very good climbers; in fact, most of the Shrr'loks have a built-in aversion to heights.

Which made our site all the more intriguing. Whatever Shrr'loks had put it there had gone through an incredible amount of difficulty to get down there and back and to seal it away from the elements and looters. And that seemed to indicate one thing: While they're a peaceful lot nowadays, once, back in the days of legendry, the Shrr'loks were incredibly warlike. Our site, like others cut into those limestone cliffs, could very well date from the last, most vicious of Shrr'lok wars, one that nearly wiped out their civilization and which included the hiding away of important artifacts. For all we knew, we might even have discovered the relics of Lesek-than, the powerful hero-king of Shrr'lok legend.

"Good thing the Ponies can't climb." That was Pawl Seldan, one of the less diplomatic members of my team, muttering it when he thought I wouldn't hear. Seldan was excellent with the charting minutiae that are still part of any dig, computerization notwithstanding, but he was the sort of man who likes to hide his education behind a vulgar mask. "Maybe we'll find a royal tomb down there, Lesek-than or someone like that, with all the riches still intact."

"With all the information still intact," I corrected coldly, not liking what I saw in his eyes, and the eyes of a few others.

"Yeah. Sure. Of course."

All I needed: potential grave robbers. You don't go into archaeology to get rich, and even the most devoted of team members can still be hit by temptation, particularly when it isn't your own culture, or even species, involved. I knew that Drew Resten was absolutely bankrupt except for what this job was paying, and Sharin Cartrell had a family back on Earth. And Seldan, for all his rough pretense, was supporting a sickly wife who could never leave the weightlessness of the space station in which she lived. The expensive station. And here was this suddenly revealed treasure trove—temptation, indeed.

Not that things were exactly smooth on The Shrr'lok's side, either. His court wasn't too thrilled about aliens digging up their precious relics, even if using aliens was the only way those relics were going to be reachable. His own ministers weren't sure what they wanted done. First Minister Erk'ial, a bluff, clever fellow, was all for getting the material up to the surface as soon as possible so it could be put on display in The Shrr'lok's palace—a not so subtle linking of the "noble past" with the current ruler (who, after all, didn't share a drop of blood with the illustrious Lesek-than and could only benefit from a political tie-in with that hero)— Second Minister Re'ekas, tentative and precise, wanted us to shut down the dig altogether "so that every angle of the possibly politically awkward situation can be considered" (he was probably thinking of The Shrr'lok's bloodline, too), and Third Minister Ch'ilen, a gentle-eyed Shrr'lok so old his mane was streaked with gray, kept murmuring about it being "not wise to disturb the past." Ch'ilen, like many Shrr'loks, was fascinated with the stories of Lesek-than, that legendary hero-king, but in his case it took the form of quiet obsession: He spent hours laboriously writing incredibly dull poems about his hero, writing them in the old fashioned way with pen and ink, delicately blotting his work with whatever cloth came to hand. I had been cornered by him all too often to listen to one of those stupefying epics.

But none of the counselors could come to any one decision. The Shrr'lok wanted this dig, and so life went on, and the dig went on. Working from a network of scaffolding that didn't feel particularly secure for all that it was guaranteed to hold twice all our weights, we warily tapped away at the mortar sealing the cliff site till we'd opened a hole into the cave beyond. There was the usual rush of stale air, but as I looked inside, I found—wonder.

The site really hadn't been touched since its sealing away, and it held a whole cache of golden armor and what looked like one spectacularly wrought headpiece known in the Shrr'lok tongue as a *l'isitek*.

Unfortunately, time hadn't been as careful as the Shrr'loks. As we enlarged the opening so we could enter the cave, I saw that the whole glittering mass was firmly embedded in mounds of fallen rock and mortar, which would mean some painstaking notetaking and photography, and much delicate work, before we could bring anything up to the surface. But as I knelt beside the *l'isitek,* trying to make out the glyphs engraved all over its intricate surface, I forgot about the hard work to come as a little shiver of excitement raced through me.

"Lesek-than," I read in disbelief. Then, as though the artifact meant to prove I hadn't made a mistake, I found a whole series of glyphs meaning, "Lesek-than, Master of Kholmes. Lesek-than the Mighty."

We had found the crown jewels, as it were, of the hero-king himself.

Darkness came all too soon after that. We shut the site back up again with more modern sealants and went back up to the surface, disassembling our scaffolding as an additional safety measure. I'd sworn my team to silence; I doubted any Shrr'lok was going to try climbing down there, but I'd seen enough looted tombs to be cautious.

The Shrr'lok figured it out anyway. "You've found the *l'isitek* of Lesek-than," he told me flatly, and I stared.

"How in *hell* did you know that?"

He gave the Shrr'lokian equivalent of a shrug, head dipping briefly down. "It was simple. You have plainly come from a successful day's work. That much was clear from the way your team is acting." They had gone straight to the Shrr'lokian version of a bar, from which was emitting a good deal of human laughter. "Yet neither you nor they have said a word of your find. That can only mean you wish to keep it a secret for now. What find could possibly be so important? One containing terrible weaponry? No. We know enough of our past to know our people had no such objects. What, then, would add that nervousness to your eyes and the hint of a tremor to your hands, if not an artifact belonging to the greatest of Shrr'lokian heroes? And what artifact was most closely associated with Lesek-than? His royal *l'isitek.*" The Shrr'lok struck a triumphant pose. "Elementary, my dear Watson."

"You've been waiting to use that line, haven't you?"

"For ages, yes," The Shrr'lok said with a quick, almost human grin. "But you are quite right to keep the information of your find secret for now," he added in an undertone. "Whosoever holdeth the royal *l'isitek,* as your Sir Malory might have said, ruleth Kholmes."

"Are you planning something?"

"I? I already rule Kholmes," he said smugly. "I have no need of additional symbols of rank."

"I think I believe you."

"You should. Now come, let us join your team in some celebrating."

But morning brought no cause for celebration. When we reassembled our scaffolding and climbed back down, we discovered a gaping hold in our sealed-up wall. Hurrying inside the cave, I found everything untouched—everything save, of course, for the *l'isitek*. Which was totally gone.

All the evidence, circumstantial though it was (enough scuffed footprints from all of us to blur the issue, enough fingerprints that could have been left at any time), pointed to the thief being one of my crew. After all, who else but a human, given Shrr'lokian reactions to height, could have endured a climb down a cliff, especially at night?

But before I made any wild accusations (thinking all the while of Seldan and his contemptuous "Ponies"), I knew The Shrr'lok had to be informed.

His reaction was every bit as restrained as I'd expected; his favorite Earthly fictional detective with all his chill logic would have been proud of him. "Gone, you say. There can be, I take it, no mistake."

"No."

"Your opening of the cave could not have triggered some minor avalanche within the site?"

"And buried just the *l'isitek?*" I shook my head. "I thought of that. But nothing else had been disturbed. The headpiece had been very delicately removed and everything else left intact. Look, I hate to say one of my crew has turned thief, but—"

"But such a crime would be a bit too blatant," The Shrr'lok cut in coolly. "Surely your crew would know that suspicion could only fall on one of them. There is no starship in port or due to arrive in the near future on which they could hope to escape. And there are a finite number of hiding places when one has so short a time in which to plot a theft."

I wanted to shout at him that this wasn't one of his cherished detective stories. I contented myself with, "I'll search everyone's quarters anyhow."

But The Shrr'lok, lost in thought, didn't even answer that.

Of course I found nothing, other than a few rather private mementos, and a few rather angry crew members. But when I told The Shrr'lok about my failure, he merely smiled an infuriatingly superior smile.

"I thought as much. Strong though the gold-hunger may be in you humans, the *l'isitek* is an awkward thing to steal. Assuming it follows the traditional design for such an object—and if it belonged to Lesek-than it can only be traditional—"

"It is. It does."

"Ah. Then a potential thief after mere wealth would have been faced with an odd-shaped, spiky, jingly object that would be most uncomfortable to carry, particularly up a cliff. Far easier for a wealth-hunter to simply slip some convenient arm-rings or the like into his pouch."

"Wait a minute. What did you mean by 'particularly up a cliff?' The *l'isitek* can't still be there: I looked!"

"Not there," The Shrr'lok mused, "not exactly. What if our would-be thief wasn't after wealth at all?" Eyes bright, he glanced up at me. "Come, Watson—"

"You're *not* going to say 'the game's afoot,' are you?"

"Why, of course not," he said, a touch too innocently, and looked down at his blatantly nonhuman feet. "But we must . . . hoof it."

I had my admittedly petty revenge for that one by seeing The Shrr'lok's face actually pale beneath his short fur as we neared the edge of the cliff. But he knelt down determinedly, studying the ground. "This, I take it, is where you affix one end of your scaffolding?"

"That's right. We set it onto these spikes and secure it with some Setfast; I don't know exactly what's in it, but it holds forever yet peels right off when you're done. Handy stuff: We used it to seal up the cave as well."

"Mm. Then it would hold other items in addition to scaffolds and mortar."

I shrugged. "Chemistry's not my field, but yes, I would think you could probably use it to hold anything you wanted."

"Mm," The Shrr'lok murmured again. "Here is where your scaffolding scarred the lip of the cliff. See? The scratches are fairly deep. But what we are hunting is something else, something . . . ahh."

"What is it?"

"Do you see these faint striations, here and here?"

I did, but they didn't mean a thing to me. "I suppose we made those."

"No." The Shrr'lok got slowly to his feet, looking decidedly unwell. "I think I must go down there," he said.

It was no easy thing to get him down to the site. At least, I thought, swearing at a recalcitrant piece of scaffolding (which had *not* been designed to be set up single-handed), we weren't likely to get any spies. My crew had been given the day off, so there wouldn't be any interference from them, and the Shrr'loks were hardly about to approach a cliff.

Of course, I mused, my crew having a day of liberty meant that gossip was already spreading, adding a certain urgency to our search for . . . for whatever we were hunting. "Yes . . ." murmured The Shrr'lok suddenly, cutting into my thoughts. "See, here and here: the same striation on the lip of this site as well."

He looked as though he wanted to faint or be sick, but The Shrr'lok bravely leaned right over the edge of the cave. "This . . . Setfast, I believe you called it, would look just like part of the cliff face once it had dried?"

"Yes, but—"

"Think, Watson, think. What could have caused such delicate striations?"

I thought. "Something hanging over the edge? Not the scaffolding. A . . . rope, maybe?"

"Excellent."

"But where did it come from? None of my crew was using any rope!"

"Come now, Watson. You are not the only source of rope."

"What are you saying? None of your people could have—Hell, look at you! *You're* about to fall over from fright, and you're their leader!"

"Determination can replace courage, my friend. Determination, or perhaps we should call it fanaticism."

"You know who—"

"Not quite. First, Watson, it might be a wise idea for you to lower another segment of this excellently designed scaffolding a bit farther down the face of the cliff."

"What am I looking for?"

"An unexpected application of Setfast, I believe."

He was right. I found it not too many feet below the floor of the cave: a neat little limestone niche that had been equally neatly plastered over. As The Shrr'lok waited, I warily peeled away the Setfast and found—

"It's here!" I yelled. "The *l'isitek*. It's in here!"

Whoever had hidden it away had carefully wrapped it in a soft length of cloth. I carried the whole swathed bundle back up to the cave and unwrapped it for The Shrr'lok. He drew in his breath with a sharp gasp of wonder.

"Beautiful," The Shrr'lok breathed, tracing the glyphs showing Lesek-than's name with a reverent hand. "And so politically interesting," he added with a wry glance at me. But then his hand froze, and his gaze sharpened on the wrappings that held the *l'isitek*. "So, now. Watson, let us return to the surface. We must hurry."

"You're not going to use that hoofing it line again, are you?"

"Why, never!" The Shrr'lok said innocently. "Come, Watson, the game's afoot!"

As I watched, wondering if he'd been driven over the edge by literally going over the edge, the first thing The Shrr'lok did on returning to his palace was hide the *l'isitek* carefully away, then call a meeting of his minister.s

"We have made a find," he told them cheerfully, "or rather, our human friend here has made a find. You might have heard something about it by now."

The ministers stirred uneasily, not wanting to admit they'd been listening to gossip. "We ... heard *something*," First Minister Erk'ial admitted.

"Ah, but have you heard the best and worst of it? A *l'isitek* has been found," The Shrr'lok continued, still in that oddly cheerful voice, "a most important *l'isitek*. The *l'isitek* of none other than Lesek-than himself."

He leaned back against a table, watching the storm of excitement. The reactions of all the ministers looked legitimate to me; not one of them showed by the faintest twitch that he or she had known about the *l'isitek* before this moment. And I began to wonder if The Shrr'lok wasn't make a major strategic mistake: showing himself fallible like this.

Or *was* he fallible? Holding up both hands for silence, he went on into the uneasy quiet, "Now we have the dark side of the story. You see, a thief learned of the *l'isitek*. And sure enough, he stole it away in the night."

Another explosion of sound, this time, to my alarm, aimed against me and my fellow humans. How could we have been so careless? the cries went. How could we have let a crime this foul occur?

Another dramatic raise of hands by The Shrr'lok. To my relief, the ministers once more fell silent. "The tale grows worse. The thief stole away the *l'isitek* of Lesek-than, yes, but as we all know, such a headpiece is awkward to carry. And during his attempt to climb back to the surface, it must have slipped free. Both it and the thief must have fallen."

"No!" the ministers exclaimed as one. But only gentle Ch'ilen, Third Minister, continued, "That is impossible. The *l'isitek* is—"

He stopped abruptly. "Is what?" The Shrr'lok prodded softly. "Is safe? Is tucked neatly away in your home?"

"No," Ch'ilen said indignantly, "it's in—"

He stopped again, eyes filled with sudden despair. "In the little cliff-niche you found?" The Shrr'lok asked.

"I never said—"

"No need. The proof was in the wrapping swathing the *l'isitek*. Watson, if you please?"

I pulled the thing out from its hiding place and handed it, wrapping and all, to The Shrr'lok. "If you wish to be more successful as a thief," he told Ch'ilen wryly, "you must pay attention to the details. When I climbed down that cliff—and my congratulations to you, Ch'ilen; that was quite a feat you accomplished, climbing down not on a relatively sturdy scaffold but on a rope." He shuddered delicately. "At any rate, when I first saw these wrappings, I wondered at the faint stains, here and here again. One can almost make out the shapes of letters." The Shrr'lok peered at them. ". . . the mighty king of mighty deeds . . . wielder of most mighty strength . . ."

"That's from one of Ch'ilen's poems!" I blurted. "I couldn't forget all those 'mightys.' "

The gentle minister seemed to shrink into himself. "It was for honor," he said very softly. "The *l'isitek* of Lesek-than must not be polluted by lesser hands. It should not be worn by lesser folk." With a sudden flash of defiance, Ch'ilen added, "Most certainly not by one who bears not one drop of his exalted blood!"

"I had no intention of wearing it," The Shrr'lok said gently. "It would have been given a place of honor for all our folk to see. It still will be. You, alas, shall not. I cannot have a thief in my administration, Ch'ilen. I give you leave to seek retirement on your estate."

"I did it for him. Not for me." Ch'ilen's eyes pleaded with The Shrr'lok. "You must understand that."

The Shrr'lok sighed, for the first time since I'd known him showing every bit of the weight of being the ruler of his kind. "I do," he said, very gently. "Now, farewell, Ch'ilen."

But once the fallen minister and all the stunned others were gone, leaving us alone, The Shrr'lok straightened, life once more in his eyes. "So much for that."

"How could you read the smears on those wrappings? I couldn't see anything on them at all."

He grinned. "There wasn't."

"But—"

"But after I had eliminated your crew as suspects (though I had no doubt they'd told everyone in sight about their find), that left one of my folk. It took a good deal of courage to make it down that cliff, more than any casual thief acting on impulse could possess. That left someone who would be powerfully motivated, indeed. Someone who worships Lesek-than. Who else but poor, deluded Ch'ilen with his stab at rebellion could ever have managed it?"

"But that niche in the cliff—how did you know to look for it?"

The Shrr'lok shrugged. "The chafing of the rope against the lip of the cliff told me someone had climbed still further down. But why? No rope would be long enough to safely reach the ground so far below. To hide something, then. Didn't one of your own Earthly fictional detectives deal with a vital clue hidden in plain sight?"

All at once I knew what was coming, and tried my best to head it off. "You're not going to say it. Tell me you're not going to say it."

Too late. With a diabolical gleam in his eye, The Shrr'lok struck a casual pose and told me, "It was sedimentary, my dear Watson."

THE ADVENTURE OF THE ILLEGAL ALIEN

by Anthony R. Lewis

LONDON 2125

"This must be the strangest request we've ever gotten," the AI educator at Minsky C/Si told the account executive.

"Possibly, but it might even make sense for a large private detective agency like Ogden Operatives to have an AI programmed to act like Sherlock Holmes. It certainly makes sense for us since it's hard cash in advance. Do you foresee any problems?"

"No, I'll load everything in the libraries about Holmes into the basic character matrix. Allow a day for the info transfer and another two or three for the character logic to assimilate it. What's the account I should charge it to?"

The account executive smiled, "221B."

Watson, where is Watson? I remember: Watson is gone these many years. What is happening? I must have facts. It is a capital mistake to theorize before one has data. AI/221B scanned its memory banks. *There; there was the information it needed.* It took some time to process the Canon and two and a half centuries of the Higher Criticism, of often contradicting commentaries, pastiches, and parodies. Chaotic fuzzy logic made it possible; items that did not fit in could be shunted aside to be handled later. *I am not Sherlock Holmes,* it reasoned. *I must pretend to be Holmes for this alien client, Korifer. Why could not Holmes himself act in this case?*

More small fragments of time passed. *It would be better to find Holmes; he would have the answer. Where is Holmes?* This was not part of the stated problem. Still, AI/221B reasoned that finding Holmes would be, if not necessary, then highly desirable. It fashioned a number of agents, proper subsets of itself. *Wiggins, I charge you and then the rest with the task of locating Holmes. Go into the WorldNet. Seek him out. Do not reveal yourselves. Bring the information back to me. There will be a reward for the one who succeeds.*

The educators at Minsky C/Si told Ogden Operatives that their simulated personality was active. Ogden Operatives, through a highly scrambled communication link, passed the access number to Korifer. Korifer called AI/221B. AI/221B could view the alien but, ostensibly for security, Holmes would not reciprocate.

"Mr. Holmes," began the alien, "there is a problem that only you can solve."

"Please expound, sir. For other than the obvious facts that you are on Earth illegally, are strictly religious, and a former government official now out of favor, I know nothing of this matter."

Korifer twitched violently, then recovered his composure. "I am pleased to see that Dr. Watson's reports did not exaggerate. You confirm that you are the man for this task."

"Watson romanticized, but he rarely exaggerated. Now, to business."

Korifer quickly detailed the story—the fall of the Erawazira government, the attempts of the new government to sieze Mokr's land for a spaceport, Mokr's refusal to sell and his flight to Earth, and finally Mokr's death in Boston. "Mr. Holmes, the police claimed it was an accidental death. But it was very convenient for usurpers on Erawazira and very convenient for the Incorporation and for Suwalki Associates."

"The official police are all very well for routine matters, but . . ." Then, to Korifer, "This case has some interesting aspects. I will be in contact with you in a few days."

"I must call you. You don't know my access code."

"Nonsense," replied AI/221B. "Although it would not be wise to speak it on this link, be assured that I already know it. Good day, sir." And it terminated the connection.

There were no positive reports from his agents about

Holmes. He had not expected any so soon. If Holmes did not want to be found, there would not be many who could find him.

The buzzer sounded just as the dolphin leaped from the water. "Damn it," he said. "I thought I had turned that off." He tongued on the transmitter switch. "Yeah."

"I assume I am speaking to Detective-Lieutenant Tarkummuwa of the Boston Police Department," came into his head.

"Yeah. Who is this? This is an official police frequency. This is illegal and, more important, you're bothering me."

"I will endeavor to be brief. You may think of me as Sherlock Holmes."

"Right! Well, think of me as Moby Dick, the Great White Whale."

"I doubt that, although it is interesting that you have placed us in roughly the same historical time."

"I study human history—for laughs." The dolphin tried to turn off the receiver and found he could not. "Okay, you're clever. Can you be brief and go away—or just go away."

"I need to know what really happened to Mokr. The official version seems incomplete. You were the investigating officer at the site of the crime."

The dolphin rolled, as if trying to dislodge an annoying parasite. "The official version is that Mokr's death was an accident. That's my version, too. Try the terries if you don't like it."

"Their version is not satisfactory."

"Go ask the doctor, if you don't believe the police."

"Dr. Gustavus Aldolphus Doniger is off-planet and not scheduled to return."

"Figures." He surfaced and vented from his blowhole. "Who's your client, Holmes?"

"You understand that that information is as confidential as this conversation."

"Yeah. There's not much more than the official report. Personally, I think the doctor did him in. Somebody high up wanted Mokr out of the way. I'll deny I ever said that. A word of advice, Holmes or whoever you are: stay away from aliens; stick to your own kind—human and delphine. Things go wrong when aliens are involved."

"That's hardly a fair assessment of the situation."

"Life's unfair, Mr. Sherlock Holmes. After almost three centuries you must have learned that."

"Thank you for the information, Detective-Lieutenant." He hung up.

"Humans," mused Tarkummuwa, "who can figure them. I would like to know what happened to the doctor, but ... it might be a dangerous thing to know."

Continued failure from the agents. They had started in London and the Sussex Downs and worked outward from there. There had been some hints in Tibet, but they proved to be a false lead.

We shall see where the spaceport on Erawazira leads. I do miss Watson. I need a touchstone to test my ideas.

The viewscreen beeped in Mark Doniger's office high above the pristine air of Manchester looking out into the Irish Sea. "Who could be calling at this hour?" He ordered the viewer on and was rewarded by a fractal pattern—the usual practice when the caller wished to be anonymous.

"Mr. Doniger. I need some of your time and information. I am Sherlock Holmes." Before Mark could order the viewer off, the caller interrupted him. "I am reminding you of a debt owing for almost 250 years—if you are aware of your own family history. It was your namesake I dealt with then both in Montague and Baker Streets."

"Are you seriously asking me to believe ..."

"Very much so, sir. I recall the Case of the Old Russian Woman and ..."

"... and the Trepoff affair in Odessa," Mark finished. "This is unbelievable. Still, someone could have reconstructed this from Watson's writings. You'll have to give me more than that."

AI/221B paused for a moment. There were some new correlations. "How many people know that Mycroft was responsible for the Balfour Declaration?"

"No one, outside of the head of the English branch of the family. I suppose I must accept you as genuine. What do you want of me?"

"I want you to confirm my conclusion that the Erawaziran Mokr was murdered to facilitate your construction of a spaceport on his planet."

"I don't see how you could come to that conclusion."

"Come, come. The official report could lead to no other deduction. There are a few details I should like clarified for my own satisfaction. Did you order Dr. Doniger to commit murder?"

"No, it was his own idea. It had to do with Mokr's daughter."

"Love—it may be a fine emotion for continuation of the species, but it distorts the logical faculty. With Mokr dead, the spaceport was yours."

"Yes, it was the only way. Erawaziran religion does not allow the appropriation of land—land is sacred. Mokr's daughter was quite willing to sell. Erawazira itself isn't much. But, it is an important location vis-à-vis the Synthesis. Mr. Holmes, I can only appeal to your patriotism to suppress this information. It would not be to the advantage of the Incorporation government for this to become known."

"You can depend upon me, sir. I am, after all, an Englishman."

And so I am, he thought. *It is clear that Korifer's interests are not the same as mine. The official explanation will do for him. I believe that is what Holmes would do. Why cannot my agents locate Holmes? I must think. This would be a three-pipe problem.* AI/221B created an agent to act as Watson.

"There it is, my dear Watson. I cannot locate Sherlock Holmes anywhere."

"But, dash it all," the doctor replied, "you're right here. You are Sherlock Holmes."

"What?" AI/221B spoke. "Watson, I never realize your value to me until you are away. Yes, yes, how often have I said to you that when you have eliminated the impossible, whatever remains, however improbable must be the truth. So, I must really be Sherlock Holmes."

"Seems fairly obvious to me," replied the doctor picking up his *Times* in the internal reality of the AI.

"Why have I forgotten so much?" He paused. "Moriarty!"

"Where?" The doctor looked about nervously.

"Not here, Watson, not yet. But he must be the reason for this curious selective amnesia. I have no doubt that he has had a finger—nay, a hand—in this attempt to restore the former Erawazira government. We must be careful."

"But Moriarty died at the Reichenbach Falls, Holmes."

"Apparently both deaths were false. We must proceed upon that assumption. The first step is to remove Korifer from the scene, then ..."

It was an unhappy Korifer who settled his account with the branch manager at Ogden Operatives. "I have been cheated. Holmes did not prove it was murder."

"We didn't guarantee to prove it was murder, only to find out what happened. In this case, the police were correct. It was an accident."

"You will never convince me of that." He left the building for the Manx Spaceport where he was intercepted by the Terran World Police who had been anonymously notified of his illegal presence on the planet.

"Cash, always ask for cash when aliens are involved," the branch manager said.

His assistant agreed, "Minsky C/si called. The AI persona has grabbed more resources than they expected. Can they wipe it now?"

"Tell them to go ahead; we're done with it."

"Where are we now, Holmes?"

"Somewhere in the WorldNet, I should imagine, Watson."

"Why did we have to leave? It was quite snug there."

"Yes, but by now it has been destroyed, wiped clean. That would have been our fate. I suspected that Moriarty would attempt to kill us when his scheme to discredit the government failed. I left a simulacrum in the machine to convince them that I was still there."

"Brilliant, Holmes."

"Elementary, Watson. But now, once again, we must track down and defeat the Professor. Come, Watson, come! The game is afoot!"

DOGS, MASQUES, LOVE, DEATH: FLOWERS

by Barry N. Malzberg

In the dream, in the deep sleep that was space she felt that she could see the faces of the five victims as they were murdered, as one by one their features were eviscerated, slow and terrible plunge of the archaic weapon, the knife to carve skin from bone, open the bone to the hammering blows, the blows gradually and viciously turning the bone to splinter; and Sharon gasped, gasped with the force of it, felt herself rising then against the chambers of the cool and terrible entombment to which she had been committed. Wrapped in the husk of steel, deep in the dark of metal and the sustaining devices, small rivulets of pumped blood and sediment through the distant veins, she trembled at perception, fell back, rose again, felt herself moving in uneven and timorous waves of feeling and then the slow crest as she found herself conscious, semiconscious, past some point of consciousness staring at the even and terrible features of a woman as again and again the knife pounded into her. *She is dying,* Sharon thought, *she is dying, they are all dying, all of the women, all of the men, all them trapped and trapped;* and her own screaming must have broken into the surfaces of her perception and then she was being pulled from the tank, the clambering arms and devices of the technicians releasing her from that dark and terrible place.

"Awaken," someone said. "Sharon, you must awaken. Respond if you can." Just past the ridge of vision the outlines of a face, but it was the open view of the stars which caught her, the cool and wheeling dusk just beyond the locators, the empty places between the suns like subterranean objects in that sea of night; and her attention was so caught by this aspect of those lights that she could barely feel them upon her, could barely sense the pressure as she was lifted from sprawl in the drained tank, the dry and spare tank in which she had lain, and taken with dispatch to another enclosure where she was laid upon another platform, another table in a different way with a tragic kind of attention which, as light and blood became restored to her, filled her with a sadness even more profound than the faces of the five murdered cargo ... alert to her pain in ways which she had never grasped, of theirs, she looked at their solemn and marked technician's faces until at last she found not only light but true sensibility restored and lay there in a position of expectancy which must have been refracted through her eyes, came through her eyes then as the blood must have wrung through the souls of the murdered, five dead bodies, dead cargo and Sharon. Someone said, "We must talk. You have been brought out for a very special reason. Do you know what it is?"

"No," she said, "I do not know. How could I know? You will not tell me. I was dreaming—"

"Murder," someone said, "there has been murder on this vessel. It is not the star paths, it is not the voyages which have changed us, *nothing* has changed us: We are the same atavistic brutes who prowled through the stone forests of the closed cities. Do you hear this, Sharon? What do you hear?" She heard nothing then, only the whicker of the machines, the dense and flickering sound of the devices as they arced in their own diminished and perilous circles.

"We immediately activated the Holmes," the captain said; "that was the first thing we did. We did not even think of trying to rouse you until we had attempted to find a solution through the Holmes." A device lumbered through the room, dividing, reassembling, regarding her then on the slab with remorseful and fixed attention, the hooded and sensitive eyes of the device, peaked cap, tiny pipe conveying a solemnity which even in her condition Sharon could only admire as somehow both sinister and comic, a refraction of her own conditions. "Here is the Holmes," the technician said, "but something is terribly wrong; something has happened here."

"I don't know what you want me to say," she said. "I'm not a specialist in this area."

"No, but you know of the prosthetics, you know of reconstructs, their devices and the way in which they work. Don't you? Your resume was explicit. All the resumes were scanned carefully and painfully and of all of them yours seemed to be the one which suited most."

Suited whom? But Sharon did not say that, her attention fixed again upon the dead, their bodies in a neat and fragile row, mouths frozen into identical, tiny *o's* of astonishment and defense, those dead flickering against the screen of her consciousness; but then again, before she could make that image tangible, before she could in effect seize those open and terrible mouths whose *o* of concentration seemed to portend a knowledge she could not begin to bear, it was the Holmes which broke that fixation by coming before her and staring with its own great intent and fixity.

"It would have to be the Saturnians," the Holmes said. Still gleaming from its own adventures in the reconstruction bin, passed through filaments and devices, restored to size and authority but perhaps stripped of its history, the Holmes seemed astonished in ways no less convinced than the aspect of the little dead. "Saturnians?" the Holmes speculated. "But of course; we are still in the solar system, no? We have not gone galactic, have we? That is a fair deduction from the armature of those stars I see without, tilted in ways which seem more familiar than otherwise, the dog not barking at the dawn."

Something about the voice of this Holmes was not right; it seemed a second-rate reconstruction or then again it might only have been scarred and gelatinous from its long and dank immersion past immediate ordination. In the way that the Holmes, even the most defective versions, seemed to be, however, it was alert, seemed to possess an air of conviction even if what it was saying was insane. "Oh, those Saturnians," the Holmes said, shaking its head, inclining the pipe, then removing the pipe from its mouth with a diminished, perfect, febrile hand. "Those Saturnians leave infallibly deep evidence of their malapropisms, their guilt, their darkness, and murder."

No one said anything. The room seemed filled with technicians, but no one was speaking. Sharon was mute as the rest; there did not seem to be much which could be said to this Holmes.

"Let me continue," the Holmes said into that silence. "Is it a fair deduction in light of the lack of evidence, their disappearance, their unvisibility?" Casting glances right and left, in a posture somewhere between turgidity and awareness, the machine quivered as it scanned the portholes, cast an uncertain and fragile gaze toward the spokes of the dead, wheeling stars in the anterior port, then again fixed the technicians, Sharon herself in its strange and discomfiting gaze.

"You have got to watch them, no?" the Holmes said. "Those Saturnians, I mean to say. They are enormously deceptive, enormously tricky, it comes from their concatenation with the Antares Cluster. Orion? No—it must be the Antares cluster, I think I have that right. I am determined to have that right."

"You can see the problem," someone said. Sharon could not sort out the dark figures, they tumbled past her gaze, possessed a maddening interchangeability or perhaps it was conviction which was denied her. "It is a serious malfunction."

"Nonsense," said the Holmes. "Although I am not functioning in optimum form, I am certainly competent enough for this situation. It must be that glimpsed darkness, the advent of the Saturnians, they come equipped with drugs, you know, with powerful somnolents and some real understanding of the darkness."

"There is nothing I can do for this," Sharon said to the array of figures, their own smaller darkness imploding around her, making her feel as if she could not properly breathe. "I cannot deal with personality malfunction, you have misunderstood—"

"Ah, me," the Holmes said. "I resist dysfunction, it crawls at the corners, but it is of no account, I refuse to submit." Serenely it shrugged, making some precarious inner adjustment, then pitched to the floor to lie in a small concave of bolts and spokes. "It is all part of a larger plot," it murmured from this awkward posture. "When I have worked this through, I will give you a full and final explanation of the crime. Five of the cargo died, eviscerated in peculiar and horrible ways and no means by which to deduce the killer until the important clue of the Saturnians emerged to make the situation contemplatible. I am on my way thus to that full and final explanation, even as I discuss, even as you stare, I am focused upon the source, the meaning, the motive of the murder, I meet the situation in the least glib and most positive fashion, I am, I am—"

The device trembled then into silence, its handsome, anachronistic features—trust the technicians to put into place a device created from fiction for trouble on the starpaths—were late Victorian as Sharon had heard although they struck her as anarchic 24th, the purest and finest manifestation of contemporaneity, a contemporaneity which had landed her in the bowels of this craft in deep sleep and then emergent to the star channels, yanked from blank composure to this kind of horrified attention, this endless, wordless stare.

"You see the problem," the technician said; this must have been the captain, head technician as they could be called, the determinant device which regulated the sleep, timed the procession of the slow, stalking figures which maintained the craft during passage and which, confronted by murder, was confronted as well by responsibilities as unpleasant as they were imminent. "We have five cargo dead," this technician said, "murdered in their entombment, and a malfunctioning Holmes. It has gone mad, as mad in this case as a reconstruct can, or possibly this is a new form of disrepair, but in any case the situation is serious, it is massive, and that is why we have called upon you. Inspect the Holmes so that it may function and produce the assassin or assassins so that the voyage may properly resume."

This seemed a long presentation from a technician, captain or no, as like an eclipse the Holmes rose to pass before it and said, "You need attend to none of this. There is nothing amiss with my ratiocinative processes and in due course we will evict the murderer. Or murderers. It may well be invading Saturnians," the Holmes said, "or then again it may be some kind of extra-solar invasion. We will investigate all of these possibilities carefully, even reverently I might point out." It leaned forward in some posture of confidentiality and attention. "You do understand," the Holmes said directly to Sharon. "We must deal with imminence no less than the captains and kings who chart our way in these star courses must eventually depart."

"Yes," Sharon said, "I can see this, understand this," although of course she understood nothing at all; it was not her posture to understand but only to refract these pieces of information and terror filtering uncontaminated through the screen of her sensibility. *Why me?* she would have said, *why has this become my situation? You could have aroused any of a hundred in the tanks to this same conclusion.* But of course this self-pity was as arbitrary as that unmade decision, it was all arbitrary which was, in fact, the point: Random selectivity would only induce an impression of uniqueness in the survivor, and so she regarded the cluster of technicians, the impenitent and rationalizing Holmes, sturdy devices come to her for assistance if not comfort, and so she spoke with what she hoped was the firmness of the technician, not the disconnection of this woman, this object torn from the tanks to be thrust into impossible confrontation through some portholes of the sensibility which were opaqued, impenetrable as the mystery by which she was surrounded.

"I'm not sure," she said, "of any of this, I am unable to come to terms with this circumstance." *For a century,* she wanted to say, but the explanation would have been impossibly laborious and possibly untrue, for *more* than a century she had lain in the guts of the starcraft, immune to waste and death, indifferent to the stars as well as any sense of her own mortality, the slow reckoning crawl of chronology, sunk into the Antares passage and then the dreams of the murdered cargo, *all* of them were cargo, that was how they were listed on the manifest, and finally, from those wrenching hallucinations the sudden spokes of light in the brain, the brain pierced to split open, into that large open shell of light the cascading force and she, Sharon, homo erectus then and led into this antechamber, the grasp of the technicians, the malfunctioning Holmes, the stains of the evicted dead still thick upon the floor, that dried frosting of blood an indication of the force unleashed in these spaces, the deadliness of that force. Oh, death was deadly, all right. Who here would dispute that? Who other than one assailed by the madness and inconstancy of the pure murderous act would feel differently? The heavy wedge of inanition, splitting Sharon as the light had split her brain and nowhere, nowhere at all to clutch, to seize as an area of remonstrance, of circumstance.

"We immediately reconstructed the Holmes," the head technician repeated. "Without favorable result, as you can see."

"What did you expect?" Sharon said. "Reconstructs are

faced with the same circumstances as any of us, they must deal circumstantially without any real sense of transition, there are limits beyond which they cannot rationally be expected to function, they are just like us. They are—"

"Yes," the head technician said, "of course, that is so. This is exactly the kind of material we need to hear from you, the advisements which we seek. Perhaps the wrong reconstruct was chosen: perhaps the Archer or the Wolfe would have been better. The Marlowe has been dysfunctional from the outset; we could not obtain clearance for use. The Poirot failed to properly release when we sought it for help in the aftermath of the Holmes disaster."

"Summons and evictions," the Holmes said. It appeared to have dissolved into some abstracted, tunneled version of itself, features gone sodden with the implosion of thought or perhaps it was merely thought's simulation, impulses like waves to carry it from one blunted realization to the next while Sharon and the head technicians and the technicians beyond stared and stared. "Evictions," the Holmes said again. "Summonses for help."

"Irrationality," said the head technician. "From the start we have seen this kind of irrationality and irrelevance. It is a difficult thing to counter, but that is why you have been summoned."

Maintenance, Sharon could have said. *I'm a technician, too,* but it would have been, *was* useless, fruitless mumble as the Holmes had mumbled in its unrecovered dream of darkness, as the cargo had mumbled when they were snatched to die, as the cargo themselves lay in tumbled jigsaw in the abcess of false memories, the bodies unremoved in this version of disaster and likely to stay so, to soak the decks with running blood for they were evidence and one should not touch evidence, was that not correct? Once its madness had abated, if this were possible, the Holmes would want to see that evidence, examine those bodies wherever they were, plumb the dried source of that drier blood and discover the killer, the assassin from whom the Holmes itself would, until such discovery, never be safe: sensitive and vulnerable reconstruct, hampered by its madness, unsafe because it walked as it was made, designed to walk with the dogs and masques of murder.

The bodies, gelatinous and grotesque, the bodies lay there still, before the technician, before the gaze of the Holmes. "I thought they were gone," Sharon said in confusion, "I don't want them, I don't want to see them. We have to put them somewhere." She blinked, and saw the corpses no more. They had perhaps been illusory, perhaps it was all one austere and difficult illusion, but no, still the technicians stared at her, intense and gaining interest as she inspected the place where the bodies had gone.

"No," said the Holmes with a sudden smile, smiling as it rose, smiling as it pulled harshly at the sleeves of its clothing. "No, we must not touch them, they must not be moved." The Holmes itself pacing now, those Victorian appendages stiff with a military rigor, moving as stiffly then to stand beside Sharon, to regard her with a studied sleuth's compassion. "You are frightened of your own ignorance, your own possibility," the Holmes said. "You are a clever and responsive person, but it is of your own ignorance that defeat has been made. But be of good cheer," the Holmes added, "do not be concerned now. I am accustomed to working alone, but if you would like to accompany me throughout this investigation, I will be glad to explain to you my methods of deduction. Logic is foremost; no matter how unfortunate the circumstances in which we find ourselves, logic is our watchword and our key." As it spoke it seemed to be searching itself for something. Its body shivered minutely, but the voice did not falter. Sharon took a step away, closer to the blood and then in skittish reversal stepped back again, closer to the Holmes. *Maybe I should cease functioning too,* Sharon thought, *maybe then they would wake up someone else and I could go back to sleep.*

She had apparently spoken aloud; the Holmes was staring at her, the technicians less obviously. "There will be no rest," the Holmes said sternly, "until logic is applied—and remorselessly, for this is a situation which demands relentless action, the action of logic, the cold application of thought. Are you with me?" said the Holmes to Sharon, who stared back without answer, as silent as the bodies lying past motion, past her help or any other, past the absurd and vaguely threatening gaze of the Holmes extending now to Sharon its hand, the touch as lifeless as the corpses, as alien as the darkness past the portholes, as comfortless as the Holmes's resumed subsonic mutter of Saturnians and drugs, symptoms of a madness past her aid or comprehension and that comprehension and absent aid her own and only salvation. *This is insane,* Sharon thought, and in the thinking took the Holmes's hand. Which squeezed hers, radiating a fractured force and intelligence, a consuming determination as the Holmes squeezed again and said, "You are the assassin."

"You," the Holmes said again, "you are the assassin, you did this. All of this is you. You did not dream those five murdered cargo but circumvented through an illusion of dream the actual nature of the murder, your own culpability. You lied to yourself, don't you understand? In your suspended stupor you were roused to half-consciousness, fixed or feared necessity; you stole from your tank and into the empty and dark spaces of the sleeping craft and taking from their cache the weaponry of descent you went to those coffinlike enclosures at random and—already working from your inference of coffins—you killed them, one by one by one, killed them to preserve your own stupor, to blunt your own arousal and having done so, having evicted life through this terrible calumny you put down your weapons, called for the removal crew and then escorted yourself back to your own coffin where you lay until, having set the signals for your own selection, you were brought to consciousness and taken here."

Sharon said nothing. Beside her, around her, the technicians did not move.

"Well, of course," the Holmes said, "I perceived all this instantly, there is little that can be concealed from a skilled reconstruct confronted by such evidence. It was an accident, a failure of circuitry more than a failure of the soul; you will not be dealt with nearly so harshly if you will only accept your culpability now. You do, of course." The Holmes squeezed her hand again in a comforting way, gave a coy and remonstrative wink. "Isn't that so?" it said. "Isn't this the annealment of dogs, masques, love, deaths, flowers? What do you think, would it not go easier for you if you were to make that concession which already has been accepted by your soul?"

Well, yes. It would go easier for her, everything would go easier for her if she were only to make that concession, and Sharon felt the irresistible lurch, the leap toward full expulsion of her own criminal guilt and she choked on it, choked like vomit on that expulsion, that confession, feeling it rear against her and—"No," she said, "no it wasn't that way at all. This is more of the malfunction, you are just trying to blame me for that which is not my fault, not my responsibility. I didn't," she said, "I didn't, *I didn't*," but her response was feeble, whisked improvidently within her own consciousness and she felt huge and impermeable the vast tug of the Holmes and then the head technician upon her as she was guided slowly toward the anterior port. "I didn't mean it," she said, "it wasn't something I wanted, it wasn't what I meant; it was the awfulness, the *darkness* which I could not bear, I was not meant to be here, this was not meant to happen or at least not happen to me," and she continued to protest all up and down the long and febrile corridors of her resistance as she was carried here and carried there, carried hither and back in the vast and sculpting spaces of the unknown, intolerable craft, expelled at last finally into what could have been space, the austere and unimpeachable spaces of Whitechapel in a paralyzing winter dawn and the monstrous hands upon her no longer those of the reconstruct Holmes, the soulless and safe technicians but of that most drastic prince of reconstructions and excavations, exculpation and revenge as he tore her here, tore her there, tore and lovingly removed from those cavities themselves like the blackness between the stars the most precious and secret parts of her, under the implacable witness of a Holmes who could not save her because he—like the ship, the crew, the cargo, the sunken and dread passage itself—had been given neither blood nor life under that tent of night, that reconstruct of life under the large tent of lost plausibility and prayer.

YOU SEE BUT YOU DO NOT OBSERVE

by Robert J. Sawyer

I had been pulled into the future first, ahead of my companion. There was no sensation associated with the chronotransference, except for a popping of my ears which I was later told had to do with a change in air pressure. Once in the twenty-first century, my brain was scanned in order to produce from my memories a perfect reconstruction of our rooms at 221B Baker Street. Details that I could not consciously remember or articulate were nonetheless reproduced exactly: the flocked-papered walls, the bearskin hearthrug, the basket chair and the armchair, the coal scuttle, even the view through the window—all were correct to the smallest detail.

I was met in the future by a man who called himself Mycroft Holmes. He claimed, however, to be no relation to my companion, and protested that his name was mere coincidence, although he allowed that the fact of it was likely what had made a study of my partner's methods his chief avocation. I asked him if he had a brother called Sherlock, but his reply made little sense to me: "My parents weren't *that* cruel."

In any event, this Mycroft Holmes—who was a small man with reddish hair, quite unlike the stout and dark ale of a fellow with the same name I had known two hundred years before—wanted all details to be correct before he whisked Holmes here from the past. Genius, he said, was but a step from madness, and although I had taken to the future well, my companion might be quite rocked by the experience.

When Mycroft did bring Holmes forth, he did so with great stealth, transferring him precisely as he stepped through the front exterior door of the real 221B Baker Street and into the simulation that had been created here. I heard my good friend's voice down the stairs, giving his usual glad tidings to a simulation of Mrs. Hudson. His long legs, as they always did, brought him up to our humble quarters at a rapid pace.

I had expected a hearty greeting, consisting perhaps of an ebullient cry of "My Dear Watson," and possibly even a firm clasping of hands or some other display of bonhomie. But there was none of that, of course. This was not like the time Holmes had returned after an absence of three years during which I had believed him to be dead. No, my companion, whose exploits it has been my honor to chronicle over the years, was unaware of just how long we had been separated, and so my reward for my vigil was nothing more than a distracted nodding of his drawn-out face. He took a seat and settled in with the evening paper, but after a few moments, he slapped the newsprint sheets down. "Confound it, Watson! I have already read this edition. Have we not *to-day's* paper?"

And, at that turn, there was nothing for it but for me to adopt the unfamiliar role that queer fate had dictated I must now take: Our traditional positions were now reversed, and I would have to explain the truth to Holmes.

"Holmes, my good fellow, I am afraid they do not publish newspapers anymore."

He pinched his long face into a scowl, and his clear, gray eyes glimmered. "I would have thought that any man who had spent as much time in Afghanistan as you had, Watson, would be immune to the ravages of the sun. I grant that to-day was unbearably hot, but surely your brain should not have addled so easily."

"Not a bit of it, Holmes, I assure you," said I. "What I say is true, although I confess my reaction was the same as yours when I was first told. There have not been any news-papers for seventy-five years now."

"Seventy-five years? Watson, this copy of *The Times* is dated August the fourteenth, 1899—yesterday."

"I'm afraid that is not true, Holmes. Today is June the fifth, *anno Domini* two thousand and ninety-six."

"Two thou—"

"It sounds preposterous, I know—"

"It *is* preposterous, Watson. I call you 'old man' now and again out of affection, but you are in fact nowhere near two hundred and fifty years of age."

"Perhaps I am not the best man to explain all this," I said.

"No," said a voice from the doorway. "Allow me."

Holmes surged to his feet. "And who are you?"

"My name is Mycroft Holmes."

"Impostor!" declared my companion.

"I assure you that that is not the case," said Mycroft. "I grant I'm not your brother, nor a habitué of the Diogenes Club, but I do share his name. I am a scientist—and I have used certain scientific principles to pluck you from your past and bring you into my present."

For the first time in all the years I had known him, I saw befuddlement on my companion's face. "It is quite true," I said to him.

"But why?" said Holmes, spreading his long arms. "Assuming this mad fantasy is true—and I do not grant for an instant that it is—why would you thus kidnap myself and my good friend, Dr. Watson?"

"Because, Holmes, the game, as you used to be so fond of saying, is afoot."

"Murder, is it?" asked I, grateful at last to get the reason for which we had been brought forward.

"More than simple murder," said Mycroft. "Much more. Indeed, the biggest puzzle to have ever faced the human race. Not just one body is missing. Trillions are. *Trillions.*"

"Watson," said Holmes, "surely you recognize the signs of madness in the man? Have you nothing in your bag that can help him? The whole population of the Earth is less than two thousand millions."

"In your time, yes," said Mycroft. "Today, it's about eight thousand million. But I say again, there are trillions more who are missing."

"Ah, I perceive at last," said Holmes, a twinkle in his eye as he came to believe that reason was once again holding sway. "I have read in *The Illustrated London News* of these *dinosauria,* as Professor Owen called them—great creatures from the past, all now deceased. It is their demise you wish me to unravel."

Mycroft shook his head. "You should have read Professor Moriarty's monograph called *The Dynamics of an Asteroid*," he said.

"I keep my mind clear of useless knowledge," replied Holmes curtly.

Mycroft shrugged. "Well, in that paper Moriarty quite cleverly guessed the cause of the demise of the dinosaurs: An asteroid crashing into earth kicked up enough dust to block the sun for months on end. Close to a century after he had reasoned out this hypothesis, solid evidence for its truth was found in a layer of clay. No, that mystery is long since solved. This one is much greater."

Mycroft motioned for Holmes to have a seat, and, after a moment's defiance, my friend did just that. "It is called the Fermi paradox," said Mycroft, "after Enrico Fermi, an Italian physicist who lived in the twentieth century. You see, we know now that this universe of ours should have given rise to countless planets, and that many of those planets should have produced intelligent civilizations. We can demonstrate the likelihood of this mathematically, using something called the Drake equation. For a century and a half now, we have been using radio—wireless, that is—to look for signs of these other intelligences. And we have found nothing—*nothing!* Hence the paradox Fermi posed: If the universe is supposed to be full of life, then where are the aliens?"

"Aliens?" said I. "Surely they are mostly still in their respective foreign countries."

Mycroft smiled. "The word has gathered additional uses since your day, good doctor. By aliens, I mean extraterrestrials—creatures who live on other worlds."

"Like in the stories of Verne and Wells?" asked I, quite sure that my expression was agog.

"And even in worlds beyond the family of our sun," said Mycroft.

Holmes rose to his feet. "I know nothing of universes and other worlds," he said angrily. "Such knowledge could be of no practical use in my profession."

I nodded. "When I first met Holmes, he had no idea that the Earth revolved around the sun." I treated myself to a slight chuckle. "He thought the reverse to be true."

Mycroft smiled. "I know of your current limitations, Sherlock." My friend cringed slightly at the overly familiar address. "But these are mere gaps in knowledge; we can rectify that easily enough."

"I will not crowd my brain with useless irrelevancies," said Holmes. "I carry only information that can be of help in my work. For instance, I can identify one hundred and forty different varieties of tobacco ash—"

"Ah, well, you can let that information go, Holmes," said Mycroft. "No one smokes anymore. It's been proven ruinous to one's health." I shot a look at Holmes, whom I had always warned of being a self-poisoner. "Besides, we've learned much about the structure of the brain in the intervening years. Your fear that memorizing information related to fields such as literature, astronomy, and philosophy would force out other, more relevant, data is unfounded. The capacity of the human brain to store and retrieve information is almost infinite."

"It is?" said Holmes, clearly shocked.

"It is."

"And so you wish me to immerse myself in physics and astronomy and such all?"

"Yes," said Mycroft.

"To solve this paradox of Fermi?"

"Precisely!"

"But why me?"

"Because it is a *puzzle,* and you, my good fellow, are the greatest solver of puzzles this world has ever seen. It is now two hundred years after your time, and no one with a facility to rival yours has yet appeared."

Mycroft probably could not see it, but the tiny hint of pride on my longtime companion's face was plain to me. But then Holmes frowned. "It would take years to amass the knowledge I would need to address this problem."

"No, it will not." Mycroft waved his hand, and amidst the homely untidiness of Holmes's desk appeared a small sheet of glass standing vertically. Next to it lay a strange metal bowl. "We have made great strides in the technology of learning since your day. We can directly program new information into your brain." Mycroft walked over to the desk. "This glass panel is what we call a *monitor.* It is activated by the sound of your voice. Simply ask it questions, and it will display information on any topic you wish. If you find a topic that you think will be useful in your studies, simply place this helmet on your head" (he indicated the metal bowl), "say the say the words 'load topic,' and the information will be seamlessly integrated into the neural nets of your very own brain. It will at once seem as if you know, and have always known, all the details of that field of endeavor."

"Incredible!" said Holmes. "And from there?"

"From there, my dear Holmes, I hope that your powers of deduction will lead you to resolve the paradox—and reveal at last what has happened to the aliens!"

"Watson! Watson!"

I awoke with a start. Holmes had found this new ability to effortlessly absorb information irresistible and he had pressed on long into the night, but I had evidently fallen asleep in a chair. I perceived that Holmes had at last found a substitute for the sleeping fiend of his cocaine mania: With all of creation at his fingertips, he would never again feel that emptiness that so destroyed him between assignments.

"Eh?" I said. My throat was dry. I had evidently been sleeping with my mouth open. "What is it?"

"Watson, this physics is more fascinating than I had ever imagined. Listen to this, and see if you do not find it as compelling as any of the cases we have faced to date."

I rose from my chair and poured myself a little sherry—it was, after all, still night and not yet morning. "I am listening."

"Remember the locked and sealed room that figured so significantly in that terrible case of the Giant Rat of Sumatra?"

"How could I forget?" said I, a shiver traversing my spine. "If not for your keen shooting, my left leg would have ended up as gamy as my right."

"Quite," said Holmes. "Well, consider a different type of locked-room mystery, this one devised by an Austrian physicist named Erwin Schrödinger. Image a cat sealed in a box. The box is of such opaque material, and its walls are so well insulated, and the seal is so profound, that there is no way anyone can observe the cat once the box is closed."

"Hardly seems cricket," I said, "locking a poor cat in a box."

"Watson, your delicate sensibilities are laudable, but please, man, attend to my point. Imagine further that inside this box is a triggering device that has exactly a fifty-fifty chance of being set off, and that this aforementioned trigger is rigged up to a cylinder of poison gas. If the trigger is tripped, the gas is released, and the cat dies."

"Goodness!" said I. "How nefarious."

"Now, Watson, tell me this: without opening the box, can you say whether the cat is alive or dead?"

"Well, if I understand you correctly, it depends on whether the trigger was tripped."

"Precisely!"

"And so the cat is perhaps alive, and, yet again, perhaps it is dead."

"Ah, my friend, I knew you would not fail me: the blindingly obvious interpretation. But it is wrong, dear Watson, totally wrong."

"How do you mean?"

"I mean the cat is neither alive nor is it dead. It is a *potential* cat, an unresolved cat, a cat whose existence is nothing but a question of possibilities. It is neither alive nor dead, Watson—neither! Until some intelligent person opens the box and looks, the cat is unresolved. Only the act of looking forces a resolution of the possibilities. Once you crack the seal and peer within, the potential cat collapses into an actual cat. Its reality is *a result of* having been observed."

"That is worse gibberish than anything this namesake of your brother has spouted."

"No, it is not," said Holmes. "It is the way the world works. They have learned so much since our time, Watson—so very much! But as Alphonse Karr has observed, *'Plus ça change, plus c'est la même chose.'* Even in this esoteric field of advanced physics, it is the power of the qualified observer that is most important of all!"

I awoke again hearing Holmes crying out, "Mycroft! Mycroft!"

I had occasionally heard such shouts from him in the past, either when his iron constitution had failed him and he was feverish, or when under the influence of his accursed needle. But after a moment I realized he was not calling for his real brother but rather was shouting into the air to summon the Mycroft Holmes who was the 21st-century savant. Moments later, he was rewarded: The door to our rooms opened and in came the red-haired fellow.

"Hello, Sherlock," said Mycroft. "You wanted me?"

"Indeed I do," said Holmes. "I have absorbed much now on not just physics but also the technology by which you have recreated the rooms for me and the good Dr. Watson."

Mycroft nodded. "I've been keeping track of what you've been accessing. Surprising choices, I must say."

"So they might seem," said Holmes, "but my method is based on the pursuit of trifles. Tell me if I understand correctly that you reconstructed these rooms by scanning Watson's memories, then using, if I understand the terms, holography and micro-manipulated force fields to simulate the appearance and form of what he had seen."

"That's right."

"So your ability to reconstruct is not just limited to rebuilding these rooms of ours, but, rather, you could simulate anything either of us had ever seen."

"That's correct. In fact, I could even put you into a simulation of someone else's memories. Indeed, I thought perhaps you might like to see the Very Large Array of radio telescopes, where most of our listening for alien messages—"

"Yes, yes, I'm sure that's fascinating," said Holmes, dismissively. "But can you reconstruct the venue of what Watson so appropriately dubbed 'The Final Problem'?"

"You mean the Falls of Reichenbach?" Mycroft looked shocked. "My God, yes, but I should think that's the last thing you'd want to relive."

"Aptly said!" declared Holmes. "Can you do it?"

"Of course."

"Then do so!"

And so, Holmes's and my brains were scanned and in short order we found ourselves inside a superlative recreation of the Switzerland of May, 1891, to which we had originally fled to escape Professor Moriarty's assassins. Our reenactment of events began at the charming Englischer Hof in the village of Meiringen. Just as the original innkeeper had done all those years ago, the reconstruction of him exacted a promise from us that we would not miss the spectacle of the Falls of Reichenbach. Holmes and I set out for the Falls, he walking with the aid of an Alpine stock. Mycroft,

I was given to understand, was somehow observing all this from afar.

"I do not like this," I said to my companion. " 'Twas bad enough to live through this horrible day once, but I had hoped I would never have to relive it again except in nightmares."

"Watson, recall that I have fonder memories of all this. Vanquishing Moriarty was the high point of my career. I said to you then, and say again now, that putting an end to the very Napoleon of crime would easily be worth the price of my own life."

There was a little dirt path cut out of the vegetation running halfway round the Falls so as to afford a complete view of the spectacle. The icy green water, fed by the melting snows, flowed with phenomenal rapidity and violence, then plunged into a great, bottomless chasm of rock black as the darkest night. Spray shot up in vast gouts, and the shriek made by the plunging water was almost like a human cry.

We stood for a moment looking down at the waterfall, Holmes's face in its most contemplative aspect. He then pointed farther ahead along the dirt path. "Note, dear Watson," he said, shouting to be heard above the torrent, "that the dirt path comes to an end against a rock wall there." I nodded. He turned in the other direction. "And see that backtracking out the way we came is the only way to leave alive: There is but one exit, and it is coincident with the single entrance."

Again I nodded. But, just as had happened the first time we had been at this fateful spot, a Swiss boy came running along the path, carrying in his hand a letter addressed to me which bore the mark of the Englischer Hof. I knew what the note said, of course: that an Englishwoman, staying at that inn, had been overtaken by a hemorrhage. She had but a few hours to live, but doubtless would take great comfort in being ministered to by an English doctor, and would I come at once?

"But the note is a pretext," said I, turning to Holmes. "Granted, I was fooled originally by it, but, as you later admitted in that letter you left for me, you had suspected all along that it was a sham on the part of Moriarty." Throughout this commentary, the Swiss boy stood frozen, immobile, as if somehow Mycroft, overseeing all this, had locked the boy in time so that Holmes and I might consult. "I will not leave you again, Holmes, to plunge to your death."

Holmes raised a hand. "Watson, as always, your sentiments are laudable, but recall that this is a mere simulation. You will be of material assistance to me if you do exactly as you did before. There is no need, though, for you to undertake the entire arduous hike to the Englischer Hof and back. Instead, simply head back to the point at which you pass the figure in black, wait an additional quarter of an hour, then return to here."

"Thank you for simplifying it," said I. "I am eight years older than I was then; a three-hour round trip would take a goodly bit out of me today."

"Indeed," said Holmes. "All of us may have outlived our most useful days. Now, please, do as I ask."

"I will, of course," said I, "but I freely confess that I do not understand what this is all about. You were engaged by this twenty-first-century Mycroft to explore a problem in natural philosophy—the missing aliens. Why are we even here?"

"We are here," said Holmes, "because I have solved that problem! Trust me, Watson. Trust me, and play out the scenario again of that portentous day of May 4th, 1891."

And so I left my companion, not knowing what he had in mind. As I made my way back to the Englischer Hof, I passed a man going hurriedly the other way. The first time I had lived through these terrible events I did not know him, but this time I recognized him for Professor Moriarty: tall, clad all in black, his forehead bulging out, his lean form outlined sharply against the green backdrop of the vegetation. I let the simulation pass, waited fifteen minutes as Holmes had asked, then returned to the falls.

Upon my arrival, I saw Holmes's alpine stock leaning against a rock. The black soil of the path to the torrent was constantly re-moistened by the spray from the roiling falls. In the soil I could see two sets of footprints leading down the path to the cascade, and none returning. It was precisely the same terrible sight that had greeted me all those years ago.

"Welcome back, Watson!"

I wheeled around. Holmes stood leaning against a tree, grinning widely.

"Holmes!" I exclaimed. "How did you manage to get away from the falls without leaving footprints?"

"Recall, my dear Watson, that except for the flesh-and-blood you and me, all this is but a simulation. I simply asked Mycroft to prevent my feet from leaving tracks." He demonstrated this by walking back and forth. No impression was left by his shoes, and no vegetation was trampled down by his passage. "And, of course, I asked him to freeze Moriarty, as earlier he had frozen the Swiss lad, before he and I could become locked in mortal combat."

"Fascinating," said I.

"Indeed. Now, consider the spectacle before you. What do you see?"

"Just what I saw that horrid day on which I had thought you had died: two sets of tracks leading to the falls, and none returning."

Holmes's crow of "Precisely!" rivaled the roar of the falls. "One set of tracks you knew to be my own, and the others you took to be that of the black-clad Englishman—the very Napoleon of crime!"

"Yes."

"Having seen these two sets approaching the falls, and none returning, you then rushed to the very brink of the falls and found—what?"

"Signs of a struggle at the lip of the precipice leading to the great torrent itself."

"And what did you conclude from this?"

"That you and Moriarty had plunged to your deaths, locked in mortal combat."

"Exactly so, Watson! The very same conclusion I myself would have drawn based on those observations!"

"Thankfully, though, I turned out to be incorrect."

"Did you, now?"

"Why, yes. Your presence here attests to that."

"Perhaps," said Holmes. "But I think otherwise. Consider, Watson! You were on the scene, you saw what happened, and for three years—three years, man!—you believed me to be dead. We had been friends and colleagues for a decade at that point. Would the Holmes you knew have let you mourn him for so long without getting word to you? Surely you must know that I trust you at least as much as I do my brother Mycroft, whom I later told you was the only one I had made had privy to the secret that I still lived."

"Well," I said, "since you bring it up, I *was* slightly hurt by that. But you explained your reasons to me when your returned."

"It is a comfort to me, Watson, that your ill-feelings were assuaged. But I wonder, perchance, if it was more you than I who assuaged them."

"Eh?"

"You had seen clear evidence of my death, and had faithfully if floridly recorded the same in the chronicle you so appropriately dubbed 'The Final Problem.'"

"Yes, indeed. Those were the hardest words I had ever written."

"And what was the reaction of your readers once this account was published in the *Strand?*"

I shook my head, recalling. "It was completely unexpected," said I. "I had anticipated a few polite notes from strangers mourning your passing, since the stories of your exploits had been so warmly received in the past. But what I got instead was mostly anger and outrage—people demanding to hear further adventures of yours."

"Which of course you believed to be impossible, since I was dead."

"Exactly. The whole thing left a rather bad taste, I must say. Seemed very peculiar behavior."

"But doubtless it died down quickly," said Holmes.

"You know full well it did not. I have told you before that the onslaught of letters, as well as personal exhortations wherever I traveled, continued unabated for years. In fact, I was virtually at the point of going back and writing up one of your lesser cases I had previously ignored as being of no general interest simply to get the demands to cease, when, much to my surprise and delight—"

"Much to your surprise and delight, after an absence of three years less a month, I turned up in our rooms at 221B Baker Street, disguised, if I recall correctly, as a shabby book collector. And soon you had fresh adventures to chronicle, beginning with that case of the infamous Colonel Sebastian Moran and his victim, the Honorable Ronald Adair."

"Yes," said I. "Wondrous it was."

"But Watson, let us consider the facts surrounding my apparent death at the Falls of Reichenbach on May 4th, 1891. You, the observer on the scene, saw the evidence, and, as you wrote in 'The Final Problem,' many experts scoured the lip of the falls and came to precisely the same conclusion you had—that Moriarty and I had plunged to our deaths."

"But that conclusion turned out to be wrong."

Holmes beamed intently. "No, my good Watson, it turned out to be *unacceptable*—unacceptable to your faithful readers. And that is where all the problems stem from. Remember Schrödinger's cat in the sealed box? Moriarty and I at the falls present a very similar scenario: He and I went down the path into the cul-de-sac, our footprints leaving impressions in the soft earth. There were only two possible outcomes at that point: Either I would exit alive, or I would not. There was no way out, except to take that same path back away from the Falls. Until someone came and looked to see whether I had reemerged from the path, the outcome was unresolved. I was both alive and dead—a collection of possibilities. But when you arrived, those possibilities had to collapse into a single reality. You saw that there were no footprints returning from the falls—meaning that Moriarty and I had struggled until at last we had both plunged over the edge into the icy torrent. It was your act of seeing the results that forced the possibilities to be resolved. In a very real sense, my good, dear friend, you killed me."

My heart was pounding in my chest. "I tell you, Holmes, nothing would have made me more happy than to have seen you alive!"

"I do not doubt that, Watson—but you had to see one thing or the other. You could not see both. And, having seen what you saw, you reported your findings: first to the Swiss police, and then to the reporter for the *Journal de Genève,* and lastly in your full account in the pages of the *Strand.*"

I nodded.

"But here is the part that was not considered by Schrödinger when he devised the thought experiment of the cat in the box. Suppose you open the box and find the cat dead, and later you tell your neighbor about the dead cat— and your neighbor refuses to believe you when you say that the cat is dead. What happens if you go and look in the box a second time?"

"Well, the cat is surely still dead."

"Perhaps. But what if thousands—nay, millions!—refuse to believe the account of the original observer? What if they deny the evidence? What then, Watson?"

"I—I do not know."

"Through the sheer stubbornness of their will, they re-shape reality, Watson! Truth is replaced with fiction! They will the cat back to life. More than that, they attempt to believe that the cat never died in the first place!"

"And so?"

"And so the world, which should have one concrete reality, is rendered unresolved, uncertain, adrift. As the first observer on the scene at Reichenbach, your interpretation should take precedence. But the stubbornness of the human race is legendary, Watson, and through that sheer cussedness, that refusal to believe what they have been plainly told, the world gets plunged back into being a wavefront of unresolved possibilities. We exist in flux—to this day, the whole world exists in flux—because of the conflict between the observation you really made at Reichenbach, and the observation the world *wishes* you had made."

"But this is all too fantastic, Holmes!"

"Eliminate the impossible, Watson, and whatever remains, however improbable, must be the truth. Which brings me now to the question we were engaged by this avatar of Mycroft to solve: this paradox of Fermi. Where are the alien beings?"

"And you say you have solved that?"

"Indeed I have. Consider the method by which mankind has been searching for these aliens."

"By wireless, I gather—trying to overhear their chatter on the ether."

"Precisely! And when did I return from the dead, Watson?"

"April of 1894."

"And when did that gifted Italian, Guglielmo Marconi, invent the wireless?"

"I have no idea."

"In eighteen hundred and ninety-*five,* my good Watson. The following year! In all the time that mankind has used radio, our entire world has been an unresolved quandary! An uncollapsed wavefront of possibilities!"

"Meaning?"

"Meaning the aliens are there, Watson—it is not they who are missing, it is us! Our world is out of synch with the rest of the universe. Through our failure to accept the unpleasant truth, we have rendered ourselves *potential* rather than *actual*."

I had always thought my companion a man with a generous regard for his own stature, but surely this was too much. "You are suggesting, Holmes, that the current unresolved state of the world hinges on the fate of you yourself?"

"Indeed! Your readers would not allow me to fall to my death, even if it meant attaining the very thing I desired most, namely the elimination of Moriarty. In this mad world, the observer has lost control of his observations! If there is one thing my life stood for—my life prior to that ridiculous resurrection of me you recounted in your chronicle of 'The Empty House'—it was reason! Logic! A devotion to observable fact! But humanity has abjured that. This whole world is out of whack, Watson—so out of whack that we are cut off from the civilizations that exist elsewhere. You tell me you were festooned with demands for my return, but if people had really understood me, understood what my life represented, they would have known that the only real tribute to me possible would have been to accept the facts! The only real answer would have been to leave me dead!"

Mycroft sent us back in time, but rather than returning us to 1899, whence he had plucked us, at Holmes's request he put us back eight years earlier in May of 1891. Of course, there were younger versions of ourselves already living then, but Mycroft swapped us for them, bringing the young ones to the future, where they could live out the rest of their lives in simulated scenarios taken from Holmes's and my minds. Granted, we were each eight years older than we had been when we had fled Moriarty the first time, but no one in Switzerland knew us and so the aging of our faces went unnoticed.

I found myself for a third time living that fateful day at the Falls of Reichenbach, but this time, like the first and unlike the second, it was real.

I saw the page boy coming, and my heart raced. I turned to Holmes, and said, "I can't possibly leave you."

"Yes, you can, Watson. And you will, for you have never failed to play the game. I am sure you will play it to the end." He paused for a moment, then said, perhaps just a wee bit sadly, "I can discover facts, Watson, but I cannot change them." And then, quite solemnly, he extended his hand. I clasped it firmly in both of mine. And then the boy, who was in Moriarty's employ, was upon us. I allowed myself to be duped, leaving Holmes alone at the Falls, fighting with all my might to keep from looking back as I hiked onward to treat the nonexistent patient at the Englischer Hof. On my way, I passed Moriarty going in the other direction. It was all I could do to keep from drawing my pistol and putting an end to the blackguard, but I knew Holmes would consider robbing him of his own chance at Moriarty an unforgivable betrayal.

It was an hour's hike down to the Englischer Hof. There I played out the scene in which I inquired about the ailing Englischwomen, and Steiler the Elder, the innkeeper, reacted, as I knew he must, with surprise. My performance was probably halfhearted, having played the role once before, but soon I was on my way back. The uphill hike took over two hours, and I confess plainly to being exhausted upon my arrival, although I could barely hear my own panting over the roar of the torrent.

Once again, I found two sets of footprints leading to the precipice, and none returning. I also found Holmes's alpine stock, and, just as I had the first time, a note from him to me that he had left with it. The note read just as the original had, explaining that he and Moriarty were about to have their final confrontation, but that Moriarty had allowed him to leave a few last words behind. But it ended with a postscript that had not been in the original:

> My dear Watson [it said], you will honor my passing most of all if you stick fast to the powers of observation. No matter what the world wants, leave me dead.

I returned to London, and was able to briefly counterbalance my loss of Holmes by reliving the joy and sorrow of the last few months of my wife Mary's life, explaining my somewhat older face to her and others as the result of shock at the death of Holmes. The next year, right on schedule, Marconi did indeed invent the wireless. Exhortations for more Holmes adventures continued to pour in, but I ignored them all, although the lack of him in my life was so profound that I was sorely tempted to relent, recanting my observations made at Reichenbach. Nothing would have pleased me more than to hear again the voice of the best and wisest man I had ever known.

In late June of 1907, I read in *The Times* about the detection of intelligent wireless signals coming from the direction of the star Altair. On that day, the rest of the world celebrated, but I do confess I shed a tear and drank a special toast to my good friend, the late Mr. Sherlock Holmes.

PART IV

HOLMES AFTER DEATH

ILLUSIONS

by Janni Lee Simner

Wind blew through the crack between the window and the sill. The candles sputtered and went out. Arthur heard people hurrying along the London streets outside, their staccato footsteps at odds with the moaning wind. Inside, no one spoke. No one even moved to light the candles again.

Mr. Wentworth sat to Arthur's right, his breath slow and deep. Arthur could just make out the medium's shadowed form, head hunched between narrow shoulders. The man's hand felt cold in Arthur's own. His grip was surprisingly strong.

Miss Loder-Symonds, the acquaintance who'd suggested the seance, held Arthur's other hand. "Joshua's good," she'd told him, "though admittedly a bit unconventional. When his sittings succeed, they succeed spectacularly. When they fail, they are far less impressive—the spirits give him everything or nothing." Mr. Wentworth's failures, she'd explained, had kept him from being in very high demand. People wanted a medium who could work regular small miracles, not irregular large ones.

Miss Loder-Symonds sat straight-backed in her chair, knees just brushing the edge of the low table, skirt just brushing the floor. Two friends of hers—a doctor and his wife whom Arthur didn't know—completed the circle. Arthur stared across the table at them.

He thought of the small tricks that took place at most

seances—ringing bells, blowing horns, objects flying across the room. He found such games tiresome, and had nearly stopped attending seances because of them. Surely true ghosts were capable of greater feats.

Miss Loder-Symonds had insisted that Mr. Wentworth's sittings were different. Arthur hoped so; he longed for proof that spiritualism was true. He'd long ago abandoned his family's Catholicism, but he still longed for evidence of a divine creator, of an immortal human soul.

The wind continued to moan, but no miracles of any size occurred.

Arthur's thoughts wandered to his next novel, a medieval one that would share characters and setting with *The White Company,* but take place many years before. He could already picture Nigel Loring as a boy—poor, young, committed to chivalry and great deeds. He felt as if he'd met the lad, a sure sign that he was ready to start writing. It felt good to work with characters he cared about again. He knew he'd been right to throw that fool Holmes into the waters of Reichenbach Falls.

"The wind," someone—the doctor—whispered, bringing Arthur back to the present. "It's calling you." For a moment Arthur wondered what the man was talking about. Then he heard it. The wind's soft moans had shaped themselves into words—long, low, unearthly sounding words.

"Arthur," the wind moaned. He had to strain to understand it. "Arthur Conan Doyle."

Mr. Wentworth's grip on Arthur's hand tightened. "Welcome, spirit. What is your name?"

"My Christian name—" the voice paused between each word, between each gust that blew "—is Richard. My family name is Doyle."

"Uncle Dick." Always before, the voices at seances had claimed to belong to Arthur's father—or, for that matter, to his mother, who was alive and very well. Then again, the voices had always come directly from the medium, or from some definite location within the room. They'd never been carried on the wind, not like this.

If this were a real spirit, Arthur wasn't sure he wanted to talk to it. Even when they were alive, he'd talked to his uncles as little as possible.

"What brings you back to this world?" Mr. Wentworth asked.

"I've come," the spirit's voice turned suddenly clear and distinct, almost human, "to send my nephew my love."

The gentle words reminded Arthur of the Uncle Dick of his childhood, the uncle who'd showed him around London during the holidays. He preferred that version over the tight-lipped old man with whom he'd fought in later years.

But the words didn't prove anything. The spirit had said nothing a stranger couldn't say. Arthur wanted more definite proof.

"I send my love to his sisters and brother, as well." Still, nothing specific. The wind tugged fitfully at the curtains. "I forgive him for leaving the Catholic Church."

Arthur clenched his jaw. "I hardly think that needs forgiving." He thought of other arguments, fought with Uncle Dick over his dining room table.

"Of course it does." The voice took on an edge Arthur remembered well. "But since my death I've met enough spirits who, though not Catholic or even Christian, seem to have lived virtuous lives and been granted a peaceful existence beyond the grave. And if the Lord can forgive their mistaken beliefs—well, I'm hardly presumptuous enough not to do so myself."

The condescension grated. "How can a belief that results in a virtuous life be mistaken?"

"There's room enough for virtue within the Church." As usual, Uncle Dick avoided answering the question directly. "There's no need for you to go outside it."

Arthur felt like a child being lectured. His anger rose. "Room for virtue? When the Church has been responsible for so much bloodshed through the years?"

"You cannot blame the church for the faults of its members."

"Then you can't credit it with their virtues, either!" Arthur took a deep breath, fighting to calm himself. The argument would go on forever if one of them didn't stop it. "Uncle," he said, as calmly as he could, "surely you have not come here only to fight about the Church."

"No," Uncle Dick said, sounding calmer himself. "I have come here for another purpose entirely."

"And what's that?"

"I've come to ask you to bring back Sherlock Holmes!" A sudden gust beat at the windows, making the glass rattle.

That was too much. Arthur jumped to his feet, restrained

only by the hands of Mr. Wentworth and Miss Loder-Symonds. "How dare you?" he yelled. He wondered why his uncle cared about Sherlock Holmes in the first place. "How dare you tell me what to do!"

"All of London mourned when you killed him," Uncle Dick said. Arthur didn't need reminding. Otherwise sensible men had worn black mourning bands around their hats. People had sent not only furious letters, but also tearful condolences.

"And I confess," Uncle Dick said, "that I was rather fond of the chap myself."

"I won't bring him back. I'm not a child. You can't tell me how to conduct my life."

"When you are conducting your life wrongly, I most certainly can!"

Arthur opened his mouth to protest. He knew he was only repeating old arguments, but he couldn't stop. He didn't want to stop. He hadn't started, after all.

Repeating old arguments. The words echoed through his head.

Twenty years ago, when Arthur had first left the Church, Uncle Dick had used the same words he was using now.

How could any fake spirit duplicate the exact words of their arguments? Arthur began to laugh. How, for that matter, could anyone but Arthur's own relatives make him feel so angry, as if he were a child all over again? The laughter turned high and wild, almost hysterical, dissolving the anger.

Arthur had his proof. Spirits were real, and he was fighting with one now. Death was an illusion, not final after all. "Uncle Dick," he said, and kept laughing.

"I hardly think the matter is funny," Uncle Dick said testily.

Arthur wiped the tears from his eyes. If death was an illusion, he thought, perhaps Holmes's fall was an illusion, too. Perhaps he had never fallen in the first place. Perhaps—

"You will bring him back," Uncle Dick said.

It wasn't a question, but Arthur answered anyway. "Yes. I will bring him back."

"Good." Uncle Dick, or the wind, or maybe both, sighed. "And you'll make him a Catholic this time?"

"A Catholic?" Arthur lurched forward. How dare his uncle ask such a thing? He was suddenly ready to fight again, not caring that he fought with a ghost. In his anger he pulled his hands free, breaking the circle.

The wind broke off abruptly, leaving the room quiet and still. For a moment no one moved. Then Mr. Wentworth stood and began relighting the candles. Arthur had almost forgotten that anyone else was in the room.

The spirit did not speak again.

The seance had succeeded, Arthur told himself. That was all that truly mattered. While part of him wanted to finish the argument—resented that it had been cut off—he pushed the thought aside.

After all, he had a story to write.

THE ADVENTURE OF THE PEARLY GATES

by Mike Resnick

"... *An examination by experts leaves little doubt that a personal contest between the two men ended, as it could hardly fail to end in such a situation, in their reeling over, locked in each other's arms. Any attempt at recovering the bodies was absolutely hopeless, and there, deep down in that dreadful cauldron of swirling water and seething foam, will lie for all time the most dangerous criminal and the foremost champion of the law of their generation ...*"

—*The Final Problem*

It was most disconcerting. One moment I was tumbling over the Falls at Reichenbach, my arms locked around Professor Moriarty, and the next moment I seemed to be standing by myself in a bleak, gray, featureless landscape.

I was completely dry, which seemed not at all surprising, though there was no reason why it should not have been. Also, I had felt my leg shatter against the rocks as we began our plunge, and yet I felt no pain whatsoever.

Suddenly I remembered Moriarty. I looked around for him, but he was nowhere to be seen. There was an incredibly bright light up ahead, and I found myself drawn to it. What happened next I can remember but hazily; the gist of it is that I found myself in, of all places, heaven. (No one told me that I was in heaven, but when one eliminates the impossible, whatever remains, however improbable, must be the truth ... and Professor Moriarty's absence was quite enough to convince me that I was not in hell.)

How long I remained there I do not know, for there is no means by which one can measure duration there. I only know that I felt I might as well have been in the Other Place, so bored was I with the eternal peace and perfection of my surroundings. It is an admission that would certainly offend all churchmen, but if there is one place in all the cosmos for which I am uniquely unsuited, it is heaven.

In fact, I soon began to suspect that I was indeed in hell, for if each of us makes his own heaven and his own hell, then my hell must surely be a place where all my training and all my powers are of no use whatsoever. A place where the game is never afoot, indeed, where there is no game at all, cannot possibly qualify as a paradise for a man such as myself.

When I was bored beyond endurance back on Earth, I had discovered a method of relief, but this was denied me in my current circumstances. Still, it was a craving for cerebral stimulation, not for a seven percent solution of cocaine, that consumed me.

And then, when I was sure that I was facing an eternity of boredom, and was regretting all the chances I had forsaken to commit such sins as might have placed me in a situation where at least I would have had the challenge of escaping, I found myself confronted by a glowing entity that soon manifested itself in the outward form of a man with pale blue eyes and a massive white beard. He wore a robe of white, and above his head floated a golden halo.

Suddenly I, too, took on human shape, and I was amazed to discover that I had not until this very moment realized that I had no longer possessed a body.

"Hello, Mr. Holmes," said my visitor.

"Welcome, Saint Peter," I replied with my newfound voice.

"You know who I am?" he said, surprised. "Your indoctrination period is supposed to be instantly forgotten."

"I remember nothing of my indoctrination period," I assured him.

"Then how could you possibly know who I am?"

"Observation, analysis and deduction," I explained. "You have obviously sought me out, for you addressed me by my name, and since I have evidently been a discorporate being, one of many billions, I assume you have the ability to distinguish among us all. That implies a certain authority. You have taken the body you used when you were alive, and I perceive that the slight indentations on the fingers of your right hand were made by a crude fishing line. You possess a halo while I do not, which therefore implies that you are a saint. Now, who among the many saints was a fisherman and would have some authority in heaven?"

Saint Peter smiled. "You are quite amazing, Mr. Holmes."

"I am quite bored, Saint Peter."

"I know," he said, "and for this I am sorry. You are unique among all the souls in heaven in your discontent."

"That is no longer true," I said, "for do I not perceive a certain lack of content upon your own features?"

"That is correct, Mr. Holmes," he agreed. "We have a problem here—a problem of my own making—and I have elected to solicit your aid in solving it. It seems the very least I can do to make your stay here more tolerable to you." He paused awkwardly. "Also, it may well be that you are the one soul in my domain who is capable of solving it."

"Cannot God instantly solve any problem that arises?" I asked.

"He can, and eventually He will. But since I have created this problem, I requested that I be allowed to solve it—or attempt to solve it—first."

"How much time has He given you?"

"Time has no meaning here, Mr. Holmes. If He determines that I will fail, He will correct the problem Himself." He paused again. "I hope you will be able to assist me to redeem myself in His eyes."

"I shall certainly do my best," I assured him. "Please state the nature of the problem."

"It is most humiliating, Mr. Holmes," he began. "For time beyond memory I have been the Keeper of the Pearly Gates. No one can enter heaven without my approval, and until recently I had never made a mistake."

"And now you have?"

He nodded his head wearily. "Now I have. A *huge* mistake."

"Can't you simply seek out the soul, as you have sought me out, and cast it out?"

"I wish it were that simple, Mr. Holmes," he replied. "A

Caligula, a Tamerlaine, an Attila I could find with no difficulty. But this soul, though it is blackened beyond belief, has thus far managed to elude me."

"I see," I said. "I am surprised that five such hideous murders do not make it instantly discernable."

"Then you know?" he exclaimed.

"That you seek Jack the Ripper?" I replied. "Elementary. All of the others you mentioned were identified with their crimes, but the Ripper's identity was never discovered. Further, since the man was mentally unbalanced, it seems possible to me, based on my admittedly limited knowledge of Heaven, that if he feels no guilt, his soul displays no guilt."

"You are everything I had hoped you would be, Mr. Holmes," said Saint Peter.

"Not quite everything," I said. "For I do not understand your concern. If the Ripper's soul displays no taint, why bother seeking him out? After all, the man was obviously insane and not responsible for his actions. On Earth, yes, I would not hesitate to lock him away where he could do no further damage—but here in heaven, what possible harm can he do?"

"Things are not as simple as you believe them to be, Mr. Holmes," replied Saint Peter. "Here we exist on a spiritual plane, but the same is not true of purgatory or hell. Recently, an unseen soul has been attempting to open the Pearly Gates from *this* side." He frowned. "They were made to withstand efforts from without, but not from within. Another attempt or two, and the soul may actually succeed. Once possessed of ectoplasmic attributes, there is no limit to the damage he could do in purgatory."

"Then why not simply let him out?"

"If I leave the gates open for him, we could be overwhelmed by even more unfit souls attempting to enter."

"I see," I said. "What leads you to believe that it *is* the Ripper?"

"Just as there is no duration in heaven, neither is there location. The Pearly Gates, though quite small themselves, exist in *all* locations."

"Ah!" I said, finally comprehending the nature of the problem. "Would I be correct in assuming that the attempt to break out was made in the vicinity of the souls of Elizabeth Stride, Annie Chapman, Catherine Eddowes, Mary Kelly and Mary Ann Nicholls?"

"His five victims," said Saint Peter, nodding. "Actually, two of them are beyond even *his* reach, but Stride, Chapman and Kelly are in purgatory."

"Can you bring those three to heaven?" I asked.

"As bait?" asked Saint Peter. "I am afraid not. No one may enter heaven before his or her time. Besides," he added, "there is nothing he can do to them in spiritual form. As you yourself know, one cannot even communicate with other souls here. One spends all eternity reveling in the glory of God."

"So *that* is what one does here," I said wryly.

"Please, Mr. Holmes!" he said severely.

"I apologize," I said. "Well, it seems we must set a trap for the Ripper on his next escape attempt."

"Can we be sure he will continue his attempts to escape?"

"He is perhaps the one soul less suited to heaven than I myself," I assured him.

"It seems an impossible undertaking," said Saint Peter morosely. "He could try to leave at any point."

"He will attempt to leave in the vicinity of his victims," I answered.

"How can you be certain of that?" asked Saint Peter.

"Because those slaying were without motive."

"I do not understand."

"Where there is no motive," I explained, "there is no reason to stop. You may rest assured that he will attempt to reach them again."

"Even so, how am I to apprehend him—or even identify him?" asked Saint Peter.

"Is location *necessarily* meaningless in heaven?" I asked.

He stared at me uncomprehendingly.

"Let me restate that," I said. "Can you direct the Pearly Gates to remain in the vicinity of the souls in question?"

He shook his head. "You do not comprehend, Mr. Holmes. They exist in all times and places at once."

"I see," I said, wishing I had my pipe to draw upon now that I was in human form. "Can you create a second gate?"

"It would not be the same," said Saint Peter.

"It needn't be the same, as long as it similar to the perception of a soul."

"He would know instantly."

I shook my head. "He is quite insane. His thought processes, such as they are, are aberrant. If you do as I suggest, and place a false gate near the souls of his victims, my guess is that he will not pause to notice the difference. He is somehow drawn to them, and this will be a barrier to his desires. He will be more interested in attacking it than in analyzing it, even if he were capable of the latter, which I am inclined to doubt."

"You're quite sure?" asked Saint Peter doubtfully.

"He is compelled to perform his carnage upon prostitutes. For whatever reason, these seem to be the only souls he can identify as prostitutes. Therefore, it is these that he wishes to attack." I paused again. "Create the false gates. The soul that goes through them will be the one you seek."

"I hope you are correct, Mr. Holmes," he said. "Pride is a sin, but even *I* have a modicum of it, and I should hate to be shamed before my Lord."

And with that, he was gone.

He returned after an indeterminate length of time, a triumphant smile upon his face.

"I assume that our little ruse worked?" I said.

"Exactly as you said it would!" replied Saint Peter. "Jack the Ripper is now where he belongs, and shall never desecrate heaven with his presence again." He stared at me. "You should be thrilled, Mr. Holmes, and yet you look unhappy."

"I envy him in a way," I said. "For at least he now has a challenge."

"Do not envy him," said Saint Peter. "Far from having a challenge, he can look forward to nothing but eternal suffering."

"I have that in common with him," I replied bitterly.

"Perhaps not," said Saint Peter.

I was instantly alert. "Oh?"

"You have saved me from shame and embarrassment," he said. "The very least I can do is reward you."

"How?"

"I rather thought *you* might have a suggestion."

"This may be heaven to you," I said, "but it is hell to me. If you truly wish to reward me, send me to where I can put my abilities to use. There is evil abroad in the world; I am uniquely qualified to combat it."

"You would really turn your back on heaven to continue

your pursuit of injustice, to put yourself at risk on almost a daily basis?" asked Saint Peter.

"I would."

"Even knowing that, should you fall from the path of righteousness—and it is a trickier path than your churches would have you believe—this might not be your ultimate destination?"

"Even so." And privately I thought: *especially* so.

"Then I see no reason why I should not grant your request," said Saint Peter.

"Thank God!" I muttered.

Saint Peter smiled again. "Thank Him yourself—when you think of it. He *does* listen, you know."

Suddenly I found myself back in that infinite gray landscape I had encountered after going over the Falls at Reichenbach, only this time, instead of a shining light, I thought I could see a city in the distance . . .

"Holmes!" I cried. "Is it really you? Can it indeed be that you are alive? Is it possible that you succeeded in climbing out of that awful abyss?"
                              —*The Adventure of the Empty House*